JO...

"Refreshing and ... ...last. Beautifully done!"

—*Fresh Fiction* for *One Fine Cowboy*

"HOT, HOT, HOT...with more twists and turns than a buckin' bull at a world-class rodeo, lots of sizzlin' sex, and characters so real, you'll swear they live down the road!"

—Carolyn Brown, *New York Times* bestselling author, for *Cowboy Fever*

"A sassy and sexy wild ride that is more fun than a wild hootenanny! Don't miss it!"

—*The Romance Reviews*, 5 Stars for *Tall, Dark and Cowboy*

"A fast-paced, delightful read that will leave readers longing for a cowboy of their own."

—*Night Owl Reviews* for *Cowboy Crazy*

"Packs a powerful, emotional punch...nobody does it better."

—*Booklist* for *Cowboy Tough*

"Emotionally driven, extremely heartfelt and beautifully executed."

—*HEAs Are Us* for *How to Handle a Cowboy*

Also by Joanne Kennedy

COWBOY
SUMMER

JOANNE
KENNEDY

sourcebooks
casablanca

Published by Sourcebooks Casablanca, an imprint of Sourcebooks
P.O. Box 4410, Naperville, Illinois 60567-4410
(630) 961-3900
sourcebooks.com

Printed and bound in the United States of America.
OPM 10 9 8 7 6 5 4 3 2 1

To Amanda Cabot and Mary Gillgannon
with love and gratitude.

"All for one and one for all!"

Chapter 1

JESSICA JANE BAILEY CRANKED DOWN HER CAR WINDOW and let the scents and sounds of Wyoming sweep away the stale city funk of her workaday life. While the wind tossed and tangled her blond curls, she sniffed the air like a dog, savoring the familiar mix of sage, pine, and new-mown hay.

It was August, so the plains had shed green gowns for gold. Brilliant yellow rabbitbrush blazed against red rock outcroppings, and cattle, corralled behind rusty barbed wire, shared forage with herds of antelope. The cows only lifted their heads as she passed, but the antelope startled and raced away, flowing over the coulees like schools of fish.

A fox dashed into the road and paused, one paw upraised. Hitting the brakes, Jess met its eyes for one breathless instant before it darted into the underbrush.

There was something in that gaze she recognized—a kindred soul. It had been years since she'd encountered anything wilder than a pigeon, and the thrill of it surprised her. So did the swelling of her heart as she turned onto a red dirt road and felt the real Wyoming pummeling her little Miata's muffler without mercy.

Her love for this land had lain in ambush all these years. The place was so stunningly wild, so unique, so *home*, it hurt—because she was going to lose it. Every branch and flower was waving goodbye.

She'd given herself two weeks to live it, love it, and learn to let it go.

And she wouldn't let anyone see how much it hurt.

—∿∿—

Jess's dad was like a well-oiled chainsaw; pull the cord, and he was raring to go. No one ever had to wait for him to get to the point, so Jess hadn't been surprised when he'd launched into conversation the moment she'd answered her phone.

It was what he'd said that made her clutch her chest and gasp for breath.

"I'm selling the Diamond Jack," he'd announced. "Know anyone who wants to buy a ranch?"

The words had sent her white-walled office spinning like a manic merry-go-round. Backing toward her desk chair, she missed the seat and landed with a spine-rattling *thud* on the floor. The phone flipped out of her hand and bounced across the floor with all the cunning of a fresh-caught fish while she bobbled it and dropped it again.

She had no reason to be so upset. She was on the verge of a promotion at Birchwood Suites, one that would take her to their new Maui location and put Wyoming firmly in her rearview mirror.

White sand beaches. Sunset on the water. Crashing surf. And surfers…

She'd been to the ocean once in her life, and it had awed and entranced her. The vastness of it and the big sky overhead reminded her of home, and the thundering roll and retreat of the waves answered a longing deep inside her. Living and working near a beach sounded like heaven, and it was Birchwood's ultimate prize.

She'd vowed to win it, but first, she had to deal with her dad. By the time she caught the phone, he was cussing like a bull rider with a porcupine in his pants.

"Dag nabbit, Jess, you 'bout broke my corn's-a-poppin' eardrum."

"I just—I couldn't—what did you say?"

"I said dag *nabbit*. And I *meant* it."

"No, before that."

"Oh. I said I'm selling the ranch. It's not like *you* want the place," he said. "You take after your mother."

She bristled. "Do not."

Dot Bailey had run off with a slick politician from Jackson Hole when Jess was sixteen, leaving Heck with two kids to raise and a ranch to run. He'd been hurt all over again when his son chose the army over ranching and Jess took her mom's advice and moved to Denver after high school. Lately, his resentment had risen between them like dust on a dirt road, clouding the closeness Jess had always treasured.

"You know what I mean." He sounded sulky. "You like people better'n you like cows. And your brother's too busy chasin' terrorists to even think about it." He sighed. "Always thought you and Cade might get together, take the place on. That boy would've made a fine rancher if his daddy hadn't sold so much land out from under him."

"Cade got *married*, Dad, and not to me. Don't you think it's time to let go?"

"You're the one who let go. What was the boy supposed to do?"

"Well, he wasn't supposed to marry Amber Lynn Lyle."

Jess didn't like to say she held hatred in her heart, not for anyone, but Amber Lynn Lyle had always inspired some awfully strong feelings. And that was *before* she'd married Cade Walker.

Heck grunted, which sounded like agreement, but Jess sensed there was something he wasn't telling her.

"Is this Molly's idea?"

"Sort of," he said. "She's tired of ranching."

"That didn't take long."

"Now, you be nice. It's a hard life for a woman."

Jess knew her dad deserved happiness, and she wanted to like her new stepmother. But rumor had it Molly Brumbach had auditioned the marital skills of every man in town before she hit on Heck at a church pie sale. Oblivious as he was to the wiles of women, he'd probably fallen in love with her coconut cream before he'd even looked at her face. With her too-blue eye shadow and penciled brows, she looked as out of place on the Diamond Jack as a rabbit at a rodeo.

"She's looking at some retirement communities," Heck said. "You know, for the over-fifty set."

Jess winced. Her dad wasn't part of any "set," and Molly didn't know him if she thought he'd retire like some normal old man. Cowboy to the core, he sat a horse like most men sat a La-Z-Boy recliner and cared more about his livestock than his own sunbaked skin. Without horses to ride and cattle to tend, he wouldn't know who he was.

"Dad, you can't sell the ranch. You just *can't*."

"Sure I can. Molly's got it all worked out." He coughed, a brutal, phlegmy sound, and Jess wondered if he had a cold. "She sent for five brochures from retirement communities in Arizona. Now she's lookin' at floor plans and measuring the furniture."

"But what would you *do* all day?"

"Guess I'd finally have time to fix stuff around the house. Get your evil stepmom to stop nagging me."

Even Jess knew Molly was about as evil as a golden retriever, and any nagging was well-deserved. Her dad's cowboy work ethic meant everything was shipshape in the barn, but the house was a festival of deferred maintenance. The dripping faucets, sagging stair treads, and wobbly doorknobs had all dripped, sagged, and wobbled for decades. He preferred what he called "the real work of ranching," which was any job that could be performed on horseback. If he could figure out a way to get a quarter horse into the bathroom, he might get those faucets fixed. Until then, they'd continue to drip.

"What about your horses?" Jess asked.

"Molly says they can come, too. These places have community stables and riding trails."

"Yeah, for sissies." She snorted. "They probably all ride English."

She tried to picture her father's finely tuned cow horses prancing around groomed riding trails with a bunch of show ponies. For some reason, the image pushed her over the edge. She tried—and failed—to stifle a sob.

"I know you're a city girl now, with a fancy apartment, cable TV, air-conditioning—hell, I hate to ask you to leave home."

"The Diamond Jack is home, Dad."

The truth of that statement hit her heart so hard, it left a bruise. She'd been dead set on leaving the ranch when she'd graduated from high school, but Denver hadn't been the big-city paradise she'd hoped for. She'd felt closed in, trapped by the looming skyscrapers.

Home in her heart was still the ranch, with its horses and cattle and miles of fence, its endless pastures and dusty dirt roads. It was blushing-pink dawns and tangerine sunsets, the misery of riding drag and the triumph of roping a scampering calf. Home was sagebrush and wild lupine, the bright sheen of mountain bluebirds by day and coyote yodels spiraling up to the moon at night. She might not want to be there every minute of every day, but the ranch was her roots and supported her still.

"If you care so much, how come you never come home?" he said. "Molly loves you, you know, and she worries she's keeping you away."

Jess couldn't tell her dad he was right. Molly tried too hard to make Jess like her while Jess struggled to pretend she did. The tension stretched tight as the duel in *High Noon*, but Heck, who could tell a cow had a headache from thirty feet away, wasn't much good at reading women.

Molly wasn't the only problem, though. Jess had no desire to watch Cade Walker squire Amber Lynn Lyle around town in the beat-up truck where he and Jess had run over so many of life's milestones—first kiss, first promise, first...well, first everything. That truck was practically sacred, and she couldn't bear to think of Amber Lynn Lyle sitting on the bench seat, cozied up to Cade with the stick shift between her knees.

She sniffed, blinking away tears.

"Now, Jess." Her dad's voice dropped into a parental baritone. "What did I tell you 'bout crying?"

She recited one of the mantras he'd taught her growing up. "'Cowgirls don't cry, and tantrums are for toddlers.'"

It was true. Cowgirls didn't cry—but they didn't just lie down and die, either. Not without a fight. The ranch was her heritage and her dad's lifeblood. No oversexed pie lady with poor taste in eye shadow was going to take it away.

"I need to be there," she said. "I'll take vacation or something."

"I'd sure like that," he said. "Molly's just crazy 'bout these brochures, but I don't see why. The folks all look like the ones in those vagina ads."

"Dad, what are you talking about?"

"The vagina ads. On TV. For that medicine men take when they can't—oh, you know."

"It's *Viagra*, Dad."

"That's what I said, dang it. They look like the folks from the Viagra ads."

"Well, I guess they won't be bored, then."

"Nope. According to those ads, their erections last four hours or more." He snorted. "No wonder they're skin and bones. Bunch of silver foxes, like that newscaster on TV. The women are foxes, too, so Molly'll fit right in."

Jess smothered a snort. Molly was hardly a fox. In a Beatrix Potter story, she'd be a lady hedgehog, one that baked pies and seduced all the old man hedgehogs.

"You there, hon?"

"Uh-huh. I'll come home soon as I can, Dad. I miss you. And I miss the ranch."

He sighed. "We'll all be missing it soon. I'll be playing canasta with a bunch of the vagina folks in Sunset

Village every night. When the game gets slow, we'll watch the ladies fight off those four-hour erections."

She laughed despite her fears. "Sit tight, okay? And don't do anything crazy."

That was like telling the sun not to shine. Her dad was always up to something, and that something was usually crazy.

If those folks at the retirement home thought a four-hour erection was trouble, wait until they met Heck Bailey.

Chapter 2

CADE WALKER'S PICKUP LET OUT A METALLIC SHRIEK AS HE downshifted into his driveway. The old Ford, persnickety as a maiden aunt, had been raiding his wallet for months with its nickel-and-dime demands. He'd bought it a fuel pump just last week, and now it wanted a transmission. Dang thing was starting to remind him of his ex-wife.

He thumped the dashboard with his fist. "I'll trade you in for a Dodge."

It was an empty threat. He couldn't afford a new truck now. Not with the mortgage to pay.

The mortgage. The thought of it plagued him ten times a day, hammering shame into his heart so hard it felt like a railroad spike in his chest. One missed payment and the place would be gone, a hundred-acre rug ripped from under his feet.

Not even his dad, with his taste for bourbon and high-stakes gambling, had managed to lose the ranch itself. Pieces of it, sure. Tom Walker's bad habits had chipped away an acre or two at a time, until Walker Ranch was more of a ranchette than a working cattle spread. But Cade had only himself to blame if he lost what little was left.

You don't have to stay, Son. Cut your losses and get out if you're so miserable. You always were a quitter.

Cade tried to shake off the voice in his head. Maybe he was losing his mind. His father's legacy wasn't just the leavings of their once-great ranch; his voice remained as well, delivering a never-ending harangue about Cade's incompetence, his stupidity, his useless-ness and bad decisions.

But Cade wasn't a loser like his old man said, and he had proof. He'd worked his way out of the mess his father made, sold off the cattle, and gone all in for train-ing horses. Just last week, he'd gotten a job offer from one of the country's top clinicians. Most of the famous so-called horse whisperers knew more about self-promotion than they did about horses, but John Baker was one of the greats. After hearing raves from some of Cade's clients, he'd sent a letter offering the opportunity of a lifetime.

It was a chance to learn from a legend, and Cade felt validated by the compliment. But accepting the offer would mean leaving the business he'd worked so hard to build. Worse yet, it would mean leaving Jess Bailey. She was finally coming home, at least for a while, and Cade couldn't help but stay. His chance to win her back had finally come, and he had to take it.

As he neared the house, a shard of light distracted him, arcing up from behind a shed. He'd cleaned up all the old machinery and car parts his dad had left behind, along with a rusty seized-up tractor and a fifty-gallon drum full of broken glass, so there shouldn't be anything back there but weeds.

As he pulled past the shed, he saw a black car parked by the pasture fence. Long and lean with a preda-tory sheen, it sure didn't belong to any of his friends. Cowboys drove pickups, most of them rusty. A truck wasn't supposed to be pretty, just functional, so when a paint job surrendered to Wyoming's brutal climate, they slapped on some primer and kept going. But this vehicle was some fool's pride and joy. Beneath the dust from the dirt road, it was waxed to a shine.

Stepping out of the truck, Cade peered through the weeds at the car's back end. When he saw the crest on the trunk, an eerie silence settled over the landscape, as if the birds and the breezes were holding their breath.

Cadillac.

His ex-wife drove a Caddy, but hers was an SUV—an Escalator, or something like that. This was a sedan, something her daddy would drive, and that couldn't be good news. Amber Lynn's daddy owned the bank in Wynott, and the bank in Wynott owned Cade's ranch.

He glanced around, unnerved by the silence. Where the hell was his dog? Boogy should be bouncing in the front window, barking his head off. The bandy-legged, brindled boxer cross was supposed to guard the house.

He was probably hiding behind the sofa.

Cade sighed. He didn't need trouble right now. All day, he'd been looking forward to stopping by his neighbor's place—casually, of course—to see if Heck Bailey needed a hand with anything.

Like maybe his daughter.

Jess Bailey had always been the first to climb the highest tree or ride a forbidden horse when they were kids. Her sexy, reckless courage had whirled like a tempest through Cade's life, and her smooth-muscled cowgirl body, laughing blue eyes, and wild blond curls had filled his dreams, right up to the day she left him behind.

Actually, that wasn't true. She *still* filled his dreams. But she'd put much more than miles between them, following a star he couldn't see from Walker Ranch—a star that told her a high-powered job in the city was worth more, somehow, than an honest country life.

She was wrong, but a life without her hadn't been worth a dime to Cade. Maybe he should have followed her. If his father had left him with anything to offer, he might have convinced her to stay.

There you go again, blaming everything on me.

Cade shook his head hard, but the voice droned on.

I warned you it wouldn't work out with the Bailey girl, but would you listen? Not a chance. And then you up and married that other bitch. Dumbass. You should have…

A sudden clash of hooves on steel shocked the voice into silence. Jogging back to his horse trailer, Cade flung open the battered door to find his wild-eyed, tangle-maned gelding flailing toward a full-on mental breakdown.

"Easy, Pride. Settle down."

He might as well tell the horse to turn a somersault. The only thing that calmed the nervy Arabian was work, the harder the better. They'd enjoyed a busy day chasing feral cows through the canyons and coulees of the neighboring Vee Bar ranch, but the ride home had set off a collection of twitches and itches the horse needed to shed with a little bucking, a lot of crow hopping, and a gallon of high-test attitude.

Once Cade swung the butt bar aside and clipped on a lead rope, Pride calmed. Tossing his head, swishing his tail, he pranced down the ramp with the hot feline grace of a flamenco dancer.

The horse had belonged to Cade's ex, but she'd lost interest in riding like she'd lost interest in her other expensive hobbies, which had included fine wine, ball-room dancing, and sleeping with men who weren't her husband. Amber Lynn had left a mess in her wake, but he could almost forgive her, since she'd left him Pride. The horse was responsive as a finely tuned sports car, and working with him was a challenge Cade enjoyed.

What if Amber Lynn's daddy thought Pride still belonged to him?

Cade released the horse into the pasture and slammed the gate, letting the chain clang against the metal rails. Spooked, the horse pitched along the fence like a demon-driven rocking horse, then rocketed over a hill, out of sight and hopefully out of everybody's mind.

Returning to the shed, Cade strode through the tall grass and peered into the Caddie. Candy wrappers and fast-food containers littered the floor, and a bottle of wine sat on the passenger seat, cork askew.

Amber Lynn.

Sure as claw marks on a tree trunk spelled bear, junk food and expensive booze spelled Amber Lynn Lyle.

Crossing the parched lawn, he jogged up the porch steps and flung the door open, letting it bang against the wall. Boogy skulked in from the kitchen, staggering sideways like a sorry-ass drunk, his jowly face eloquent with doggie remorse.

"Aw, Boogy." Cade bent to rub the dog's ears. They stood up like satellite dishes, swiveling toward whatever Boogy was looking for—which was sometimes Cade but usually bacon.

A ripple of tension ran down the dog's back.

"She's here, huh? You're scared," Cade whispered. "It's okay. Me, too."

Sliding to the floor, Boogy rolled over, gazing up with adoring eyes as his tongue flopped out the side of his mouth. Cade had been looking for a cow dog when Boogy had turned up homeless. He'd fallen for the sturdy, smiley critter and told himself any dog could learn to herd cows. Unfortunately, he'd been wrong. Boogy couldn't grasp the difference between herding and chasing, so the folks at the Vee Bar asked Cade to leave him home.

A faint squeaking sound came from the kitchen. Standing slowly, Cade peered around the doorframe.

Amber Lynn Lyle, formerly Amber Lynn Walker, crouched in one of the battered captain's chairs at Cade's kitchen table. Her feet rested on the rungs, and she'd thrust her hands between her knees like she was cold. Dark hair hung knotted and limp around her hunched shoulders, obscuring her face.

Cade stilled, chilled to the bone. His ex had broken their vows so hard and cleaned out his bank account so thoroughly, he'd assumed she was gone for good. There was nothing left on the ranch but him, and she'd made it clear he wasn't what she wanted.

Yet here she was, looking almost as sorry as poor old Boogy. Her pose was calculated to inspire pity; with Amber Lynn, every move had a message, and every position was a pose. There was always an equation behind those green eyes, and the answer was always Amber Lynn Lyle.

He knew, sure as he knew his own name, that her timing was another calculation. Gossip spread across the county fast as wildfire in a high wind, and everybody knew Jess Bailey was coming home.

So here came Amber Lynn, staking her claim like an old dog peeing on a tree.

"Amber Lynn?"

She shivered dramatically.

He glanced up at the cabinet over the refrigerator. Hadn't that bottle of Jim Beam just called his name? Maybe he should offer his ex-wife a shot, pour one for himself. Calm things down.

But no. It was whiskey that had led him to Amber Lynn and sobriety that had set him free.

"What are you doing here?" He pulled out a side chair and straddled the seat, resting his forearms on the back. "You wanted to get married; I married you. You wanted me to pay off your bills; I hocked my ranch to pay 'em. Then you wanted Drew Covington, and I gave you a divorce." He splayed his empty hands. "What's left?"

"I'm s-sorry." She hiccupped, then dropped her voice to a whisper. "Drew was a mistake."

"So was I. Or so you said." He hated to be harsh, but hey, at least he was talking to her. He'd much rather take her upstairs and throw her out a second-story window. "How is your boyfriend, anyway?"

"Drew? He's not my boyfriend. Not anymore." With a dramatic sniff, she tossed her hair aside, revealing a nasty black eye. The skin around it looked like a stormy sunset, purple with streaks of red.

"*Drew* did that to you?"

She nodded.

Cade couldn't believe it. Drew had been a jerk, but he'd been a civilized jerk. In their only confrontation, he'd been scared as a skinny second grader facing the school bully. Cade had waved him away, told him to go on and take her. But if he'd known the man would *hit* her…

This is your fault. You should've seen he was a hitter. Not like you never knew one, right?

For once, Tom Walker's voice made sense. Poor Amber Lynn.

But as pity clouded his brain, his ex-wife bit her lip and looked away, as if something outside the window had caught her eye.

The woman was as transparent as a toddler. Cade leaned a little closer.

"Seriously? *Drew?*"

Squeezing out a tear, she shook her head. "No." She shot him a sulky glare, as if the lie was his fault. "Not Drew. It was another guy."

"Jeez, Amber Lynn. It's serious stuff, accusing a man of something like that."

"Well, it was Drew's fault." Her voice rose to a whine. "He locked me out of his house, and I didn't have anywhere to go. I knew this other guy liked me, so I went to his place, and then—he hit me."

There was something missing from that story. His ex blinked up at him with red-rimmed eyes. "Aren't you going to ask who it was?"

"I don't fight your battles anymore. I stopped that when you started sleeping around."

"I had to do *something*. You never paid any *attention* to me." She pointed toward the barn the way another woman might point at a bar or a strip club. "You were always out there with the horses, and I was always *alone*."

He'd heard this song before. She'd demand his attention, then leave in a huff just when he made time for

her. Usually, she'd gone shopping for revenge, spending what little money he had. When that ran out, she'd
forged his name on credit applications and spent money
he didn't have. When he'd been forced to take on extra
work to pay the bills, she'd hurled herself into storms of
weeping—because he never spent time with her.

"Cut it out, Amber Lynn. We've been over this."

"All right." With a final sniff, she straightened her
shoulders, took a deep breath, and blew her nose with a
honk that would have impressed a Canadian goose. She
was trying, at least, and that was all it took to make him
feel pity again.

She couldn't help who she was. Her folks had given
in to every tantrum instead of taking the time to teach
her right from wrong. Now, she survived the only way
she knew how—by manipulating people.

"I'm s-s-*sorry*, Cade."

With one more comical goose honk, she dissolved into
tears, crying so hard, he was afraid she'd pull a muscle.

Wait. Did sobbing require muscles?

He had no idea. He'd never cried like that in his life.
Not when his dad smacked him around, not even when
cancer took his mother. The only time he'd cried had
been when Jess left, but even that hadn't been an all-out,
shoulder-heaving show like this.

"I had such a bad night." She hiccupped, then burped,
and he smothered a smile. "I s-s-slept in the c-c-*car*."

She blinked her sorry sheep eyes, clueless that the
burp had made him feel closer to her than any of her
womanly wiles.

"I have n-nowhere to go." The blinking turned to all-
out lash fluttering. "Can I stay here? Just tonight?"

Boogy whined and crawled under the table.

"Why can't you stay with your dad?" Cade asked.

Amber Lynn slumped like a puppet whose strings had snapped. "That would be the first place that jerk would look. Besides, Daddy won't even talk to me because I left you. He said you're a g-good and decent man."

"Yeah, right. Last I knew, I was a low-class, redneck, white-trash bum who'd forced his precious daughter to live in a hovel. I believe that's a direct quote."

"He knows better now. You're a good man. You *are*." She choked on another burp and hiccupped. "My own daddy disowned me, 'cause I'm nothing but a tramp."

"You're not a tramp, Amber Lynn. You're just confused."

"I *am* confused." The storm cleared as suddenly as it had begun, and Amber Lynn smiled. With her face all pink from crying, she looked pretty as a prize piglet at the fair—except for that eye. "I need to get a good night's sleep and figure things out. Can I stay here? Please?"

"Why don't you get a hotel room?"

"I l-l-left my purse back at—back where…" She pointed toward her black eye, then pushed her chair back. "You're right, though. I should go back and get it." She sighed. "I don't *think* he'll hit me again."

Cade felt his resistance waning, then thought of the Cadillac parked behind the shed. It had to be her father's car, and if Jasper Lyle would loan her the car, why wouldn't he give her a place to stay?

Cade was pretty sure she was lying. Matter of fact, he was sure of it, because her lips were moving.

"I'm sorry, but no," he said. "You can't stay."

The sniffling started up again. He raised a hand, palm

out, as if it could hold back her tears. "I need to go out. You can rest a little. Take a nap and maybe a shower, okay? But then you have to go."

She opened her mouth, no doubt to ask where he was going, but Cade wasn't about to tell her. She'd throw herself on the floor and pitch a fit if she knew he was helping out at the Diamond Jack and hoping to see Jess Bailey.

"You can use my soap, okay? Shampoo, too. But be gone before I get home, around sundown, okay?" He answered for her. "Okay. Come on, Boogy."

When they reached the truck, Boogy jumped up into the shotgun seat while Cade gripped the wheel, his head spinning. Had he been firm enough? Would Amber Lynn be gone when he got back?

Probably not. When Amber Lynn wanted something, she was stubborn as a rusty gate. But he couldn't deal with her right now. He'd made a promise to Heck Bailey—one that just might put him in place to welcome Jess back home where she belonged.

Turning to Boogy, he rubbed the dog's flat head. "You're a good dog, but you're useless, you know? I ought to replace you with a Rottweiler."

Boogy panted and grinned, oblivious to the threat, his mind on the wonders of truck riding.

"I'm not any better, though. We're both softies at heart, and you know what?"

The dog perked up, as if Cade had said "ball" or "play."

"It's going to get us in trouble, Boogy. All kinds of trouble."

Chapter 3

JESS ROLLED INTO THE DIAMOND JACK WITH A SMILE ON HER face and a song in her heart. She had two weeks off. Her boss seemed to understand this was a family emergency, and she didn't think he'd hold it against her when it came to the Hawaii position.

She hoped not, because she wanted that job. She'd chosen a degree in hospitality hoping for a ticket to see the world, and now she had her chance. Birchwood Suites was expanding, and their more exotic locations were prizes her colleagues vied for in a fierce but unspoken competition—one Jess intended to win.

Turning into the drive, she paused beside the familiar old ranch sign with its crudely painted, peeling jack of diamonds. Maybe she'd fix that up while she was here. She'd never had the heart to tell her brother the jack looked like he had a stomachache. And if they were selling the ranch…

No.

They wouldn't sell the ranch. They couldn't. Probably her dad was just tired; it was a lot to deal with on his own, and Molly wasn't much help. In fact, Jess didn't know why her stepmother didn't just go back to her teaching job. There was no reason for her to hang around the ranch all day if she couldn't do the work.

Jess would cheer up her dad, pitch in with the chores, and everything would go back to normal. She'd just have to come home a little more often. And Griff—well, she hoped her brother made it back from whatever wild part of the world he'd been sent to in the endless fight against terror. He could help on the ranch or not. She didn't care. She just wanted him home.

Pulling into the drive, she checked her phone. No calls from work, but she'd better check in. It would be impossible to tear herself away from family once she stepped inside.

Her assistant answered the phone in two rings.

"Birchwood Suites Denver. Your comfort is our business. How can I help you?"

"Nice greeting, Treena! It's Jess. How's it going?"

"Great. We had a little hiccup when that new maid didn't show up, though. Mrs. Donnelly had a fit."

"You can't be afraid of her," Jess said. "You're in charge, remember?"

"Oh, don't worry," Treena said airily. "She doesn't scare me, and now she knows it. We had a good conversation about people skills. I pointed out how much she cares about doing a great job and how that makes her too hard on the staff sometimes. She agreed to try to be more positive. I think it'll really help."

Treena was right. If the head of housekeeping could just stop barking at the maids, everything would run a lot smoother. But Jess had had that conversation with Mrs. Donnelly a dozen times, and though the woman would improve for a day or two, her new attitude never lasted.

Treena didn't need to hear that, though.

"Good job." Jess put a smile in her voice. "Sounds like you handled the situation really well."

"I learned it all from you!" Treena could be a bit of a brownnoser, but that was part of the game. "How's your vacation going?"

Jess winced. "It's not a vacation. It's a family emergency."

"Right. Okay, well, have fun! I'll call you if I need you."

Jess hung up the phone, feeling dismissed. She wondered if Treena was doing that on purpose or genuinely trying to be nice.

There was no point in worrying. She was home now, amused as always by the house's wild and whimsical architecture. It had begun as a simple homesteader's cabin, but each generation of Baileys had added rooms in the style of their time, creating an architectural mishmash that ranged from rustic cabin to High Victorian. Mismatched windows were flanked by crooked shutters, the front porch leaned slightly to the left, and the roofline ranged from sober slopes to wild, winged gables. There was even a tower, which held a breakfast nook on the first floor and Jess's bedroom on the second.

Stepping out of the car, she clutched her hair as the Wyoming wind slapped her upside the head, flinging grit that stung her skin. Some people might have gotten back in the car and hightailed it for someplace more hospitable, but Jess was a Wyoming girl, accustomed to winds strong enough to overturn semis on the interstate.

She gathered her curls in one hand and shaded her eyes with the other, sipping a long, slow drink of home. All the empty places inside her filled with peace and pleasure, as if she'd downed a whole pitcher full of blue skies garnished with wildflowers and sunshine.

Hawaii, schmawaii. This was her favorite place in all the world.

A friendly voice hailed her from a rusty flatbed parked by the barn. Painted letters on the driver's door, nearly obscured by rust and flaking paint, read JEB JO SON HAY & FE D.

"Hey, Jeb!"

Jeb Johnson had been working with her dad since Jess was knee-high. Racing to the truck, she hopped on the running board and reached through the open window to drag his weathered face to hers and lay a smooch on his grizzled cheek.

He reached up and touched his face with shy reverence. "Oh, girlie, it's good you've come home." His eyes, normally bright with mischief, were glossy with— could that be tears? "They need you 'round here."

"I need them, too. I've missed them. My dad, I mean. And you." Grabbing the steering wheel for support, she popped up on tiptoe and peered inside the cab. "Got snips?"

"Forgot 'em at the last place." He nodded toward the barn. "He went in to grab some."

"Oh good. I'll surprise him."

She hopped off the running board and considered the load on the flatbed. Hay bales were stacked high and wide, bulging over the edge of the bed, barely contained by baling wire.

Since she'd been a little girl, Jeb had made a game of letting her choose which wire to cut. If she chose the right spot, the bales would tumble safely off the far side of the truck. Choose wrong, and they'd tumble all around her, bouncing to the ground like giant, hairy hailstones. But she needed snips to play.

Heading for the barn, she hugged herself with glee. Her dad, stepping out of the dark tool room, would be blinded by the sunlight. She'd surprise him, all right.

Jeb called after her. "Now, honey, I'm not sure…"

Shushing him, she pressed her back to the sun-warmed barn. The paint would rub off on her shorts, but a barn-red butt was a small price to pay for scaring her dad into one of his creative cussing streaks.

She heard the rasp of wood on wood, then *bang*—a drawer slammed shut. Tensing, she tightened her smile to restrain the laugh trapped high in her chest.

Footsteps hit the hollow floor, approaching the door. She counted.

Five, four, three, two…

"*Arooooo!*"

With a crazed coyote howl, she leapt for the shadowy form in the doorway, knowing with giddy certainty her daddy would catch her, like he always did.

The wire cutters rattled to the ground, and a masculine grunt greeted the impact of her body.

She was caught, all right. The only trouble was, that wasn't her father's grunt. It wasn't his body, either.

It was Cade Walker's.

Cade had pictured his reunion with Jess waking, and he'd pictured it in dreams. He'd pictured it happy, and he'd pictured it hard. But he'd never pictured it quite like this.

Momentarily blinded when he stepped out of the dim barn, he was shocked, even scared, when a howling bundle of womanhood slammed into his chest. He'd almost pushed Jess away—but then she'd kissed him.

It was a family kind of kiss, not a romantic one, and it landed on his cheek instead of the other body parts that would have been happy to host it. But it was still a kiss from Jess, and that made it electrifying. He caught the familiar scent of her—grass and flowers, summer sun and peaches—and his heart sailed away on an ocean of happy memories.

But the seas were choppy. She was fighting him like a cat in a bathtub.

"*Let…me…go!*"

He couldn't. For one thing, he needed to look at her—just drink her in like a tonic that warmed his heart, plus a few places further south. Jess wasn't a classic beauty, being taller and stronger than most movie-star types. But with her wild blond curls tumbling down her back, her blue eyes sparkling with energy, and her lithe, fit body warm and strong in his hands, she'd always been his feminine ideal.

She managed to wrench herself away, but he kept his grip on one firm thigh. The ground sloped steeply to the rocky drive, and she'd fall if he didn't hang on.

Floundering for balance, she hopped madly down the slope.

"Let go," she snarled, slapping his arm. "I thought you were my *dad*. Let me *go!*"

She always reminded him of some sort of wild critter. Usually, it was something sweet, like a rabbit or a deer. But there were times she was a cat—slinky, smooth, and lovely to look at, but all claws and teeth if you got too close.

This was one of those times, and he was apparently way too close.

Course you are, said his father's voice. *Baileys think they're better'n us. Got all that money, all that land…*

"Wait." Pushing the voice out of his head, Cade released her leg, but he braced his hands around her waist so she wouldn't fall. "Calm down, okay? Listen."

He pulled her a little closer, knowing he risked getting hurt, but miraculously, the anger in her eyes flickered and died. The bobcat turned into a bunny, and there she was, back in his arms—the Jess he remembered.

And oh, did he remember. The last time he'd seen her, she'd come back for Christmas after two years away. He'd already started seeing Amber Lynn by then, but he'd jumped at the chance to share Christmas Eve dinner with the Baileys.

Jess had told story after story of her adventures in the city, her hilarious mistakes, and the friends she'd made. By dessert, he knew his chances of keeping her home were slim to none.

They'd said a polite goodbye at the front door, and he'd gone to bed early that night. He hadn't hit the whiskey bottle. It had gotten to be too much of a habit, and Jess wouldn't like it. Even with her gone for good, her opinion mattered.

He hadn't expected the tap at his window a couple of hours later. He hadn't expected to see her standing in the winter night with flakes dusting her hair and lashes tipped with snow. He hadn't expected his brave, wild Jess to cross the pasture in a pair of pajamas to see him again.

One more time, she'd said.

He didn't like to think of those city guys putting their hands on her, so he'd done his best to heat her up so she'd stay warm for a while. And then...

His thoughts snapped back to the present as the scent of her fruity shampoo flooded his senses. Combined with his Christmas memories, it sparked a rush of adrenaline that collided with a hefty dose of testosterone, setting his body on high alert.

High alert. He shifted against her, hoping she hadn't noticed his flag was up and waving for attention.

"You attacked me," he murmured. "I almost knocked you down in self-defense."

She gave him a cockeyed smile that reminded him of those double-dog-dare summer days. "You couldn't knock me down if you tried."

"You think?" He leaned forward, then leaned a little more. He was just trying to scare her, but he scared himself—and fell.

Every cowboy knows the safest way to fall. Jerking her sideways, he made sure he'd hit the ground first, landing on one hip. Everything was fine until her body slid neatly between his legs and...

Bam!

The breath whooshed out of his lungs. Stars winked and danced before his eyes, and little cartoon birds sang, they really did, flitting around his head in happy circles while the world went black.

Chapter 4

THE LITTLE BIRDS TWITTERED AWAY AS CADE OPENED HIS eyes to a blurred, watercolor world. Maybe it was heaven, because Jess's blue eyes were fixed on his, just inches away.

"Are you okay?"

She was close, so close, and when he looked into those eyes, he was lost—because *oh*, she was right there, right where he could kiss her.

He wanted to slip his fingers through her hair the way he used to, sweep it back from her face so he could see her, really *see* her, and then kiss her till she writhed against him, wanting more, always more. He knew just how it would feel—the pillowy give of her lips, the warmth of her skin. He could almost taste her—but wait.

Wait.

She reached out a hand to stroke his hair, then pulled back, frowning.

He ought to say something. Something funny. That would cut the tension, and *then* he could kiss her.

But he wasn't much of a talker at the best of times, and the hard hit to his vitals must have knocked his brain off-kilter. All he could do was stare up at her, dumb as a rock, and hold out his hand.

Miracle of miracles—she took it.

With that touch, the world he'd lost came rushing back in glorious technicolor. His heart stirred like a hibernating beast, sensing the promise of spring, stretching in the sun after a long, cold winter.

For the first time in forever, it felt good to be alive.

———ᴡᴡ———

Jess pulled Cade to his feet—and boy, was *that* a mistake.

While she'd been in the city among the desk jockeys, Cade had been busy working the ranch, building muscle as only a cowboy can. He'd earned the powerful shoulders, sinewy biceps, and bulging, muscular forearms of a *Men's Health* model, but he was no Hollywood wannabe. His muscles were real, and so were his suntouched hair and tanned skin—testaments to long, hard cowboy days in the western sun.

The thought of long, hard cowboys set off a wild clamor of bells in her head. It sounded like a celebration, and her body was ready to join in. Intimate moments, some sexy, some sweet, rose up and drifted through her mind, spinning out in warm detail, wrapping around her thoughts, reaching for her heart as it softened and yearned.

This is wrong. He isn't yours.

When he stood, she dropped his hand like it was hot. *Her* Cade wouldn't have looked twice at a woman like Amber Lynn Lyle. Either he'd fallen for a human Barbie doll, or he'd married a woman he didn't love, and that wasn't the Cade she'd known—the Cade she'd loved.

"Here." He held up the wire cutters, reminding her this was about the hay. About the ranch. How had she gotten caught up in memories so fast? Memories, fantasies—she needed to get a grip.

He tossed her the snips. As she snatched them from the air, he caught her gaze and held it. His eyes were pale gray, almost silver, like ice on a frozen pond, but there was something broken there, like shattered glass.

Dang. Had he looked like this when she left? How— and *why*—had she ever walked away? Maybe it had been a mistake, but today, she'd have to walk away again before she screwed up both their lives even worse.

She practically ran for the truck, where Jeb was grinning like a squirrel at a nut party.

"You two done?" he asked.

She flashed him a smile she didn't feel. "Show's over."

"You 'member how to do this?"

"I sure do."

She strolled around the truck, considering the puzzle, wielding the wire cutters like a weapon as she searched for the perfect snipping spot.

Cade pointed to the back of the load. "Here," he said. "This one."

Dang it. Now she remembered why she'd left the Diamond Jack. Ranching was a man's world, and men— Cade, her father, her brother—always acted like she was the *dumb* kind of blond. She'd had to leave home to prove herself. Now she managed a major hotel, hosting thousands of travelers, setting up international conferences for important organizations. She didn't need Cade Walker to tell her what to do.

As if acting on their own, her snips flashed out, cutting the closest wire. The blades cracked like a gunshot, halting the buzz of a nearby bee as suddenly as if she'd flipped a switch. Whatever birds were singing shut their beaks and fled, leaving room for one profound thought that thundered through her mind.

Uh-oh.

Covering her head with her hands, she ducked, squeezing her eyes shut as bales tumbled all around her. One thudded onto her bowed back, exploding on impact and showering her with fine, fresh hay that slid down the neck of her top and into her cleavage, where it itched like live bugs. She didn't dare move while the rest of the load thumped to the ground in her own personal hay-pocalypse.

When it was over, she dusted herself off, doing her best to act as if she was bombed by hay bales every day of her life. Jeb, leaning out the truck window, nodded at the exploded bale lying in the dirt.

"I'll refund your daddy for that one. But you really shoulda listened to Cade." He shook his head. "You been gone too long, girlie. Aren't you a cowgirl anymore?"

He was teasing, but the words stung. She knew she'd never been a real cowgirl—not even to her dad. She'd tried hard and been willing to work, but roping wasn't one of her talents, and he'd always laughed at her efforts, like she was cute or something.

She glanced at Cade, sure he'd be laughing, but he was already carrying two bales to the barn. With biceps bulging from the torn sleeves of his T-shirt and strong thighs flexing under his Wranglers, the man was one fine personification of the cowboy work ethic.

She wanted to poke her eyes out so she'd stop looking.

She'd dated amazing men in Denver, she reminded herself. Lawyers. Stockbrokers. Entrepreneurs. Sophisticated men with fat bank accounts and bright futures. Why hadn't any of them made her feel this way?

Cade was married. *Married.* To Amber Lynn Lyle, of all people.

Setting his load against the barn wall, Cade headed back to the truck with a loping stride that made her want to bite his spectacular cowboy ass.

She'd better get to work before she got herself in trouble. Clutching a single bale to her belly, she waddled along like she was ten months pregnant with a gigantic hay baby.

"Where's Dad?" she asked.

"Inside, I guess."

"Is he sick?"

Cade set his load in place and went back for more. "Ask him."

Winded, she set her bale on the growing stack and lifted her hair off the back of her neck, gathering it in her fist so the air could cool her skin. Tiny shreds of hay dropped from her fingers and drifted down the back of her shirt, adding to the itchiness.

Cade returned, carrying two bales like they were light as throw pillows.

"You don't have to do that." She followed him back to the truck, trotting to keep up. "I can get it stacked."

"I know."

"Dad said he's selling the ranch." Grabbing another bale, she stutter-stepped to keep up with his long stride. "It's not true, though, is it? He'd never do that."

"I hope not. Things around here wouldn't be the same without Heck and Molly."

"Without Heck." The words leapt out, a fierce protective reflex. "Molly doesn't belong here."

Setting two more bales in place, he paused in the cool

shade of the barn, shoving his hands in his pockets and staring out a window beside the barn door.

His silence got under her skin worse than the flecks of itchy hay. He was probably on Molly's side. Cade needed mothering, and now that Molly didn't have students to smother, she'd probably taken Cade under her wing. Why else was he hanging around, working for free? Couldn't her dad stack his own hay, the way he always had?

Maybe not. Something was wrong; she could feel it.

If there was bad news, she'd just as soon hear it now, from Cade. He was so strong, so stable. His scent alone had always calmed her—that soothing blend of hay and sage and saddle leather. She'd known half her life she could stand up to anything as long as he stood behind her.

But there'd be no more holding or standing or smelling. Not anymore. Leaving had been her choice, but *damn* Amber Lynn Lyle for making it a permanent one.

He finally spoke, staring through the window's rippled glass at a funhouse version of the fields and hills.

"I can get this done. Go talk to your dad, okay?"

She watched him, willing him to tell her what was going on, but being Cade, he didn't jump to fill the silence like most people would. Finally, she gave up and left the barn, but as she headed for the house, a different kind of itch started up between her shoulder blades.

He was watching her. She'd always been able to feel his gaze, sure as if he'd touched her.

When she spun around, he looked away—but not before she saw his eyes. The broken look remained, but there was pity there, too. It made her feel as if those hay bales were still tumbling off the truck, bouncing all around her, threatening to knock her flat in the hard, dry dirt of the Diamond Jack.

Somehow, she'd stay standing, and she'd do it without Cade Walker's help.

Chapter 5

THE WIND SLAMMED THE SCREEN DOOR SO HARD, IT FELT like the house was giving Jess a spanking—maybe for being gone so long, or maybe for having lustful thoughts about a married man. Either way, she deserved it.

Stepping into the front hall, she took a deep breath. It smelled like childhood, like happiness, like home. If the house were a fine wine, it would be a rich, robust red, with notes of lemon Pledge and Murphy's Oil Soap, plus undertones of saddle leather, hay, and horse.

But the place was dead quiet. Naturally, there was no one in the front room, the one her mother had called "the parlor" and furnished with expensive Victorian antiques. Dot Bailey had declared it was "the one civilized room in the house," but with everything upholstered in cream-colored silk, no one ever felt quite civilized enough to use it, except for Jess, who'd spent hours there after her mother left, dreaming up a future that might lure Dot Bailey home.

There, she'd resolved to become the kind of woman her mother respected. She'd dreamed of a swanky apartment, an important executive job, and a cultured life in the city. Trouble was, she didn't feel any more civilized in Denver than she did in the parlor, and her mother remained unreachable, too busy with her new husband and Jackson high society to talk to the daughter she'd left behind.

Kneeling on the antique fainting couch under the window, Jess gazed at the view her mother had called barren and dull. Her mom hadn't cared that there were seven different kinds of grass in that view alone, and she wouldn't have noticed the butterfly dancing over the pasture or the crows that flew past, cursing in their comically harsh voices.

But Jess noticed it all, and it made her heart rise and sing. The Wild West of the Diamond Jack was a miracle, a gift from God. Anyone who loved that prim, stuffy parlor more than the magnificent plains could never have been happy here.

Maybe it was time to lose the little girl who'd tried to impress her absent mother with false sophistication. Her country roots glowed like a skunk stripe down the middle of her back anyway; she'd always be Jess Bailey, daughter of the Diamond Jack. Deep down, that made her proud.

She finally found her dad on the screened porch, snoozing behind the Cheyenne paper. Molly sat at a table nearby, clipping coupons from the advertising section. She set down her scissors as Jess entered.

"Hi!" She turned to her husband. "Heck, honey, Jess is here."

A snort emanated from the newspaper, which jerked spasmodically and fell away. Jess, who'd spun around to plop herself in his lap like the daddy's girl she was, stopped dead and stared.

Her dad had lost nearly half a Heck in weight. His usually ruddy complexion was a pallid shade of gray. Dark pouches hung below his eyes, and crumbs from a recent meal had gathered in the corners of his mouth. He looked old, sick, and sad—three words Jess had never, ever used to describe her vital, irascible dad.

She attempted a smile, but it trembled at the edges. "How are you, Dad?"

"Terrible. Your evil stepmother's driving me to an early grave with this talk about retirement." He grabbed a stack of pamphlets from a side table, waving them in the air. "Did you see the people at these places? Bunch of phonies with golf clubs."

"You haven't even met those folks." Molly resumed her coupon clipping. "You don't know they're phony."

"*You* don't know they're phony," Heck said. "*I* can tell by looking at 'em."

"Well. Look at the time!" Molly cut off the argument as cleanly as she'd clipped her coupons. "You must be starving after that long drive, Jess. Let's rustle up some sandwiches."

"I'll have roast beef," Heck said. "And none of that danged artichoke."

"It's avocado, and it's good for you. You're having turkey. Come on, Jess."

Jess followed reluctantly. She hated watching her stepmother in her mother's kitchen, bustling around like she owned the place. As the woman unpacked the fridge, Jess eyed her selections.

"Dad likes hummus?"

Molly laid out two slices of bread and slathered them with the spread. "Dad doesn't know what's good for him. Jess, he's not well."

"I noticed that." Jess leaned against the counter and folded her arms over her chest. "What's going on? He looks terrible, and this talk about selling the ranch is ridiculous." She shot her stepmother a glare. "It's been in our family for four generations. He *can't* sell it."

"Well, he can't stay. He's killing himself." Refusing to meet her eyes, Molly slammed the avocado onto a cutting board and jerked a butcher knife out of Dot's knife block. "He works too hard, riding off to God-knows-where on horseback. Anything could happen."

"He's a rancher. That's what ranchers do."

Molly whipped the knife around the avocado, then twisted it neatly in half. "What if he fell off? He could hit his head. We'd never find him out there."

"I'll ride out with him, then," Jess said. "Or Cade."

"Cade's got his own work, and you can't give up your career, hon. You have a right to your dreams." She paused with the knife upraised and stared dreamily out the window. "Every woman does. A job you love can be so fulfilling."

You don't even know what my dreams are. Jess opened the refrigerator and grabbed a grape tomato, popping it in her mouth. As its sweetness spread, she pictured herself as an old woman rancher, blue eyes bright in a face tanned to leather, hair flying in tangles as she galloped a tall horse across the prairie.

For some reason, she had these wild thoughts about growing old in Wyoming every time she came home. The way the place tugged on her heart was one reason she stayed away.

Her dreams had nothing to do with horses, she told herself. Her dreams were of Hawaii.

"What's wrong with Dad?" she asked Molly.

The other reason she stayed away flipped the pit out of the avocado and coaxed the pale flesh from the peel. "He's a walking heart attack."

"What does the doctor say?"

"Your dad skipped his last appointment, so I don't know. But just look at him." Turning away from her work, Molly leaned against the counter and covered her face with her hands. "Oh, Jess. I can't lose him. I *can't*. I don't understand ranching, but I love this place for his sake, and now it's *killing* him, and I hate it for that. I *hate* it." She looked up, eyes narrowed. "I hate the grass, I hate the trees, I hate the sky, and I hate, hate, *hate* the damned horses."

Jess stared at her, shocked. The horses were the heart of the ranch and held much of the heart of Heck Bailey. Obviously, he'd reserved some portion for Molly, but in a contest between his wife and horses, Jess thought horses would probably win.

"I know he loves the horses." Molly's damp eyes were defiant. "But they're going to take him away from me. I just know it."

"Call Cade," Jess said. "He could use some extra grazing land, I'll bet, and we don't use it all. He'd probably make some kind of trade. Or maybe Dad could hire him."

"Cade does a lot, but he won't take a job. We've asked." Molly slanted a sly smile toward Jess. "Why? Are you and Cade—you know…"

"Of course not."

Jess had heard Molly was shameless in her youth, but Cade was a married man. What was she thinking?

Oblivious to her shock, Molly cut the avocado into thin, even slices. "Well, your dad might feel different, but I'm glad you're not putting your eggs in that basket. I saw a car over there today—a Cadillac. I think it's Amber Lynn's car."

Of course it's Amber Lynn's car. She's Cade's wife.

"This isn't about Cade, anyway." Jess turned so Molly wouldn't see the hot flush spreading over her face as she remembered that tumble outside the barn. Cade's body had been heavy on hers, hard muscle on soft curves. She could almost smell the grass crushed beneath her, the hay on the breeze, his killer cowboy pheromones. "It's about Dad."

A pathetic little kitten squeak made her turn to see Molly smothering sobs as she stacked slices on the sandwich.

"I'm sorry," she sniffed. "This isn't what I wanted. I know you love this place. I don't want to be the one who takes it away, but your dad won't make a decision. He keeps going, day after day, like some miracle's going to happen, but it's not. It's *not*." She flapped her hands helplessly as if shaking off water. "I wish it would, honey. I really do. Maybe you and Cade—oh, I don't know."

"Me and Cade are done, in case you hadn't noticed."

Jess remembered looking into his eyes, so changed, so sad, and knew she'd never be truly done with Cade Walker, but nobody else needed to know that, least of all him. She'd moved on, and she'd keep moving.

"I'll talk Dad into going to the doctor." Jess pictured her father's face, so drawn and pale. "I wish I hadn't stayed away so long. I should have been here, checking on him."

"You can't blame yourself," Molly said.

Oh yes, I can.

While her father had been struggling with his health, Jess had been lapping up praise at work and enjoying Denver's nightlife. Seeing him now, she realized nothing was worth losing time with her dad—not even Hawaii.

Once, she'd hoped her success would bring her

mother back, but now she knew her dad was all she had. And if he and Molly moved to some retirement community, the connection would never be the same. Much more than the ranch would be gone.

Looking out the kitchen window at land she'd loved all her life, she realized how much she had to lose and how helpless she was to save it.

Molly sliced the sandwich in half and handed the plate to Jess.

"It's healthy food, but getting him to eat it is a whole 'nother thing." She grinned. "Tell him *you* made it."

Jess looked down at the sandwich. Avocado slices and spinach leaves poked out the sides, waving and screaming *Healthy! Healthy! Healthy!*

"Got any barbecue sauce?"

Molly fetched a bottle of Red's Red-Hot Brown Sugar BBQ Sauce from the fridge. She glanced at the label. "It's loaded with sodium and sugar."

"Yeah, but it'll get him to eat."

Popping the top off the sandwich, Jess dumped sauce over every trace of green, then sprinkled the whole deal liberally with pepper.

"You're a genius." Molly gave her a thumbs-up. "Thanks, hon."

As Jess stepped out on the porch and set the sandwich on the table, she felt her world tilt sideways. Her dad had always taken care of her, but now their roles had reversed. She'd moved from one phase of life to the next without so much as a speed bump to warn her.

Losing the ranch was the least of her problems. She was going to have to grow up, and she wasn't sure she was ready.

Chapter 6

IGNORING THE MONSTER SANDWICH, JESS'S DAD FOLDED HIS paper and heaved himself to his feet. His breath came hard, and blue veins bulged in his forehead.

"Sorry, hon, but I can't eat right now. I spotted some runny-assed calves in the north pasture on my way home from town. Gotta go doctor 'em." He sighed. "Thought these Highlanders would be tougher'n that. Should have gone for the Dornod Mongolians."

"Dad, those were so expensive." Jess resisted the urge to roll her eyes. Her dad couldn't raise Black Angus like any other rancher. He'd always been convinced some exotic breed would be the key to success. Mostly, he'd been wrong, although the Highland cattle were his best bet yet. "What were you doing in town?"

"Breakfast."

Standing at the door, Molly frowned. "He eats at Wynott Willie's three days a week with his cronies."

Jess knew those cronies. They'd been gathering at the diner for years, a rotating group of old cowboys on the edge. Some of them still clung to their purpose in life, but others had been forced into retirement, either passing their ranches on to family or selling out to some corporation. One would die, and another would take his place, marching toward his final fifteen minutes of fame at the Wynott Funeral Home. She shuddered to think of her father sitting at that table, telling his tall tales, unaware of the swift down-hill slide.

"The food there's pure cholesterol," Molly said. "Bacon, eggs…"

"You invoke the holy words like they're evil." Heck winked, and Jess couldn't help grinning. This was the father she knew, playful and rebellious.

A saucy tune bounced across the patio. Clapping one hand to her back pocket, Jess whirled away.

"What was that?" her dad asked. "Sounds like you got a band in your butt."

"Phone. Sorry." She wasn't surprised to see Treena's name on the screen. "Hello?"

"Jess? I'm not calling with a problem this time. I dealt with it. I just wanted to make sure I did it right."

She described a difficult guest and how she'd handled him.

"Perfect!" Jess said. "Great job."

"So see? You don't have to worry."

"You know me. I always worry."

"You should just relax," Treena said. "Gotta go! Enjoy your vacation."

"It's not…" Jess glanced down at the phone. Treena had already hung up.

It was true—Jess never stopped worrying about work, and Treena's constant references to vacation weren't helping. She hoped her boss didn't think she'd just wanted a break. She'd told him about her family issues, but maybe he thought they were just an excuse.

Hawaii seemed to be floating farther and farther away.

When she returned to the table, her dad still hadn't

eaten a bite. "We've got to get some electrolytes into those calves," he fretted.

"Tell Cade about it. He'll take care of them." Jess pushed the sandwich closer. "You could trade him a couple bales of hay."

"He won't take it, and I won't let him work that hard for nothing."

"I'd do it, Dad, but I'm beat from the drive."

"Aw, honey, you can't do it." Catching her frown, he scrambled to cover his gaffe. "You've been driving all day."

"I can do it." She grinned and punched him gently on the arm. "You can come watch in the morning."

She hadn't roped a calf in five years, but she'd do it, all right. She had to, if only because he'd said she couldn't.

"Aw, I know you'll try, honey. You always do."

Jess winced at the backhanded praise. What her dad meant was she always tried but usually failed.

She pointed to the sandwich. "Eat. Come on. It's my favorite." She searched her mind for a clever sandwich name. "It's a Tildy's Truck Stop Turkey-Town Special. They make 'em at a place just outside Denver, and I think I figured out the recipe. You tell me if it's good."

She was sort of telling the truth. She'd seen a sandwich called a Turkey-Town Special at a truck stop once, and the waitress's name had been Tildy. She had no idea what the original sandwich was like, but it sounded like something Heck would eat.

"I hope you can stand it." She heaved a dramatic sigh. "That barbecue sauce you have is way spicier than theirs, and I might have used too much pepper. It's probably too hot for you."

He sat back in his chair. "If it's so good, how come you didn't make one for yourself? I heard you tell your ma you were starving."

She's not my ma.

"Here you are, honey." Molly bustled out of the kitchen bearing a sandwich, the twin of Heck's. "You were so busy with your dad, you forgot your own, um, Turkey-Town Special."

Resigned, Jess took the sandwich in two hands and chomped a big bite.

"Mmm, good." She hadn't lied about the hotness. Even without the pepper, she could barely stand it. "Just look out. It's spicy."

Her dad took one bite, shrugged, then took another. When he pushed his plate back after eating half, she pouted.

"Don't you like it?"

"It's terrific, honey." Mopping his forehead, he manfully chomped at the second half. "Not hot enough, though. Not even close." Finally, he shoved his empty plate toward her like a child seeking approval. "Come on," he said. "Let's go for a ride. We can check those calves, get a closer look."

"Jess?" Molly called from the kitchen. "Cade got that load of hay stacked, and he's about to go. Could you thank him for us?" She came to the doorway, holding up hands decked in rubber gloves and dripping with soapsuds. "I'd go, but I'm in the middle of dishes."

Jess had told herself to stay away from Cade, but her dad's illness changed everything. She needed to talk to him, and this would be better than stopping by his place. The last person she wanted to see was Amber

Lynn Lyle—Amber Lynn *Walker*—keeping house at Cade's.

"Go," her dad said. "Thank the man. And be nice to him, okay? Cade does a lot for us."

She went, mulling over what Molly had said and wondering what was wrong with her father's heart. There was certainly nothing wrong with her own. It was beating jackrabbit fast, making her dizzy and a little faint.

Shoot, it was just Cade. And she was just saying thank you. Nothing could possibly happen, because he was married.

Married.

She wished she could pound that fact into her brain like a nail, so the pain would remind her of the truth every time she thought of him—him and those shattered crystal eyes, those manly muscles, and that utterly spectacular cowboy ass.

Heck watched his daughter walk away with a sigh of relief and a pang of guilt. He'd pretended to be disappointed when she wouldn't go out and chase cows, but the fact was, he didn't have the energy. He didn't have the strength to do much of anything these days.

Molly bustled in from the kitchen and gathered the plates. She was always bustling, and no wonder. She was a spirited forty-five years young, while he was an old man of sixty-four, so all the work of the big house fell on her soft shoulders.

At least he'd talked her into quitting her teaching job. Crazy woman had wanted to keep working, but Heck

Bailey could support his own wife, thank you very much. No wife of his would ever have to work.

He felt a flutter in his chest and put a hand over his heart. Long as his ticker held out, they'd be fine. He'd felt like a man in the prime of his life when he'd met her, and he'd mocked her fears about the sometimes dangerous work he did on horseback. But then he'd come face-to-face with mortality, and they'd had a long, serious talk about the future.

He hated long, serious talks. And these days, he didn't much like the future, either.

Canting one hip, Molly gave him a flirty smile and nodded toward the barn.

"Looks like our little plan worked."

"Of course it worked." He made a pistol with his finger and pointed it her way. "You're a devious woman, Molly Bailey."

"Oh, pshaw." She waved a plump, pretty hand in the air. Dimples blossomed when she smiled, and darn if she didn't look as pretty as a spring heifer sleeping in the sun. "I just know how women think. Jess was too proud to come back home, especially after Cade got into that mess of a marriage. She needed a reason to come, and we gave her one."

"So here she is. Now what are we going to do with her?" Heck sighed. "I told you, her mother poisoned her mind when it comes to ranching. She'll go back to the city soon as she can kick off her boots."

"It all depends on Cade." Molly glanced out the window toward the barn. "I think she'll stay in the end. You know they're meant to be together. And that girl belongs here, in a way I never will."

"I always thought so, but she thought different."

"Well, I'll just egg her on by leaving these brochures where she'll see 'em." She fanned a handful of pamphlets from various retirement communities in a half circle on the table. "There. Just a little nudge."

Heck reached over and grabbed one, holding it up to show its dog-eared cover. "Is this the one you like? What's it called, Moony Mind Manor?" He flipped through the pages, scene after scene of old fogies having what passed for fun in the so-called twilight years. "I'm thinking you'd like this place."

"Now, honey, it's Sunset Acres. And those pamphlets are just props for the plan." The dimples bloomed again, but he thought he caught a shadow behind that smile. "You know it's just to get Jess home. Once she and Cade get back together, you'll have a son-in-law to help you, and we won't ever think about retirement again."

"And if they don't?"

She looked away, a frown flitting across her face before she caught herself and smiled. "We'll cross that bridge when we come to it."

"Not the bridge to this place." He glanced at the cover, grunted with disdain, and tossed it back on the table. "Can't imagine living there."

"I know, honey." She slipped the pamphlet in with the others, straightening her display. "But lots of people do."

"I s'pose." He glanced out at the barn. "Jess didn't seem all that happy to see Cade. Holding back, I'd say."

"She's hurt. You and I were surprised he married Amber Lynn, so just imagine how Jess felt."

"Doesn't matter. He caught his mistake, and the

coast is clear. Girl ought to jump at a second chance with him."

"It's smart to be careful. Make sure that little sneak's really gone for good." Molly bit her lower lip. "I wasn't going to say anything, but I saw Amber Lynn's car over there earlier. She must've heard Jess was coming home, gone to stake her claim."

"Cade ought to run that woman off," Heck said. "She dang near ruined his life."

"He's too softhearted. Cade's a good man."

"Be better if he was a smart one."

Smiling as if he'd made a joke, Molly headed back to the kitchen. But Heck knew he was right. Cade had been manipulated up, down, and sideways by a woman, and now Heck wondered if the same might be happening to his own self. Molly's plan to get Jess to come back was brilliant, but it was also devious, underhanded, and manipulative. If his new wife ever turned that mind toward Heck himself, he'd be wrapped around her pretty fingers before he knew what hit him.

Maybe he already was. Maybe the plan wasn't about his daughter at all. It had been, at first—he was pretty sure. But once he'd had that heart attack, Molly started getting awfully serious about those brochures. When the dust cleared, he was afraid his daughter would be back in the city and he really *would* be living at Sunset Acres.

It all depended on Cade.

"You go, Son," he muttered under his breath. "Don't blow it."

—◆—

Cade crouched in the barn's wide entryway, rubbing Boogy's furry chest and trying to imagine the Diamond Jack belonging to anyone but the Baileys. He couldn't.

He could imagine Jess naked, though. Matter of fact, he couldn't seem to stop.

Twisting his shoulders, he tried to wriggle off the hay that had drifted down his collar. Finally, he tugged the T-shirt over his head and used it to slap at his shoulders. Savoring the cool air, he dried the sheen of sweat that glossed his back and chest, tossed the shirt to the ground, and bent at the waist, shaking his head and running his fingers through his hair. More hay showered into the dirt.

"So you still take cowboy showers."

He looked up to see Jess standing right where they'd tumbled together just an hour before. He'd relived that encounter with every bale he'd stacked, revising it in his head, trying out different responses. In his mind, he was one suave and clever cowboy. In real life, not so much.

"Molly and Dad said thanks for taking care of the hay. Me, too." She bent down and scratched Boogy's ears. "Plus, I need to talk to you."

He felt uncomfortable standing there bare-chested, but the shirt, damp with sweat, was too disgusting to wear. Tossing it over a stall door, he grabbed his hat from a peg on the wall and clapped it on his head, tugging the brim low over his eyes. A man didn't feel so naked with his hat on.

Jess perched on a hay bale just inside the wide barn doors. She looked tense, like a lark on a fence post, ready to take flight at the slightest threat.

Boogy trotted over and sat on her foot.

Good dog, Boogy.

"So what did you want to talk about?" he asked.

Avoiding his eyes, she stroked the dog's ears. "Molly said you won't work for Daddy."

Boogy threw his head back, letting his tongue flop out the side of his mouth, grinning his toothy grin. Jess smiled back, and Cade vowed to give the mutt a treat when they got home.

"I do what I can," he said. "It's just that I've got all the work I can handle at home."

"Your place keeps you that busy?"

Did she have to sound so surprised?

"I didn't see any cattle in your fields, so I thought..."

"I quit the cattle business." He sat down beside her, close but not too close. Resting his elbows on his knees, he clasped his hands and carefully looked away. Calming body language worked for horses; he hoped it would calm Jess, too.

"I work over at the Vee Bar now and then, but mostly I'm training horses. Cutting's big these days, and team roping. I take on mounts for clients and have a few prospects of my own. There's a good market these days for all-around ranch horses." Hat or no hat, he still felt naked, so he tugged it down to hide his eyes. "Your dad helped. He used a couple geldings I trained as pickup horses at Wynott Days. They performed like aces, got me a lot of business."

"It figures Amber Lynn wouldn't want a farmer for a husband."

"The change was my choice, not Amber Lynn's." He kept his tone mild, but it wasn't easy. "I had to do something. She left a lot of bills behind."

Jess turned, blinking as if she'd just stepped into the sun. "She *left* bills *behind*?"

"Yeah." He wondered why she'd be surprised. Everybody knew how Amber Lynn was with money. "I wish I could do more for your dad, but she had a pile of maxed-out credit cards when we—you know."

He couldn't say *when we got married*. Not to Jess.

"She hasn't paid a dime since she left, so I'm working pretty hard." He stared down at the scuffed toes of his boots. "I help your dad when I can, but I wish I could do more."

Jess was still blinking. She spoke in a strangled voice. "Did you say since she *left*?"

"Yeah. Since the divorce."

"*Divorce?*" She stared at him, openmouthed, and the facts clicked together in his head. He understood her reluctance now, her anger, the new awkwardness between them.

She didn't know.

She didn't know about the divorce.

His heart leapt so high, he had to swallow so it wouldn't jump out and land in her lap. He pictured it dancing a joyful rhumba there, turning cartwheels.

"I thought you knew," he said. "I tried to call, but then—I figured somebody'd tell you."

"I don't really see anybody from home. I'm always at work." She shook her head. "What happened?"

"She said I was always working. I didn't talk enough, she said, or show her affection. According to her, I wasn't cut out to share my life with another person. So she found somebody else, carried on with him behind my back. When I found out, well…"

Jess glanced at him, then stared out at the prairie, blinking as if she was holding back tears.

Dang it, maybe Amber Lynn was right. He wasn't good at sharing. He should have tried harder, left a message—but he'd pictured a sleek answering machine piping his voice into Jess's city apartment, and he just couldn't do it. He wasn't sure it would be welcome.

It had been easier to let it drop, let fate take its course, and hope somehow, someday, they'd see each other again.

Well, someday was here. And he'd better make the most of it.

Chapter 7

THE BRIM OF CADE'S COWBOY HAT HUNG LOW OVER HIS eyes, which left Jess staring at a shred of hay caught in the blond hairs strewn across his chest. It gleamed in the sunlight that poured through the window, and her fingertips itched to flick it away.

Once, she'd touched this man every day. She'd worn his love like an old shirt, casual and comfortable. The trouble was, she'd treated him like an old shirt, too.

They'd been friends since childhood, then lovers, together so long, it had been hard to tell where she ended and he began. She'd chafed at that and felt trapped by everyone's assumption that she'd marry him, stay in Wynott forever. She'd wanted to see the world—or at least Denver. And she'd started to wonder who she'd be without him.

Well, she'd found out. She was the same person she'd always been—only lonelier. She compared every man she met to Cade Walker, and every one came up short. But once he'd married Amber Lynn, it was too late to change her mind.

Until now.

Holy cats, what was she going to *do*? She wasn't ready for this. She'd come home to help her father, and now...

"Well, I ought to go." He stood and stretched, stepping out into the sunshine. "You probably want to spend your time with your dad."

Oh God. She'd been staring at him with her mouth hanging open for how long? She wasn't sure. But she probably looked like a sun-stroked calf.

Rising, she joined him. "I've got lots of time."

Her voice came out husky. She sounded like the kind of woman who dragged men to the hayloft and ravished them. Come to think of it, she'd been that kind of woman a time or two. But that wasn't a good idea now.

Was it?

She scanned his face and caught that shattered look in his eyes again. Maybe he'd loved Amber Lynn. Did he miss her? Had he found something in her he hadn't gotten from Jess? Amber Lynn had always been sexy and wild, a sleek cat to Jess's big-eyed, clueless fawn. That fawn had been a complete innocent when she and Cade had first made love. He'd had to teach her everything she knew.

He hadn't had much experience either, but they'd figured things out. The thought sparked a smile, and she reached out, running the back of her fingers down his chest and knocking that bit of hay to the ground. It was a gesture from the past, the ghost of an old habit come to life. He took her hand and held it, gazing into her eyes.

If she was going to resurrect old habits, she might as well dig up the fun ones. Tilting her head ever so slightly, she licked her lips. It was a question without words, and he answered.

He didn't use words, either.

The moment their lips touched, her world rushed away as if they were streaming into the past on a runaway train. Old fears surfaced and pressed the brakes, but memory raced on, rushing backward in a blur.

He's changed. He's been married, divorced. He's not yours anymore. And Molly saw Amber Lynn's car. Wasn't that just now? Or did I dream that?

Brakes, brakes, brakes, but the train sped on. Nothing mattered but the smooth, slow glide of his tongue, the warmth of his mouth, the press of his lips on hers. And his body—that body!—pressed to her own, making her feel all warm and melty.

There was no barn, no hay, no horses. No divorce, no sick father, no stepmom, no job in Denver. Her fear of losing the ranch faded away, and so did Amber Lynn Lyle. There was nothing but Cade in the whole wide world. He filled her empty places, warmed her cold spots, and chased off all her fears.

He kissed her as if he was dying and she was the air he needed to live. She wondered how he could have even looked at Amber Lynn if he felt this way, let alone married her.

The question hauled her up from the warm world of the kiss and tossed her into reality. Twisting in his arms, she tried to free herself, but that brought the unmistakable push of his arousal against her, hard, hot, and demanding. Her determination to push him away somehow transformed into a desperate need to close even the smallest space between them, and the train gathered speed.

When the kiss finally ended, she backed away, tripped over a half-buried rock, and sat down hard against the barn. Dangling her hands in her lap, she let her head drop back against the sunlit wood and gazed up at the sky as if the answers to everything were written in the clouds. He joined her, hands clasped, staring at nothing.

She didn't know about him, but she was too dazed to speak.

Questions, though. Questions.

"Why Amber Lynn?" She did her best to smile, keep it light. "You knew she was about my least favorite person in the world, right?"

"Yeah." Letting his hat tilt over his face, he rubbed the back of his neck. "Guess I thought it didn't matter anymore. Maybe something inside me wanted to punish myself or punish you for leaving. I don't really know." He glanced at her, then looked away. "I thought I could finally be like other guys about women." He swallowed hard. "With you, I was always after forever. I wanted something casual, you know?"

Yeah, she knew. She'd wanted to taste that freedom, too, wanted to care a little less, make love without her whole future twisted in the sheets.

"I didn't care about a damn thing after you left." He was studying the horizon as if he needed to memorize the mountains for a test. "Most of my life, things only mattered if they mattered to you."

She started to speak, but he shook his head.

"I know that isn't fair, and it might be part of why you left. I hung my whole life on you. Maybe it was too much."

"No. I just got selfish," she said. "I wanted casual, too." She felt her lips tip into a mirthless smile. "It's overrated, far as I can tell."

"It sure is. I started to understand my dad—why he drank so hard once my mother was gone."

"He always drank."

"He did, but after she died, he drank like he was

gunning for the grave." He shook his head. "I'm not saying that was right, and I always swore I wouldn't be like him, but you mattered too much when I was sober. So I got drunk. Great coping skills, right?" He plucked a black-eyed Susan from the weeds and stared down at the yellow wheel of petals. "Then Amber Lynn came along." Avoiding Jess's gaze, he spoke to the flower. "I don't know why she wanted me, but she did, and she was relentless. She went after me like she went after being rodeo queen."

"Oh crap." Jess's sudden laugh surprised them both. "You were doomed, then. She didn't know a horse's ass from a big-mouthed bass, but she went after that sash like a tiger on steroids."

"That sash belonged to you. You rode better than she did, and you did a lot more work behind the scenes, too."

"Yeah, but she looked better. She was good at fashion and a real whiz with makeup." Jess shrugged. "Besides, it wasn't worth it. You wouldn't believe the under-handed stuff she did. Bubble gum in my hair, salt in my coffee… When I caught her in Buster's stall, I gave up. I didn't know what she planned to do, but I cared more about that horse than about riding in some parade."

"Well, she didn't put bubble gum in my hair, but she scared me all right. Stalked me, I guess. I'd turn around, and there she'd be, usually half undressed for some reason I never could figure out. Then she followed me home one night, and well…" He pulled a petal from the flower and let it twirl to the ground, then glanced up at her with those eyes. "Men are weak, you know? I thought it was just a fling, but she kept pushing for more. I was about to pull the plug, but then there was the baby."

Jess's blood stalled in her veins. "Baby?"

"You didn't hear about that either? The gossips are slipping up." He plucked another petal off his flower, then one more. "She said she miscarried after the wedding, but I don't think it was real."

"But you believed her. And you married her."

"Thought I might have a son or a little girl." A wistful look softened those eyes. "Can you imagine?"

She couldn't. Not with Amber Lynn. But she'd dreamed of the children she'd have with Cade half her life. Named them even.

Staring down at the fallen petals, he shook his head. "I loved that mythical baby. Dumbass, right?"

She plucked a flower of her own, a daisy. Its petals fanned out, neat and even. *Loves me, loves me not.* Suddenly, life made sense again.

She'd believed Cade must have changed in some essential, dramatic way. How else could he have chosen Amber Lynn? She'd wondered how the man she'd known so well, a man who'd respected her for her intelligence, not her body, had fallen for a human Barbie doll.

Now she knew he'd just been Cade—*her* Cade— trying to do the right thing for a child.

"So that's the sad story of me and Amber Lynn." He grimaced. "Thought I was taking a one-week cruise and ended up with a life sentence in the brig. Well, almost. But I gotta tell you." He frowned as he tore off another petal. "I was a dud at being married."

"She cheated on you. How is that your fault?"

"The blame went both ways. I cheated, too, in a way." His gaze dropped to the ground, and he refused to meet her eyes. "I never stopped loving you, not for one day, one hour, one minute." The last petal fell, spinning, to the ground. "I did my best. Swore an oath and tried to keep it." He sighed. "I'm glad we're here. I'm glad I'm free. But I still feel like I failed."

He handed her the flower, now a drooping, ruined stem. "I won't fail again. I'm about as wrecked as this flower, but I'm still here, okay? And still yours, whether you want me or not."

Molly's busy hands stilled as she watched Jess and Cade from the kitchen window. Jess had caught Cade cleaning himself up.

Well, that ought to do it. Even she, an old married lady, could appreciate the sight of that man with his shirt off.

She felt like a peeper, but not so much she'd walk away from the window. They were so sweet, out there by the barn, finding their way back to each other under the summer sun. And they looked so right together—Jess, with her blond curls and long legs, Cade so muscular and manly.

Maybe this would turn out all right.

Boot heels struck the floor behind her, and she felt familiar hands on her hips. The warmth of her husband's palms spread straight to her lady parts, and she wondered, not for the first time, how a man so much older could warm her to the core.

"What do you think?" She twisted to see his face and

was surprised to see his brows drawn low over his eyes. "It looks like they might make it, hon."

"They'd better." Heck sounded his age, his voice high and fretful. "I don't like the look of those brochures, Molls. I need to tell you, I'm not moving to one of those places."

Patting his hands, she kissed his cheek. "I know, sweetheart. But stop worrying." She nodded toward the two kids. "It might take Jess a little time, but whatever happens with Cade, she'll find her way back to the ranch. You can see in her eyes how she loves it." She patted his cheek. "And how she loves you."

"She hasn't thrown a rope in five years. Ridden a horse in, what, three? Four? And she was never rodeo ready. Not like Griff."

"Give her time. You said she always tried hard, and doesn't that matter more? You have to *want* to throw the rope."

He grunted in response, and she knew she'd hit a nerve. Griff had been a disappointment to his dad. The boy was a soldier, something to be proud of, but Heck had wanted to pass the ranch on, and when it came to gender roles, he was a regular Neanderthal. He thought western women ought to be traditional ranch wives, cooking for the crew, keeping house, bottle-feeding calves, and raising little cowboys to take over from their daddies.

But Molly would change him. She *would*. She'd convince him his precious daughter, strong woman that she was, deserved as much of a chance as his son. With or without Cade.

Molly hadn't been raised a cowgirl. She couldn't

ride or rope or doctor cows. But she knew Jess could, and if her stepdaughter could tear herself away from the city and come back where she belonged, she'd find one heck of a cheerleader in her new stepmother. Sure, it would help Heck keep the ranch, but Molly thought it would make Jess happy, too. And that was all Molly wanted.

Well, not all.

She sighed. "I just want her to love me, hon. Without my job, I miss the kids, and—I miss that bond, you know?"

"You don't need that job." Heck nuzzled her neck. "And Jess'll figure it out. Give her time."

"I don't know. She seems so set against me."

His grip tightened on her hips. "She been rude to you?"

"No, it's not that. I probably want too much, too soon. You know. *Babies*."

Molly hadn't even finished being a virgin when the doctor had told her babies would never happen for her. She'd done her best to find a silver lining, but that was when the trouble started. Infertility had made it easy to say yes to any man who offered a wink or a smile, and she'd looked for the love she craved in sex instead of family. She'd prayed some man would love her enough to overlook the fact that she couldn't give him kids, but that didn't happen.

Oh, there'd been a couple of guys she'd gotten serious with, men who'd been glad she didn't want to discuss baby names over dinner. But she knew they'd change their minds someday, and she wasn't about to deny them their God-given right to have a child.

She'd never compromised and rarely complained, even to herself. She knew some women at church called her white trash behind her back—partly because she'd grown up in Springtime Acres trailer park, and partly because she'd dated so, well, so *widely,* and maybe a bit, er, *enthusiastically*. She'd always held her head high, happy with her homey little single-wide, her job as a substitute teacher, and her busy social life.

But dear Lord, how she'd wanted babies.

She turned, lacing her hands around Heck's neck. "You are the answer to my prayers," she said. "You *and* your kids."

He kissed her, and she felt that thrill again, the one that always crept up on her and made her dizzy. She thought about dragging him off to the bedroom, but Jess might come in. He must have had the same thought, because he released her when she turned to the window.

"Whether they come around or not, I feel blessed you chose me, Heck Bailey." She gazed at the barn and the pasture beyond, at horses grazing peacefully and the mountains in the distance. "And I've learned to love this place, too. It'll work. You'll see."

She watched Cade hand Jess a flower, then turn and walk away, his back bowed under the weight of what looked like unrequited love. She wondered if Jess realized how rare it was to have a man who treasured you like that. The girl should requite that love, and soon, if she wanted to find what mattered in life.

Turning back to her husband, she found it for herself. "You've made me so happy, sweetheart. And I would do anything to return the favor."

She looked out at the plains, the barn, the mountains. Her husband's whole being was planted in this land—his heart, his soul. And hers was with him, always and forever.

She'd do anything to keep the land he loved.

Chapter 8

IT WAS HARD FOR CADE TO LEAVE HIS DREAMS BEHIND THE next morning—dreams of Jess and a future he'd long thought impossible—but he folded his blanket, set it on his pillow, and stretched his legs, which ached from sleeping on a sofa so much shorter than he was.

The sofa. Momentarily confused, he looked down at the lumpy cushions, then scanned the room for clues. Why had he slept on the sofa? His days of passing out drunk in front of the TV had ended along with his marriage to Amber Lynn.

Amber Lynn. That's why.

She'd taken a shower after he'd left, all right, but then she'd gone to bed. *His* bed. On discovering her sleeping form, he'd backed out of the room, unwilling to sully his still-fresh memories of Jess by having an argument with his ex.

Now, he sought refuge in the barn, taking his time feeding the horses. He brushed out a knotted tail here, checked a cut leg there. When he couldn't delay any longer, he headed for the house, where he was welcomed by a resounding crash from the kitchen. Boogy shrank back, alarmed.

"It's okay, bud."

Reassured, the dog sniffed the air and grinned. Cade wasn't so smiley, but he smelled something, too. Burnt toast and…was that bacon?

The kitchen looked as if half a dozen caffeinated toddlers had invaded, spilling juice, dribbling crumbs, and sprinkling the counters liberally with flour. Or was that sugar?

In the center of it all, Amber Lynn struck a June Cleaver pose at the stove top, presenting a plateful of food. She'd made a valiant attempt to hide her black eye with makeup, but the effect was hardly appetizing. She still looked a little like a Hollywood zombie.

He spoke cautiously. "Somebody's been busy."

"It was *me*." She flashed him a thousand-watt smile. "I made *breakfast*."

"Wow." He eyed the plate. "How'd you get the bacon so, um, shiny?"

Her lower lip trembled, and he rushed to cover his mistake.

"I'm just asking 'cause I haven't seen bacon that way before," he said. "All limp. You know, like noodles."

"Oh." The frown returned. "I boiled it and boiled it, but it just wouldn't brown."

He was relieved when his phone interrupted him. He checked the screen.

Bank, it said.

Cade's stomach clenched. It might be about the mortgage, but more likely it was Amber Lynn's father poking his nose in Cade's business. Maybe he was looking for his daughter or his car. Hopefully, he'd forgotten about the horse.

Cade almost handed the phone to his ex, then thought better of it. Walking swiftly to the bedroom, he grunted a hello.

"Howdy there, Son!"

Somewhere out on the endless plains, a cell tower was trembling, while here on the Walker Ranch, things were getting weirder and weirder.

Jasper Lyle had never called Cade "Son" before. In fact, when Cade had asked for permission to wed Amber Lynn, he'd said no, calling Cade a ne'er-do-well and a country bumpkin. He'd enumerated Tom Walker's many crimes and heaped the sins of the father on the son as if Cade would inevitably inherit every one of the old man's vices.

Finally, old man Lyle had decided having a punching bag for a son-in-law wasn't such a bad thing, and besides, there was that mythical baby. He'd agreed the two should wed, but from day one, he'd berated Cade for everything Amber Lynn did, as if Cade had been the one to raise her.

"How are things at the ranch?" Jasper Lyle asked as if he cared—and maybe he did. If Cade missed so much as one payment, the ranch would belong to the Wynott Bank and Trust, which belonged to Jasper Lyle.

"Fine," Cade said. "Keeping busy."

"*Cade?*" Amber Lynn hollered from the kitchen. "*Who is it?*"

Twisting the lock on the bedroom door, Cade settled on the bed. Something was up here, and he was going to find out what.

"I bet you're busy," Jasper Lyle said. "That's what I always admired about you."

What?

"You're willing to work for what you want," Lyle continued. "Bet you worked hard to win my little girl's heart, didn't you? Must have been a sorry day when she left you."

"Yes, sir." Cade wasn't fool enough to disagree. "But I know you disapproved of me, sir. You made that clear."

"Well, yes." Lyle cleared his throat. "Seems I was wrong."

The world stopped turning, but only for a second. Cade guessed old Jasper had seen Amber's black eye when he loaned her the car. He probably viewed Cade as the lesser of two evils—or however many evils Amber Lynn had managed to find.

"It's kind of you to say so, sir. Glad to hear I'm a step up from a man who hits women."

Jasper cleared his throat. "I'm saying I'm sorry, Son."

Well, glory hallelujah. It's about freaking time.

"Thank you, sir."

"I want you to know I've taken the note on your home loan and torn it up."

"You *what*?" Cade fell backward onto the bed as if shot.

"You heard me, Son. That loan is paid in full."

Cade heard a loud *thunk* and pictured Jasper smacking the desktop with his hand. It was a habit, one that had always annoyed Cade. But right now, it sounded like music.

"Is that for sure, sir? You're not going to change your mind?"

"You have my word. Your debt is paid." Lyle chuckled. "Or maybe I should say my daughter's debt."

Something was going on here. Jasper Lyle cared more about money than his own immortal soul. There was no way he'd forgiven Cade's debt out of the goodness of his evil, money-grubbing heart.

"I appreciate this, sir. I hope you know I'm careful with money, and I've never missed a payment."

"I know that, Son." Jasper chuckled. "I also know it was my daughter's careless spending that forced you to take out that loan. I suppose her wild ways with money are my fault. I never could say no to my little girl." Cade heard a creak and pictured the old man leaning back in his high-backed "executive" desk chair. "But she and I've had a talk, and she's promised to be more careful."

Cade felt a slow burn smoldering in his gut. The day he'd taken out the mortgage on the ranch had been the most shameful day of his life. The mortgage rep at Lyle's bank, a fat man in a checked suit, had chided him mercilessly, treating him like a child with lectures on reckless spending.

Cade's sense of honor hadn't allowed him to tell the man it was his wife who'd spent the money or that his wife was the bank president's daughter. It wouldn't have been right to tell a stranger how she'd spent most of it before he'd even met her or how Lyle refused to pay her bills because he wanted to teach her a lesson by making her husband miserable.

Now old Jasper seemed to think it was some sort of joke. But hey, he'd torn up the loan—or so he said.

"Thank you, sir."

"No problem. I sent you an email, Son, with the zero balance. The deed is done." He smacked the desktop again. "Ha! Get it? The deed. It's done."

"Good one." Putting his phone on speaker, Cade checked his email. Sure enough, there was a note from Jasper Lyle. He opened it to find written confirmation: the loan was gone. Paid in full.

"Consider it a gift on this happy occasion."

Cade figured the happy occasion must be Jasper getting dead drunk. Nothing but near unconsciousness could make him part with that kind of money.

"Cade?" Amber rapped on the door. "Who is it, honey?"

"I heard that. Better go see to the little woman."

"Right, sir."

Mr. Lyle chuckled again. He seemed to be in a chuckling mood. Or a drunk one.

"One more thing."

"Yes, sir?"

"There'll be no running off to the courthouse this time, okay?"

The man's tone was jocular, as if wagging a finger, but Cade had no idea what he was talking about. The courthouse? Was there some way he could sue the Lyles for damages? He'd never thought of that. But with the divorce final and the mortgage gone, it didn't matter anymore, and he'd never been big on revenge.

"Don't worry, sir," he said. "No courthouse."

"This time, my little girl will have the wedding of her dreams. The dress, the cake, the country club—the works. I'll do right by you this time, Son."

A high, hot ringing clanged in Cade's ears, and the slow burn deep in his stomach burst into flame.

Surely, surely, Lyle couldn't believe Cade would marry his daughter *twice*? That would be like asking an escaped circus lion to step back into its cage and get whipped a little more.

"Son?" Lyle tapped the receiver. "You there?"

"Ah, that's great, sir. Amber Lynn deserves that. The wedding of her dreams."

"*Cade*," Amber Lynn shrieked through the door. "*It's time to eat! Get off the phone!*"

The caged lion feeling returned. He had the ringmaster on the phone, and the lady with the whip was in the kitchen. Wild calliope music rang in his head, high and off-key. *Doot-doot diddle-iddle-oot-doot doo-doo…*

"I have to go, sir, but I sure appreciate this talk. And I'm grateful about the mortgage."

"Well, I know what it's like trying to keep a woman in line." Jasper huffed out a phony, man-to-man laugh. "My Mona sure does love to shop."

Mona. Of course. That's what this is all about.

Amber Lynn's daddy had recently married for the fourth time—or was it the fifth? The woman was half his age and probably didn't want Amber Lynn around. That's why Jasper was desperate to unload his daughter on the nearest low-class, redneck, white-trash bum with a hovel.

But it wasn't going to work—not for Cade and not for Amber Lynn, who'd made it clear throughout the divorce that she hated Cade. He wondered where Lyle had gotten the idea they'd try again. It must have been a misunderstanding.

It was time to get off the phone and tell Amber Lynn about the mistake. They'd laugh, and the incident would be over.

Hopefully, that dead mortgage wouldn't spring back to life when Lyle found out that no way, no how was Cade Walker taking Amber Lynn off his hands.

Amber Lynn jiggled the doorknob. "Cade, you get out here!"

"I'd better go," Cade said to Jasper.

"Sure, sure." His ex-father-in-law let out a laugh that set Cade's teeth on edge. "Get back to my daughter. You're one lucky son of a bitch, Walker, you know that? When she told me, you could've knocked me over with a feather."

"Wait. *She told* you we were getting married?"

"Sure, Son. Did you think a little birdie told me?"

No wonder Amber Lynn wanted him off the phone. She probably knew it was her daddy, calling before she'd had time to spring some trap she'd set.

"I sure was surprised," Jasper said.

"Yeah. I'm surprised, too."

Cade realized he was smiling. He might not be into revenge, but this was strangely satisfying. Amber Lynn and Mona must be fighting like cats in a bag, and suddenly, Jasper Lyle, bank president, desperately needed Cade Walker, a no-account, common cowboy.

But Cade didn't need the Lyles. He never had, not even to pay off Amber Lynn's debts. His reputation as a horse trainer was growing with every client, so he could take care of the mortgage on his own if he had to.

But he wouldn't have to. He had written proof it had been paid.

"Well, thanks, Mr. Lyle." Cade couldn't help sounding sarcastic any more than he could help smiling at the ceiling. "And congratulations. Who's the lucky guy?"

"I beg your pardon?"

"You said Amber Lynn was getting the wedding of her dreams. I'm wondering—who's the groom?"

"What? Why, it's…she said…"

Cade jumped in before Jasper could stop stammering. "I'll be sure and send something special for a gift, but

I won't be coming to the service. I'm the ex-husband, after all, a country bumpkin and a—what was it? A ne'er-do-well, that was it. So I really can't imagine I'd be welcome."

And if I ever saw your daughter in a wedding gown again, I'd run screaming from the room.

A series of bumps and thumps, followed by a crashing sound, reverberated over the line. It sounded like Lyle's desk chair might have spun out of control and tossed him through a window.

Gently, with a feeling of great satisfaction, Cade hung up the phone.

The bumping and thumping continued, but now it was Amber Lynn pounding on the door.

"Cade? I need to talk to you. Now! Who *is* that? It's not my dad, is it?"

"Sure was." Cade leapt from the bed and opened the door. "Good news. He forgave my loan. And hey, you're getting married!"

Chapter 9

JESS ROSE EARLY TO A BLUEBIRD DAY DRENCHED IN sunshine. She had a good horse, fine weather, and a mission of mercy to save sick baby calves.

The only cloud in her sky was her dad's health. She'd seen sweat bead on his forehead when he tacked up and heard a raspy sound in his chest. But after a brief pause for breath, he swung into the saddle like his old self.

Jess was feeling like her old self, too. She loved seeing the ranch from the back of a good horse, and while her quarter horse gelding might be getting old, he was the only creature on earth, outside her family, that she loved without reservation. All through her teen years, Buster had offered a listening ear, a shoulder to cry on, and a healthy distraction from drinking, boys, and all the other temptations that prey on small-town kids with nothing to do. She'd ridden him for miles, lost in her thoughts, reins slack in her hands. He'd always kept her safe.

Her dad nudged his mount into motion, and Jess followed, enjoying the creak of saddle leather and the warmth of the sun on her back. She didn't see why her stepmother was so worried. Heck was riding like a grandpa today, so slowly old Buster was prancing and champing at the bit.

"You must be fired up about something to make him act like that," her dad said.

"Nope." Her crazy kiss with Cade had crept into her mind again, but she didn't need to share that with her dad. "I'm fine."

"You and Cade didn't fight, did you?"

"No." She couldn't help smiling. "We got along just fine."

"Used to be a lot more'n fine." He shot her a sidelong glance.

"Uh-huh."

She didn't want to discuss Cade with her dad. That kiss had been a stroll down memory lane—such an enjoyable stroll, she had to squeeze her legs around her horse's barrel even now, just thinking about it. But it hadn't changed anything, because nothing *could* change. She'd dedicated years of energy to climbing the corporate ladder. She had to admit she was a little bored with her job in Denver, but the Hawaii location would take care of that problem. Nobody could be bored on a beach, right? But Cade's life was here, and that would never change.

She closed her eyes, trusting Buster, and pictured an endless expanse of sand and white-topped waves rolling in and out with their slow, rumbling thunder. She pretended the cry of a hawk was a seagull overhead and imagined exchanging the scent of sage for that salty, fishy smell that should be gross but wasn't.

But when she opened her eyes, the clear blue sky, the gleaming shafts of sun-bleached grass, the sunflowers dancing on their long stems, and all the other wonders of the West shoved Hawaii right out of her head.

Buster tossed his head and danced. "He needs to run, Dad."

"Can't do it. Your stepmother laid down the law. It's not safe."

"Right." She nodded toward his flashy palomino, who was sidestepping like Seabiscuit at the starting gate. "That's why you picked that horse."

"Oh, he's safe. He's one of Cade's." Her dad patted the animal's neck. "Trust me, that boy's horses are bombproof when he gets done with 'em."

"That's Cade's?" Jess eyed the horse's perfect conformation. "Looks expensive."

"One of his clients' horses. He likes me to give 'em some ranch work now and then. Calms 'em down, helps 'em focus."

"He's doing well, then?"

"Sure is." Heck glowed as if Cade were his own son. "Earned the trust of some of the best in the business. That boy's going places, Jess."

Jess thought about Cade and all the places he could go. Her bedroom. The hayloft. The back of his pickup, parked under the stars down by the quarry. She'd gone all those places with him and enjoyed every trip. Maybe they could have a private high school reunion, just the two of them.

She sighed. "He might be going places, but he'll never leave here. And I've got other plans, Dad. I'm in line for a promotion. This job lets me travel and meet so many people—I just love it."

"That's great, hon. I'm proud of you. But I'm proud of Cade, too." Her dad gave her a sideways look. "He's making a good living doing what he loves to do, right here at home."

Home. The word echoed in Jess's mind as they

plodded up a rock-strewn hill. Twisting in her saddle, she watched the house grow small in the distance as the valley celebrated all around it, dancing to a tickling breeze. Dressed in rust and gold, sap-green and sage, swaying aspen rattled leafy castanets. Beyond them, white patches on the mountains warned that snow would fly before long and everything would go cold—just about the time Jess lost the warmth of home.

She watched the petulant, old-man look leave her dad's face, proving the ranch itself was the cure for what ailed him. That made her wonder if her stepmother was on Heck's side at all. Maybe this was all about money or a more leisurely lifestyle. Molly didn't have to work now, but she probably wanted to live in a swankier neighborhood, with other people around. She'd become one of those ladies who lunched, spending her husband's money while he—well, Jess didn't know what her dad would do.

Heck opened the gate to the next pasture, a wide, flat acreage scattered with boulders the size of small houses. It looked like a giant stone baby had abandoned his toys beside the deep ravine, where a creek fed undergrowth so thick it would hide their bovine patients forever.

The Highland cattle were solitary beasts who nursed their young alone rather than hanging in a herd. They were absurdly cute, with flat pink noses, ginger Beatles moptops, and wide, branching horns. They looked ridiculous, but her dad claimed their lean beef commanded a high price.

She wondered how this latest experiment in exotic livestock was going. Better than the alpacas, she hoped, or the emus. Or the camels.

Oh God, she hated to even *think* about the camels.

"See, they're all spread out." Her father nodded toward what appeared to be reddish-brown hummocks in the distance. "Should be able to rope these babies one by one, without spookin' the rest of 'em."

"Should's a big word, Dad." Jess touched her rope nervously. "I'm really out of practice."

Up ahead, a mama cow nuzzled a calf that bore the telltale signs of scours, a disease known to cowboys everywhere as the dreaded "runny ass." It could kill a calf in a matter of days if it wasn't treated.

"This one's mine," Jess said and nudged Buster into a sidelong walk. She and the horse avoided eye contact with the moptopped baby and his redheaded mama. She wished her dad raised Herefords or Black Angus—or any breed without horned heifers—but the thought flew out of her head as she kicked Buster into a lope.

Her dad let out a loud cowboy whoop behind her, and joy rose with it, free and unfettered on the wind. Jess hadn't ridden in years, let alone roped, yet it felt so right. Maybe it was like riding a bicycle, and you never forgot how.

As she neared the so-called baby, she realized he was more of a teenager, and a bull calf to boot. He bolted, of course, but Buster, cow-smart and cunning, cut him off from his mama on dancing, darting hooves while Jess clung to the saddle horn and prayed. Anyone who thought cowboys didn't pull leather had never ridden a working cow horse. It was a challenge just to stay in the saddle.

When the horse brought her into position, she felt her skills click into place one by one. Forming a loop, she twirled it overhead.

As she sent it spiraling into the sky, her world narrowed until all she saw was the rope and the calf. She didn't notice the heifer until the beast darted forward and scraped one of her boots out of the stirrup with its horn. Surprised, Buster spun a sudden circle. Jess grabbed the saddle horn again, but the world dipped and wobbled and—*whump!*

Breathless, she stared up into the hairy face of Mama Cow, whose mournful *mooo* wafted the scent of half-digested cud into Jess's face.

Those horns looked a lot bigger from the ground. Staggering to her feet, Jess found Buster right beside her. Sticking one foot in the stirrup, she grabbed the saddle horn and hauled herself onto his back.

The fluid grace of the motion made her feel like a real cowgirl again. Sure, she'd been tossed, and her loop missed by a mile, but she hadn't gotten hurt, and most important, she hadn't cried.

Her butt was going to be sore for a week, though.

"You think she would have gored me, Dad?"

"Naw. But she's running that calf toward the ravine. Better get going."

Buster put on the gas, almost jerking Jess from the saddle before she gathered her wits and her rope, throwing a spinning loop that settled neatly, perfectly, miraculously over the bull calf's head.

She was so stunned by her success, she paused, and the calf ran halfway through the loop. The neat catch turned awkward, circling the head and one foreleg. But he was caught.

Leaping from the saddle, she raced down the rope while Buster backed slowly, keeping it taut. Grasping one furry ear and some loose skin at the calf's flank, she summoned all her strength and strained to lift him.

"*Bawww*," said the baby.

They danced a long and clumsy waltz, Jess hauling and shoving, the calf bawling and balking. It was a familiar feeling—incompetence on the plains. Maybe she'd been right to trade her saddle for an executive desk chair and a story about how she *used* to be a cowgirl.

But no. She would always be a cowgirl. *Always*.

Determined, she hooked one foot around the calf's hind leg and tugged him off-balance. *Whump!* again— but this time, it was the calf who hit the dirt.

At a rodeo, she would have been disqualified six ways to Sunday, but this was real life, and there were no rules except to be as gentle as possible with His Runniness while making sure he took his medicine. It would be nice if she could avoid rubbing up against him while she did it, but that wasn't really a rule, nor was it possible.

Pressing the bawling beastie to the ground, she dragged his legs together and whipped the piggin' string around his bony ankles, then pulled the knot tight as a familiar, cud-laden breath bathed her face with the scent of rotten vegetation.

"Oh no." She jumped to her feet, waving and dancing. "Git, Mama. Git!"

The bull calf bucked and strained, the mama cow mooed, and Buster held his ground without so much as a twitch while Jess raced to her saddlebags, dancing like a spastic leprechaun to keep Mama Cow at bay. She could hear her father's laughter, but she was getting the job done, wasn't she?

Returning to her patient, she thrust a drenching

tube into his mouth midbawl and shoved the plunger home. Mama backed off while Jess cleaned the baby's nasty bottom.

"Yeah, you don't want to do that part, do you?" Jess slashed the calf's hide with a fluorescent marker. "Not so worried now."

"One down," her dad said. "Good job, hon. Wasn't pretty, but it worked."

Climbing back into the saddle, Jess grinned. She was bruised and breathless, sticky with sweat and streaked with unmentionable cow leavings, but her heart swelled with a sense of accomplishment she'd never found at Birchwood Suites.

"How many to go?" she asked.

"Not sure." Her dad glanced around as if the calves might come out and stand for a count. "We had sixty, but there were coyotes."

"Ouch. Better get going."

Ride, rope, wrestle, repeat. As the sun rose in the sky, sweat ran down Jess's back and between her breasts. She could swear Buster grew an inch every time she dismounted. Why else was it so danged hard to get back in the saddle? A real cowgirl would be ashamed of the way she climbed on stumps and rocks so she could haul herself onto the horse. Then again, real cowgirls got the job done, no matter what. It only looked pretty in the movies.

She was relieved when her dad turned toward home.

"You did good, hon."

As she turned to answer, the wind whipped up and caught the curls that had escaped her ponytail. She swiped them out of her face and grinned. "I'm rusty, but I'll get better."

"It's no work for a woman, though. Not on her own."

She had a sudden urge to toss a loop over her father's stubborn head and talk some sense into him. She thought again of the few lady ranchers in the county who, through widowhood or sheer orneriness, ran big spreads on their own. Their brand of beauty never aged; they became bright-eyed, leather-skinned spirits of the plains, wise in the ways of wind and rain, cattle and coyotes. Maybe she could become one of them.

Yeah, and maybe Buster could open a restaurant.

Clicking her tongue, she let her dad eat a little of her dust while she loped Buster up the hill and calmed herself.

At the summit, they rested their forearms on their saddle horns, enjoying the view and inhaling the sweet, sage-scented air. The ranch spread out below them, with crooked fences stitching together quilt squares of green and brown. Scrub and tall grass lined each patch like lace, and winding trails crisscrossed the whole panorama, leading from barn to house, house to garage, garage to barn.

How many times had she tramped those trails, lugging hay, toting water, hauling grain? Her brother had hated the hard, heavy work, and she had to admit she'd done her share of grousing. But lately, she'd missed it with a country-girl ache that never died.

Maybe, by some miracle, her dad would get better, and the family land wouldn't slip out of her loop like a randy bull calf bent on escape.

Chapter 10

"You okay, sugar?"

"Yeah." Feeling the heat of tears behind her eyes, Jess pulled the brim of her hat down and looked away. "I missed this place so much, Dad."

He sighed. "Enjoy it while you can."

A thousand protests rose to her lips, but she bit them back. It would be better to use her skills, draw on the accounting courses she'd taken to assess the business and find solutions. If she could find the funds to hire someone before she left, her dad wouldn't have to do the heavy work.

"This here's what matters, Jess." He gestured away from the house at the acres of rangeland, dotted with cattle, wreathed by the silver ribbon of Willow Creek. "Nothing but this land."

She laughed. "You sound like the dad in *Gone with the Wind*." Laying on a dreadful Irish accent, she quoted, "*It's the only thing worth workin' for, worth fightin' for, worth dyin' for…*"

"He was right, wasn't he?"

"I think so, but you apparently don't, since you're selling this place to please a woman." She faked a saucy smile, but her lips quivered, and she had to look away.

"Now, don't be like that."

"Like what? Like honest?"

"Like mean-spirited."

"Sorry. I didn't mean to say it out loud. But don't you want to know what I'm thinking?"

"Not when you're thinking like that."

Drinking in the view, she calmed herself with the breadth of the sky, the acres of grass, and the knowledge that the land would endure whether it belonged to the Baileys or not. Besides, she'd be in Hawaii, slathered with suntan lotion, holding an umbrella drink, and watching the waves roll in.

She just didn't want to come back and find it hacked up into two-acre lots, cluttered with tacky houses, and sliced into alleys and cul-de-sacs.

Grimacing, she turned her horse toward home. "Ready to go?"

"Not yet." Her dad spun his mount and gave her a devilish grin.

"Oh no. I know that look." She shot him a glare. "We're not racing."

Ignoring her, he whooped and dug in his heels. Rearing, the palomino plunged downhill as if somebody'd popped the clutch.

Jess forgot to stop him, forgot to follow, forgot everything in the pleasure of watching her dad ride like— well, like her *dad*. Molly's warnings flashed through her mind, but she brushed them away like pesky flies. As he rose in the stirrups to urge his horse on, something small and mean inside her was glad Molly didn't own every part of him.

Joining the race would only encourage him, so Jess held Buster to a trot. When she topped the next rise, she was surprised to see the palomino had slowed and was staggering through the boulder field like a drunk.

She urged Buster forward, heart pounding. Her dad's horse pinned its ears as she grabbed its cheek strap, but she wasn't worried about the horse. Her dad's skin had an unhealthy sheen, with dark circles around his eyes standing out like bruises. As he slid from the saddle, Jess thought of Molly's warnings again with a painful lurch of her heart.

He goes off to God-knows-where on that horse, and anything could happen. Anything.

"Hold on, Dad."

Sliding from her saddle, she did her best to slow his fall, but he poured from the horse's back, boneless as a bucket of mud.

She leaned him against Buster's side and tried to hold him up, ignoring a twinge in her back when his knees buckled. He might have lost weight, but he was still a big man. The best she could do was prop him against a rock, where he slumped like a broken doll. Every breath he took sounded painful, as if torn from damaged lungs.

"What is it, Dad? Your heart?"

He didn't answer, just closed his eyes.

Dammit, she was so selfish. She'd upset him, talking that way about Molly. She'd had a moment of delight when the dad she knew and loved emerged from the hollow husk she'd found on the porch. But what if that husk was all she had?

He gasped, fumbling at his collar, and she undid a button, but his fingers tangled with hers until she realized he was dragging out a leather thong he wore around his neck. An old coach's whistle dangled from his fingers.

"Blow."

She couldn't see the sense in it, but she blew. The shrill shriek shocked the birds to silence, leaving only the grasshoppers clicking in the grass.

But how could a whistle do any good? Molly was too far away to hear, and if she did, what would she do? The two of them couldn't get Heck home. Of course, her stepmother might want to hold her husband as he drew his last breath. Jess wanted to slap herself for being so thoughtless.

Squatting beside her father, she felt for his pulse. It was weak but beating, and his breath was ragged.

A tear slid down her cheek and landed in the center of his palm; his fingers closed over it tightly, as if she'd dropped a diamond. At that, she lost the battle, leaning her forehead against the rock beside his shoulder and weeping.

"You are the best, best father. I should have told you every day." She took his hand. "Oh, Dad, I should have stayed. I love you. I love the ranch. Mom..." She realized she had nothing to say about the mother she barely knew. "Don't leave me, okay? You're all I have. I know that now." She smothered a sob. "I'm sorry."

He squeezed her hand, so he was still with her. He was so strong, so stubborn.

It had never occurred to her he might leave her one day.

Chapter 11

AMBER LYNN POSED IN CADE'S BEDROOM DOORWAY, offering the sleepy, smoky gaze that had doomed him into their disastrous marriage. Lobbed across crowded barrooms like casually tossed grenades, her sulky stares had pierced his loneliness when nothing else could, and when she'd encouraged him to stow his sorrow in her warm, willing body, he hadn't cared who she was or what she wanted. They'd never talked or walked or done anything together besides drinking and dirtying the sheets, but he hadn't cared. He'd just wanted to forget Jess Bailey. It hadn't worked, and it wasn't working now.

He waved the phone. "Your dad said you're getting married. Who's the lucky guy?"

"Don't listen to Daddy. Listen to me. *Look* at me." She minced into the bedroom with a lilting gait and stroked the sheets with one perfectly manicured hand before sitting down beside him. She was wearing a loose top with a wide V-neck that gaped to show all but the tips of her breasts. "It's just you and me, cowboy. Right here, right now."

She was trotting out all her tricks, but he knew every move, and the only one he wanted to see was the one where she walked out the door.

"Amber Lynn, I told you to go."

She pouted. "Don't be mad. Daddy messed up my plan. He wasn't supposed to call so soon." She licked her lips, but the black eye seemed to change minute by minute like a Technicolor sunset, and she looked like a TV zombie, hungry for brains.

She let her hair tumble to one side, hiding the bruise. "Did Daddy tell you he's going to give you a job at the bank? He thinks you're terrific." Running her finger down his chest, she parsed out words one button at a time in a breathy whisper. "And so. Do. I."

He grabbed her hand.

"Knock it off, Amber Lynn." He set her hand firmly on her lap and stood, but she rose with him, and he wound up jammed up against her, chest to breasts, hip to hip, groin to—well, right there. "Come on. You have way more to offer than—than this."

"Do I?"

"Sure you do."

She pressed into him, the movement as hard and angry as her expression. "It's all you ever wanted from me. All anyone ever wants."

"That's because it's all you offer."

She shoved him away. The backs of his knees hit the bed, and he crashed to the mattress with Amber Lynn clinging to him like a motherless spider monkey. For the second time in two days, he found himself lying under a woman through no fault of his own. But this time, it was the wrong woman. He rolled away, then looked back to see if she was all right.

She was. The only hurt was in her eyes.

"You wait." She leapt to her feet. "I'm gonna tell Daddy to call in that loan. What do you think of that, cowboy?" She hissed the last word as if it was something to be ashamed of.

"I think your daddy's word's worth more than that," Cade said. "You always said he was a 'man of honor,' remember?" He waved the phone, showing her the email her dad had sent. "If he goes back on his promise, there isn't a rancher in this town who'll do business with him."

He watched Amber's dignity deflate. Her shoulders slumped, and a tear welled from her wounded eye, streaking down her blue, bruised cheek.

"I'm going to tell everyone you did *this*." She pointed to her wounded eye. "They'll see what you're really like, and you'll be broke and everyone will hate you."

"Folks know me," he said. "And they know you, too. I'm not worried."

She burst into tears. "I was so s-s-sure you'd take me b-back." She sniffed. "I mean, you were always so nice to me, no matter what I did. Nobody's ever been that n-n-nice to me." She pressed the flesh around her black eye with her fingers and winced. "*He* sure wasn't. But you—I want you b-back. I made a m-mistake."

"Amber Lynn." He clapped his hands on her shoulders and shook her gently. "You don't want me. I'm never going to be rich, and you need—stuff."

Okay, so he wasn't eloquent. But he spoke the truth.

"Daddy gives me all the stuff I need," she said. "I just need…" She glanced around the room. "I don't know. Something's m-missing." She plopped herself down on the bed. "I just want to stay here."

"Why? You hate it here."

"But it's—I don't know, it's nice."

She glanced dubiously around the room, which was done up in Middle American Thrift Shop, with mismatched dressers and a mangy braided rug. When he was alone, he never noticed the lingering odors of horse and dog that clung to his clothes and furniture, but right now, it was overwhelming.

His ex looked up at him with wide, blinking eyes. Even with the bruise, she looked sweeter and more innocent than usual. That was never a good sign.

"It's just that *he* can't find me here," she said.

Cade sighed. In her way, Amber Lynn was naïve, a poor little rich girl who had no idea how the big world worked. He couldn't imagine the kind of monster who would hit her. She must have been so scared.

He sighed. "Why can't your dad take care of you?"

"My dad has Mona. He doesn't care about me anymore." She shoved her lower lip out in a pout. "All that 'my little girl' stuff was just an act. He never really loved me. He just gave me money to shut me up."

Sadly, she was probably right. Her eyes filled, and he figured the waterworks were about to start, but to his surprise, she blinked a couple of times and took a deep breath.

"But you know what? You don't need to protect me. I can take care of myself. I just need a place to stay." She fluttered her lashes, then wiped a hand across her face as if erasing the gesture. "Sorry. I didn't mean to flirt. Just let me stay, and I promise I won't try to seduce you." She held up her fingers in a *Star Trek* Vulcan salute. "Scout's honor."

He glanced wildly around the room for something that would save him. He tried to send a bat signal to Boogy, but for once, the dog failed to release one of the silent-but-deadly farts that used to send Amber Lynn screaming from the room.

But did Cade really want to chase her off? Amber Lynn was right. He'd used her, the same way other men had. The only difference was he'd married her, but that almost made it worse. He hadn't done right by her.

Maybe it was time to start.

"You know what, Amber Lynn? I think you *can* take care of yourself. You don't need to depend on anybody else."

"That's what I said." She tilted her chin, looking offended, but it was all an act. She really didn't believe she could survive without a man. It was like her beauty had hijacked her brains, and she'd never learned to use them.

"Can't you stay at a hotel?" he asked.

"I don't have my purse, remember?"

She'd probably left the purse behind on purpose—if she'd left it behind at all. For all he knew, she'd clocked herself in the eye with a two-by-four so she could get what she wanted out of him.

The problem was, he couldn't be sure. Nor could he be sure she'd have sense enough to run to her dad if he turned her away. So he had to let her stay. Women got killed for going back to their abusers, and he couldn't let that happen.

"One more night." He held up a finger. "Just *one*. But then we need to fix this. You can't keep relying on men to help you. Wouldn't you rather take care of yourself? You're more than smart enough to be successful on your own."

She turned those big eyes on him, blinking, all innocence, as if she couldn't grasp the concept of independence.

"We're going to have a talk tomorrow. Find a way to make things better, okay?"

"Okay." She smiled, and it was like a cluster of dark

clouds had been whisked from the face of the sun. That was how she got her way; a man just wanted the skies to clear.

"Thank you, Cade. I'd kiss you, but I promised, so…"

She blew him a kiss. Dutifully, he caught it and slapped it to his cheek. A ritual from their dating days, it almost made him smile. There'd been a time when he'd believed he might learn to love this woman, get over Jess, and move on. He'd figured if pretty, sexy Amber Lynn couldn't do it, nobody could.

Now he knew—nobody could. One look at Jess had brought joy whooshing back into his world. And that kiss—the thought of it gave him strength.

But as Amber Lynn sashayed from the room, he realized Jess would have a fit if she found his ex here. She'd understand once he explained about the abuse, though. Wouldn't she?

"I have to get my stuff."

As Amber Lynn left the room, Boogy rose from the throw pillows he'd hauled into the corner. The parts that weren't tattered were soaked with drool, and the dog's carefree doggy grin showed he was proud of his work. Cade kept the local thrift stores in business, buying pillows for Boogy to destroy.

"Don't smile yet, bud. She's coming back. And if you think she'll be happy staying just one night, think again." He gave the dog a speculative look. "You weren't much help back there. I'm thinking you need a digestive aid. How 'bout some broccoli?"

As Amber Lynn left the room, Cade heard a shrill *tweet*.

She glanced out the window. "What was that?"

"A whistle." Cade raced back to the kitchen and floundered through the crap on the counter. Bills, energy bars, paperwork—and finally, a bottle of pills. Shoving them in his pocket, he grabbed his fire department radio.

It was a rare rancher who didn't volunteer for one of Wyoming's rural fire departments. The Wynott district consisted of Cade, three other able-bodied firemen, a couple of EMTs, and a rickety chief whose advanced age didn't prevent him from making it to dang near every call.

Paging dispatch, Cade relayed directions to the Bailey ranch. Remembering Heck's vow to help the sickly looking calves in the north pasture, he gave the dispatcher a few landmarks to steer by. He didn't have to tell them they'd need a helicopter; that was standard procedure. The nearest hospital was in Grigsby, over forty miles by road.

Running for the barn, he slipped a bridle on Pride, grabbed a fistful of mane, and vaulted onto the horse's back. He was halfway to the road before he dared to look over his shoulder.

Amber Lynn was hauling a pink suitcase the size of a hippo across his lawn.

Damn. How long was she planning to stay? And wait—no purse, but a suitcase in the trunk? What was the real story here?

Amber Lynn was lying—that was the one thing he knew for sure. But right now, Heck was in trouble. He wouldn't blow that whistle unless things were bad. Really bad.

Bending low over the horse's neck, Cade urged the animal on.

———~~~———

Lub dub, lub dub.

Closing her eyes, Jess rested her head against her father's chest and prayed to the rhythm of his heart.

Let it beat harder, faster...

Her prayers were answered when the palpitations picked up speed.

Lubbity dub, lubbity dub, lubbity dub.

Didn't it just figure his heart would sound like a galloping horse?

The beat grew louder, faster, then stumbled.

No, wait. That really is *a horse.*

She looked up to see a horseman cresting the hill. The animal wore no saddle; a rider's body stretched low over its neck as it raced downhill in a flat-out, ground-eating lope. She'd seen a horse race at Crow Fair once, up in Montana, where the men and their mounts had melded into one perfect creature, all speed and strength of will. She'd only ever seen one other man ride like that.

Buster neighed at the newcomer. Meanwhile, the palomino fretted and pranced, spooked by Heck Bailey's hat, which had become a plaything for the breeze. Cartwheeling across the rocky plain, it struck a sagebrush and hung there, trembling.

Running to catch it, Jess snatched it up and waved it frantically in the air. As Cade approached, she traded it for her own. It was big as a bucket and dirty to boot, but she didn't care how she looked. She didn't care about anything but her dad.

Her dad and Cade, who was coming to save the day.

Chapter 12

CADE PUSHED OFF PRIDE'S NECK, SAT BACK ON HIS SEAT bones, and tugged the reins. The horse slammed to a stop and shied, almost dumping him in the dirt. That was understandable, since Jess, wearing Heck's huge hat, looked like an animated mushroom, while Heck, lying at her feet, looked—well, he didn't look animated at all.

Sliding to the ground, Cade dropped to his knees, whispering a prayer while he slipped his hand beneath the collar of Heck's shirt. There was a pulse, but it was faint, and the rhythm seemed off. Maybe it was angina, maybe anxiety, maybe a combination of both.

Fishing out the pills, he shook one into his hand. Heck opened his mouth like a baby bird, and Cade dropped the tablet on his tongue.

"What was that?" Jess asked.

Heck's eyes were bright, begging him not to tell, but Cade had kept his secrets long enough.

"It's nitroglycerine. Should help until Lifelift gets here."

Lifelift was a volunteer force of retired Black Hawk pilots from a nearby air force base. They'd bought an old weather copter from a Cheyenne TV station and retrofitted it with lifesaving equipment.

"Nitro-what?" Jess asked. "What's it for?"

"Arrhythmia."

"Whatever that is."

"Irregular heartbeats."

The air began to throb as if the earth's own heart was pounding all around them. Pride tossed his head and screamed as a helicopter rose over the hill like a giant insect, its unseeing eyes reflecting the landscape as it slanted its body and swept straight toward them, blades slapping the air.

The Arabian sidled closer to Buster, tossing his head, but the palomino stood firm. Cade allowed himself a mental cheer; a month ago, that horse would have shied at an eggbeater.

As the spinning blades flattened the grass in every direction, Cade grabbed the palomino's bridle, along with Pride's. Jess left her dad and helped move the animals to a circle of rocks a short distance away. Clapping their hands onto their hats, she and Cade raced back to Heck as the rotors slowed.

Heck groaned. "Wave 'em off. I don't need 'em. Just had to rest, that's all."

He struggled to a sitting position and launched into a fit of coughing so violent, Jess fell to her knees by his side. With her help, he lay back down, looking paler than ever. Jess pushed his hair back and patted his cheek, but he swatted her away.

"Aw, fussbudget. Leave me alone. Got somethin' caught in my throat, that's all." He lifted his head to watch two EMTs leap from the back of the helicopter. "Don't let 'em take me to the hospital. I hate that place."

He didn't stop whining until one of the EMTs began pelting him with questions about his health.

Cade tugged Jess away. "Let 'em do their job. They've got it under control."

She stared sightless toward the horizon, blinking fast. "We went for a ride. And then he… It went wrong, that's all. I had no idea he was this bad." She suppressed a sob. "Molly told me he had heart trouble, but I figured like a blood pressure problem or maybe high cholesterol. I had no idea…" Nodding toward the pills in his pocket, she pointed. "What are those again?"

He handed them over, and she glanced at the label.

"His name's on the bottle. How come you had it?"

Shoving his hands in his pockets, he stared down at the ground. "In case he had another heart attack. He forgets to carry his meds, so Molly made sure I had some, and we gave him that whistle…"

Jess interrupted. "*Another* heart attack?"

Heck propped himself up on his elbows. "Don't worry, hon," he said. "It was just a little one."

"Don't *worry*?" Tears tumbled out like a flash flood filling a canyon. "I didn't. Not one bit. Because I didn't *know*." She broke off on a sob, mastered herself, and swatted the tears from her eyes with one hand. Jutting her chin, she turned her fury on Cade. "I had no idea anything was wrong. And he's my *father*."

Cade splayed his hands, feeling helpless. "It was his decision to keep it quiet."

"And you thought it was a good one?"

Cade felt a hot wind blow through his heart. "I didn't hide anything, Jess. Nobody did. If you'd been here…"

She collapsed like a punctured balloon, the fight leaking out of her. He wished he could somehow gather it up and stuff it back in, straightening her backbone and reconstructing the strong Jess who stood up for herself.

"I was busy," she said. "Working hard, trying to make him proud."

"He doesn't care about that stuff. He just wants to see you."

"I know, but..." She tugged her hair back from her face. "I guess I was mostly trying to make my mother proud. As if she gives a damn." She sat down hard, covering her face with her hands. "I don't know why I even tried."

Cade knelt beside her, wishing he could soften the blow. But maybe it was time for her to face the consequences of walking away from the people she loved—the ones who loved her back.

"This was my fault," she mumbled.

"He's sick, Jess. You didn't do that."

"No. You don't understand." She shook her head, curls whisking wildly from side to side. "I made him mad, and he ran off, tried to race me to stop what I was saying. You know how he is."

Cade nodded. Heck hated conflict of any kind.

"I didn't stop him. I should have tried harder."

The roar of rotor blades saved him from having to agree.

"Wait!" Jess rose and stumbled toward the machine. "I'm going with him. *Wait!*"

With its expressionless staring eyes, the helicopter tilted onto one runner, then rose into the sky. Jess took off her dad's huge hat and watched it go.

Cade reached out and touched her arm, and the past faded away in the glance that passed between them.

"Oh, Cade." She sounded helpless, and that broke his heart.

"Come on," he said. "I'll take you to the hospital."

Chapter 13

WITH ITS SHINY WHITE FLOORS, FLUORESCENT LIGHTS, and antiseptic stench, the Grigsby Hospital was the opposite of a barn. And a barn was where Heck belonged. Hadn't Molly told him so a hundred times?

He opened one eye, hoping his wife would be there, but found Cade instead, slouched in a plastic chair with his arms folded and his ankles crossed. He looked bored, like he'd been there a while. Beside him, Jess was faking absorption in a decorating magazine, which made Heck want to laugh. There wasn't a domestic bone in that girl's body. She was still his cowgirl. Might not be able to rope worth a dang, but she had the spirit, and that was what mattered.

He could see her true self flowering, the layers of city sophistication falling away. After her mother had left, she'd taken to watching *Sex and the City* like she was studying a foreign culture. He'd been afraid she'd take off and join the Kardashian family the way other kids ran away to join the circus, and when he'd gone to see her in Denver and found a sharp-dressed professional woman, he'd worried his little tomboy was gone for good.

But Molly said all Jess needed was a nudge, a little warning that she might have a lot to lose, and a reminder of who she was. Sure enough, his cowgirl had come riding home.

Sometimes Molly's intuition made him a little nervous, but so far, she had used her powers only for good.

The room was spinning, and as he watched Jess, it seemed to speed up. He felt like he was on a danged merry-go-round, and he hated that feeling. When he closed his eyes, memory flooded his senses.

He'd been three, maybe four, and his folks had set him on one of those wooden horses with the pole through its belly. They had acted like it was a treat. He'd known what to do, of course, so he'd kicked his heels and clicked his tongue. They'd laughed while he'd scowled at the motionless horse with its stiff wooden mane, feeling cheated. Then the music had begun, wild and a little off-key, and the thing had started moving.

It didn't run like a real horse; it rose and fell with a sickening lurch, gliding faster and faster, out of control. He'd pulled the rope reins, but the critter wouldn't stop. Glancing around in a panic, he'd realized his parents were gone. Just *gone*. The world beyond the platform was a spinning, streaking blur. Faces rushed past, none of them familiar.

Good Lord, how he'd bawled. And he wanted to bawl now. The chimes and bells in the hospital hallway reminded him of the carousel's crazy music, tinkling eerily as the world spun by, too fast, too far away, and fully out of control.

If the world would buck like a rank horse, he could spur it and subdue it, but this spinning was making him sick. He fixed his gaze on his daughter, anchoring the world on her pretty face as she flashed dirty looks at poor Cade.

It was hard not to just take her aside and tell her what to do. It seemed simple enough to him. *Be nice to Cade. Remember, the boy's loved you all his life. Marry him, take over the ranch, have beautiful babies, and be happy.*

But Molly said he had to let Jess figure things out for herself. Make her own mistakes.

Well, she'd made 'em all right. Watching her rope calves this morning, with her face all flushed and her grin lighting up the land, it had been clear she didn't belong in some stuffy office in Denver. She belonged on the Diamond Jack, same as she belonged with Cade. Heck wanted to jump up and tell the pair to stop wasting time, treasure what they had, and let themselves love each other, dang it.

He tried to speak, but his heart stepped up and swung a hammer at his ribs. *Bam, bam, bam.* Maybe he'd better calm down. Didn't want to blow the pump.

He closed his eyes again, and the hospital sounds closed in. Bells rang, machines whirred, and nurses were everywhere, gabbling like chickens. He'd seen some of 'em on his way in, dressed in their baggy clothes, and wondered what had happened to the crisp uniforms he remembered from his rodeo days. Back then, the pain of a broken bone had been eased by pretty girls in crisp white dresses, with neat caps pinned in their hair. Nowadays, nurses dressed like Walmart customers. Might as well wear pajamas.

Sure was loud in here. He wondered why his hearing was so good all of a sudden. He had hearing aids but never used the dang things. They felt like somebody was sticking their thumb in his ear, so he'd stuck 'em in a drawer and forgotten about 'em. But everything was loud and clear, like he was young again.

Didn't that happen just before you died?

Aw, hell, he said silently, to God.

He knew he shouldn't go cussing at God, but he cussed at everybody. God probably knew that, so he wouldn't take it personal.

Don't let me die now. I got things to do.

God didn't answer, but Heck was used to that. He figured God was a lot like his own father had been—a good listener, but not much for answering questions. And strict. The kind of dad who was always saying, "Well, what do you think? Work it out for yourself."

But even thinking made his heart pick up the hammer again. *Bam, bam, bam.*

He tried to relax and think of his old John Deere, with its low diesel throb. He imagined pulling the throttle out, letting the engine idle, and sure enough, his breathing slowed, his heartbeat, too. Calm flowed into his mind, easing out the worry, pushing out the pain. The tractor was his happy place.

He heard Cade sigh. "I'm just glad you're here this time." He must be talking to Jess, 'cause surely he wasn't glad Heck was in the hospital. "I should have called you the first time."

"It's okay." Jess heaved a heavy sigh, as if the weight of the world was on her shoulders. "I know how he is. Stubborn as a mule. It's not your fault."

Holy cats. Was Heck that bad?

"I sure do miss your brother," Cade said. "You heard from him?"

Good boy. Change the subject. Don't be talkin' about me, 'cause I'm listening. Kind of scared what I'm liable to hear.

"Griff? Yeah. I found an app where I can text him," Jess said. "He sounds okay. He's a big tough soldier now."

Heck felt as if his eyelids were heating up on the inside and knew he'd better be careful or he'd cry like a girl. He wasn't a crier—he was a rancher, for God's sake, tough as nails—but he missed his son so much, it felt like he'd lost a limb. He'd heard amputees got phantom pains, and maybe fathers did, too, after their sons left home. Because thinking of Griff hurt, every blessed time.

"Remember that time we broke up, and you tried to go out with Bill Hancock? Griff took care of that in a hurry," Cade said.

"Oh yeah. Bill took me down to the quarry instead of to the movies like he was supposed to, but Griff knew how he operated. He was right there waiting and popped out of the bushes in full Rambo gear—face paint, camo, the works."

Heck had been upset when Jess had gone out with Bill, who wasn't one-tenth the man Cade was. Now he knew why their first date had been their only one.

"Bill took off," Jess continued. "Left me behind to get killed, I guess. He almost got hit by a car." She giggled. "I think he messed himself."

Heck tried to hold back, but his laughter shot up like a geyser erupting at Yellowstone.

"Dad!" Jess stood and stared down at him.

Busted.

Squeezing his eyes shut, he let his head flop to one side, hoping Jess would think his laugh had been some sort of spasm, but she bent down and lifted one eyelid. The white light was painful.

"I know you're awake, you big faker."

"Knock it off." He pushed her hand away. "I can deal with my own darn eyeballs."

"We'll see about that," said a new voice.

A girl stood in the doorway, dressed in all her Walmart glory in a green flour sack and a puffy hat that matched. Wrapping a cuff around his arm, she pumped it up 'til it hurt. She looked about twelve years old, but she was doing a danged good job playing nurse. Tucking a stethoscope into her ears, she squinted as the needle twitched its way down the scale.

Removing the cuff, she wagged a finger at him. "No more steak and potatoes for you."

Heck harrumphed. "We'll see what the doctor says 'bout that."

The twelve-year-old laughed. "I *am* the doctor."

"Sure you are. Now bring me a real one. Playtime's over."

"Oh, Dad."

Jess rolled her eyes while the so-called doctor gave him a snake-eyed stare that told him she was older than he'd thought—and tougher, too. She'd be a worthy adversary.

Because that's what doctors were. Adversaries. They wanted to filter all the fun out of life until all you could do was sit around and drool in your soup. Hadn't he seen that happen to half his friends? With a new young wife, Heck had to keep his strength up. That's why he avoided the damn leeches and took care of himself. It took a lot of steak and potatoes to keep up with Molly.

He closed his eyes, faking sleep so Doogette Howser would leave him alone.

"What was going on when this happened?" the doctor asked.

"We were out roping calves," Jess said. "My dad's a rancher."

"You didn't know he had a bad heart?"

"I should have, I guess. My stepmother told me, but I thought she was exaggerating."

"Molly doesn't exaggerate," Cade said.

Heck wanted to cheer. Cade always defended Molly, and no wonder. If ever a boy was in need of mothering, that boy was Cade, and Molly made it her mission to fuss over him.

"What was I supposed to think?" Jess said. "He calls to tell me he's selling the ranch he's loved all his life, and when I come home, his new wife's got some ritzy retirement place picked out. Nobody told me he was this sick, so I figured she was trying to make a change in her lifestyle." She lowered her voice. "I still think so. They took blood earlier, right?"

"Yes," the doctor said.

"Will they check it for toxins?"

She thought she was being sneaky, but Heck heard her just fine. He moved his lips, but something was stuck in his throat. It felt like his heart, hot and full, making him mute. Tearing away the chest strap, he jerked upright.

Immediately, the room filled with beeps and whoops while the yellow light outside the door spun and blinked.

He wagged a finger at Jess. "You listen. Let me tell you 'bout Molly."

He'd worked up a stirring speech about his wife's finer qualities, but before he could get started, he slid sideways off the gurney.

"Look out!" The doctor raced for the gurney. "He's going to fall!"

Flailing his arms, Heck knocked a monitor to the floor while a dozen taped-on sensors tore from his chest and arms, along with half his body hair. He hadn't noticed the IV in his arm, but he sure felt it now as it tore through his skin.

He'd almost hit the ground before Cade hauled him back onto the cot, muscles bulging, face red with effort. Meanwhile, Jess had braced her feet against the wall and kept the bed from rolling out from under him.

"Nice one, Jess," Cade grunted. "Really nice."

"What?"

"He heard you. So did I. You've got him all upset."

"Well, I'm upset, too. All of a sudden, she's saying he's too sick to run the ranch. He was fine when I left." Her eyes were brimming with tears.

"It wasn't sudden at all," Cade said. "This has been going on a long time. You just haven't been here to see it."

"I'll let you folks talk this out." The doctor set a sheaf of wires across a steel cart. "Somebody'll be right in to put these back on."

Jess and Cade were red-faced, facing off over the gurney. Anger simmered between them, so strong, Heck could feel it in the air.

Molly complained sometimes that he was difficult, but he'd always been secretly proud of his cantankerous personality, as if it were a superpower. But look what he was doing to the people he loved.

Staring up at the ceiling, he ignored the crew of nurses that came in and rewired him, closing his eyes. But deep inside, he made himself a silent vow.

He'd turn over a new leaf, starting today. From now on, he'd think of his children and his wife before he thought of himself. He'd think before he spoke, too. That would be a new experience for him, one that was long overdue.

"Jess, honey." He opened his eyes and took a deep breath, swallowing his anger. "Molly's my wife. She's been by my side through this whole heart thing, and I can guaran-dang-tee she's not trying to kill me. If she says I'm sick, I'm sick, and that's all there is to it."

The doctor loomed into sight, frowning as she checked his electrodes. "That's right," she said. "You should listen to his wife."

Heck nodded. Maybe this doctor wasn't so bad after all.

"His wife says he should sell the ranch and retire," Jess said. "Quit doing what he loves and sit around and do nothing. That won't help him get better."

"I'd say his wife knows him best." The doctor touched Heck's shoulder. "Isn't that so?"

He nodded, glad to hear someone support Molly.

"So if she says you need to retire…" She splayed her hands as if the rest of the sentence was obvious.

And damned if it wasn't.

Dang it, Heck had dug himself a hole, and Doogette had tossed him in and covered him up like a seed in the springtime.

He'd felt faint earlier, when he'd thought life might be leaving him, but now he felt the desperate dizziness that comes with being cornered. Lying on the gurney, his chest aching, his heart pounding on his ribs like one of those heavy metal drummers, there was nothing he could do but take what the world dished out.

The notion of selling the ranch had originally been a
ruse, a way to get Jess back home. But this latest episode
had him thinking he might be ready for Muddletime
Manor after all. Maybe he should take another look at
those brochures.

Just the thought of giving up and going to one of
those places made his heart pound so hard, it hurt, but
he had to do what was best for Molly. And if Jess didn't
want to stay…

Cade put a hand on his shoulder. "Easy, Heck. You
can beat this, but you need to relax. Let us help, okay?"

Heck gasped out a few shallow breaths. Everybody
was staring at him, and he felt deeply, profoundly
ashamed. He was nothing but a problem for the people he
loved. "I know, Son. I know. I'll get better, I promise."

He'd repair all the damage he'd done, smooth things
out, and help his family understand what mattered. Jess
was giving Cade the evil eye and suspecting Molly of
terrible things, Cade was frustrated with Jess, and poor
Molly was sinking fast under the pressure.

Then there was Griff. Heck knew, deep down, that
he'd driven the boy away by demanding he take over
the ranch. He'd never listened to the boy's hopes and
dreams. Hell, Heck never listened to anybody.

But he would, starting today.

The room had stopped spinning, but everything
had grown smaller and sharper, as if he were looking
through the wrong end of a telescope. At the large end of
the telescope was his own heart, which felt big enough
to hold the whole room. He felt it swell with every beat,
as his love grew for his children, his wife, his life.

Silently, he made a promise to God. Not only would

he stop aggravating his family, he'd stop cussing, too, if he could just live long enough. But life was a struggle, more and more, day by day.

He remembered a flag he'd seen back in Vietnam. Somebody'd raised it high above a battlefield, and it had been shot to rags. Bit by bit, scraps tore off and whipped away while the edges frayed and raveled.

His heart felt like that flag. He needed to leave the battlefield and find a foxhole where he could hold onto what tattered shreds of himself remained. Where he could treasure the miracle of his glowing, beating heart and nurse it back to health before time and old age shot it all to hell.

Chapter 14

JESS WATCHED HER DAD STRUGGLE FOR BREATH AND FOUGHT a flurry of emotions. Love became helplessness, helplessness became fury, but the whole mess circled back, always, to love. She wanted to help him, but all she could do was hang on, squeezing his hand.

Just this morning, she'd thought the ranch was the key to his health. Now, she had no idea how to help him, but one thing was for sure: the ranch was good as gone. The doctor was right. He needed to slow down and stay safe.

Above the din in the hallway, Molly's voice rang out, asking where was Heck Bailey and was he all right.

Jess was stunned when a flood of relief swept through her like a cleansing wave. When had she ever been glad to see the woman who'd tried—and failed, of course—to take her mother's place? Every time Jess saw Molly standing in her mother's kitchen, sitting in her mother's chair, or driving what should have been her mother's car, she felt a cold chill of resentment. But now, in a crisis, Molly was somehow—well, *needed*.

For her father's sake, of course.

"Hey, baby."

Molly's brow was furrowed with concern, but her smile was bright, dimples flashing like twin stars. She was a plus-sized woman, but Jess had to admit her sunny attitude made her attractive. More importantly, she saw her father light up at the mere sight of her.

Placing a bundle of wildflowers on her husband's lap, Molly gave him a kiss on the lips—one that lingered a little.

"Don't rile him up." Cade grinned. "He's liable to throw himself off the gurney again."

"Oh, he won't do that." Molly patted Heck's knee through the thin blanket. "He's a very good patient."

Jess started to snort, but looking at her dad, she realized Molly was right—at least for the moment. All the fight had ebbed out of him, and he was looking at Molly like a hound dog looks at bacon. If he'd had a tail, it would have been wagging.

"If good patients pitch themselves off the gurney, then I guess you're right," Cade said.

"Sorry about that, kids." Heck sighed. "I'll try to do better."

Sorry? What?

Who was this man, and what had he done with her cantankerous dad? Heck was always right. He blustered his way through even the worst of his mistakes, never, ever admitting he was wrong.

"And Molly? Don't you worry." He took his wife's hand. "This old heart beats for you, darlin', and it's not done. I promise you that."

Jess tried not to make gagging sounds. She wasn't sure about Molly's motives, but it was obvious her dad had moved past the coconut cream pie stage. He'd executed an all-or-nothing dive into the deep end of love and saw his new wife through a watery haze of adoration. Jess might as well get used to having the woman around.

"And that plan we had?" Jess's dad looked miserable,

and she knew he was talking about selling the ranch. "I think maybe it's a good idea. For real."

Molly shook her head and started to speak, then bit her lip. Tears welled up in her eyes as she patted her husband's hand. "Don't you worry about that right now," she said. "Jess, why don't you and Cade go get something to eat?" She smiled down at her husband. "I'll take care of this guy."

"No, I'll stay," Jess said.

"You do what you want, hon, but you have to eat, and so does that man of yours." Molly stepped around the gurney and gave Jess a hug as comforting as a squishy pillow. "I'm just so glad you were with Heck when it happened. Having you here is such a blessing."

Molly was a full head shorter than Jess, who had to hold her breath so she wouldn't sneeze at her stepmother's trademark scent—a mix of perm lotion, hairspray, and drugstore perfume. For some reason, she felt an almost irresistible urge to confess, but she didn't tell Molly about the race. She didn't say how Heck had taken off before Jess had realized what was happening, how she hadn't stopped him, how one mean little part of her heart had been glad, *glad* Molly couldn't control him.

"It was Cade that saved him," she said instead. "Dad blew the whistle, and Cade gave him one of those pills." She looked up at Cade, startled as a realization dawned. "I think he saved Dad's life."

"It wasn't me, it was Molly," Cade said. "She thought up the plan, with the whistle and the pills, and it worked."

A dark-haired nurse about the size of the average Cub Scout pushed in a cart laden with electronic doodads. She had a heavy unibrow over piercing dark eyes and wore scrubs spattered with abstract renditions of SpongeBob SquarePants. Glancing from Heck to Molly, she caressed a sheaf of electrical leads like Dr. Evil stroking his cat. Jess wondered why she'd never noticed SpongeBob's manic grin before or his menacing, buggy eyes.

"I'm Joanie." The nurse's dark eyes sparked. "I'll need that gown open in the front."

Heck looked panicked. "You gotta go, Jess. Open in the front, she says."

"I won't look." Jess wasn't about to leave her father alone with Satan's Little Helper, even if she did have an official hospital name tag.

"You're not staying here while they hook me up to machines," Heck said. "Leave me a little dignity."

Jess sighed. When he put it like that, she couldn't say no. Besides, Molly would be there. Any suspicions about toxins and ulterior motives had been burned to ashes in the light of the woman's smile. Jess's stepmother was a small, plump steamroller, mowing down the world with her goodhearted charm.

And Jess, in spite of herself, was utterly, thoroughly flattened.

Time to go home and get some rest. She could see her father again the next morning, then finish drenching those calves in the afternoon. The hard work would do her good and give her time to think.

To plan.

~~~

"The way that little girl squealed, you'da thought she caught that fish all by her own danged self!" Heck said, finishing a story about Jess. He'd been moved to a room of his own at the hospital the night before. This morning, his face was pale, but he was more like his cheerful self.

Molly laughed. Hearing Heck's family stories eased an ache inside her. She could almost pretend Jess and Griff were her own kids.

"Aw, no." Heck's face paled to the pasty white of a trout's belly.

Turning, Molly saw Grigsby's one and only cardiologist, trailed by his silent entourage of interns and residents. The students stood in a circle around their instructor, wearing servile expressions that reminded Molly of Heck's cows.

"Got those test results back." The doctor frowned at his clipboard while his students competed for the Most Grave Yet Attentive Expression Award.

"Not good." The doctor shook his head slowly. "Not good at all."

He stared down at the clipboard so long, Molly thought he'd gone into a trance. Finally, she cleared her throat.

The doc jerked his head up. His cold blue eyes regarded her with barely suppressed fury, as if she'd interrupted a Nobel Prize–winning daydream.

Molly glared back. "Not good? What does that mean?"

"Your husband needs a pacemaker." Again, he consulted the clipboard. "These episodes can't continue. Unhealthy diet, I'm guessing."

Her mind filled with excuses. *I haven't known him for long. We just got married. I try to get him to eat healthy foods. It wasn't me that fed him those steaks, those potatoes; it was Dot.*

"Surgery will be on Monday."

He turned and began ladling out jargon to his students, explaining the intricacies of Heck's heart to a bunch of strangers who didn't care if her husband lived or died. To them, he was a lesson in their textbook come to life—easily studied, easily learned, and soon, most likely, gone.

A little swirl of rage rose in her heart, spinning like a dust devil in a harrowed field. Leaping to her feet, she followed the doctor as he left the room.

"I have a question."

"And I have a schedule." With an officious tilt of his wrist, he checked his watch and upped his pace.

The dust devil spun a little faster. Molly didn't get mad often, but once someone brought her whirling dervish to life, it was hard to control.

She touched the doctor's arm.

Okay, maybe she *grabbed* it.

That would explain why he curled his lip and gazed at her over a pair of half-glasses as if she were some sort of bug he'd like to squash. Men thought those glasses made them look smart, but to Molly, the doc just looked silly, like an owl in a storybook. The thought made her giggle, and the interns stared like she'd farted in church.

Whipping the glasses off, the doctor cleared his throat and fixed her with the full force of his owly eyes. Molly smothered another giggle.

"A question?" he asked.

She searched the soupy stew of stress that was sloshing around in her brain and grabbed the first question that floated to the top.

Whoooo are you?

No, that won't do. Try again.

She cleared her throat. "Um, how long will the surgery take?"

"Could be four hours, could be seven." He shrugged his narrow shoulders. "There can be complications."

"So you don't know."

As one, the students' brows lowered. She half expected them to moo and paw the ground, but picturing them as cows gave her courage. She'd been a little afraid of Heck's cattle, with their long horns and shaggy coats. But he'd pointed out how calm they were and how they protected their young. He'd taught her how to exude confidence so they'd respect her, and to her surprise, it had worked.

Tears stung her eyes, and for a moment, she couldn't speak.

"I'll tell you how you can help him," the doctor said.

Molly almost grabbed him again. "Please."

"Heart patients need *rest*." The doctor enunciated clearly, as if she were a dolt.

"I know," she said. "That's why, as soon as he gets home, we're making some changes. We're going to sell…"

"That's not soon enough." The doctor looked like an angry owl now. "He needs rest now, and he's not getting any. He won't, as long as you insist on camping in his room all day."

Molly felt as if he'd slapped her. "I'm his wife. I need to be here."

He looked her up and down, lips pursed. "A man doesn't want to appear frail in front of his much-younger wife. You need to find something else to do. Don't you have a job?"

Molly hung her head. "He doesn't want me to work. I'd like to, actually, but—well, he's too proud."

She hated admitting that in front of all these people. She'd never been the sort of woman who let a man tell her what to do, but Heck was old-fashioned.

"Besides, he wants me here. I know he does."

The doctor gave her a cold owly stare. "Do you ever see him sleep?"

"Sometimes." She fiddled with her collar, flustered. "When I come back from the cafeteria or the powder room, he's usually nodded off. I try to be quiet, but— well, he always wakes up when I come in." She sighed. "I guess you have a point."

"Limit your visits. Two hours in the evening, at most." He frowned. "Find something to do."

"All right."

She stumbled back into Heck's room, smoothing her hair and surreptitiously wiping her eyes. He was sleeping, of course.

Don't you have a job?

She used to. She'd loved it.

She missed it.

Doctor's orders.

Gathering her things, she headed home, a glowing ember of happiness warming her heart.

She could find something to do all day. Heck wouldn't like it, but what he didn't know wouldn't hurt him. As a matter of fact, he'd be healthier.

And God knew, she'd be happier.

Chapter 15

CADE DIDN'T GET MUCH SLEEP, THANKS TO DREAM JESS, who danced through his head like Salome waving her seven veils. It should have been a good dream, but it wasn't. For one thing, Jess was about as comfortable on a dance floor as a fish flopping around on dry land. For another, he wanted those veils gone, and Dream Jess took her time. Slowly, slowly, she shed one, then another, and before she could finish, his dad stepped into the dream, shaking his head, tossing Cade a disgusted look.

You're not good enough for the Baileys. Never were. Never will be.

Cade launched himself from the bed and barked his shin on the coffee table before he remembered he'd slept on the sofa again. There was a crick in his neck and a cramp in his back. Muttering an oath at his father's ghost, he threw on a T-shirt and headed for the barn.

An hour later, horses grazing contentedly, he loaded Pride into the trailer and headed back to the house. Jess had probably forgotten about her father's sick calves, so he'd take care of them. Just grab a cup of coffee and...

There was a light on in the kitchen.

Shoot. Amber Lynn.

What the hell was she doing up this early? She usually did her prowling at night, with all the other predators.

As his heart sank into his boots, he heard her crooning

a Britney Spears song. She'd mastered Britney's breathy, nasal inflection, but her singing was wildly off-key.

"*Hit me, baby, one more time!*"

Remembering the black eye, he shook his head. "That song's a little on-the-nose, don't you think?" he asked Boogy.

The dog whined, staring at the truck, then up at Cade.

"Yes, you'll get to go. But first, we have to face the music."

The dog lifted one eyebrow.

"I know. You can hardly call it music."

Amber Lynn was staring down the coffeemaker like it was her worst enemy when he walked in. She spun around with a smile fixed on her face.

"Good morning."

"Uh-huh." He wasn't trying to be rude. He just wasn't awake enough to have a conversation. Not with Amber Lynn, anyway.

To his surprise, she didn't turn his grunt into some unforgivable slight. In fact, she smiled at him, then reached for the stove and presented him with yet another plate of fried eggs and bacon. This time, at least the bacon was cooked right. It looked crispy and smelled terrific, but the eggs were profoundly undercooked.

"Oh, thanks." He looked down at the plate and watched the egg yolks wobble. His stomach churned. "I'll have to eat on the run, though."

"You're leaving?"

"Yeah." He gave her a narrow-eyed stare. "I have stuff to do. You, too, right? Do you need help packing?"

She gave him a doe-eyed stare, her lower lip trembling. "You said we were going to have a talk."

"We are, Amber Lynn. But right now, I have to go to—um, to work." He wasn't about to tell her he was going to the Baileys'.

She blinked slowly, as if struggling to understand. "Oh. So I should stay, and we should talk later."

"No." He glanced wildly around the room and saw nothing that would save him. Exasperated, he sat down at the table. "We'll talk now. Okay?"

"Okay." She took a deep breath. "So I looked on the internet, and I found out how to cook bacon. You don't boil it. You cook it in a pan. But you didn't tell me that."

Cade shrugged. "I didn't want to hurt your feelings. You tried, and it was okay."

"It was gross." She tossed her hair. "You didn't tell me because you think I'm stupid. So why were you going on about how smart I am? I don't need to be patronized."

He was tempted to point out she was using awfully big words, but that would be…patronizing.

Maybe she had a point.

"You're plenty smart, Amber. You just cover it up."

She was smarter than him, that was for sure. She'd spent another night in his bedroom while he tossed and turned on the couch, trying to figure out how to pry her out of his house. And now she'd managed to change the subject, while he could barely remember what they were supposed to be talking about.

"You really think I'm smart?"

Oh yeah. They were talking about her. Of course they were.

"Sure," he said. "You're more than smart. You're ambitious, you're observant, and you're, well, ruthless."

"And *pretty*."

"Right. All that would make you one hell of a businesswoman."

"A what?"

She gave him a practiced look, lips parted, eyes wide. It was designed to make her look dimwitted, and she pasted it on whenever anyone asked her to do anything beyond being decorative.

"A businesswoman," he repeated. "You sell yourself short, Amber Lynn. You shouldn't have to depend on me or your dad or that asshole who hit you. *You*." He jabbed a finger at her, earning a surprised gasp. "*You* should be the one in charge."

"I used to be." She pouted. "I was with *you*."

He wiped his hand down his face. The day hadn't even begun, and she'd exhausted him already. He was a fool to feel sorry for her; she'd taken everything he had.

But maybe she'd had to. Despite her privileged upbringing, Amber Lynn didn't have a damned thing of her own. That was her father's fault, and if Cade had anything to say about it, Jasper Lyle was going to pay for neglecting his only child. Cade would hit the man where he lived—which had never been at home with his daughter. The man lived at the bank, where he could feed his bloated ego by bossing his employees around.

Boss this, *Jasper*.

"Listen." Cade leaned against the counter beside Amber Lynn. "You said your dad had a job for me, right?"

She nodded, staring at the floor. "But you don't want it."

"Nope. I'd die in an office. You have to dress up and

look nice, and you have to understand people and talk them into doing what you want."

"What's wrong with that?"

"Nothing, for you. I'm awful at it, but you'd be great." She gave him a rueful smile. "You *are* kind of hopeless."

"So tell him *you* want the job."

"Me?" Amber Lynn was still playing dumb, but he caught a spark of interest in her eyes.

"Sure. You'd be good at it. Manipulating money's a lot like manipulating men."

He thought he might have gone too far, but Amber Lynn looked thoughtful. "It probably is. But more direct."

"Right," Cade said. "And, whoa, I can see you with a corner office, wearing high heels and a suit like one of those lady lawyers on TV."

"Like Princess Meghan. I *would* look good, wouldn't I?"

"You sure would. And everybody'd listen to you and do what you say. You'd be the boss. That's what you were born to be."

"The *boss*." She spoke the word lovingly, as if tasting it for the first time.

He had a feeling a star had just been born.

"You're your father's daughter. He owes you this chance. And then you'd have your own money. Mona would be *so* jealous." He gave her a playful push. "Go pack your stuff. You don't belong in a dump like this. Never did."

She scanned the room, frowning at the torn coverlet he'd tossed over the sofa, the three-legged coffee table propped up on a stack of horse training books, and Boogy, who'd drooled a puddle on the scarred wood floor.

"You're right. What was I thinking? I'm better than this. *So* much better." To his horror, she threw her arms around his neck and kissed him on the cheek. "Thank you. I think you're right. It's just what I need—and I'll look so *good*."

"All right, then." He patted her back, feeling awkward but strangely touched. "Guess I'll see you at the bank, right? You sure you don't need help packing?"

"No." She blinked and gave him a trembling smile. "I can do it."

"That's right," he said, trying to sound hearty and encouraging. "You can do anything."

The coffee was ready, thank God. Filling his mug, he grabbed his plate and headed out the door, the greedy-eyed Boogy behind him.

Climbing into his truck, he set the plate on the dashboard. Boogy hopped up to ride shotgun, and as they bounced down the drive, the dog watched the eggs jiggling and sliding around the plate with drooly determination. The whole mess made Cade feel a little nauseous, but Boogy's pleading eyes made him feel downright mean.

Cade grabbed one strip of bacon, leaving the rest for the dog.

"Go ahead."

Boogy went all right, propping his paws on the dash and slurping up the greasy breakfast in seconds. He turned to give Cade a grateful doggy grin. A string of egg yolk dangled from his jowls, swinging with the motion of the truck.

"You'd better not puke on my upholstery," Cade said. Of course, his upholstery was Walmart seat covers he'd bought on clearance, decorated with pink butterflies. They might be improved by a little strategically placed vomit, but Cade was a sympathetic puker.

Boogy slurped up the egg yolk string and burped. Cade felt himself go green.

He felt even sicker as he reran his conversation with Amber Lynn in his head. Had she ever really said she was leaving? He should have made her call and set up a meeting with her dad right then and there. He needed to know for sure she'd be gone when he got home tonight.

Because once he'd helped Jess with those calves, he'd be her hero, right? She'd be grateful, and maybe she'd come home with him. Maybe she'd kiss him while they stumbled in the door, shedding clothing as they went. Maybe they'd make love right on the sofa, where he'd left his blanket and pillow. Maybe…

Maybe he'd better make sure Amber Lynn was good and gone before he risked having Jess anywhere near the house. Even if his ex talked her way into a job, it would take her a while to find an apartment. She could hardly live at the bank.

But that wasn't his problem. Anyway, with Heck in the hospital, the Bailey home would be empty most of the time. Jess's bedroom was still decorated as it had been when she was a girl, all pink and frilly, with a canopy bed that had inspired all sorts of fantasies for Cade over the years, mostly about making love in an actual bed, like the married couple he hoped they'd be someday. Married sex might not be the most imaginative sexual fantasy in the world, but for Cade, it held more promise than any wilder dream.

There would be no veils between them then. There'd be just him and Jess, the real Jess, *his* Jess, the one he'd loved for so long.

Chapter 16

MOLLY WAS AT HECK'S BEDSIDE FIRST THING THE NEXT morning. No matter what the doc said, she needed to see for herself that his chest was rising and falling and hear that familiar snore. Once she was satisfied, she slipped out of the room without waking him and headed for a public restroom.

Glancing in the mirror, she gave herself a tentative smile. She still had dimples, and the delicate skin under her eyes was still smooth. Her eyes were bright, her skin clear, and her hair—well, her hair could use some work. Fluffing the fine brown curls, she thought about what the doctor had said.

A man doesn't want to look weak in front of his much-younger wife.

It had been nice to hear she still looked young. She'd been through so much lately, she felt every bit as old as Heck. And she was starting to realize her husband was, indeed, an older man. She'd married him because she loved his sense of humor and his adventurous spirit, but those qualities were fading along with his heart. And now she wasn't even allowed to spend the day with him.

Don't you have a job?

She'd spent all night staring at the ceiling, wondering if she dared to take the doctor's advice. By morning, she'd decided she would.

Tugging her cell phone from her pocket, she brought up her contacts.

David Burton. 555-6238.

How many times had she longed to dial that number? Before she'd met Heck, David had been the man she turned to when life got complicated. Of course, Heck wouldn't approve. Talking to David would be a betrayal in his eyes.

Heck's not here. And besides, it's doctor's orders.

Dodging into a stall, she felt like a spy contacting her handler or a teenager calling her bad-boy crush.

A tinny ring sounded in her ear.

"Dave Burton."

Oh, he sounded so professional, so above it all. With Dave, she could be her old self—her best self.

"Are you busy?" She injected a teasing tone into her voice, hoping he'd remember her.

"Molly!"

He recognized her voice! She let out her breath in one long, relieved whoosh.

"Blow in my ear and I'll follow you anywhere." His voice was pitched low, in a humorously flirtatious tone.

"Oh no." She felt her heart flutter. Talking to him always made her so nervous. "I didn't mean to— I didn't..."

"Just joking, Molly. It's good to hear from you." The flirty tone was gone, the professionalism returned, but he sounded wonderfully warm and sincere. "How have you been?"

"Fine," she said. "Mostly. But Heck had a heart attack, and he's in the hospital. He has to have surgery."

"I'm sorry."

A long, uneasy silence followed. Maybe she shouldn't have mentioned Heck.

Finally, he spoke again. "We've missed you around here."

"I've missed you, too. And the children." She sighed. "I've missed them terribly."

"You could come back."

"Really? You'd still want me?" This was what she'd been hoping for, and she hadn't even had to ask.

"Sure." Again, his voice vibrated, low and—dared she say it?—sexy. "Come see me tomorrow."

"I can't. How about Friday?"

"That would work."

They laid down the details—time, place, and plans. She hoped so hard she could fit into Dave's world again. She'd been a fool to leave.

"Thank you," she said. "For taking me back."

"No, thank *you*," he said. "You made my day."

As she exited the restroom, she realized someone else was in the next stall. They probably thought she was crazy, talking on the phone from a toilet stall. Either that or they thought she really was a teenager calling her boyfriend.

The thought made her giggle. Washing her hands, she appraised her looks again. She wasn't vain, but she wondered if she should color her hair before Friday.

Oh, pooh. It looked fine. *She* looked fine. There was a happy flush in her cheeks, and her eyes were bright. No wonder the doctor had said she was Heck's "much-younger wife."

Trilling a few lines of a sappy love song, she danced out of the restroom and into the hall.

—◦◦◦—

From her perch on the toilet, Jess lowered one foot to the floor, then the other.

As soon as she'd realized it was Molly in the next stall, flirting on the phone with some stranger, she'd pulled her feet up and crouched on the toilet, hoping her stepmother hadn't heard her come in.

It was a good thing she'd decided to visit her dad this morning. Good thing she'd come to the restroom just then and learned the truth.

Molly had married for money, just as Jess had suspected. And maybe, just maybe, she'd convinced her new husband to sell the ranch so she could claim half the proceeds before running off with Mystery Man. That would leave Jess's father alone in the world, without his ranch *or* his new young wife.

But Jess couldn't tell him, for fear of causing heart attack number three.

Cursing under her breath, she left the restroom and headed for home. She couldn't face her father right now.

It was a good thing she'd called that morning and talked to her boss at Birchwood. He'd been kind and understanding when she'd told him about Heck's heart attack and agreed she should take family medical leave. She'd stammered a few words about her dedication to her job and how she wouldn't stay in Wyoming if it wasn't a matter of life and death. He didn't really respond, and she felt the Hawaiian islands drifting away, the white sand slipping through her fingers.

She'd taken a deep breath and told him straight out that she was concerned her leave would lose her a promotion. To her relief, he'd told her he was moved by her dedication to her dad. He hadn't said right out that he was still considering her for the promotion, but he'd sounded very encouraging.

She sighed. Her father needed her, so none of that mattered. For the moment, she needed to shift her priorities to the ranch and get those calves drenched. It would be tough on her own, but she couldn't let the little buggers suffer.

She thought again of Molly's voice back in the restroom—her flirty tone, the things she'd said. Jess needed to doctor those calves tomorrow, but on Friday, she'd follow her stepmother and find out exactly what was going on. Her dad would never believe her unless she had proof.

Once that happened, she had no idea what she'd do. Losing Molly would be a terrible blow, and he was already sick. How would she go back to work at all? How could she leave him behind?

Chapter 17

JESS MOUNTED BUSTER AND HEADED FOR THE NORTH pasture, wondering who would fail her next. Her stepmother was apparently cheating on her dad. Her dad, who'd been the single solid rock in her life, was fading fast.

She couldn't understand it. He'd been polite, he'd been kind, and he hadn't cussed for a whole day, so either he was dying and aiming to make it to heaven, or he was so sick, he couldn't be himself. What if she lost her dad *and* the Diamond Jack? The thought made a sob tighten her throat.

And then there was Cade. A big part of her wanted to pick up right where they'd left off, but another, bigger part held her back.

Hawaii. She could see it if she closed her eyes—the clean white sand, the white-capped waves, the seagulls soaring overhead. She pushed Cade into the picture, shirtless of course, racing with her into the waves. They were holding hands, laughing...

But no. Cade never traveled. Staying with him meant staying here, giving up everything she'd worked for. And that would be plain dang stupid. Either Cade would have to change, or they were as doomed as Romeo and Juliet.

As she reached the pasture where her runny-assed patients waited, she shoved her love life out of her mind and thought about the task at hand. She'd tell her dad the calves had all been medicated on her next trip to the hospital. He'd be so relieved, he'd cuss out a doctor, and all would be right with the world.

All was not right, however, with her roping skills. Apparently, the success she'd enjoyed with her dad had been a textbook case of beginner's luck. Today, her luck had changed, plus she'd pulled a muscle somewhere. By lunchtime, she could barely raise her hand above her shoulder, and her roping efforts were a series of very bad jokes.

She found a perfect picnic spot—a flat rock under an old tree twisted by decades of endless wind—but Buster spotted a calf sprinting for a ravine and put on the gas before she could signal him to stop. Setting her heels, she sat back and pulled on the reins.

The calf had plunged down the rocky slope into the underbrush that bordered a seasonal creek. It would be twice as hard to catch later, but her sore shoulder didn't care about later. It cared about *now* and whether she'd be able to lift her sandwich to her mouth. Her arm ached, her butt had been paddled by the saddle, and her thighs burned like twin flames. The calf could wait. Letting Buster loose to graze, she rested against the tree and unpacked her food.

Moments later, the sandwich hung limp in her hand, and her head lolled against the tree. The world flowed past her and away, all those uncaught calves receding into the distance as she sank into blessed sleep.

A sharp sound jolted her awake. For a second, she wondered where she was, but then her thighs screamed out some two-part harmony, her shoulder joined in, and she remembered the scampering calves.

Struggling to her feet, she squinted into the distance.

The sun seemed awfully low in the sky. How long had she slept? And where was Buster? Putting her fingers to her lips, she whistled and waited.

And waited.

Her heart tripped, stumbled, and revved up to a nervous cha-cha beat. Buster always came to her whistle. Always.

Maybe he was hurt. Maybe he'd followed that last calf into the ravine. He could have snagged his leg on a root, tripped over a rock, broken a leg.

Ten minutes and seven increasingly frantic whistles later, she edged over the rocks that guarded the deep slash in the earth. Picking her way down the slope, she set her feet with care. Cowboy boots were made for riding, not hiking, and the slick leather soles would become twin skateboards if she slipped.

She was halfway down when a jay hoisted his jaunty tail and screeched out a warning. At the same moment, something smacked her ankle, hard.

Jumping back, she lost her footing and slid, cussing wildly, downhill. Grabbing a sturdy branch, she skidded to a stop and glanced back just in time to catch the furtive glide of a rattler pouring bonelessly off a rock. Saluting her with a final shake of its God-given maracas, it disappeared into the grass.

No. Surely her luck couldn't be that bad. Clutching her ankle, she heard her father's voice in her head.

Folks rarely die from snakebite. But boy, can it make you sick.

She needed to keep her cool. Panic only make the blood flow faster, helping the venom do its deadly work. Tugging off her boot, she found two small punctures in the leather, right where she'd felt the strike.

She tried to remember first aid for snakebite as she tugged off her sweaty, stubborn sock. Number one — keep antivenom close. But it was too late for that. Her dad always made sure they had some in the fridge in the barn, but that wasn't close enough.

Number two — slash the punctures and suck out the blood. That was actually an old wives' tale, but sometimes those old wives knew their stuff. Bending to examine her ankle, she searched for the wound. There were two faint bruises where the fangs had struck but no blood, no broken skin.

No puncture, no poison.

Relief flooded her brain so fast she thought she might faint, but she was far from safe. Her horse was still missing, and the weather had shifted while she'd slept. Thunderheads puffed behind the mountains, mirroring the worries stacked up on her mental horizon. Her horse. Her dad. Her cheating stepmother. This land, so soon to be lost forever. Plus she was halfway to the base of the ravine, where a heavy rain could cause a flash flood. And Buster, her Buster, might be trapped down there.

The storm clouds billowed and broke. All her losses, past and future, crashed around her with the summer storm. She was glad she was alone, miles from anyone who could hear or see her, because sometimes a girl just had to let go. Deep sobs escaped in guttural moans while rain pelted her hair, her skin, her shirt.

Minutes later, she sniffed, stood, and brushed the mud from her butt. Buster was somewhere in the storm, alone, maybe hurt. She pictured her big gelding lying at the bottom of the slope, helpless in the rain. Flies would buzz at his sweet, soft eyes, and buzzards would tear at his shining hide. It would be all her fault for quitting when he was still eager to chase calves, for falling asleep when she should have been watching him, and for trying to do a job that was way too big for her cowgirl britches.

You should have asked for help. Cade would have come.

Swatting the thought away like a pesky fly, she resolved to take this one step at a time.

Step one: Find her horse.

Step two: Quit crying.

Step three: Figure out what the heck step three was.

Chapter 18

JESS'S SOCK WAS DAMP WITH RAIN AND SWEAT, BUT SHE wrestled it on while she sorted through the sounds of the prairie—the tinkle of a songbird, the blatt of redwing blackbirds in the willows, and the splat of raindrops hitting the dry earth.

There was another sound, though. Something different—and welcome. She stood, her heart lifting.

Hoofbeats, faint but getting faster. Scrambling to the brink of the ravine, she caught sight of Buster and hoisted herself up over the rocks to greet him. *He* was a welcome sight—as opposed to the mounted horse behind him.

Cade.

She should have been relieved, but the stress of the past half hour made her inexplicably annoyed as he smiled down on her, all white teeth and summer tan. His ridiculously pretty horse seemed to be smiling, too, as if he knew what a fool she'd just made of herself.

Apparently, she wasn't done, because the sight of Buster made a great, shuddering breath escape her as she swallowed a mighty sob of relief.

Dammit, she needed to stay cool so Cade wouldn't know how bad she'd screwed up. She swiped at her tears, remembering too late how dirty her hands were. She'd probably pawed a streak of dirt across her cheek, which must look charming, what with her hair being drippy from the rain and her shirt wet through. When it rained in Wyoming, it really *rained*. Storms might not have staying power, but they were thorough.

"Need help?" Cade asked.

Deep inside her, a little voice cried *Yes! Please!*

But an old defensiveness born of too many dumb blond jokes reared its head and struck like a rattler.

"I'm *fine*."

She was tired of men who patronized her, as if she couldn't perform simple, everyday tasks. Maybe the task at hand wasn't so simple, and maybe she'd been bested by a bunch of bovine babies, but *still*.

She brushed dirt off her jeans with her muddy hands, then grabbed her snakebit boot and hopped around awkwardly, trying to put it on. "Just fine."

"Fine?" Cade grinned, looking her up and down. "I noticed that."

His gaze stroked her like the palm of a warm hand, trailing a shimmer of lust from the top of her head to her toes. She was acutely aware that her shirt was wet through. Probably see-through.

His sure was. As she faced him, the sun emerged behind him and the rain cloud passed. The little voice started shouting again.

Give up. Go home. And take that cowboy with you!

She distracted herself by petting his horse while she clenched her thighs to cut down on the shimmering.

"Is this a client's horse?"

"Nope." He slid his gaze sideways. "He was Amber Lynn's."

"Figures. His eyelashes are longer than mine." She stroked the velvet muzzle and felt the comfort of the horse's scent, his soft eyes, his sturdy if spindly presence. "He looks like Barbie's Dream Horse."

"He's Ken's Dream Horse." Cade faked a childish pout. "Barbie's horse is pink."

"Oh, right. He's so manly. What's his name?"

Cade grinned wider. "Pride. Like I said, he was Amber Lynn's. Get it?"

It took her a second. "Oh. So he goeth before a fall?"

"Sure does."

She laughed as Buster pushed his muzzle into her hand, searching for a treat.

"I think Buster's in love with him," Cade said. "He's been following us around for the past fifteen minutes. Where were you?"

"Resting."

She stared off over a landscape brightened to brilliance by the rain. The Highlanders had emerged with the sun, and the pasture was dotted with cow-calf pairs, dozens of them. Just looking at them made her so tired and frustrated that she was almost afraid to open her mouth. She was afraid a petulant *mew* would escape and finish shredding her dignity.

Swallowing, she managed to speak.

"You didn't have to come looking for me, you know."

"I wasn't looking for you." He moved his head, and a pool of rain in his Stetson poured, in a single silver stream, from the brim. "I was looking for those calves Heck was worried about." His brow furrowed. "Is that why you're here? Were you trying to do this job on your own?"

"Are you?"

"Well, yeah. But I haven't been living in the city for the past few years."

At least he hadn't brought up her lousy roping skills. She supposed she should give him credit for tact, but her feminist ire had collided with the shimmering, and she was too confused to be anything but grumpy.

"I'm fine. It's like riding a bicycle."

He rested his forearms on the saddle horn and fixed his eyes on hers. "You're not fine, and that horse is not a bicycle." He sighed. "It's Buster, though, and you know what they say. Good horses take care of fools, drunks, and children."

"I am not a child."

He gave her an indulgent smile, the kind a favorite uncle might bestow on a three-year-old. "I didn't call you one."

She shook back her hair, trying not to wince when a small waterfall cascaded down the collar of her shirt. "I'm not a drunk either."

He gave her a level stare from those clear gray eyes while rain dripped in big, fat drops from the brim of his hat. "That rules out two out of three. Gee, what's left?"

She set her fists on her hips, giving him a mock glare. "Are you calling me stupid?"

His brows lowered. "Anyone's a fool who'd be out here alone. What if Buster throws you?"

"What if I'm struck by lightning? What if Buster grows horns and a forked tongue? What if the devil rises up from the canyon and hauls me off to hell?" She blew out an impatient sigh. "I told you, I'm fine."

It really wasn't fair, arguing with a man sitting high in the saddle while she stood there flatfooted. He looked handsome and confident, forearms on the saddle horn, hat tilted up, those pale, sky-lit eyes seeing everything. She almost broke down and told him she couldn't do this.

Almost.

But she could. The strength to get this job done was at the core of her. So what if that core had shrunk down to the size of a peanut? A very small peanut, which she seemed to have misplaced?

Another sob, left over from her snake-induced panic, welled up like a knuckle-sized rock in her throat. The shimmering was still there, mixed with annoyance in a toxic stew garnished with terror of the snake and frustration with the prancing calves. Leaning her forehead against the swells of Buster's saddle, she felt her self-reliance pour out in a moan that was a whole lot louder and more pitiful sounding than she'd planned.

He had his arm around her shoulders in an instant, his eyes filled with concern.

"What happened, hon? What can I do?"

"I'm just tired." The part of her that had no pride collapsed into him. "I whistled, and Buster didn't come, and I thought he was dead. And my dad's sick, and the ranch is going to be sold, and it's all gone wrong." Sorrow squeezed her heart so hard, she could barely squeak. "I love this place. I love my dad. Nothing's right. Nothing."

Cade put his arms around Jess. They stood in the mud, rocking together while she cried. She never let herself lean on him like this, and he knew she'd start fighting her feelings in ten, nine, eight, seven...

"Oh God, I'm such a *girl*." Shoving him away, she

ran her hands over her face in a vain attempt to erase her tears. "I'm fine. I'm okay."

He tilted his head, considering her muddied knees and hair, her damp shirt, her dirty face. "What were you doing down there, anyway?"

"Nothing. But look—you won't believe this."

Balancing on one leg, she removed her boot, tugged down her sock, and held out her foot to show him a bruise on the fair skin of her ankle.

"What did you do?"

He bent to take her foot in his hands. What was left of the rain poured out of his hat brim, right onto her bare foot. Yipping, she pulled away.

"Look." Picking up her boot, she pointed to two faint holes in the leather. "It was crazy. A snake..."

The breath left his body as if he'd been punched in the gut. "What? What kind?"

"Rattler. But..."

He snatched the boot away and grabbed her arm. "I thought you said you were okay."

Frog-marching her toward the horses, he swore and hoisted her roughly into his arms when she stumbled on her half-socked foot.

"Cade, stop. What are you doing?"

"What am *I* doing? What are *you* doing?" He hoisted her higher against his chest. "It's like you were *born* in that damn city. Don't you remember rattlesnakes?" He dumped her beside the horses.

Teetering on her one boot, she grabbed his arm to keep from falling. "Be careful."

"Careful?" He was so mad that the words got all jammed up in his throat. They made a growling sound, then burst out before he could think. "*You* be careful, dammit. You could be dead. You may be yet, because you're too damned stubborn to ask for help."

"I can do it," she said in a small voice. "I don't know how long Dad'll be in the hospital, and the work has to be done."

"Exactly! But does it ever occur to you I might *want* to help?" Waving the boot in the air, he pointed at the puncture holes. "Tell you what. Take a couple days off. But Saturday, we work *together*." He bit off every word like buffalo jerky. "I'll meet you at your place in the morning. We'll doctor those calves as a *team*. And we'll *stay* a team for as long as you're here."

Teardrops hovered on her lashes, and he wanted to drag her to his chest and kiss her, but he knew she'd push him away. So he stared her down, his mouth a thin, grim line.

"All right." Her shoulders slumped. "You win."

"I don't want to *win*." Savagely, he kicked a stone and sent it skittering across the prairie—which sent Pride skittering, too. "We don't have time for this. That foot's not swelling yet, but it will."

"No, it won't."

He waved the snakebit boot. "You think you're immune or what?"

"I think I'm not bit." Balancing on one foot, she tore off her sock. "It didn't break the skin. I checked. And if I *was* bit, I'd have died five minutes ago, while you were going on about how stupid I am."

She stood there, wobbling on one leg with her hand on Buster's saddle, holding up her bare foot. All around her ankle, he saw the bruise blossoming in shades of blue, purple, and green—but there wasn't so much as a scratch.

Relief blended with a complicated cocktail of anger, fear, and dread. For a moment, he didn't know what to do—but he had to do *something*.

Rearing back, he wound up like a big-league pitcher and threw the boot into the sagebrush, hard as he could.

And then he took her in his arms and kissed her with everything he had.

She fell against him, letting go little by little. He could feel the remnants of her anger simmering under his hands, but she kissed him with equal passion, and his heart rose like a bird winging into the sky—until she jerked away, pressed both hands to his chest, and shoved him onto his butt in the sagebrush. He missed a prickly pear by inches, and his heart folded its wings and fell out of the sky, landing beside him with a *splat*.

He looked up, stunned. "Hey."

"Hey yourself." She started to laugh, giggles bubbling up like bubbles in a spring. "Sorry. Didn't mean to push that hard. But you'd better go find my boot." She climbed into the saddle and turned her horse toward home. "Meet me at the house. No, the barn." She clicked her tongue, spun her horse, and was gone.

He watched her go, scratching his head, then strode out into the brush. He found the boot and carried it back to Pride, who shied at the sight of it. His stupid rage had obviously reminded the horse that humans were foolish and sometimes cruel.

"Sorry, pal."

He let the horse smell the boot and mumble his soft lips over the leather until he lost interest in it. Then Cade climbed wearily into the saddle. He set the boot upside down on the horn and followed Jess, barely noticing how the sun's last rays warmed the damp earth, making the scent of the plains rise all around him. The sharp tang of rabbitbrush blended with the scent of the earth itself, nourished by the rain.

As Jess's fleeing figure topped the ridge and disappeared, he rode slow, images of her flashing through his mind like a flickering nickelodeon film. When he finally noticed the gold and pink hues of the sunset, her eyes seemed to float there, behind the clouds.

She was as much a part of this land as he was, but the road to a life with her would always be rocky and steep, pocked with potholes and racked with switchbacks.

But if he kept on climbing, if he pushed and struggled and did all he could, he might catch a glimpse of heaven in those eyes that floated up there, out of reach—at least for now.

Chapter 19

CADE PULLED PRIDE TO A STOP ONCE HE REACHED THE Diamond Jack. There was no sign of Jess, but a light burned in the barn, and the wide front doors stood open.

Night made the cavernous building a mysterious realm. Releasing his horse into a stall, he gazed up at the thick wood supports that stretched into the dark. Scattered hay glittered like gold confetti in light cast by a caged bulb that hung from a high crossbeam.

"Jess?"

Horses shifted in their stalls as he passed, one blowing out a soft breath, another thudding a hoof against the wooden stall door. A sleepless dove throbbed and muttered in the rafters, and mice skittered and chirped among the hay bales. The plains' twilight sonata drifted through the stall doors—whippoorwills repeating their sad refrain, the yip of a coyote, the whirr and cry of nighthawks diving for moths.

A rustle too big for a mouse made him glance up at the hay loft, and there she was, next to the ladder, dangling her legs over the edge. Somewhere along the way, she'd kicked off the other boot, and her feet were bare.

Hadn't he just told himself heaven floated above him?

And this time, there was a ladder.

Jess stood, her bare feet gripping the edge of the loft, and took a few steps, dipping her outside foot like a gymnast on a beam.

"Careful," he said.

"Won't fall. Never do."

Arms outspread, she paced to the far end of the loft, spun gracefully, and danced her way back. Looking down, she laughed at his furrowed forehead.

"Quit worrying, Cade. You're like an old woman."

The comment stung. He probably wasn't as much fun as he'd been back when they were kids. Then, he'd thought of nothing but love. He would have climbed any mountain, forded any stream, and fought a dozen mountain lions for her.

Now, he had responsibilities, goals, and due dates for the horses he'd taken in training. Up until yesterday, he'd had a mortgage—but he apparently didn't have to worry about that anymore. Just taxes, upkeep, and feed, plus a hundred other everyday distractions.

The trick to love, though, was *not* to be distracted. To focus on what mattered. And what mattered stood at the top of the ladder, her nimble fingers dancing down the front of her shirt, undoing one button after another. When she reached the tail, she shimmied her shoulders, and the shirt slipped away, revealing a white tank top, still damp from the rain, stretched tight over her breasts. In the warm yellow light, it was almost transparent.

Turning, she headed toward the front of the barn, where the loft widened in front of the big square window at the peak of the roof. Her steps were slow and graceful, her hips swinging a sexy rhumba.

It was as if a gust of wind had blown through his mind and cleared out the cobwebs. He forgot due dates, responsibilities, and every goal but Jess. Grabbing a clean horse blanket from the stack outside the tack room, he climbed the ladder.

She lay sprawled across a blue Native American blanket she'd tossed over a soft bed of hay. Her arms were crossed above her head, and her blond hair blended with the gleam of clean straw. The denim that hugged her curves was worn to white in all the right places. She might think she was a city girl, but he bet those city boys saw the difference. She'd never lost her horsewoman's thighs or the toned arms she'd earned bucking hay.

He memorized the moment—the drape of her limbs, the lashes shading her laughing eyes. But then she licked her lips, and his brain shorted out as if she'd zapped him with a cattle prod. Toppling into the straw, he caught himself just in time, so their bodies meshed instead of mashing.

"Hey." She swept her fingers through his hair, just the way she used to, and just like that, they were Cade and Jess again. He remembered how proud he'd been of the love they'd shared—a grown-up kind of love, deep and warm, unlike the raging fires of adolescent obsession that had burned among their friends. Those fires flared up and died, gone in a flash. He and Jess had been the one permanent constellation in the ever-changing astrology of Grigsby High.

And then their star had burned out. She'd headed for the city while he'd stayed, trying to make something of Walker Ranch. He wished things could have been different, but she'd had to follow her bliss, and he'd had to stay. Or so he'd thought.

Resting his cheek on her hair, he inhaled her intoxicating country-girl scent—the tang of sweat, a hint of cut grass, and the lingering warmth of the summer sun. It drew him out of the past and into the present—right where he wanted to be.

He kissed her forehead, her eyelids, the bridge of her nose, then moved to her lips and down, sipping and savoring, planting a dozen more kisses along her jawline and down her neck. Dipping his tongue into the warm, throbbing hollow of her throat, he smiled into her skin when she mewed in response.

Her tank top was nothing but a scrap of cloth with strings for straps; a flick of his finger bared one shoulder, then the other. He kissed the soft spot below the bone, then worked his way down her arms, silky and smooth below, the tops bronzed to gold. Love had been a banked fire, burning steady inside him all these years. Now the flames were rising, high and wild, need heating the embers to a white-hot glow.

Kissing the tops of her breasts, he slipped the straps down her arms, then glanced up to check her eyes, her smile. Did she want this? Heavy-lidded, long-lashed, her eyes said yes.

Yes to everything.

Pulling the soft, stretchy fabric away, he cupped his hands around her breasts, savoring the sweet soft heft of them, the subtle slope of her cleavage, and the pink summits that peaked beneath his tongue. Her hair tumbled over her face and shielded her eyes, but her lips, wet and slick, lured him back for a kiss.

In the kiss, he felt her tension dissolve, softening her limbs as she gave in to desire and tore open the snaps of his shirt. Sweeping her hands over his chest in slow figure eights, she brushed his nipples on every pass, making him shiver before she stroked low toward his hips and the danger zone.

Biting the tip of her tongue between her teeth, she ran one finger slowly across the top edge of his belt.

"Cade, *now*." Her voice was a breathy whisper as she shimmied out of her jeans. "Now."

Rolling over, he pulled off his own. Her striptease had been so sweet; his was a clumsy wrestling match with fumbling hands.

When he turned, she lay naked in the straw, watching him with a come-hither smile.

Smiling back, he said a silent prayer thanking God for sending her back home. For a long time, he'd been sure he'd ruined his life by letting Amber Lynn hijack his desperate heart, sure as if he'd shot himself and died. But now he'd come alive, along with all the hopes and dreams he'd kissed goodbye.

He played Jess like a cello, stroking the dips that bracketed her belly, the insides of her thighs, the soft skin behind her knees. And she touched him in return, proving she knew his body as well as he knew hers. As she worked her way from his temples to his neck and trailed her fingers down his chest, then his hips, he squeezed his eyes shut and tried to think of those goals and due dates so he wouldn't explode. A stallion reared in the round pen of his mind, and a white mare raced through a grassy field. But pretty things always brought him back to her.

He rolled her under him, rose above her, and looked a question into her eyes while he fished in his pocket for the foil packet he'd stowed away in a fit of hopefulness. She nodded and he fumbled around, so rushed he barely got the thing on, before surrendering to the long, slow glide inside. The grace of their giving and taking erased all his doubt and pain and regret, all his anger and self-recrimination. The past was gone, burned to ashes, blown away.

Her cries bounced off the rafters and rattled the windows. But it wasn't just her; he shouted, too, as the world spun off course and swept them into a windstorm, hot and wild. They clung together, riding the high until the strength of their emotions wore them out and tossed them, like ragdolls, spent and blinded on a straw-strewn shore.

He memorized the moment, holding it in his mind like a globe of fragile glass, a treasure lost and miraculously found, and prayed she felt the unbreakable rightness of it.

The two of them could grow old, together or apart. She could leave a thousand times, return, and leave again. But nothing could come between them—not for long. Love would always be like this for them, perfect and solely, miraculously theirs.

Jess felt as heavy as a stone tossed in a stream. She'd flown high, splashed, and settled, rocking into a perfectly formed and fitted spot. Warm water stroked and soothed—Cade's love, calming her body and clearing her mind.

Never leave him. Never leave this place…

The words seeped into her soul, along with the sounds of doves cooing in the rafters, a faint breeze swishing through the eaves, and the celebratory songs of tree frogs by the creek. Sweet scents floated on the damp night air—clean straw, old wood, sunbaked shingles cooling in the night.

She heard Cade breathing beside her, first hard and fast, then slower. She knew he was looking at her, but she kept her eyes closed so she wouldn't have to talk or even smile. The moment felt so perfect, and perfection was fragile.

She'd broken that perfection when she'd left, but she'd had to see what the world had to offer before she could appreciate what she had. She didn't regret her few flings with other men. There'd been a lawyer who'd taken her to the best restaurants in town but was a bust in bed. Then, an older man from Boston she'd met at the hotel had known a dozen sleek sexual tricks but seemed to practice them all by rote. Last came a hot Italian chef who barely spoke English but loved her with a tenderness that had surprised her. He'd been the best, but they'd had nothing in common, not even a language.

Rich, experienced, passionate—but none came close to eclipsing Cade. Steady as he was, solid and hardworking, he was still the hottest lover she'd ever had.

Probably because he loved her.

How could you not know how much that mattered?

She wanted to slap her forehead at her foolishness, but she was too comfortable to bother.

Blinking, she stretched and smiled, wondering if he'd flown in the same sky, had the same love-inspired epiphany. He'd propped himself up on one elbow to watch her, but now he threw himself back in the straw as if shot.

"Jesus, Jess, give a man a break. I'm lost already, but when you do that…"

"Do what?"

"I don't know. That thing you just did."

"I stretched." She did it again.

"Like that. I swear, all you ever have to do is look that satisfied, that sleepy, and I'm yours." He took her hand, and his smile turned serious. "I am anyway."

A little voice in the back of her mind spoke.

And you're his.

No, she wasn't. She couldn't be. There was a reason, she was sure of that, but she couldn't remember what it was, because the reason for everything was lying beside her with love in his eyes and no clothes on.

How was a girl supposed to make sensible decisions when the man looked that good naked? How was she supposed to do anything but kiss him and see if he could still do it twice in one summer evening?

"I'll see you Saturday, right? If not before."

"Saturday?" she asked.

"Our deal. First thing. I'm helping you, you're helping me. Remember?"

She gave him a sly wink. "I thought that's what we just did."

He grinned. "I'm hoping I don't have to wait until Saturday for that." To her intense regret, he reached for his clothes and began dressing. Once he'd floundered into his shirt and tugged on his jeans, he rose and offered a hand. "You know, Jess, we could help each other more than you realize. This place—if you stayed, I'd help you any way I could."

"But your business, my job…"

He pulled her to his feet. "Like I said, we could help each other. With you here and me helping out, Heck could stay."

"But I can't stay."

She turned and pretended to look out the window so he wouldn't see she was lying. Right now, her heart had hijacked her brain, and she damn sure wanted to stay.

And why not? It wouldn't be the future she'd envisioned for herself. She might never get to Hawaii, never live on a beach. But she'd be with Cade, and wouldn't that be better?

Maybe. Her brain flashed a caution light, telling her this happiness couldn't last. You couldn't depend on love, no matter how much someone cared. Look at her mother—surely, the one person in the world she should have been able to trust. But when something better had come along, Dot had left without a backward glance.

Then there was Molly. She'd vowed to love Jess's father forever, for better and for worse, and now she was flirting on the phone with some stranger. Even Cade had shifted his affection to Amber Lynn Lyle once Jess was out of sight. She needed to build a life that was bulletproof and all her own.

But Cade...

"Give that brain of yours a rest, would you? I can see all the doubts chasing through your mind. Just trust me." He paused, holding her at arms' length and looking into her eyes. "You do trust me, don't you? It felt like you did."

She looked away, swallowing hard. Unfazed, he pulled her close and kissed her, a brief, sweet benediction, then pressed his forehead against hers to look into her eyes.

"Everything's going to be all right, okay?" he said. "Whatever you decide to do, I'm on your side. So quit worrying."

She nodded, but she lowered her lashes so he couldn't read her eyes.

Chapter 20

Molly sat by Heck's hospital bed, listening to his slow, steady breathing. It was late, and the room was dark but for a shaft of light that angled through the half-open door.

Her husband. Sometimes it still struck her as a miracle she'd found someone who loved her with such complete acceptance. Someone who didn't care about where she'd grown up or how many men she'd known or that she couldn't bear him babies.

She loved him so much, it hurt.

She wanted to tell him, but she remembered the doctor's warnings. Heck needed his sleep, and that was fine. She'd taken some time to talk to Jess. The girl had seemed happier today than she'd ever seen her, though she was still painfully wary of Molly herself.

"Aw, Heck, I try," she said softly. "I love her to pieces whether she loves me back or not. But I don't know why she can't at least like me, just a little bit. It would be nice if she'd talk to me in words of more than one syllable."

She sighed. "If only she knew I didn't really want to sell the ranch. It was always just a way to bring her home. You know that. But now..." She glanced out the hospital window at the black macadam parking lot, tacky small-town high-rises, and cracked concrete sidewalks. "Now, I don't know what we'll do. With your heart...

I just don't see how we can stay unless Jess does. And
Cade. You need somebody, honey. I know you hate that,
but you do."

An impossible wave of tenderness rushed over her.
"It's going to be okay, hon. You know Cade can do anything he sets his mind to. They just need time, and it's
up to us to make sure they get it."

She scanned his face, so very tired, like a weary child.

"It's up to *me*," she whispered.

She sat there, holding his hand, listening to the hush
of the hospital and thinking about the way Jess and Cade
had looked when they'd come in from the barn. It was
obvious what had happened and even more obvious
they'd enjoyed it.

What would it be like to make love in a barn? It
wasn't the cleanest place in the world, but maybe sometime she could bring a nice clean blanket from the house
and a picnic basket with dessert and some wine.

Coconut pie, maybe. That was Heck's favorite,
because of how they'd met.

She imagined lying in the cool darkness, moonlight
slanting through the windows, stars glittering in the
spaces where shingles had been blown off by the wind.
Heck would finish his pie, and then he'd give her that
look, the one that warmed her to her toes, and they'd...

"Dammit, woman, you oughta be home in bed!"

She smiled into the darkness. "No. I need to be with
you." She sighed. "I was thinking we should make love
in the barn."

"The barn?" His sleepy voice sounded a little more
alert. "Like where in the barn?"

"Maybe the hayloft." She fumbled to find his hand in

the sheets he'd twisted in his sleep. "It's working, Heck. Our plan. You wait. There'll be wedding bells, and Cade and Jess will take over the ranch, and you won't have to worry anymore."

"Well, good," he said. "But I wasn't worried anyway."

"You weren't?"

"Nope." He squeezed her hand. "Even if we have to move, I'll still have you."

"That's sweet." Sweet, but hard to believe. Heck loved his land and his horses and being a cowboy. She wasn't sure where in his pantheon of great loves she belonged, but she'd always assumed she took second place to his work. It was who he was.

"It would be better if Jess and Cade had each other, too," she said. "I know family's important to you."

"You're right." He pulled her hand closer, placing it right where he wanted it. "But why are we talking about Jess and Cade?"

She giggled. "Because it's important. It's a good reason to celebrate."

"Okay, but I don't really need a reason." He moved her hand back to the mattress with a sigh. "When we get home, we're going to celebrate every night."

In answer, she bent and kissed him, gently but deeply. She was thrilled when he responded with more enthusiasm than he'd shown since his first heart attack.

"We can do it wherever you want," he said. "In the barn, in the pasture. Good gravy, we could do it on the tractor if you want." He lifted her hand to his mouth and kissed it. "But you need to know, our life's about you and me. Not Jess and Cade, not the ranch, not the cattle. You're all I need. I mean it."

"Oh, Heck." She smiled. The nickname made it sound like she was swearing, when really, she was doing the opposite.

Because to her, his name was a blessing—one evoked with love, reverence, and a happy heart.

———

Jess called her office every day, first thing. It seemed wise to start the day with a reminder of her *real* life—the one where she was *good* at her job. The one where she made a living. The one she needed to get back to, just as soon as she could.

And it seemed wise to remind her boss that she cared. And sometimes, she thought it was a good idea to remind Treena—and herself—that she'd return to Birchwood Suites.

There were times when she wanted to stay at the Diamond Jack so badly it hurt, but she knew that wasn't practical long-term. She needed to get her father healthy and find him a good life that wouldn't strain his heart or break it. She needed to see him safe and well so she wouldn't have to worry. Putting even a small part of the ocean between them seemed crazy right now, but things would get better. Or so she hoped.

She was just about to dial her boss when she heard her stepmother clattering around in the kitchen and remembered today was Friday, the day of Molly's assignation.

Quietly, Jess eased herself down the stairs and watched her stepmother from the landing. The woman was waltzing around like a happy lunatic, singing Patsy Cline's "Crazy" in a thin but enthusiastic soprano. She wasn't wearing the jeans she'd adopted since her marriage to Heck. Instead, she was dressed to impress—by Molly standards, at least—in a white shirt with roses embroidered on the collar, a navy skirt, and a pink vest decorated with appliqued flowers. She looked like one of those flags people put in their gardens to announce various seasons. This would be spring. Was Molly celebrating a new beginning?

Jess went back to her room and waited until she heard the Camry crunching down the gravel drive. Her stepmother was on her way to the meeting she'd set up on that phone call, and Jess was determined to follow. She'd call the office later.

Pausing by a rack of keys by the back door, she chose the one for her dad's truck. Molly would know Jess's little red car, but there were lots of red Ford pickups in town.

She was flying out the door, intent on her secret mission, when the phone rang. She was tempted to let it go, but a quick glance told her it was the hospital calling.

"Is this Molly?" said a stern female voice.

"No, this is Jess. Are you calling about my father? Is something wrong?"

"He's asking for her, that's all. I assume Molly's his wife?"

"Yes." Jess wondered how long that would be true. If Molly was off to see some lover in a no-tell motel, she wouldn't be Heck's wife for long.

"She needs to be here. He's in a temper, and his blood pressure's sky-high."

"I'll find her," Jess said. "I'll get her there."

Slamming the receiver down, she raced out the door. She had a twofold mission now: first, find Molly and reveal her cheating ways; second, drag her back to the hospital to save the husband she was cheating on.

When Jess reached the main road, the Camry was already out of sight. Making a quick guess, she turned toward town. A mile farther on, she caught sight of her stepmother up ahead and began tailing her in earnest, dodging around like a private eye on TV. She felt silly, but then she remembered Molly's voice on the phone in the restroom—nervous and giggly as a teenager with a crush.

As they neared the town of Wynott, the sagebrush flats gave way to neat front yards. Jess was sure her stepmother was heading for one of the cheap hotels that catered to oil rig workers, but the Camry sailed past them and took the highway ramp. Jess followed, allowing a couple of semis to get ahead of her, then accelerated when she saw the Camry take the Grigsby exit.

Grigsby was a bigger town than Wynott, with a more industrial flavor. Instead of a grain elevator and quaint, brick-fronted Main Street, it was cluttered with pole buildings and crumbling brick garages. Molly finally turned into an empty parking lot that surrounded a yellow brick building, the largest in town.

Grigsby Elementary.

Surprised, Jess slowly passed the school. Maybe Molly, a long-time substitute teacher, had arranged to meet with a former coworker. It seemed like an unlikely spot for an assignation, but there was no accounting for taste. And it was summer, so the building was probably empty.

Jess parked her truck on a side street behind a tree as Molly walked into the school, which was apparently unlocked. In moments, a van pulled into the lot.

Dang. Jess should have brought binoculars. She could barely see the outline of the driver as the van stopped in front of the door, and the vehicle blocked her view of whoever emerged from the back seat and entered the school.

The van drove off, which seemed odd. Had someone dropped off Molly's paramour? How many people were in on this affair, and how would her dad feel if the whole town knew about it?

Shutting off the ignition, Jess watched the entrance for a while, wondering what to do. It was summertime, so school was out of session. Maybe Molly was having an affair with a teacher she'd worked with before she got married.

Suspicion coiled and circled in Jess's mind like a snake about to strike as she stepped out of the truck and stared at the now-closed door. Now that this was actually happening, she felt suddenly rooted to where she stood, unwilling to confront her stepmom and learn the truth. It would change everything—for her and for her father.

Her belly burning with indignation, she marched across the parking lot. She didn't know what was going on, but she aimed to find out—and save her father from making the biggest mistake of his life.

Chapter 21

STEPPING INTO THE SCHOOL, JESS WAS SWEPT AWAY BY A wave of nostalgia. The mingled scents of paste, crayons, and floor wax carried her back to a simpler time, when teachers had told her what to do and she'd obeyed without question. She'd admired her teachers, all of them, but she had a feeling that image was about to be shattered.

Heading down the hall, she peered into the narrow sidelight beside each closed classroom door. Old-fashioned oak teachers' desks still fronted neat rows of Formica-topped ones for kids. The color scheme of the plastic chairs was turquoise and orange, like an old Howard Johnson's motel.

The hall turned sharply to the right, and a child's voice intruded on the silence, reading aloud, stumbling on the hard words.

Huh. Must be summer school.

There was a pause in the reading, then a rustling of small bodies and scraping of chairs before a new voice took over. This one was smoother than the first, adding dramatic flair to the story.

Jess peeked into the classroom to see a boy standing at the teacher's desk with that back-bowed, tummy-first posture peculiar to little boys. Despite thick-lensed glasses, he held a battered paperback book so close to his face that he risked pinching his nose in the crease.

He occasionally paused, sniffed, and pushed the glasses up the slope of his freckled nose.

When Jess moved a little closer to the window, he glanced over and widened his eyes.

"There's someone at the door, ma'am."

Fudge. Now Jess would have to explain why she was there. If the teacher knew Molly, the rumor mill would start churning. The Baileys had provided plenty of grist when Jess's mother had left. With Molly's betrayal, they'd be big news all over again.

She wanted to cry. Either that or kill somebody. Preferably her stepmother.

"Tell them to come in, Josh."

Huh. That sounded like—

"Okay, Mrs. Bailey." The kid waved. "Come in, ma'am."

Jess set her face in a pleasant smile, but she had a feeling she looked stunned, awkward, and guilty. "Um, Molly?"

"Jess!"

Six boys and one girl sat at the child-sized desks, with Molly in the back row. Smiling, she scrambled to her feet and scampered to the front.

"Class, this is wonderful! I told you we'd get to know each other, and what did I say was the most important thing about a person?"

"Family!" shouted a boy in a Harley T-shirt at the back.

"That's right. Family is the biggest and best part of a person's life. Sometimes you're born with a family; other times, you create one of your own."

Jess realized at least a couple of the kids were probably from Phoenix House, Wynott's home for foster kids. The van must have picked them up, brought them to summer school.

She felt like a fool. She *was* a fool.

"This is Jess Bailey, and she's my stepdaughter," Molly continued. "Does anyone know what that means?"

"She isn't your *real* daughter," shouted a skinny kid with braces.

"Hmm. She looks real to me." Molly cocked her head and smiled. "It means she's not my blood relation. We're family because we *chose* to be. And that's very, very real."

Jess flushed as her stepmother continued.

"Jess is a very important part of our family, because she helps my husband run the ranch. She rides horses better than anyone I've ever seen."

Jess's eyes stung. She'd built a tower of assumptions, including a firm belief that her stepmom was a liar and a cheat. Obviously, she'd been wrong.

"Maybe you could come sometime and tell the class about your horse." Molly turned back to the class. "His name is Buster. He's the most beautiful animal, and he comes when she whistles!"

Josh, the smooth reader at the front of the room, burst into the conversation.

"My friend Jeff has a horse like that. It used to be bad, but now it does everything he says, and it comes when he calls it. It's a yellow horse, but Jeff says it's *golden*."

"That horse sounds marvelous, Josh. I think you might call him a palomino. Is that right, Jess?"

Molly turned to Jess with such an earnest expression that what little remained of the tower of assumptions crashed to the ground.

"Um, yeah. That's right. Or maybe a buckskin."

"Now I think Jess must want to talk to me, since she followed me here." Molly's eyes sparkled, and Jess wondered if Molly knew why she'd come. Thank goodness she had a genuine message from the hospital for an excuse.

Molly pointed to the lone girl student, whose hair was styled in beaded braids that clicked when she glanced up. There was guilt in her brown eyes, as if she was used to being in trouble.

"Destiny, you're in charge."

Destiny widened her eyes in panic, but Molly stayed calm.

"Please lead your classmates to the art table." Molly lowered her voice to a conspiratorial tone. "Your mission is to draw a picture of the horse you'd like to have for yourself. It doesn't have to be a *real* horse. Remember we talked about imagination?"

The class nodded.

"There'll a prize for the most original drawing," she continued. "Show me just how wild your imagination can get, and draw a horse like I've never even dreamed of!"

Jess watched the little gang march to the back of the room under Destiny's leadership. They gathered art supplies with minimal tussling, and soon six heads bent over sheets of paper. The only sound in the room was the gentle scrape of crayons. The only laggard was Josh, who shuffled reluctantly to the back of the room.

"I'm not a good drawer," he said as he passed Molly.

"Nobody's good at everything, and you're a wonderful reader," Molly said. "Just remember 'most original'" is about ideas, not how well you draw. I think a *golden* horse would be a good start."

Shrugging, Josh sat in the one remaining chair and began fishing through the crayons as Molly led Jess out into the hall, her face shifting from perky and smiling to grave and concerned as soon as the door closed behind them.

"Is your dad all right?"

"His blood pressure's sky-high." Remembering the nurse's clipped tones, Jess felt a little more confident in her mission. "The nurse said he's upset because you're not there."

"Oh dear." Molly glanced through the narrow window at the kids and wrung her hands. "I was afraid that would happen."

"What are you doing here?" Jess asked. "I mean, they're cute kids and all, but Dad's sick. He needs you."

"The doctor said he didn't." Molly thrust her hands into the pockets of her skirt and stared at the floor like a chastened child. "He said your dad wouldn't sleep when I was there, and he was so stern, Jess. He said, 'Don't you have a job?' And I didn't, because your dad wanted me to quit, but…" Leaning back against the wall, she sighed. "I feel like I'm cheating on him just by being here, but it was doctor's orders. Your dad—I know supporting me is a point of pride for him, but I've missed the kids so much. So I called David and asked to come back."

I miss the children.

Jess resisted the urge to smack her own forehead and groan.

"Who's David?"

"The principal. He was looking for someone to help

with the boys from Phoenix House and a couple kids from Springtime Acres whose parents can't afford child care." She lowered her voice. "We call them the Loose-Ends Gang, because they don't have anything to do when school's out. And you know what they say about idle hands."

"I need red! Where's the red crayon?" a boy bellowed from the classroom.

Molly and Jess watched through the window as Destiny threw a stubby crayon toward the boy, missing him by a mile. Three boys took the opportunity to race across the room, chasing the crayon as it rolled across the floor.

Molly edged the door open. "Boys."

Shamefaced, they returned to their seats and resumed work.

Molly closed the door gently. "That darn doctor. How am I going to get out of here?"

She glanced at the boys, nibbled on her thumbnail, then turned a thoughtful gaze on Jess.

"Oh no." Jess put her hands up as if to stop an oncoming train. "Call that David guy or something. I'm no good with kids."

"It's less than an hour. You'd just have to judge the contest, supervise lunch, and then get them to the bus."

"I'm not a teacher."

"You don't have to be. David was using volunteers before I called."

Jess peered into the classroom. The kids were behaving remarkably well, but beneath their furrowed foreheads and protruding tongues as they colored, she could see the tough little nuts they really were.

"They'll be good," Molly said. "You just have to have confidence. If you believe in yourself, they will, too." She giggled. "It's like walking through cows."

"What?"

"Like walking through cows," Molly repeated. "Your dad had a whole bunch of them gathered up for branding one time, and didn't he forget something in the house and send me back to get it? I had to wade through all those cows. Big as Buicks, every one, but your dad said to pretend I wasn't scared. And you know, it worked." She smiled. "Kids are just the same."

Molly sailed back into the room. Gathering up her handbag, she turned to the class and clapped her hands. Immediately, their chattering hushed.

"Class, I need to go take care of an emergency, so Miss Bailey's going to judge your work and have lunch with you." She showed Jess a brown paper bag on her desk. "There's a sandwich for you there." She turned back to the class. "Miss Bailey's going to report back to me on your behavior for the rest of the day, and I don't want to hear that any of you treated her with disrespect, okay?"

"Okay." The response was grudging but unanimous.

Jess felt a rush of panic. "Molly, I'm no good at this," she hissed.

"You'll be fine." Molly patted her cheek. "Remember, it's like walking through cows."

For half an hour, Jess watched the kids work. They seemed to be on their best behavior, and it was a lot more fun than she'd expected until she had to decide whether a horse with wheels and handlebars was more original than one with wings like a fighter jet. She had to smile at Destiny's picture; it was clearly inspired by Barbie's Dream Horse and looked a lot like Pride.

She solved her dilemma by having the kids vote, and three creations made the cut. The boys said there had never been a three-way tie before and seemed impressed with her judging ability.

Lunch went well once she quashed their attempt to test her mettle with a food fight. A tossed cookie was returned to its owner without comment, and the shenanigans stopped as she entertained them with stories about Buster the Wonder Horse.

They almost missed the bus because she lost track of time. After herding the last kid into the van, she walked out to her dad's truck and headed for the hospital with shame and relief warring in her mind, making her a little light-headed.

She'd been convinced Molly was cheating. Before that, she'd resented her stepmother for sponging off her dad. But she'd been wrong on both counts. In fact, she had to admire her soft-spoken stepmother for managing the Loose-Ends Gang so well, for loving her work so much, and for being so wise about the art of walking through cows.

When had she started expecting the worst from people—even people who loved her? Her dad wouldn't choose a woman who lied and cheated, and Molly wasn't gunning for the Bailey family fortune. She'd given up work she loved to make Jess's father happy.

Hauling her hair back in her fist, Jess gave the resulting ponytail a painful tug and told herself Molly had her dad's best interests at heart. And she was right; he would never give up the work he loved as long as he lived on the ranch. The idea of a retirement community was a good one. A *safe* one, if not the one Heck would choose himself.

But maybe there was another way. She remembered Cade's eyes, the warmth of his hands on her skin, the way they fit together, as if nothing had ever changed. As if they were meant to be together.

We could help each other more than you realize. With you here and me helping out, Heck could stay.

All of a sudden, the ocean waves that had loomed so large in her mind seemed to recede from the shore. Hadn't she heard Hawaiian beaches were always crowded? And that ocean smell was kind of fishy. Did she really want to give up her home, her horse, and her cowboy for that? When she imagined waking to Cade every morning, kissing him before she slept each night, she wondered why she'd ever left.

She'd been wrong about Molly, and she'd been wrong about Cade. Was it so hard to believe she'd been wrong about herself and what she really wanted?

It was time to trust people more, to open her heart and let love in.

Chapter 22

JESS'S DAD WAS ASLEEP WHEN SHE REACHED THE HOSPITAL. Molly, sitting by his bed, looked a little peaked. She gave Jess a weary smile.

"The doctor gave him something to help him sleep. He wouldn't notice if an elephant walked in the room."

"Good."

It was like talking to a stranger. Jess's evil stepmother was gone, leaving Jess herself the villain in this story—the evil stepdaughter, turning the fairy tale on its head.

No wonder she hadn't found her own happy ending. She didn't deserve one.

"You and I need to talk. I thought the coffee shop would be good." Molly sounded a little stern. "Your dad won't notice we're gone."

Jess glanced at her father, who looked strangely angelic with his eyes closed, a serene smile on his face. The little hair he had left curled around his head in tousled disarray.

"Okay. I could use a latte."

Jess thought she'd covered up her undercover mission with the message from the hospital, but it was obvious Molly had figured out her motives. She was a little worried about the upcoming conversation. Molly was a teacher, after all, and they always had a unique ability to show you all your mistakes.

At the café, Jess angled through the crowd to grab

a corner table while Molly stood in line. Clearing off some empty coffee cups and crumpled napkins, she pretended to study the courtyard outside while her mind raced through possible excuses for her behavior.

It was a short race. She really had no excuse, and by the time Molly set a tray bearing two lattes and a pair of enormous chocolate chip cookies on the table, Jess was so worked up, she jumped like a nervous cat. Molly simply smiled.

"It's been a hard day. I thought we deserved cookies."

You deserve cookies. I deserve a swift kick in the pants.

Opening her latte, Jess blew on the hot liquid and tried to calm the thoughts that stampeded through her mind like panicked horses. She felt a flush rising to her face, but it felt like anger, not embarrassment, and she wasn't sure why.

"What's the matter?" Molly asked.

"I don't know." Jess sipped her drink and replaced the lid, wishing she could cool her feelings that easily.

"You're upset I left your dad alone today."

"It isn't that." Jess searched her mind for the source of her emotions. "It's just—why didn't you react when you saw me at the door? You had to know something was wrong, but you let that kid keep reading. It was like they mattered more than my dad." She sighed. "I'm sorry. That's awful. They're kids, and they matter more than anybody. It's just…"

"Everybody matters." Molly broke a cookie in half and took a bite. "But you're right, these kids matter a lot. Two are on the autism spectrum, one has a really severe case of ADHD, and the others—well, they tend to act out. They need a teacher who's calm and in control. I wanted to react, believe me. But I can't let my personal issues ruin their chance to learn."

Jess felt about an inch high. "I didn't realize," she said. "They seemed so—good."

"They *are* good. They just need someone to believe in their goodness."

Jess was beginning to wonder why she hadn't believed in the goodness of her own stepmother when the woman seemed so willing to believe in everyone around her.

"They're my kids, you know?" Molly said. "I never had any of my own, so I love them the way I would if…"

"Why didn't you?"

The question had been lurking in the back of Jess's mind, her inner witch brewing suspicion in a big iron cauldron. The contents of the cauldron said Molly had been waiting for a rich enough husband who could give her an easy life, so she wouldn't have to trade up like Jess's own mother had.

"It's a medical thing. Endometriosis," Molly said. "For a while, I was hoping you and Griff could be…" She waved her hands as if erasing her words. "I'm sorry. That's not fair. You already have a mother. One who's beautiful and successful, from what I've heard."

Jess huffed out a sarcastic little laugh. "My mother left us like a litter of stray kittens once somebody richer than Dad came along. I rearranged my whole life to win her back, but I've finally figured out she doesn't care." She picked up her napkin and began cleaning a smudge off the table as if her life depended on it. It did, in a way. She just might die of shame if she had to look Molly in the eye.

"I'm sure she had her reasons," Molly said gently. "But I think she's made it hard for you to trust people with your heart."

Jess shrugged. She'd obliterated the smudge and moved on to folding her napkin into a perfect square.

Molly reached over and placed her hand on Jess's, stilling her. "It's okay," she said. "But think about it. What your mother did—I don't want to criticize her, but it changed you. Maybe you need to think about that, see if it helps you open up a little."

Jess finally met her stepmother's eyes. "You're not talking about opening up to you, are you?"

"No." Molly gave her a coy, looking-up-while-looking-down smile that reminded Jess of Princess Di. "I'm talking about Cade. He loves you, you know. I think he could make you happy."

"I know. Everybody thinks that. Sometimes I do, too." She wondered if Molly was right. Maybe her mother was the reason handing over her heart felt like jumping across the Grand Canyon without a net. "I live in Denver, though, and he can't leave here. So it's impossible."

"Aren't you getting a little ahead of yourself? The future has a way of forming on its own. Wait and see what happens." Molly took another bite of her cookie. "Love doesn't have to be a big, momentous decision. Just enjoy it for what it is."

Jess stared down at the table, her forehead creased. She felt like she'd been handed an impossible math problem, one so complicated she couldn't even begin to solve it.

"I'll try. But I do have to think about the future. I'm hoping for a promotion to a new location." She frowned.

She couldn't bring herself to tell Molly how far away that location was. In the light of her stepmother's smile, it seemed selfish to go so far away, just so she could live on a beach. Because truth be told, she was starting to think she shouldn't leave her father that far behind.

Shoot. How was she supposed to decide?

Molly was wrong. Jess couldn't let the future form on its own. She had duties. Obligations. But most importantly, she plain dang loved her dad.

Molly was still smiling, oblivious to the tempest raging in Jess's heart.

"That's great about the promotion, hon," she said. "Just remember, though, money's not everything. Sooner or later, you're going to want a family. Don't get so busy and ambitious you forget."

Jess remembered what Molly had told her about being unable to have children. Then she remembered Cade's mythical baby and the little Cades and Jesses that had danced through her mind at the thought.

"I don't mean to tell you how to live your life," Molly said. "I just want you to be happy."

Once again, Jess could feel the stepmother she'd constructed in her mind shriveling in the light of truth. The sultry siren who'd seduced her father and fixed her evil eye on a life of leisure had been replaced by a sweet and dedicated schoolteacher who loved him. Who seemed to love everyone, even her suspicious stepdaughter.

They stood, as if by some prearranged signal, and began gathering their cups and napkins. As they took turns pitching them into the trash can, Molly gave Jess an impish grin.

"You thought I was cheating on him, didn't you?"

"Shoot, you can never fool a teacher," Jess said. "You guys can read minds."

Molly chuckled. "I can't read minds, but I'm glad you're so protective of your dad. Lord knows, he needs protecting."

Jess couldn't help laughing.

"But I promise you I'm not the cheating kind," Molly said. "That man is the love of my life. I feel lucky beyond words to have him."

Jess pretended she had something in her eye. It seemed like she was always on the verge of tears these days. It was never like that at work, where she was always caught up in a whirlwind of accomplishment. She didn't have time for pesky distractions like feelings. Love.

Or happiness, come to think of it.

"We should probably get back to him." Molly glanced up at the ceiling as if she could see through the acoustic tile and all the floors between, clear up to Heck's hospital bed. "I'd hate for him to wake up and find us gone."

"I'll go home, I think," Jess said. "It's you he wants to see."

To her horror, a sob escaped. With it, all the emotions she'd been holding inside gushed out like water from a fire hydrant.

Molly turned with a little sob of her own. She opened her arms, and Jess walked into them, resting her head on Molly's poufy hair. This woman might not be her mom, but she sure *felt* like one. And God knew, Jess could use one.

"Your dad needs you, too, you know," Molly said. "He told me you did real well with those calves. Said he was proud of you." She pushed Jess away, holding onto her shoulders and looking into her eyes. "But that doesn't mean you have to change your life for us, okay? Don't even think about that. You're young. Your life should be about you, not about old folks, okay?"

Jess nodded, a lump forming in her throat. Molly really could read her mind. Because she'd just been thinking that her life might actually *need* to change. That she might be concentrating on all the wrong things. Material things and accomplishments, rather than family and home. And thoughts of family and home invariably conjured up Cade.

As she left the hospital, her heart felt buoyed—which was surprising, because shouldn't it be heavier? There was more in it, after all. Now that she understood who Molly was, she'd found herself a new person to love.

But the empty hole her mother had left behind ached a whole lot less, and she could feel a new kind of happiness hovering right above her as if angels held a magic wreath over her head and were just waiting for her to become a good enough person to wear it. It was a happiness that didn't have a thing to do with promotions, money, or success. It didn't depend on whether you lived by the ocean or in the mountains, in the city or the country.

It was the simple happiness of being loved and loving in return.

"I'm working on it," she said aloud. "I'm doing my best."

A stranger turned and stared, frowning, and she realized she ought to go home and get some sleep instead of talking to imaginary angels like a crazy lady.

Chapter 23

It was dark when Jess's alarm clock shocked her from sleep. Moaning, she slammed the clock with one hand, then glanced out the window at the silver light of dawn.

It was Saturday, and she was supposed to work with Cade. She'd been sulking because he wouldn't let her do things on her own, but after her experience the other day, working together felt like a good idea.

Especially since she'd decided to open her life, to think less about work and success and more about *life*. Cade was a big part of that, and she'd decided Molly was right. Love was love, and there was no harm in letting it live.

Besides, it wasn't like she had a choice. It was with her every day, growing bigger with every beat of her heart. She might as well take Molly's advice and follow her heart straight to Cade Walker—at least for a while. Like Molly said, she'd let the future form itself, as long as it formed around her family and the things that really mattered.

Dressing hastily, she glanced at the clock. Five thirty was probably way too early, but darned if she could remember what time Cade wanted to meet.

She couldn't remember *where* they were supposed to meet, either—at the Diamond Jack or at his place. But since she was up so early, maybe she could surprise him. If he was still in bed, she'd let him know her decision in the warmest way possible—under the covers.

She remembered the Christmas Eve she'd crossed the pasture and tapped at his window. That time, she'd been saying goodbye, but this would be a tentative hello. She didn't know where it would lead, but every time she thought of their sweet union in the hayloft, she knew their love deserved a chance.

Saddling Buster with care, she enjoyed the way the golden light from the barn reflected off his shining coat. Every jingle of his bridle, every stroke of the brush, every coo of the doves in the rafters, was amplified by the near dark.

She mounted and nudged him with her heels, watching the sun cast searching fingers of light over the landscape, blessing every blade of grass. The dawn chorus had begun, small birds tuning up in the willows before the blackbirds chimed in like raucous electric guitars crashing a bluegrass jamboree.

Buster's hooves swept the long grass, thudding on the dew-soft ground. When she reached Walker Ranch, Cade's truck was parked beside the house, and no lights burned. She dismounted, leaving Buster at the gate and creeping to the bedroom window to tap gently on the glass.

She waited, holding her breath, trying to avoid the thorns on a rosebush that had always bloomed outside Cade's window. The smell reminded her of times they'd spent in his room, of summer heat wafting the scent of the roses over their bodies. She tapped again.

Nothing. He must still be sleeping.

Biting her lower lip, she rapped harder, picturing him rubbing sleep-tousled hair and struggling to identify the sound, too drowsy to think.

The curtains shook as if he were clawing his way through them. Impishly, she put her face to the window, opening her eyes wide and sticking out her tongue.

That'll wake him up.

Again, the curtains moved, and then a hand groped at them before jerking them open.

Jess started, banging her head on the window—and then she screamed. The quiet serenity of dawn was torn apart as a second voice ripped through the little house, joining Jess in frantic two-part harmony. Panic screamed across the plains, startling the birds from their perches and silencing their songs.

Amber Lynn Lyle was a screamer. Cade had known that since day one of their relationship—or, more accurately, night one.

The screaming had been welcome at first. Believing it was a rave review of his skills, he'd outdone himself night after night. But once the thrill of the new relationship faded, he realized she screamed for effect.

So when she started screaming that morning, he ignored her as long as he could. It was probably a spider or a mouse, or maybe Boogy had finally managed one of his toxic gas attacks. Whatever it was, running to her rescue would only encourage her.

He clutched a pillow over his head and tried to go back to sleep.

"Cade! Cade! *Cade! Aaaaaieeeeeee!*"

He heard the scrape of a window opening, then more screaming.

"No! Wait! It's not what you think! *Cade!*"

Tossing the pillow to the floor, he strode to the bedroom, where she stood by the open window, her hands over her face.

"Oh God, Cade, it was *her*!" She clutched his arm. "There was a knock at the window, and I was half asleep, so I…"

A knock at the window?

The past washed over him with the words, sweeping away the warmth of his favorite Christmas Eve memory in a cold flood of dread. He parted the still-swaying curtains to see nothing but a dark trail through the dew.

Jess. Oh, Jess.

Racing through the house, he flung the door open just in time to see the love of his life thundering off like Secretariat exploding from the starting gate. He raced out into the field with the crazy notion of chasing her down.

"Jess, wait!" he called. "Let me explain. It's not…"

He stopped and stood there in the tall grass, watching her go. She couldn't hear him, and she wouldn't listen if she could. Maybe it was just as well, because he wasn't sure she'd care why Amber Lynn was in his bed.

He'd been given a rare second chance with the woman he loved, and he'd thrown it away. *Why?*

Because he was saving a victim of domestic violence? Was that *really* the reason? Or was he just avoiding a fight with Amber Lynn? The truth was, even after all she'd done to him, it had been easier to let her stay. And she knew it.

Cold rage swept through him at the sight of her sitting at his kitchen table.

"Cade, I'm so sorry. I'll go over there and tell her

why I'm here. Honestly." Her voice rose into the familiar whine that had cut through his life like a power saw, sending his sanity flying like sawdust from the blade. "She just scared me, okay? But I'll fix it. I will."

Grabbing her arm, he marched her to the bedroom and shoved her through the door.

"Pack," he said as she stumbled inside. "Your dad'll take you in."

"But Mona…"

"Mona's *your* problem, not mine." He felt his fingers curling into fists, his jaw jutting. "Get your life straightened out on your own. I've done what I can for you. Now do this for me." He grabbed her empty suitcase and hoisted it onto the bed. "You have to go."

"But…"

"Pack. I'm not going anywhere until you're out of here."

Sniffling as if she was the wounded party, Amber Lynn began cramming clothes in her suitcase. In five days, she'd managed to throw enough stuff around the room to dress a Broadway chorus line. If Jess had looked past her and seen the condition of the room, she'd think Amber Lynn had been there for a month.

A few days ago, he'd won back the love of his life. The future he'd always dreamed of had unfurled like a banner that had been rolled up in the dark. Happiness had blared like trumpets in his mind; the light had been brighter, colors deeper, sunlight warmer.

Now love was gone on a galloping horse, while he stayed behind, trying to tame a life that had lurched out of control. A man could usually ride out a bucking horse. Even if he got tossed, he could catch it and saddle up one more time.

But Cade had blown his reride, and he had a feeling his chance was gone for good.

———

Climbing the porch steps, Jess felt like she was climbing a mountain. She'd been so sure this morning would change her life.

And it had. Just not in the way she'd expected.

She remembered herself and Cade as they'd been when they were kids, as sure of each other as the sun in summer. She saw him smiling, working, laughing with her, loving her, season after season, year following year.

She'd started to think they could bring that love back to life, find the future she'd so carelessly discarded. She'd started to think she had a second chance with him.

She'd been wrong.

His marriage to Amber Lynn wasn't just a blip on the radar, a problem that had passed them by. It was a stain, like blood, that would never wash out.

The screen door slammed, and she turned to see Molly, cute and comfy in a plush robe, carrying two steaming mugs of coffee.

"Thanks."

She smiled at her stepmother as best she could, hoping Molly wouldn't notice how her lower lip trembled. She wasn't ready to talk about what had happened. Molly would probably make excuses for Cade. Maybe there was an excuse, but Jess knew she could never forgive this or forget. If her hopes had flown a little less high, if her heart had been a little less eager, she might have been able to withstand the shock. But the higher your emotions climbed, the further you had to fall—and the worse it hurt when you got dumped in the dirt.

Fortunately, Molly was oblivious to her mood. Unfortunately, her perkiness grated on Jess's frayed nerves.

"Every night, I forget how beautiful this place is, and every morning, I'm surprised all over again. It's so pretty."

Jess stifled a snort. *Pretty*.

Molly was sweet, but she had no concept of what this land meant or how it mattered. The view was stupendous, momentous, a gift from God. Sunrise bathed the pasture in peach and ivory, azure and gold. Every blade of grass stood tall and straight as a soldier while the pond beside the barn reflected the flawless blue of the sky like a mirror. Sorrow had a way of intensifying light and color, so the rich red of the barn, the deep green of the pines, and the vibrant yellow of the sunflowers tumbling over the fence burned into her brain like a brand.

She wished she hadn't come, hadn't fallen in love all over again with the land, with Cade, with the horses and the work and the thousand little details that hit her heart at every turn.

A sob rose in her chest, aching with a truth she thought she'd smothered before she'd even arrived. She'd been fantasizing about staying—about accepting Cade's love, moving back home, taking up the life she'd left behind. She loved her job, but she'd loved him more, and she'd realized Hawaii would never be home, any more than Denver had been. This was where she belonged, and that mattered more than the deepest ocean or the most pristine beach.

But all those dreams had to end now. Staring out at the mountains, she knew she had to leave as soon as she could. She'd bury herself in work while she was here—clean up the house, put it on the market, get the place sold, settle her dad and stepmom into a new home. There was no longer a chance she and Cade could save the Diamond Jack. It was as good as gone.

Then she'd go back to the life she'd chosen and fight for that promotion. If she couldn't score Hawaii, maybe she could transfer to Chicago. Or New York. Maybe San Francisco.

Somewhere far, far away, so she'd never see Cade Walker again. Because her love hadn't died at the sight of Amber Lynn; it had dug deeper inside her, changing from a blessing to a wound. New and raw, it had to be cleaned, closed, and healed, or it would scar her forever.

Chapter 24

JESS NORMALLY TOOK HER COFFEE BLACK, BUT MOLLY, OF course, had added milk and sugar. Like the woman herself, it was a little too sweet, and Jess shuddered at the cloying taste and slimy texture before discreetly pouring it over the railing. Sweetness felt like blasphemy when she was so damn sad.

She turned to see Molly standing in the doorway, head cocked, eyes questioning.

"What happened?" She scanned Jess from her muddy boots to her flyaway hair. "Where have you been? Did something happen with Cade?"

"No." Jess looked away. "Nothing new."

Nothing that hasn't happened before. Cade slept with Amber Lynn. Big deal. I should have expected it.

"Come on, now," Molly said. "We worked this out. You can trust me, hon."

"I can't trust anyone."

The moment the words left her lips, Jess knew she'd said too much.

"You can trust Cade, hon. He's a good man. Whatever happened, surely you can talk about it."

"I don't care about Cade." Jess clenched her fists at her sides and struggled to bring her emotions under control. Breathing deep, she spoke more softly as the grass and hills before her blurred like a watercolor painting. "But you're right, Molly, something's bothering me."

She sighed. "You and Dad are right. You need to sell this place and move somewhere safer." *Somewhere I'll be safe from falling for that cheatin' cowboy all over again, like some loser in a bad country song.* "That's what I came for, and I haven't done a thing to help."

"Jess, no." Molly laid her hand on Jess's arm. "That's not what I really want. And your dad…"

"Don't tell me no." Jess barely resisted the urge to shake her off. "Dad's not well. He can't keep the place going."

"But you came back to save it," Molly said. "I know you did. You want to keep it in the family, and, Jess, that's all we needed to know." She hesitated. "And we thought Cade—"

"I thought a lot of things about Cade, too, but they were wrong. I'm sorry, Molly. I know you love him." Jess looked up at the sky, wishing God would send her a solution or strike her dead. Either would be equally welcome. "I loved him, too."

"You still do," Molly said.

"I can't. Not anymore." Jess did her best to force out a little laugh. "I was trying to recapture my childhood, I guess. Haven't you ever fallen for an old flame?" She swiped at her eyes, wishing she didn't cry when she got mad. Because that's all it was—she was *mad*. "People change, and you have to move on. This is about Dad now, about what *he* needs."

"What he needs is you."

Jess pointed a finger at Molly. "Don't do that to me. You're the one who came up with the solution, and it's going to work. We'll find an over-fifty community where he can have horses. It'll be perfect." She sighed. "But perfect costs money. We have to sell this place first."

"But you…"

"It's not about me." She gave her stepmother the best smile she could. "Besides, I'm no cowgirl. Not anymore."

She stepped back and spread her arms, as if her to show off what a city chick she was. But looking down, she remembered she was wearing an old western shirt with the pocket torn off over a pair of Wranglers smudged with dirt and worse. She realized how tan she'd become, how much muscle she'd put on in the short time she'd been home. She looked about as cowgirl as a woman could.

"Oh, never mind." She couldn't help laughing at herself, miserable as she was. "I'm trying to face facts. This place is dangerous for Dad, so let's put it on the market. I'll find an agent, and you guys can start looking at those retirement places." She paused, struggling to control the storm of rage inside her. "It's not like I'm going to stick around. Not after finding Amber Lynn in Cade's bed this morning."

Molly gasped, one hand fluttering to her throat. "No."

"Yes." Jess wiped her eyes. Okay, it wasn't anger. It was sorrow, pure and permanent.

Her stepmother was regarding her with open-mouthed horror.

"Don't worry." Jess tried to sound casual. "I'll be fine. I have to be. I'm on my own, and I've got things to do, and…" Slamming her cup down on the railing, she clapped a hand over her mouth and raced upstairs.

—∿∿—

"Honey, we've got trouble."

Heck turned in his hospital bed, shocked at the tone of Molly's voice. His wife was always cheerful. She fought cheerfully, complained cheerfully, even lectured him on his shortcomings cheerfully. But today, she was slumped into the chair beside his bed, nursing an air of defeat.

"What kind of trouble?" he asked.

"Jess is calling real estate agents right now. Something happened with Cade. She says she's ready to help us sell the place."

"No."

Heck plucked at the sheet that covered his chest, wishing he could tear it apart, wishing he could leap from his bed like some heart-attack Superman. He hated being helpless. He hated being sick. He really hated being stuck in the hospital, where he couldn't control what was going on at home.

He'd thought about breaking out but wasn't sure he could walk down the hall, let alone make it home. He was so miserable, he was actually looking forward to his surgery.

He couldn't understand it. All his life, he'd thought nothing of vaulting into the saddle of his favorite horse and riding for miles. Hell, he'd won the bulldogging at Cheyenne Frontier Days back in 1989. That had required not only vaulting onto a horse but diving onto the horns of a racing steer, braking with the heels of his boots, and wrestling the animal to the ground—all in ten seconds or less.

So how was it possible that he could barely stand? The way he felt this morning, he had no business ranching at all. Deep down, he was worried he'd taken his last ride.

He ran a hand over his face as if he could wipe away the wrinkles of old age. "I really thought gettin' her home would work. Thought Cade would set things right between 'em, and they'd be hitched by June."

"I thought so, too."

"What the ding-dang muck bucket happened?" His voice rose to a querulous old-man whine; he hated the sound of it, but he couldn't help it. "Last I heard, those two were all lovey-dovey in the barn."

She stared down at the floor, shaking her head. "I told you, Amber Lynn's car was over there."

"There's no way that boy would be fool enough to take that little bitch back. Damn near ruined his life, and he knows it."

"So you'd think. But I saw the car, and well…"

Her voice trailed off, and he knew she was hiding something from him. Could Cade really have been fool enough to fall for Amber Lynn again? If he had, no wonder Molly was hiding it. He'd be obligated to go over there and punch the boy's lights out, and he didn't feel up to that right now.

He sighed. He'd been sure his daughter would lasso Cade, drag him to the altar, and set up housekeeping for the two of them, either at the Diamond Jack or at Cade's place. They'd run the ranch, and Heck could give 'em advice. He had lots of advice.

That was about all he had.

"Maybe it's inevitable," Molly said. "Ranching—I don't know. I always feel like we live in the past. I'm not sure it's a viable way of life anymore."

"Why the hell not? It's *my* way of life and always has been."

Molly started to speak, probably to apologize, but he bulldozed right over her.

"*My* way of life, and Jess's, too. She's my daughter. It's up to me to make her happy. And instead, we came up with this crazy plot, messed with her life, and broke her heart all over again." He jabbed a finger at Molly's face, making her flinch. "I never had secrets from her until you came along."

"Oh, for heaven's sake." She stood and shot the glare right back. "Now *I'm* the problem?"

Nervously, he clutched the sheet, wondering if he'd gone too far.

"I was doing my best to help," Molly said. "But since you think I'm the problem, I guess I'd better get going and fix this, too."

Turning, she stalked out of the room.

"It was all your idea," he called after her. "I never should've agreed to it."

He thought maybe she'd come back, if only to defend herself, but he'd apparently pissed her off good this time.

"That's just fine," he muttered. "Don't go messing with my life again. It's mine. My mess."

He loved Molly, but she'd screwed up his life with this crazy scheme when he'd planned to simply *tell* Jess to come home, *tell* her to give Cade and the ranch another chance. The boy would make her happy, and she belonged on the Bailey land.

He remembered how Molly had laughed when he'd told her that.

"You can't tell a woman who to love," she'd said. "Or tell that daughter of yours what to do."

She'd been right about the last part, he supposed, but her idea hadn't worked any better. Now they'd have to sell the ranch, the only home he'd ever had, and Jess would walk away mad. Especially if she found out how he and Molly had manipulated her.

A thundercloud of misery, full to bursting, floated over his mind and cast his whole life into shadow. Catching a sob in his throat, he glanced over at the chair out of habit to make sure Molly hadn't heard.

But she wasn't there. She'd stormed off mad, and he wasn't sure when she'd come back. Or *if*.

She'd been gone more and more lately. Sure, he slept a lot, but he felt bereft whenever he woke up to that empty chair.

Maybe he was losing Molly, too.

Chapter 25

MOLLY SPUN THE CAMRY INTO CADE'S DRIVEWAY LIKE Dale Earnhardt zipping across the finish line. Gravel spattered against the shed's worn siding as she slid to a stop.

It felt good to make a racket, to express herself, to take control. Anger was a rare emotion for her, but Heck had fired it up, and she was ready to give Cade a piece of her mind.

And if Amber Lynn was around, she'd *kill* her.

Emerging from the car, she glared at the familiar black Cadillac. It was right in front of the house, gleaming shamelessly in the morning light like some predatory sea creature—a glossy manta ray, or a man-eating shark. There was a figure slumped in the driver's seat, and the flame of Molly's anger rose.

Little bitch. Spoiled brat.

Molly would never let herself say such things aloud, but a million curse words hammered at her brain. She wanted to spit them out like the car spat gravel, flinging them against the Cadillac's shiny paint job, against Amber Lynn's smug little face.

Squinting through the Caddy's tinted windows, she noticed Amber Lynn's hair looked lank and dirty. Her shoulders were shaking. Was she crying?

Good.

Molly hoped she was crying about Cade. Hoped he'd finally stood up to her.

She headed for the house. Amber Lynn rolled down her window as she passed, but Molly walked right past her, up the stairs to the front door, and hammered on it with her fist.

This being mad thing was kind of fun. She'd always thought she was a forgiving person with no anger in her heart, but it turned out she'd just been saving it up.

"Cade? I need to talk to you. *Now*." Flinging the door open, she almost hit him in the face. "What the hell's going on?"

He looked shocked. He'd probably never heard her swear before.

"Why is Amber Lynn here?" she continued. "And why is my daughter crying her eyes out at home when *she* should be the one who's with you?"

"She—I…" He lifted his hat and scratched the back of his head, then looked out at Amber Lynn's car and frowned. "It's really not a good time to talk. I promised Jess I'd help her with those calves today. I need to load up my horse and—"

"Cade, Jess is crying in her bed. I don't think she's thinking about calves."

He tugged his hat back down. "Then I'll do it myself. Need to get going before it starts getting hot."

Molly shoved her foot in the door. "You're not going anywhere until you tell me what's going on."

He stared at her a moment. The boy looked exhausted, and she felt a little bad for him. But she wasn't done being mad, so she just gave him a look. The kind of look teachers reserved for problem students.

Sighing, he held the door open. "Come in, then."

Molly glanced back at Amber Lynn, then gave Cade a Dirty Harry squint. "*She's* not coming in, is she?"

"Nope. She's leaving."

"Good."

Molly stepped into Cade's little house, and her heart broke all over again. She could picture Jess prettying it up, cooking with Cade. They wouldn't be the kind of couple where the wife did all the housework while the husband worked outside. Jess's life here would center on all the things she loved. Wyoming. Horses. Cade Walker. And someday, babies.

She doesn't know it, but that's her world.

"What's going on?" She sat down at the table and looked into Cade's honest gray eyes. He met her gaze without flinching, which meant he probably wasn't actually sleeping with Amber Lynn. "Why is your ex-wife here?"

"She was here when I got home one day, and she wouldn't leave."

Outside, Amber Lynn was gunning the Cadillac's engine. She was probably upset nobody was paying attention to her.

"Some guy hit her, Molly." Cade grimaced. "I couldn't send her back to him."

"Why couldn't she go to her dad?"

"She figured that was the first place the guy would look."

"Why wouldn't he find her here?"

"He might. But I was here if that happened." He looked down at his feet, as if fascinated by the stitching on his boots. "She'd been abused. *Hit*, Molly. I couldn't turn her away."

Molly sighed. "I can understand that. But Jess won't."

"I know." He dropped into a chair and held his head in his hands. "She came over here and tapped on my bedroom window this morning. It's something we used to do, back when—you know. But I let Amber Lynn use the bedroom. She opened the window instead of me."

"Oh, Cade," Molly whispered. "*No.*"

"I tried to help an abused woman, that's all. I need to make Jess understand that." Reaching across the table, he palmed a pig-shaped pepper shaker with a smiling face that mocked the hopelessness in his eyes. "I know I should have kicked her out, but there was that black eye, and her hair—she hadn't been taking care of herself, and that's so unlike her." He stroked one finger along the pig's snout. "It didn't matter who she was. I couldn't turn a battered woman away." He looked up and met Molly's eyes. "You know my dad hit my mom."

Molly nodded. She hadn't known for sure, but she'd suspected.

"Mom stayed because she didn't have anywhere to go." Setting down the pepper shaker, he sighed. "I couldn't turn any woman away. Not even Amber Lynn."

Molly, her anger fading, patted his shoulder. "Jess is mad, but she knows you. She'll come around."

"Would you?"

"Would I what?"

"Come around, if you came home and found Dot in Heck's bed."

"No, I guess I might not. But you have to try."

"I will. I told Amber Lynn to go to the bank, ask her

dad for a job. Then she'd be able to take care of herself, without depending on a man."

Molly sighed. "Those poor tellers."

"I know, but she needs something to do besides chase after men. And I think she'd be good at it."

There was a soft tap at the door, and Amber Lynn poked her head inside. Her eyes were swollen from crying, her hair a nest of tangles.

"Cade? Can I just clean up here? I can't go see Daddy looking like this."

Cade threw Molly a hopeless glance.

"No." Molly scowled. "You can't."

The waterworks were on full force now, and Molly saw how the girl had gotten to Cade. She didn't sob or gulp, and her face didn't turn red. She just stood there in the doorway with tears streaming artfully down her face, looking like a sad and very beautiful Madonna.

"I d-don't have anywhere to g-go. My dad married a woman who hates me, so I can't go home, so if I can't stay here, I'm *h-h-homeless*."

"I can fix that." Molly rose from the table and took Amber Lynn's arm. "I have the perfect place for you. Cade, you go take care of those calves. Amber Lynn and I will go find her a place to live."

The girl jerked her arm away as if Molly was threatening to haul her off to hell.

"I can't go with you. Jess *hates* me."

"You bet she does." Molly took her arm again, and this time, there was no shaking her off. "And you'd better not go *near* her. Come with me."

Ignoring Cade's confusion, she marched Amber Lynn back to the Cadillac and opened the driver's side door.

Obediently, Amber Lynn slipped behind the wheel. Slamming the door on her, Molly went to the passenger side and climbed in.

"I won't stay in some shack," Amber Lynn said.

"It's no shack, but you'll need to keep an open mind."

They watched Cade come out and pull his truck and trailer up to the barn. Once he went inside, Amber Lynn sniffed, wiped her nose, and backed out of the driveway.

She followed Molly's directions, turning toward town. They passed the WELCOME TO WYNOTT sign and the mini-mart before Molly told her to turn again.

"Oh no." Amber Lynn stopped the car in the middle of the road. "Not here."

There was a brief contest between Molly's substitute-teacher glare and Amber Lynn's best pout. Molly won.

"It's a trailer park," Amber Lynn said. "I've never even *visited* here."

"It was my home most of my life," Molly said, "so watch what you say."

Frowning, Amber Lynn followed the ribbon of black-top that curved through the single-wides, braking for the speed bumps that foiled the muscle cars and four-wheelers parked at half the homes.

The last corner lot held an older trailer, painted glossy white with pretty blue shutters. A blue-and-yellow plywood butterfly gave the siding a cheerful air, and the garden was bursting with salvia, lavender, and pink begonias.

Amber Lynn pulled into the driveway and parked the car, then folded her arms over her chest and set her jaw.

"If I live here, Mona wins," she said. "Everyone will laugh at me."

"They won't laugh, and Mona will lose, because she still won't have a damn thing of her own. *You'll* be the one with the job and the bank account. This wouldn't be some man's house. Your job would pay the rent, and it would be all yours. You won't have to do some man's bidding like she does."

Amber Lynn tilted her chin up. "You have to do Heck's bidding."

"No, I don't. I had my own life and my own home, so I held out for a man who does *mine*." She gave Amber Lynn a considering look. "I suppose you have one other choice."

"Like what? A little apartment or a condo?"

"Not exactly." Molly did her best to keep a straight face. "I was thinking about that little park behind the bank. There's a bench you could sleep on, and you could keep your stuff in a shopping cart from the Safeway. Wynott's never had a homeless bag lady before, but there's a first time for everything, right?"

Amber Lynn scowled. "I guess I could look at this place." Exiting the car, she tilted her nose up in the air. "It'll be good for me to see how the other half lives."

"Honey, right now, you *are* the other half. You can either accept that or earn your way out."

Chapter 26

AFTER FINDING AMBER LYNN IN CADE'S BED, JESS WAS tempted to spend the day barricaded in her room, eating cookies and watching bad daytime TV while she cried her eyes out, but the thought of the suffering calves forced her to cut her one-woman pity party short. She and Cade had planned to drench the rest of them today, but Cade was obviously busy. She might be hurt by that, but her problems didn't outweigh their furry little lives.

After splashing cold water on her face and finger combing her hair, she headed out to the barn and saddled Buster. She considered putting him in a trailer and hauling him partway, but riding would give her time to cool down and stop crying.

As they topped the rise that bordered the north pasture, she spotted a rider already at work. He had a calf down and was working over it while his horse held the rope taut.

Jess longed to kick Buster into a pounding lope and bear down on the interloper, but again, the calves' needs trumped her own. So she walked her horse down the hill and waited a short distance away until Cade—because of course it was Cade—had finished and released the calf.

He looked up at her and grinned as if nothing had happened. "One down."

She looked down at him, glad she was high in the saddle while he was on foot and glad the brief waiting period had given her rage time to simmer down to a low boil.

She didn't need to get emotional about this. Cade had killed what they'd had together. It was over, and she needed to be practical now.

"What are you doing here?"

"What I told you I'd do. Getting the rest of the calves taken care of."

He sounded so *normal*. As if she hadn't found his ex-wife in his bed this very morning. As if he hadn't led her on, acting like she was so dang precious, while all the time, he was hiding Amber Lynn at home. She didn't even know what to say, so she just looked at him, her stomach burning, her heart pounding while she searched for words that fit the situation.

There weren't any.

She nudged Buster into taking a step forward. "You need to go home."

He sighed like she was being unreasonable. "Look, Jess, I'm sorry I didn't tell you Amber Lynn was staying at the house. Nothing happened between us, but I should have told you she was there."

"*Told* me? So you're not sorry she was there? It wouldn't have made any difference if you told me or not. Facts are facts."

"Then let me tell you what the facts are, okay?" His tone was so mild and reasonable, she wanted to scream. "She needed help. That's all. Nothing was going on."

"Then why'd you keep it a secret?" The tears were gone. Jess's rage had turned to a cold, hard layer of anger that froze her feelings and let her face Cade's lying eyes without blinking.

"Look, I apologized for the secret." Cade stood with his feet apart, arms crossed over his chest. His brows arrowed down, and Jess realized *he* was getting mad. "But all I was doing was helping someone who needed a place to stay. I couldn't tell you because—well, because I knew you'd act like this."

"How am I acting? Mad? Upset? Betrayed? Because that's how I feel."

"Okay. I can understand that." All the fight drained out of him, and he stared down at the saddle horn, avoiding her gaze. "Look, I'll take care of the calves, okay? There aren't many left, and it won't take long."

She started to protest.

"Let me do it for Heck."

"All right."

She turned Buster toward home, wondering where her tears had gone. She felt so cold, so dead inside. Maybe she should go home and put her original plan into practice.

She should call the real estate agent, but the bedroom, the cookies, and the daytime TV were calling her name. If she could immerse herself in the unlikely plot of some soap opera, maybe she wouldn't have to think about Cade Walker, the ranch, or her future at all.

The coldness that coated Jess's heart only hardened on the long ride home, but that wasn't such a bad thing. She realized she needed to get down to business, not waste her time feeling sorry for herself, so once she'd taken care of Buster, she fired up her laptop and dove into Google. She'd heard about a farm and ranch specialist in Grigsby who'd sold a neighbor's place for major money.

Val Hadley. That was the one.

She picked up the phone and dialed.

"The Bailey place?" The agent sounded thrilled. "That's the Diamond Jack, right? You're selling?"

"Yes." Jess's throat swelled nearly shut as feelings welled up inside again. She needed to have fewer feelings, or smaller ones, or something. These big ones were practically making her sick.

"Well, thanks," the agent said. "I'll be right there."

"What, *now*?"

"You want to get it on the market, right? Let's get this party started."

It sure didn't feel like a party to Jess, but maybe she should get this over with.

"See you in forty minutes," the agent said.

Hanging up the phone, Jess felt her self-esteem tick up a notch. She was doing the right thing in spite of her own needs. Sure, she was gritting her teeth so hard her ears rang. But she was doing her very best to be selfless and look after her dad.

She hoped he'd notice, and Molly. Cade, too. She hoped he'd choke on it—him and his floozy of a wife. Or ex-wife. Or, if you believed him, his roommate.

She huffed out a little laugh. No woman she'd ever known would trust a man who let his ex stay overnight.

Yeah, but it's Cade. He's different.

Nope. Men are men. Don't be an idiot.

Jess looked around the kitchen, seeing the house through a stranger's eyes. Bills from the feed store, the electric cooperative, and the farrier were stacked on the counter. Livestock magazines bearing pictures of Hereford cows were stacked on the table, and her dad had left notes, scribbled on various bits of paper, on every horizontal surface.

She'd come home to clean up the place, and instead, she'd been gallivanting with the boy next door—while he'd been gallivanting with someone else. So that had been a waste of time, and she had work to do.

She was mopping the front hall when a black Mercedes SUV pulled up next to the barn. The door opened, and a small, slim foot clad in a stiletto heel prodded the earth as if it possessed a blind intelligence of its own. It was followed by an almost child-sized woman who unfolded her angular limbs from the car like a praying mantis emerging from a shiny black egg.

When Val Hadley stood to her full height, she couldn't have been more than five feet tall. Her skin was the not-quite-real tan so popular in cities, her figure fit and trim. Honey-blond hair framed her face in two perfect curves like matching scythes, and she wore dramatic cat's-eye makeup. Glossy lipstick completed the look, emphasizing a sexy pout. She looked more like a movie star than a farm and ranch specialist.

Suddenly, Jess was painfully aware of the rusted hubcaps and broken wagon wheels that leaned against collapsing outbuildings, the broken-down machinery that crouched by the corral, and the generally unkempt air of the place. Since grass struggled to grow in the dry Wyoming summer, the lawn wasn't mowed more than twice a year, but it was late in the season, and the place looked weedy and neglected.

She'd change all that, make the place shine so they

could get a good price for Heck and Molly so she could go back to Denver, get back to work.

She closed her eyes a moment and thought of ocean waves crashing on a white sand beach. Hawaii was still the best-case scenario for her future. She needed to get everything settled fast and get back to work before her boss forgot who she was.

Shoving one of her dad's little notebooks in her pocket, she strode out to greet her guest.

"Val Hadley." The agent thrust out a manicured hand. "Sorry I'm late, but I got mixed up and stopped at the place next door. Caught some cowboy changing clothes, and I have to admit I enjoyed it." Her grin was so frankly lascivious that Jess almost liked her. "Who *is* that guy?"

"Cade Walker." Jess shook the proffered hand. "Our neighbor."

"He said he was a friend of the family." Val's high voice and shotgun delivery made it sound like she'd inhaled a helium balloon.

"He is, I guess. He and my dad are pretty close."

"If I were you, I'd get close to him, too."

"I was." Jess shoved her hands in her pockets and stared at the ground. "Once."

"Okay." Val cleared her throat. "Let's get to work. Buyers for this sort of property are looking for a certain look. Rustic, but not dirty." She glanced around, and a little line formed between her eyebrows. "It doesn't have to be perfect. It just has to *feel* that way. And it needs to be on trend. For starters, that sign?" She pointed to the Diamond Jack sign at the foot of the drive. "That's got to go."

Jess scowled. Her brother had been a kid when he'd

painted that sign. Sure, it looked a little amateurish, and the plywood layers were peeling. You could barely read it, but it *belonged* there.

Sighing, she whipped out her notebook and wrote "sign." She'd list what Val wanted and make her own decisions later.

"And those sconces by the door," Val said. "That shiny brass is out. Folks like the rubbed bronze look these days." She gave Jess a slit-eyed smile. "You don't have to buy new. Just spray-paint them."

"Isn't that dishonest?"

"This is business, honey, not Girl Scouts. Besides, you won't feel bad once you see the kind of folks who buy these places." She wrinkled her nose like something smelled bad. "Most rich folks are about as phony as spray paint themselves."

Looking at the woman's obvious spray tan, Jess wondered if she'd called the right agent.

"We were hoping to sell to a real rancher."

"Yeah, right. I got to tell you, that's not likely, and I know what I'm talking about." She canted one hip and set her fists on her hips, allowing an unmistakable air of cowgirl sass to shine through the perfect hair and sophisticated makeup. "My father was the fourth generation to ranch our place in Nebraska. I know my business, but I know ranching better, and buying a place like this isn't in most folk's budgets."

Jess nodded, swallowing. This wasn't going to be easy.

"Now, this house." Val considered the place a moment. "It's sure…interesting."

Jess sighed. The crazy, cobbled-together look of the place wouldn't appeal to everyone, and when she remembered all the repairs her dad hadn't done, she wondered if they'd ever manage to sell it.

"Hey, some buyers like character." Val tapped one high-heeled foot and frowned. "Let's start in the barn."

As they walked, Jess asked, "You don't have buyers who'd want to work the ranch?"

"Oh, they'll *say* they want to work it. And maybe they do, at the start. But they overestimate their abilities. Since they're rich, they think they're good at everything, so they don't ask for help until they've gotten themselves in trouble. Then they pay somebody to haul 'em out of the hole they dug." She sighed. "Clients looking for ranch property these days only wear cowboy boots for show. They want to *play* cowboy, not be one."

As they entered the barn, Jess glanced back at the house where she'd grown up, the land she'd loved all her life. The red dirt driveway wound into the distance, reminding her she had to leave, drive off into an unknown future. At its foot, the dyspeptic jack of diamonds her brother had painted on the ranch sign stared unseeing toward the horizon, his worn brow furrowed, his painted hands clenched as if he knew his days were numbered.

Chapter 27

UNLOCKING THE FRONT DOOR OF HER TRAILER, MOLLY turned to Amber Lynn.

"This was my home for most of my life, and I loved it. You know why?"

Amber Lynn shook her head.

"Because it was *mine*," Molly said. "Nobody could tell me what to do or how to live my life."

"I guess." Amber Lynn sounded doubtful. "It's just that I'm used to my dad telling me…" She didn't have to finish the sentence. The poor thing was so used to having men run her life that she couldn't make her own decisions.

The interior of the trailer was dark, but Molly moved quickly to open curtains. Amber Lynn stood poised on the doormat as if ready to run, but as daylight revealed more and more of the room, she slowly relaxed. The overstuffed sofa had chintz upholstery, the china cabinet was full of pretty dishes, and the tidy kitchen had faux marble counters. A silk flower arrangement stood on a neat round table in front of the bay window.

Amber Lynn turned in a slow circle.

"This is nice." She sounded dazed. "I didn't know a trailer could be like this."

Molly led her through the living room, flicking a button on the stereo and filling the place with the mellow voice of Frank Sinatra. Opening the bedroom door, she revealed a queen-sized bed covered with a frothy, lace-edged duvet. Pillows lay in flowery abundance against the headboard.

"Wow." Amber Lynn's eyes were wide. "This is so much nicer than Cade's place."

She inspected a graceful antique dresser, then wandered into the hall and flicked on the light in the bathroom, revealing the oval tub Molly had blown a month's salary on. Bottles of fancy bubble bath lined the edge, along with an assortment of scented candles.

"This looks like heaven."

"It is, after a long day's work." Molly smiled. "You want to know a secret?"

Amber Lynn turned quickly, her eyes bright, and licked her lips like a greedy child who'd just been offered ice cream. Secrets were currency to people like Amber Lynn. Molly needed to be careful, but a little truth telling might help the girl change her life.

"Sometimes I miss it," she said. "I love my husband and my new life, but it's nice to have a place that's all your own."

"I've never lived by myself." Amber Lynn spoke slowly, her eyes drinking in the little luxuries all around her. "I moved straight from Daddy's house to Cade's, and then—well, then I had another, um, friend I lived with." She looked down, suddenly shy. "That was a mistake."

"That's the good thing about living alone." Molly led her back to the living room, where they sat on the sofa. "You don't make those mistakes. You don't have to, because you can take care of yourself."

"But you're married now. Why do you still have this?"

"I can't bring myself to sell it," Molly said. "I'm so used to having my own home, and it's not easy, trusting a man. But it's time for me to move on and rent it out."

Amber Lynn walked into the kitchen and stood at the sink, where a window looked out on the plains that stretched from the back of the park to the distant highway and on to faraway mountains. A bird feeder, empty now, hung on a pole, and a cunning little park bench sat under a cluster of aspen trees.

"It's not really *in* the trailer park, is it? It's right on the edge." Amber Lynn turned. "Could *I* rent it, Molly? I'm going to get a job at Daddy's bank. It was Cade's idea. I could stay with him until I get my first paycheck—I think it would be about two weeks, right? He probably won't mind." She smiled a catlike, scheming smile. "Well, he will, but I can talk him into it."

"If you want to stay here, there are rules, and number one is that you can't stay with Cade," Molly said. "But I could give you the first two weeks rent free. How's that?"

Amber's eyes widened. "Really?"

"Go get your stuff," Molly said. "I'll help you get settled and show you how everything works."

"Why are you doing this?" Amber Lynn scanned Molly's face. "I know you don't like me."

"I don't have anything against *you*," Molly said. "I just don't like the things you *do*—using nice men like Cade. But it sounds like you're ready to change all that."

"I think I am." Amber Lynn looked down, biting her lower lip. "Cade's done so much for me. Nobody ever thinks I can do anything, but he's so sure I can handle this job, even be a boss. I don't know how I'll ever pay him back for believing in me."

"I do." Molly smiled. "You can move in here, take that job, do your best, and prove he's right." She smiled. "There's just one thing you need to do for me."

Amber Lynn looked panicked. "Do I have to mow the yard?"

"No."

"Good. Because I've seen Daddy's lawn boy do that, and it looks really hard."

"This'll be harder, but if you want to live here and build a life and a career of your own, you're going to have to put the past behind you, along with all the trouble you've caused." She lifted a hand, palm out, to stop Amber Lynn's protests. "Oh, I know you didn't mean to ruin Cade's chance with Jess. But you need to fix that."

"You know I didn't mean to?"

Molly nodded.

"Most people would think I did that on purpose, especially since—well, I have to admit I'm jealous of Jess. But going back to Cade's place made me realize he's not what I want. I care about him, though. I want him to be happy."

"You take a couple days to get started at the bank. I'll see to it Jess comes in some day, and you can explain why she should forgive that man. You know he loves her, right? So tell her. Tell her everything."

Amber Lynn frowned. "I don't know what to say."

Molly set her fists on her hips. "Figure it out, then. I don't think you'll be a success at the bank or anywhere until you take care of it. This is a small town, hon, and everybody respects and admires Cade Walker."

"I know." Amber Lynn sounded irritated. "That's why I wanted him in the first place. But I'm done with him now, I swear. I'm going to concentrate on myself, like you said." Her tone turned wistful. "And live here."

"So if Jess happens to come to the bank…"

Amber Lynn sighed. "I'll tell her I wasn't sleeping with Cade. That he helped me and encouraged me and wouldn't even look at me when I tried to flirt with him. All he thinks about is her. It's always been that way."

"Good," Molly said. "You tell her that."

Amber Lynn swallowed, hard. "And then people will like me, right? Because if nobody comes to my line at the bank, I'll just *die*."

Molly resisted the urge to roll her eyes. "It'll be fine. Now where's your suitcase? Let's get you settled in."

"Oh. I, um, left it at Cade's." She hung her head. "I know what you're thinking, and you're right. I left it there so I could go back. But I don't *want* to go back now, I swear. I'll just go pick it up, and then I'll come right here."

"I've got a better idea." Molly took out her cell phone and jabbed a few buttons. "Cade?" she said. "I'm at my old place with Amber Lynn. That's right, at Springtime Acres. We need her suitcase here. She's ready to move in." She gave Amber Lynn a quick smile. "That's okay. We'll wait."

Molly spent almost an hour showing Amber Lynn how to maintain the trailer before Cade arrived to wrestle an enormous pink suitcase up the concrete steps. Amber Lynn raced to the door to meet him. Molly thought the girl would grab her own suitcase in the spirit of her new independence, but instead, she grabbed Cade before he could even get through the door.

"Cade, I'm so excited. Have you seen this place?"

She gave his cheek a lip-smacking kiss before he could move away. "It's going to be mine, and it's all because of you."

"Okay." Shaking her off, he maneuvered the suitcase into the front door while Molly shot Amber Lynn a quelling glare. Looking past the girl, she spotted a red car stopped at the intersection just beyond the trailer. Was that…?

"Sorry," Amber Lynn said. "I forgot I'm not supposed to do that."

Molly watched as the car burned rubber, taking the turn out of the trailer park at top speed. There was no mistaking that little red sports car and no doubt who was driving it.

Jess.

Molly loved helping people, and she was good at it. She'd gotten Jess to come home. She'd gotten her together with Cade, at least for a while, and now she'd maneuvered Amber Lynn out of his house.

But life was full of complications, and it seemed like everything she did just made things worse.

Chapter 28

THE WAITING ROOM FOR FAMILIES OF SURGERY PATIENTS was right next to a set of double doors. Doctors punched through them, moving with the urgency of spawning salmon, and the doors flapped out a rapid beat that slowed, then stopped. Jess hoped that wasn't a metaphor for what was going on with her father's heart.

She was exhausted. She'd spent the weekend's daylight hours cleaning up the yard and the nights cleaning house and making repairs. Then she'd had too much coffee this morning, so every time a doctor or nurse passed, she had to restrain herself from leaping to her feet and attacking them.

How's my dad? Is he okay? Let him be okay. Make *him okay, okay?*

But the doctors rushed past, leaving her perched on the edge of a vinyl chair like a nervous bird. Finally, she curled up and pretended to read an issue of *Cosmo* so ancient, it had an article on flirting with your boss.

Across the room, Molly sat primly, ankles crossed, hands neatly folded in her lap. She seemed to be looking out the window, but Jess doubted she even noticed the leafy sycamores shading the parking lot.

Just a few days ago, Jess would have been sitting beside Molly, clinging to her hand, taking comfort in her loving presence. But while she still believed in her stepmother's love for her dad, she wasn't sure she could trust Molly with her heart after all. The image of Amber Lynn and Cade embracing on the steps of her step-mother's old trailer was burned into her mind.

Oddly, she wasn't mad. Just sad. Molly had a heart made of mush. She'd help anyone, even Amber Lynn—but that didn't make it less of a betrayal. There was only one person Jess could trust, and that person was on a cold table beyond those double doors with his chest sliced open.

The doors thumped as a masked doctor hurried through, whipping off a pair of half-glasses like a Hollywood actor in a cheap hospital drama. Jess knew from Molly's quick intake of breath this was Heck's doctor.

"Is he all right?" Molly stood and smoothed her hair. "Can we see him?"

The doctor nodded sharply. "He's just coming out of the anesthesia. Might be a little confused."

Molly and Jess followed him through the swinging doors and down a hall lined with closed doors. Finally, the doctor turned and opened one, and there he was, Heck Bailey himself, lying frighteningly still on a gurney. His face was pale, and his hair was sticking up all over in the baby-bird hairdo that normally made Jess smile. Now, it just gave her heart a hard twist.

"Dad," she breathed.

"Heck," Molly whispered.

"Wha?" Heck lifted his head from the pillow, glanced around the room, and frowned. "That goldarned doctor better get a move on. I'm not here to lie around." Fretfully, he squirmed, letting the blanket slide to the floor. "And I'd rather be naked than wear this cotton-pickin' nightie."

"It's okay, sweetheart." Molly picked up the blanket and covered him. "Your operation's all done."

"Done?" He scowled. "They didn't do a damn thing. Some stranger was in here, told me to count backward. Guess he thought I was senile or something, but I showed him." Suddenly thoughtful, he stared up at the ceiling. "I don't think I got much past 97, though. Felt kinda funny. Maybe I've got that Old-Timer's disease."

"Alzheimer's." Jess smiled. Her dad was back. Next he'd start going on about vagina people again.

A nurse bustled in and fussed with the machines surrounding the gurney. "How are you, Mr. Bailey?" she said. "That clockwork ticker's really something, hmmm?"

He glanced over, looking annoyed, then softened when the nurse turned and smiled. She was a little blond with poufy hair, soft and cuddlesome as the ducklings that decorated her scrubs. She patted his chest.

"Ow." He glanced down, surprised.

"Sorry," she said. "Did that hurt? I was just making sure you really had surgery. You look so young and handsome, I can't believe you got a pacemaker."

As she left the room, Heck's eyes followed her the way a puppy dog follows its mama, at least until Molly cleared her throat. Then his gaze skittered toward Jess— like a puppy running and hiding under the bed.

"Jess, honey." He propped himself up on his elbows. "I need to talk to you."

"Okay." Jess grinned. Her dad was totally stoned. "What did you need to say?"

"It's not what I need to say. It's what you need to *do*." He paused for dramatic effect, eyes fixed on hers. "You need to call that boss of yours and tell him you quit. Hell, invite him to your wedding. He'll understand once he sees you two together."

She laughed, but it came out crazily high-pitched. "What wedding?"

"The one you should've had years ago," he said. "To Cade."

Molly winced. "Honey, I don't think we need to talk about this now."

"We shoulda talked about it a long time ago." He collapsed back onto his pillow. "She needs to marry Cade so the two of 'em can take over the ranch. You and me'll go live in Cade's place, Molls, like we talked about. Then everybody'll be happy."

"Everybody but me," Jess said. "And Cade, probably. Considering he's still carrying on with Amber Lynn."

"Aw, no, he's not." Heck shook his head. "And anyways, think how nice it'll be. The ranch'll still be in the family, Molly and I'll live right next door, and you and Cade'll have beautiful babies." His words were soft around the edges, his eyes clouded with the effects of the anesthesia. "Wouldn't Molly make a wonderful grandma?"

Jess knew the drugs were forcing her dad to dump the contents of his brain into her lap unedited. While it irked her that he wanted to marry her off mostly so he and his new wife could be happy and enjoy the privileges of grandparenthood, she'd known for a long time that was at the top of his list.

Little Cades and Jesses danced in her head again, but they faded quickly, eclipsed by the memory of Cade and Amber Lynn embracing at the trailer. Turning away, she covered her mouth with one hand, squeezed her eyes shut, and waited out the pain.

"I'll leave you two alone," she finally blurted out and fled.

Molly found her in the hallway a few minutes later.

"I'm sorry, hon. He doesn't know what he's saying, and I can almost guarantee he won't remember when he wakes up."

"I know." Jess stared down at her red Keds, bright against the shiny white linoleum. "It wasn't what I wanted to talk about, that's all. I need to go. I'm—I'm pretty tired."

"But we need to talk," Molly said. "I need to explain…"

Pushing off from the wall, Jess shoved her hands in her pockets and hurried down the hall, following the red arrows on the EXIT signs. She didn't mean to be rude, but she couldn't bear to talk to Molly right now. She just wished somebody would put up some signs that would tell her how to exit from the mess she'd made of her life.

Chapter 29

THE NURSES WERE OBSESSED WITH WHAT THEY CALLED Heck's "vitals." They woke him at inconvenient intervals, fussed over him with wires and tubes, then left him to commune with the dark until he managed to fall asleep—just before they woke him again.

But they let him sleep in the mornings, and he woke one late afternoon feeling better. The cobwebs cluttering his mind were gone, along with the weakness that had plagued him for so long. Though he was moving slowly and his chest felt oddly pinched, he managed to dress, shave, and pack the few items Molly had brought to the hospital.

The pacemaker was working. His breath came a little hard, and the incision in his chest tugged and stung, but he was well enough to walk all the way down the hall and back. Well enough, he decided, to go home.

When Molly's cheerful face appeared in the doorway, his spirits lifted even higher. The two of them rarely fought, and though she'd seemed nothing but worried for the past few days, he'd been afraid his harsh comments about their plan might have changed their relationship or even destroyed it. He also had a vague recollection of saying something embarrassing to his daughter. He might be in some trouble there.

Molly smiled her familiar smile and clasped her hands before her like a little girl thrilled by a new doll.

"Look at you! Up and dressed." She dithered around the room, straightening pictures and shuffling flower bouquets. "You look like your old self."

"I *am* my old self. And that self's got things to do."

"Like what?"

"Like first of all, it needs to tell you I'm sorry for being a butt."

"Aw, Heck." She sat down on the side of the bed and took his hand. "I know you're frustrated. It's bound to get to you sometimes, being stuck in here."

"Well, I won't be frustrated anymore." He gave her a gentle push, and she rose from the bed. "It's time for a jailbreak. We're getting out of here, woman!"

She drew back, eyes wide. "You can't."

"Oh yes, I can." He pushed himself up to a sitting position, swung his feet to the floor, and paused to catch his breath, casual-like, as if he'd simply chosen to sit for a spell. "I can go home and talk to Cade man to man and make sure we get those two together so I don't end up living at Twilight's End." He sighed. "I know I told you I'd live anywhere with you, and I meant that. But I've got one last chance to save the Diamond Jack, and I aim to take it."

"Oh, honey. I'm working on that. There's been a bit of a—well, a bump in the road with those two, but they'll get over it." He sensed some concern hiding under her smile and wondered if the outlook wasn't quite as sunny as he'd thought. "You don't need to worry about anything but getting well."

"Darlin', I still own and operate the Diamond Jack Ranch." He knew he was being cantankerous again, but he couldn't help it. "I'm responsible for what happens there, and that includes my daughter's happiness. I aim to make darn sure she figures out where she belongs. Whatever happened between her and Cade, you're right—it's a bump in the road, and they'll get over it."

Hoisting himself to his feet, he opened the narrow closet and found his Carhartt barn jacket. A puff of dust and horsehair rose as he shrugged it on, masking the sickly antiseptic smell of the hospital.

"Come on, woman." He waved his arm and felt a pang in his chest, but it was the kind that told him he was alive, with a ticker that ticked just fine. "I've had enough of this place. These lights, that smell—it's making me sicker than I started out."

Molly stepped in close and patted his chest. "I do believe you're right. It's time to go home." She gave him a little shove. "Let's call the doctor and tell him so he can send medications home with you and instructions."

"Don't boss me, woman." Heck gave her a tough-guy squint. "He can send 'em later."

They stood nose to nose, trying to be mad, but both were stifling laughter.

"You're either with me or against me, Molls. Which'll it be?"

Molly sighed. "Honey, I've told you, it's not that easy. You can't tell Jess what to do, and what happened— well, it was a *big* bump. She might not get over it."

"Sure she will." He sounded more confident than he felt, but he believed in positive thinking. "I'm about to lose all I worked for because of some lovers' spat. If you think I'm staying here and lettin' that happen, you're wrong." He reached for her hand. "With me or against me?"

Molly took his hand and squeezed.

"I'm with you all the way, Heck Bailey."

He looked down at her small, soft hand in his calloused paw and marveled that he'd found this woman. She'd made him happy beyond his wildest dreams—but those dreams weren't over yet.

They had work to do.

Jess went home and started cleaning the barn. She wasn't happy to discover the manure shovel was missing, but mostly, she managed to find contentment in hard work. She had some blessings to count, after all. Her dad was getting better, he had Molly to keep him company, and she was filling her mind with something other than Cade. Sure, that something was horse hooey, but even poop was an improvement over painful memories.

What had Amber Lynn been doing there, anyway? Surely, the woman would rather run naked through the streets of Wynott than live in Springtime Acres. Maybe Cade had rented the place as a secret love nest. Hot dang, she'd kill the man. Or—wait.

She'd forgotten.

She didn't care.

Once she shoved the issue out of her mind, the day went fast, with one task after another around the ranch. It ended in a spectacular sunset, but as evening settled over the mountains, the darkness dimmed her optimism. Reality settled over her mind like a wet blanket as she whistled the horses in from the field and fed them. Normally, she enjoyed the familiar sounds and scents of the barn, but tonight, she performed her tasks by rote, her heart still scarred, still hurting.

In the kitchen, she opened one cabinet after another, looking for something she wanted to eat. The house felt hollow and still until a faint sound caught her attention — the grinding of wheels on the gravel drive.

Cade.

Her heart leapt at the thought of him, and she had to remind it, sternly, that he was *not* good news. Those invisible angels had been taunting her; the happiness they'd offered didn't exist. Besides, happiness wasn't something angels granted. It was something you earned through hard work and perseverance. And you earned it alone.

Ducking away from the window, she slipped upstairs and flopped onto her bed, slapping a pillow over her head.

I'm not here, I'm not here, I'm not here.

As feet crunched on the gravel below, she found herself speculating about which Wranglers he'd wear. Her brain might be over Cade, but her heart and her nether parts were taking a little longer.

A voice drifted in on a breeze. "She sure will be surprised."

That wasn't Cade. It was Molly.

Tossing the pillow aside, Jess sat up, straining to identify the faint buzz of voices as the front door slammed and footsteps clattered in the hall. A male voice mixed with Molly's, and when it rose, boisterous and familiar, Jess's heart rose with it, high and happy as a kite on the wind.

"What's a man gotta do to get a welcome home around here?"

"Daddy!" She tumbled from the bed and raced downstairs. "What are you doing here?"

There stood her father, looking more like himself than he had since she'd arrived. He wasn't quite the enormous presence of her childhood—sadly, he'd never be that again—but he stood tall, solid, and larger than life. Large enough, in fact, that she almost threw herself into his arms, as if she was still a little girl and he was still the biggest, baddest rancher in Wynott County. But a closer look caught the shadows under his eyes, so she opted for a gentle hug. His hand went reflexively to his incision, so she knew she'd been right to be careful.

Drawing Molly into the hug, she closed her eyes tightly, breathing in her dad's familiar scent. It carried her back into the past, to the days when he'd taught her to ride, helped her groom horses, shown her how to lasso the silly old roping dummy he'd dragged around the riding ring. Thanks to this man, she'd lived most of her life on solid rock. And even though she was scrambling around on quicksand now that she'd grown up, she was grateful for the firm foundation.

"Well." Her dad stepped back and looked around. "Good to see it didn't fall down yet."

She felt a flutter of alarm. What would he say about Val and the changes she wanted to make? How would he feel about putting the place on the market? Sure, he'd asked Jess to do it. But he was feeling better now, and his drug-induced confession in the surgery suite proved he hadn't been entirely honest when he'd called her home.

But now wasn't the time to talk about the ranch. She'd stick to safer topics.

"What did the doctor say about your heart?"

"Didn't say a danged thing," Heck said. "Got sick of waiting for him and staged a jailbreak."

"Oh, Dad!"

"Don't you worry about me, honey pie. You worry about yourself and that man of yours."

Jess opened her mouth to tell him Cade was no man of hers, but she closed it again. Her dad needed rest and relaxation.

"Tell you what," she said. "I happen to know somebody made a coconut pie yesterday." She winked at Molly. "So any man of mine can wait until morning while we celebrate your homecoming."

"Aw, Cade oughta be here, though," he said. "Give him a call."

"Cade's busy," Molly said, bustling off to the kitchen.

Jess watched her stepmother go, figuring Molly knew exactly what—or who—Cade was doing. But she did her best to smile while they gathered plates, forks, and the cake knife. She owed her stepmother for loving Heck Bailey and making him happy, so she'd do her best to forgive her for whatever part she'd played in that scene at the trailer. Whatever she'd done, she'd probably meant well. Jess wasn't about to assume the worst of Molly. Not again.

A half hour later, the little lamps on the wagon-wheel light over the kitchen table lit happy faces, and Jess felt absolutely safe in the center of her family. That happiness the angels had promised? Maybe this was it. And maybe—probably—it was enough and always would be. Even if they ended up sitting around a different table, in some retirement village, they'd still be happy as long as they were together.

They played a couple of rounds of gin rummy, laughing when Heck tried to cheat.

"You probably have to go soon," he said. "How long's that boss willing to wait?"

"Oh, it's no problem," Jess said. "He's very understanding."

That was a bald-faced lie. She'd spoken to her boss that morning, and he'd been dismissive and distracted. She could feel her status sliding downhill, and she doubted there was any kind of beach at the bottom. If she didn't get back to work soon, she wouldn't end up on the jewel in Birchwood's crown. She'd be down at the bottom of its bloomers.

By the fourth hand, Molly and her dad had begun to exchange meaningful glances that made Jess profoundly uncomfortable. Apparently, all those magazine articles about how old folks still liked sex were true.

"I need to go to bed." She stood and gathered the cake plates. "I've got a lot to do tomorrow."

"Like what?" her dad asked eagerly.

She didn't have the heart to tell him she'd be checking the sick calves, because he couldn't go along. Or that once the calves got well, she'd be looking into selling them, fixing the ranch up to impress buyers, and doing all the housebound chores he hated.

No more cowgirl work or cowboy work. Not for the Baileys, anyway.

"I'll tell you in the morning."

She didn't know how she'd do that. She didn't even know if she could. Because though she was doing exactly what her father had asked by "prettying up the place," she knew he'd be disappointed she hadn't found a way to save it.

Chapter 30

TWO DAYS LATER, MOLLY TROTTED TO THE RINGING PHONE to find Val on the line.

"Is Jess around?" The real estate agent sounded breathless. "I'm on my way with some clients who are dying to see your place. I know it's short notice, but they're live ones."

Molly's stomach rolled over and died. The changes in her husband's life were coming too fast. But Jess had made the call, and Molly had to face the fact that it had been the right thing to do. Cade had a point; what Jess had seen at his window was enough to send any woman running for the hills—or running back to Denver. And without the kids to help out, there was no way Heck could run the ranch. Two heart attacks were enough.

She let out a mirthless little huff of a laugh. It was ironic, really. Here they'd been scheming to get Jess home, pretending they wanted to sell the ranch, and now they actually had to do it for real. It was like karma had jumped up and slapped her in the face.

Slapped her *hard*.

"Jess isn't here," she said. "I could help show the place, I suppose."

"No need. I called that cowboy next door—the good-looking one. He offered to help the other day, so I asked him to show these folks around on horseback. I believe

this buyer's going to very susceptible to his charms—
the wife, anyway."

Molly smiled. "Sure. Cade knows the place like it's
his own."

"Okay." Val lowered her voice. "Just so you know,
we call these two the Dude and the Dudette around the
office. Totally clueless about ranching, but boy, are they
ready to play the part."

"Great." Molly tried to sound enthusiastic.

Val pulled into the driveway before Molly had even
found Heck and warned him not to wander around in
his boxers. The couple that emerged from the back of
the SUV were quite a pair, a fat man and a tall, slender
woman. They were dressed in aggressively western
clothes, but even Molly could see they were dudes.
Real cowboys didn't wear rhinestone hatbands or sou-
venir belt buckles big enough to jab your belly when
you bent over in the saddle. As a matter of fact, most
real cowboys didn't have bellies that big. Nor did real
cowgirls wear enough jangling jewelry to stampede
the herd.

"These are the Swammetts," Val said. "Glenn here is
a television producer, and Margo used to be a model."

Margo must have modeled in those upscale western
magazines where ranch work consisted of riding beautiful horses across pristine landscapes under dramatic
skies while wearing truckloads of turquoise jewelry. Dot
Bailey had probably aspired to be that kind of cowgirl,
but while Molly couldn't ride a horse or rope a calf,
she refused to be a fake. She was a perfectly capable
ranch wife, one who could whip up supper for twenty on
branding day and hold the twitch on a horse for worming

without showing one bit of the terror she felt at the nearness of its big, square teeth.

Margo's teeth were straight and blindingly white, and her cheekbones were so high, they gave her face an otherworldly cast. Her eyes were a remarkable shade of violet, and her figure was the definition of willowy. She was stunning and all the more attractive for the wide-eyed wonder with which she gazed around the ranch. A smattering of freckles across her nose kept perfection at bay, adding a touch of girlish charm and making her appear shockingly young beside her husband.

"Oh, the house, the house." Her breathy voice enunciated each word, as if reading from a language primer. "It reminds me of the house in *Days of Heaven*, honey. Remember that, the movie? Sam Shepard, he had that big old, what do you call it, the mansion?"

"I fell asleep for that one, sweetie."

"I would have, but it had Ree-shard Gere." Her smile came and went, as if it couldn't stick to her face. For a model, she seemed remarkably unsure of herself. "Oh, that Reee-shard." She fanned herself with one perfectly manicured hand. "He is so luffly." She laughed, a sudden, harsh sound. She reminded Molly of a peacock she'd seen once. It, too, had been stunningly beautiful until it squawked.

A clang of metal made every head turn. Cade, riding tall in the saddle, was unlatching the gate. His horse danced the delicate ballet to perfection, backing so Cade could bend to undo the latch, then passing through the gate and performing the process in reverse.

The buyers watched open-mouthed while Molly's heart swelled with pride. Cade was the ultimate

advertisement for the cowboy life. That horse of his was
so pretty, and judging from the way the woman's eyes
widened, she thought the man was pretty, too. Or *luffly*.

The husband stayed put, but his wife made a beeline
for Cade before he even finished with the gate. Cade
looked a little alarmed even after he realized it was his
horse she was after. Margo grabbed the animal's bridle
with both hands, and Molly froze. She was scared to
ride—horses were so *big*, especially their teeth and
feet—but at least she knew the safety rules. Quick moves
and jerking their heads were the first two deadly sins.

"Oh, I luff you!" Margo darted her face toward
Pride's nose. She was apparently trying to kiss him, but
judging from the way the horse jerked away, he thought
she was striking like a snake. Cade soothed him with a
word, so the woman lived to be foolish another day.

She didn't waste any time. Wrapping her hands
around Pride's neck, she tugged his head down and
kissed the whorl in the middle of his forehead. The horse
nearly clipped her chin as he jerked his head up.

"He is so *sweet*." She stroked Pride's neck, since his
head, lifted high and grimacing with fear, was now out
of reach. "This is an Arabian, yes? We might raise them
iff we buy here." She gave Cade a stunning smile. "Iss
he for sale?"

"No, ma'am, he's not." Cade touched the brim of
his hat and nodded politely. "But Mr. Bailey can probably help you find some fine horses. He's as good a
judge of conformation and temperament as you'll find
'round here."

"I am interested in pedigree," she said. "He is from
Spain, yes?"

"No, ma'am, he's Egyptian. Fadjur on his dam's side."

"Well, he's luffly." The woman started to step back, but one of her bracelets had tangled in the horse's mane. Pride jerked his head skyward, pawed the ground, and reared, nearly lifting her off her feet before she fell flat on her backside.

Cade kept his seat somehow as the horse nearly keeled over backward, then landed hard on his front hooves inches from where the woman sat wide-eyed in the dirt. Kicking up his heels, he did his best to dump Cade off the front. The move would have worked on most cowboys, but Cade put on a show of horsemanship that had his audience drop-jawed with admiration as he spun the animal to focus him and calm his twitching nerves.

"So spirited," Margo said. "Are you sure you will not sell him?" She turned to her husband, who'd gone slightly pale, and gave him a sad-eyed look. "He is just what I want, honey."

"Well, now, he might be a bit *too* spirited," the Dude said. "But then again, you're a spirited woman."

Molly could tell Cade was gritting his teeth as he dismounted. He took a deep breath, his eyes on the so-called spirited woman. Although he was the most even-tempered man Molly knew, he was protective of his horses, and she was sure he had something to say.

Val apparently knew that, too, and stepped in front of her clients. "Why don't you two check out the stables while I talk to Cade a minute, okay?"

The Dude had helped Margo to her feet, and the two of them disappeared into the barn. Watching them go, Cade stroked Pride's neck and spoke softly to the horse, who relaxed bit by bit.

Val turned with a grin that reminded Molly it was Shark Week on TLC. "Sorry, but this couple is hot, hot, *hot*. Normally, we like the owners to be gone when we do a showing, but Margo was dying to meet some real ranchers, and I think they'll like you folks. Make nice, because they're loaded, primed, and ready to buy."

Molly shook her head. "Seriously? The Dude and Dudette think they can run this place?"

Val smothered a smile. "This is what we get these days—dot com millionaires and media moguls. You think an honest-to-God cowboy can afford a spread like this?"

Heck emerged from the house, blinking from a nap and looking every inch an honest-to-God cowboy in his battered hat and rumpled shirt. His boots were scuffed, and Molly noticed some horse leavings on one heel. She'd have to clean the floors. Again. She wasn't sure why that made her smile, but it did.

"Mr. Bailey." Val turned on the charm. "I'm Val Hadley, your real estate agent. I specialize in properties like this." She waved toward the buyers. "That's why this couple sought me out when they started looking for a ranch."

"Well, isn't that fine." Heck smiled down at Val, and Molly couldn't help feeling proud of the courtly way he took her hand. A lot of people didn't realize how old-fashioned and polite real ranchers were.

"It's a big place," Val said. "You probably know buyers for ranches like this are scarce as…as…"

"As balls on a heifer." Somehow, Heck managed to stay courtly in spite of the ranch-raised metaphor. "I sure do, and I appreciate the effort you've put into this.

But I thought you'd want us to fix the place up first. Jess has been working hard, but we've got a ways to go." He tapped his incision gingerly. "I've had a little heart trouble, but I'll be able to pitch in and help in a couple days."

"Yeah, there's a lot to do," Val said. "That sign, for example." She frowned. "I told Jess it had to go, but it's still there. Margo really turned up her nose at it."

"My son painted that sign," Heck said. "He's in Afghanistan."

"Oh." Molly had never seen Val speechless before, but after a couple of gulps for air, she managed a smile. "Well, anyway, it's mostly the land we're selling. That alone, without the house being considered at all, will net you two million dollars, at least. I'll work up a market analysis for you and get a firm figure. I know it's irregular, showing it first, but like I said—hot, hot, *hot*."

As the couple joined them, Val nodded toward Cade. "This young man's going to saddle up some horses for you so he can show you around."

"Ooh, wonderful. I shall ride *that* one." Beaming, the Dudette jabbed a finger at Pride so suddenly, the horse shied again.

Cade stilled the animal with a touch. "He's not ready for that, ma'am, but Heck'll find you something better. Right?"

"Sure thing." Heck led the couple into the barn.

"You okay?" Molly asked Cade. "I was worried if the horse didn't kill the Dudette, you would."

"Naw, I've handled worse." He grinned. "Remember, I worked at that summer camp a couple times."

"And the kids were worse than *that*?" Molly asked.

Cade thinned his lips to a grim line. "No, not really. But I'll handle it."

"I know you will." Molly grinned. "You're so luffly."

Chapter 31

CADE GLANCED BACK AT HIS RIDING COMPANIONS. HE'D definitely need to call on his summer camp experience with children to deal with this pair, especially the woman. It would be a challenge to keep her from doing something foolish and killing her horse, herself, or both.

For someone who planned to buy a ranch, the Dude seemed awfully nervous. Maybe he was afraid of horses, or maybe he was worried he'd make a fool of himself in front of his trophy wife. Or maybe he was afraid she'd commit inadvertent suicide by horse before the day was over. Whatever the cause, his nerves were tweaking the portly roan Heck had chosen for him into a lather before they even got started.

But at least he listened to Cade's instructions and did as he was told, right down to taking deep breaths to calm his anxiety.

The woman was another story. Cade had tried to put her on one of Heck's gentler horses, but she'd insisted it was "so old, like a grandpa," and said a tall bay was more her style. Cade was worried that one's temperament wouldn't stand up to the manhandling the woman dished out, but she wouldn't take no for an answer. He knew she wasn't being cruel on purpose; if anything, she loved the horses a little *too* much.

"I haff been crazy for the horses all my life." Thrusting

one foot in the stirrup, she hopped twice and launched herself into the saddle. Her many necklaces rattled and chimed, making the horse sidestep nervously. "I luff them so much, when Glenn retired, I said, let's buy a ranch, honey! And here we are." She waved one long slender arm to indicate the landscape, making her horse roll his eyes and pin his ears. "My dream from when I was a little, little girl is come true."

Shifting in the saddle, she looked down at her legs. "These stirrups are too long. Much, much too long. My feet, they drag the dirt!" Reaching down, she shortened them until she was perched in the western saddle with her knees clenched around the horn. She looked like a jockey at the Preakness.

The bay rolled his eyes again. Cade wanted to do the same.

"They're awfully short now," he said. "Like a jockey would ride."

Her face lit with a smile. "Well, I might want to go fast." She smiled. "Racehorses are thoroughbreds, yes? We might raise them instead of Arabs. Or maybe both." She laughed. "I want all the horses, and Glenn, he can buy them for me."

In some women, the statement would have been annoying, but she seemed as surprised as anyone at her good fortune. Annoying as she was, Margo exuded a hapless innocence that made Cade want to protect her even as he longed to strangle her.

"Okay." He cleared his throat. "Let's go." The sooner he got this show on the road, the sooner he could go home. "You know how to neck rein? Horses move away from pressure, so if you want him to go left, you…"

"I know." She frowned, impatient. "I told you, I have luffed horses all my life."

Cade felt sorry for the horses she'd luffed, especially when she shortened the reins, clutched them in her fists, and hauled on both sides of the bit.

He started to say something, then swallowed his words. Heck wanted to sell the place, and Val was right—buyers were scarce. Cade had seen ranches listed for sale for years, especially when, like the Diamond Jack, they had a conservation easement and couldn't be subdivided. He needed to be nice to these people and maybe help the woman learn. He'd make it up to the horse later.

Leading the riders along the fence line, he pointed out a few landmarks, but it was impossible to carry on a conversation as Margo struggled with her horse, digging in her heels while yanking on the reins, telling the animal to go and stop all at once. Twice, the bay balked and refused to go farther. Silently apologizing to the animal, soothing it with his hands as best he could, Cade convinced her to quit hauling on the bit and let the animal take the lead.

"I trained this one myself, so you don't need to pull at the bit like that. He's a working cow horse, and cattle work can be pretty fast-moving, so you need a horse that can make its own decisions on the fly. By the time I find a way out of a scrape, the horse has usually done the work for me. So you don't need to pull at the bit like that."

"But how am I supposed to control him? He is so *beeg*."

"You don't have to," Cade said. "Let him think for himself. It's a partnership."

"Ah, a partner." She bent to talk to the horse.

"How-deee, partner!" Looking back at Cade, she smiled, and he couldn't help smiling back. She was luffly herself—but she couldn't hold a candle to Jess.

Margo kept up a constant chatter as they rode, all about horse shows she'd been to. He couldn't imagine she'd competed, but she seemed to think she was an expert. By the time they'd reached the north pasture, she'd decided to raise Morgans and miniature horses to go with the Thoroughbreds and Arabians.

Meanwhile, the Rhinestone Cowboy poked along behind them like the dude he was. Cade fell back to check on him and chat a bit. He seemed like an okay guy. He talked about his money a little too much, but he'd evidently dedicated his life to accumulating it, so why shouldn't he be proud? Cade figured he himself probably talked about horses more than he should.

Urging Pride forward, he opened the gate for the Dudette. As they rode on, she glanced back at her husband, then sidled the bay closer to Cade.

"My husband, he is a good man, but he knows nothing of horses." She gave him a conspiratorial smile. "You must be bored, yes? Going so slow?"

"No, it's fine."

"Oh, you cowboys. So polite." She turned and hollered at her husband. "Honey, the cowboy and I are going to run our horses, yes?"

The man nodded. "Sure, hon. I'll catch up."

"No, ma'am," Cade said. "I..."

Before he could finish his thought, Margo turned and smacked Pride's croup with the flat of her hand.

"Va-*moose*!" she shouted and kicked her heels hard into the sides of her horse.

Cade managed to calm Pride without much trouble, but his own temperament boiled over. What the woman had done could get a rider killed. As her horse took off, she rocked back in the saddle so hard, he thought she might tumble off the back, but she caught herself.

It was almost too bad. Good luck would teach her nothing, and she had a lot to learn.

Loping Pride after her at a steady pace, he watched as she took off her designer cowboy hat and smacked her horse's rump. She stayed in the saddle by clinging to the reins, so the horse was simultaneously frightened by the flapping hat, pushed by her clinging heels, and savaged by the bit in his mouth all the way up the hill.

Cade gunned Pride to a hard run and caught up to her. Grabbing the horse's cheek strap, he slowed it to a stop. The horse stood trembling, long ripples of terror flowing down his lathered coat.

"You see?" The woman scowled as if this was all Cade's fault. "I let him make his own decisions, and he runs away with me! I don't know what would have happened if you hadn't caught him."

"He would've killed you, ma'am." Cade tipped his hat from sheer habit and a sense of irony, but he was dangerously close to losing his temper. "No doubt about it, and the next horse you ride might do the same. It's hard for them to make a decision when you hit 'em that way."

She tossed her head as if to dismiss his words. Before, she'd seemed guileless, but a bit of spoiled princess was showing itself now. "I guess you need to train them better."

Cade saw a way out and took it. "Yeah, you know,

you're right. This one hasn't had much schooling. You ought to experience a different one. See what a pleasure a well-trained mount can be."

"Oh, I'd luff that." She narrowed her eyes, and they glowed. "*Yours* is well-trained. Let me ride *him*."

For a second, Cade enjoyed the image of Pride bucking her off and stomping her into the ground, but he shook his head.

"Not a chance, ma'am. Tell you what. Let's have you switch with your husband."

The fat man blanched. "I can't ride that runaway," he said.

"I think you can," Cade said. "I sense a certain strength in you. And sometimes, a man's gotta do what a man's gotta do to protect his woman, am I right?"

The Dude opened his mouth and closed it, opened it and closed it, until Cade wondered if he was trying to speak or catch flies.

"Uh, right," the man muttered. "Gotta do what I gotta do."

Sliding from the horse with all the grace of a bucket of mud, he hiked up his pants in a move that would have made John Wayne proud, then adjusted his belly before striding to the vicious runaway, who was cropping grass. The woman's hands tightened on the reins, ready to jerk his head up, but Cade took them from her and nodded toward the portly roan her husband had been riding.

"It's for your own safety, ma'am. I'd never forgive myself if you got killed."

Once she mounted, Cade put the reins in her hands and set them firmly on the saddle horn. "Those reins are the right length right there," he said. "Don't move your hands, don't lift 'em up, and for God's sake, don't pull on 'em. You do, you're walking home. That horse is my responsibility, and I won't see him mistreated."

"Mistreated?" Her eyes widened, then narrowed. In their depths, he saw a whole 'nother Dudette and felt a little sorry for the Dude. "I did not mistreat him." She gave her hair a haughty toss. "And by the way, you're not *supposed* to hold onto the saddle horn."

Cade pressed his lips closed and kept them that way until the Dude caught up.

"How does the ranching business work? That's what I'm interested in," he said.

"Well, it's chancy," Cade said, letting his horse shamble along the fence line. "You might want to hire somebody the first couple years to show you the ropes."

"You angling for a job? I'd be happy to set you up as foreman. Pay you real well. You could give my wife some riding lessons, too." He glanced back at his wife, who'd fallen behind, and leaned confidentially toward Cade. "She's really thrown herself into this horse thing, you know, thinks she knows all about it. But watching her—I don't know, Son. What do you think?"

Cade chewed the inside of his cheek for a moment, watching the man's face. The blue eyes were guileless, the pink cheeks flushed from the ride. He looked like a giant bald baby, and Cade didn't want to hurt his feelings.

"You're doing a fine job with that bay. I thought you could," he told him. "I also think your wife will get herself killed if you're not careful."

"Thought so. We're going to have to tread carefully, though. She's got a temper, my woman does." He patted the horse's neck in a burst of good feeling, then flinched when it tilted its ears in annoyance. "Wish there was a way we could try this ranching thing out for a bit, make sure it works out."

"Maybe a stay at a dude ranch would help."

The dude's eyes widened, making him a surprised bald baby. "I've got a notion, Son."

Cade did his best not to roll his eyes at the man's attempt at *Bonanza*-speak.

"Maybe we can find a dude ranch for sale, and you and I could go into business together. You've got a way with the public. Handled my wife just right, and she's a challenge." The man puffed his chest, as though his wife's orneriness was something to be proud of.

"I'm sorry, sir. I've got work I'm happy with. You might talk to the owner's daughter, though. She's got a hospitality degree, and she knows the ranching business."

Truth be told, Cade had been thinking about jobs lately. The letter from John Baker still sat on his kitchen table, unanswered, and he knew now he'd made a mistake in letting it go. At the time, he'd been so sure things would work out with Jess. So sure the two of them would end up together.

You're messing up your whole life over that girl. Always were a loser.

Cade grimaced. He was starting to think his father was right.

～

Jess had spent the morning chasing calves again, checking to see if they'd recovered. Most had; the only remaining patient was currently draped across her saddle, bawling pitifully. Weak from scours, he'd been unable to follow his mother down the rocky slope toward the creek. There was little chance he'd survive, but Jess couldn't leave him for the coyotes, so she'd hoisted him onto Buster's back. He'd thanked her by dispensing a generous douse of green poop down the side of her leg.

As she left the cattle behind, she spotted riders in the distance. The leader looked like Cade, but the couple strung out behind him on horseback obviously weren't locals. There was a heavyset man with a belly that jiggled whenever his horse moved and a woman built like a long-legged heron, who rode with her knees hiked up around the saddle horn like a jockey. They made a peculiar parade.

Oh boy. Jess remembered Val's warning about the kind of people who bought ranches like the Diamond Jack. *The circus has come to town*.

A sorrowful moo brought her attention back to the burden draped over her saddle. She shifted the calf to one side, trying to make the poor thing more comfortable as he continued to bawl and mess himself. She just wanted to get the little guy home where she could feed him, but she'd probably have to stop and make nice with the caravan up ahead. Since that caravan included lying, cheating Cade Walker, she wasn't looking forward to it.

"Hey, Jess." He galloped up on Pride as if nothing had happened. As if Amber Lynn had never come to his window. As if he'd never kissed her at the trailer park. As if he wasn't still carrying on with his ex-wife.

"Val brought these folks over." Keeping his voice low, he gave her a conspiratorial smile. "We call 'em the Dude and the Dudette. They're really into the ranch, so be nice, okay?"

"Oh, I'll be nice to *them*." Avoiding his eyes, she looked down at the calf, who chose that moment to dispense another load of manure down Buster's front leg.

"Orphan?" Cade asked.

She nodded.

Eyeing the mess the calf's backside was making of the horse, Jess's pants, and everything else, Cade grinned. "The romance of ranch living, right?"

"More like ranch reality."

Cade considered her left side, where the calf's head hung over Buster's shoulder. "You might want to show the buyers this side. Stay to their right."

Jess glanced at the riders and grinned an evil grin. "I don't know. Maybe they need some ranch reality. I'd hate for them to get into something they can't handle." She gave him a hard look. "Reality's always a good thing. Got to face it, you know, the sooner, the better."

"Maybe you do, but they don't." Cade's friendly face turned grim. "Your folks want to sell the place. Molly said…"

"I know." Jess waved him away. "Don't worry, I'll be good." She frowned. "Why are you here, anyway?"

"You weren't home, so Val called me over to help."

As the strangers approached, she shifted Buster so his back end faced away from them. As they approached, the baby bawled piteously.

"Oh, how precious! I luff him!" The woman looked like a Dudette all right. She was plastered with makeup, draped with jewelry, and wore jeans so tight, she was liable to split a seam. "Look, honey. A bebby *cow*!"

"We call them calves." Jess spoke slowly, as if to

an idiot, and Cade shot her a warning look. She glared right back.

One look told her this woman didn't deserve to own the Diamond Jack. For one thing, she wasn't much more than a teenager. For another, she obviously thought ranching was all baby cows and cowgirl dress-up. One look at the calf's backside would send her packing, but Cade was right—Jess had to be nice. Besides, she didn't care to be seen with fresh cow manure caking her jeans by a woman who was dressed like an over-the-top rodeo queen.

The Dudette reached out to scratch the calf's head. "Is he a boy cow or a girl cow?"

"He's a baby bull," Jess said.

"Can I hold him?"

Jess had a momentary urge to hand over the calf, who was once again actively pooping down the side of her horse, but Cade cleared his throat.

"Probably not a good idea," he said. "Bull calves can be kind of, um, difficult."

"Did you name him yet?" The Dudette clapped her hands, making her horse twitch. "Can *I* name him?"

"Sure."

Jess knew that was a bad idea. Naming critters made her love them more, and this one wasn't likely to be around for long. But Cade wanted her to play nice for these people, and a little heartache was a small price to pay for helping her dad.

"What would you like to call him?"

The woman put a perfectly manicured finger to her lips and rolled her gaze skyward, as if naming a calf required every brain cell she possessed, plus divine assistance from above.

"Hermy," she finally said. "After our accountant." She turned to the Dude. "Take his picture, honey, so we can send it to Hermy."

"Sure, honey." Fishing a smartphone out of his pocket, the Dude gave Jess a surprisingly likable grin. "Smile pretty, cowgirl."

She positioned Buster to hide the calf's mess, tipped her hat to a rakish angle, and smiled, giving some big-city accountant a hefty dose of cowgirl sass. She held the smile even when Hermy sent a projectile dose of calf poop directly into her right boot.

Cade was willing to bet that accountant wouldn't be looking at his namesake when he got the picture. With her face glowing from the ride, her ponytail undone, and curls spilling out from under her hat, Jess looked one hundred percent cowgirl—and one thousand percent beautiful.

He ought to take her aside, tell her about the Rhinestone Cowboy's dude ranch idea. He doubted she'd want to work for this pair, but she might be willing to make some big sacrifices to hang onto the Diamond Jack.

"We're just heading back to the ranch," he said. "Maybe you could answer some questions for these folks."

"Yeah, sure."

Gathering the reins, she turned Buster toward home. Cade opened his mouth to shout a warning, but it was too late; she'd thoughtlessly exposed the truth about Hermy's backside to the Dude and Dudette, and the truth was not pretty. Her right leg and Buster's hide were streaked with green manure, and Cade was pretty sure the calf had also filled Jess's boot with the stuff.

The Dudette shrieked in horror.

"Oh *no. Hermy*."

"Sorry." Jess didn't sound terribly sincere. "Hermy's not feeling well."

"Maybe I let *you* feed him." The Dudette dug her heels into the roan's sides in an effort to escape, but her horse had apparently joined Jess's ranch reality conspiracy and chose that moment to fart loudly as it ambled along.

Cade, smothering a laugh, nudged Pride toward the Dude to do some damage control. To his surprise, the man was grinning from ear to ear.

"Honey?" he called to his wife. "I think that baby needs you to cuddle him."

The Dudette let out another shriek and headed for home as fast as the portly roan could carry her—which wasn't very fast at all, despite the continuing jet propulsion.

"We won't get lost, anyway." The Dude nodded toward Jess, who'd kicked Buster into a trot. "Hermy's leaving a trail."

Cade couldn't help laughing, but the man sobered suddenly. "Hope the little thing's all right. My wife can be foolish sometimes, but she's softhearted. You let that critter die, and she'll cry for days."

"Might not be much I can do."

They were silent for a while, in a companionable way. Finally, the Dude gestured toward Jess.

"That your girl?"

"Used to be."

"Ah." The man nodded sagely. "Try jewelry. Anytime mine's mad, I just get her another necklace, and everything's hunky-dory again."

That explained all the hardware. She must get mad at her husband every day.

"It's not that. We had a—a misunderstanding." Cade sighed. "Sometimes I think she looks for excuses to give up on life before it gives up on her."

"Self-sabotage." The Dude nodded wisely. "Margo was like that. Lost her family young. Abandonment issues."

Cade nodded. That was probably Jess's issue, too. After her mother had left, she'd been desperate to change something, anything, to win Dot Bailey back. Cade had been one of many casualties.

It wasn't Jess's fault, really. It was hard for her to hand over her heart, that's all. Maybe he was an idiot—for *sure*, he was an idiot—but as long as there was a glimmer of hope, he'd stick around.

The Dude gave Cade a conspiratorial smile. "You work for me, Son, you could keep that cowgirl decked in diamonds. What is it you do for a living?"

"I train horses."

The man waved away Cade's purpose in life like the lord of the manor dismissing a servant. "I'm talking *diamonds*, Son. Sounds like you're making cubic zirconia money."

"It's very satisfying, sir."

"Well." The man harrumphed. "We'll talk later. For now, I've got some questions about this place. Do you raise your own feed? I don't want to be buying hay all winter. That's what put Big Al Johnson out of business, and I'm not about to let it happen to me."

Cade looked at the man with new respect, surprised he knew enough to ask.

"No worries there, sir. Heck grows enough hay to feed twice the stock he's got."

"That's fine, Son." The man shifted his heavy haunches, and Cade wondered if he'd be able to walk by evening.

"Who's that friend of yours?" Cade asked. "Is Big Al from around these parts?"

"No, that was in a book. I read a lot of westerns. Louis L'Amour, that kind of thing."

Cade cleared his throat, which seemed to have developed a sudden frog. And the frog was laughing.

"You can learn a lot from Louis L'Amour," he managed to say.

Like how to run a fictional cattle ranch, in the fictional nineteenth century. With fictional cows and horses and fictional weather.

He had a very strong feeling that the Diamond Jack was doomed.

Chapter 32

AFTER HIS ADVENTURES WITH THE RHINESTONE COWBOY and his lady love, Cade felt beaten down and licked. Jess was selling the place, and nothing would ever be the same. The unanswered letter from John Baker haunted him, pricking his conscience with regrets. Of course, his father's ghost had sensed his weakness and plagued him all night long. Minute by minute, hour by hour, his words taunted and harassed until Cade had clutched the pillow around his head to drown it out.

You need a goddamn woman to tell you what to do, don't you? You can't make a move without her. Why can't you stand on your own, like a real man?

You're gonna let your best chance go for a woman who don't even care. You know that, right? You'll wait all your life for that chippie to change her mind. You think that big-shot trainer's gonna tolerate that? He doesn't want some loser on the payroll.

Fortunately, the voice faded in the light of day. Maybe ghosts were allergic to sunshine or faded in the light of dawn's promise. In the east, the sky blushed to a cotton-candy pink, and a mist scented with earth, mint, and sage rose from the dew-tipped grass.

Finishing his chores, he turned out all the horses but one—a bucking, biting beauty Heck had bought at auction a year earlier. Heck had turned the impossible creature out in his far pastures for a year; he swore "letting a horse be a horse" was the best cure for the shattered, abused animals he liked to pretend were bargains.

"You're no bargain," Cade told the horse as he released it into the round pen. "He'll spend more fixing you than you'll ever be worth." The words didn't matter, as long as he spoke softly. "Sometimes I think he buys mutts like you just to keep me in business."

Carrying a long, flexible pole with a white rag attached to one end, he closed the gate, letting the high stockade walls shut out the rest of the world. From the center of the ring, he coaxed the mare into running circles around him, keeping her on the move. The plan was to short out her flight reflex. Being a herd animal, she'd look for safety in any living creature once she tired out, and Cade would be waiting, ready to prove not all men meant pain and fear.

It was going to take a while. The horse was a bundle of nerves, wily and uncooperative. Frantic, she scrambled around the pen, bumping the walls, looking for a way out.

He knew just how she felt. She was reflecting his own emotions, feeling his desperation over Jess. He struggled to calm his mind and focus on her, and she calmed somewhat, dropping her head, running steadily.

Once in a while, he'd lose focus, think of Jess again, and the mare would kick up her heels, evade the flag, and change direction. Once, she charged across the ring right at him, hell-bent on collision. He'd stood his ground, and she'd veered away at the last minute, resuming her endless run.

After a while, the sun went behind a cloud, and a breeze kicked up. The mare offered a few subtle signs that she was weakening, shooting him an assessing gaze from a questioning eye when she thought he wasn't looking or dropping her head as he stepped closer. It wasn't much, but it told him he'd succeed. Eventually.

He planned to make the mare safe enough to go back to Heck as a riding mount. The old man would appreciate the work Cade had put into her, but more important was the get-well message: *here's your horse, ready to ride. I know you're ready. I know you're back.*

Jess would be so pleased. He pictured her smile, and then...

He could have sworn he heard his father's harsh laughter floating on the wind. *She ain't smilin' at you, that's for damn sure. She don't even believe you. If she loves you so much, how come she don't trust you? You weren't doing nothing wrong.*

The horse humped up her back and crow hopped around the ring, bouncing on pogo-stick legs until Cade twitched the flag and got her running again.

Maybe he should keep this one. She threw a temper tantrum every time he thought about Jess. It was like the horse was training him.

"I get it, Redline."

Heck always had him give the horses a new name— one they wouldn't associate with their old lives. This one would be Redline, because she pushed everything to the limit.

But he could push harder.

As the sun rose higher in the sky, he kept the mare running until his arm ached. Wearily, he waved the flag while thoughts of Jess popped and hissed in his mind, fogging his thoughts like smoke bombs.

Catching the turbulence of his emotions, the horse

reacted as a person would react to stirring music, flaring her nostrils and picking up speed. He hunted through his mind for something a little less rousing, but his thoughts were as stubborn as the horse, dragging him toward Jess. Or worse, toward his dad.

She won't even give you a chance to explain, will she? Might as well quit making a fool of yourself, letting her lead you around like one of them horses.

Maybe his father was right. If Cade was smart, he'd go to California, spend a couple of years learning from the best in the business. He'd come back with the kind of experience that would let him take on his own apprentices and make some real money. Jess would wait, or she wouldn't.

Who knew? Maybe if he walked away, she'd follow.

Probably not. But at least she'd appreciate what she'd lost. And we could both move on.

That wasn't his dad. That was his own thought, and the notion made his tension ebb. Surprisingly, giving up felt good.

The horse slowed and stilled, fixing a wary eye on him. Her ears were still pressed against her skull, but the eye on Cade's side had ceased rolling in its socket, and when he let out a long, slow breath, she stretched her neck, lifting her lip and sniffing the air like a connoisseur.

"Maybe it's time to let her go," he said softly. "What do you think?"

Tilting her head to one side, Redline slowly closed one eye in a wink. And he could swear she smiled.

He considered her tangled mane, her chipped, worn hooves, and the wild, wary look in her long-lashed eyes. She'd been a horse for a while, all right. A wild one. But now, separated from her herd, she needed a friend.

She took a step toward him.

He took a step back.

She took more steps, stretching her neck toward him. The more he stepped away, the worse she wanted him.

Just like a woman. Right, Son? Get it?

After a while, Redline leaned over and nibbled his shoulder with her soft, flexible lips.

"You done?" he asked her. "You figured this out?"

She blew out an exhausted raspberry.

He reached out a hand and let her smell it, then slowly stroked her neck, admiring the clean, smooth muscles, the straight, solid legs. She trembled once or twice but stood firm, her eyes soft. She was his now, and he hadn't forced her. The secret with horses was walking away. The choice to join up had to be theirs.

Obviously, a woman was not a horse. But Jess was as skittish and high-spirited as Redline, so maybe if he left and lived his life, she'd follow. If not, he'd be in the world he loved—the round pen, the range, and the rodeo. There were worse fates.

After stroking Redline all over, he lifted each foot, then led her in a few slow figure eights. She was calm but weary, so he clipped a lead rope to her halter and led her out of the ring. When he released her into the pasture, he sensed a lightness in her that hadn't been there before, as if she'd lost the fear and tension from her past. As if she'd finally found someone to trust.

Maybe he'd stick to dealing with four-legged females from now on. He had more success with them. He couldn't control Jess, or her feelings, but he could better his own life—if it wasn't too late.

Chapter 33

JESS HEADED OUT TO THE BARN WITH A BOTTLE FOR HERMY. The calf had been holding his own for two whole days despite a continuing case of the trots. He was a smelly little guy, but he had an endearing personality, and his helplessness tugged at her heart.

He must have been feeling better, because when she reached the barn, he wasn't in his stall. Jess shouldn't have been surprised—the latch was kind of wonky—but she hadn't thought he had the strength to wobble to the door, let alone open it and wander off.

Moving slowly through the barn, she was trying to moo like Hermy's mother when a car door slammed outside.

"Anybody home?"

She peered out a barn window to see the Dude himself, big as life—or maybe a little bigger. He was followed by the Dudette, the two of them traipsing up the porch steps. With nothing more than a cursory rap on the screen door, the couple walked into the house as if they already owned the place.

But they *didn't*. If Jess had her way, they never would.

By the time she reached the house, she was out of breath, and the buyers were in Heck's study. The Dude was admiring a trophy Jess had won at a 4-H rodeo. It was a typical cheap plastic prize, with the usual motif of a gold-painted cowboy subduing a bucking horse atop a column engraved with "First Place, Goat Tying."

Swammett turned guiltily, setting the trophy down quickly as if he'd been caught stealing the silver. "Guess your dad was quite the rodeo star in his day."

"That one was mine," Jess said.

Wonder and admiration bloomed on the Dude's face, and she smothered a laugh. He actually believed she'd ridden bucking horses. While there were women who did that, they were rare. Riding critters that didn't want to be ridden was kind of a boy thing.

Goat tying, however, was a girl's sport. The guys made fun of it, but it demanded real skill. And cooperative goats.

"Thought we'd stop by," said the Dude. "Had a few questions."

"Sure. Sorry about the mess." She tried to sound sincere, but it was hard to hide her annoyance. No doubt they'd arrived unannounced to see the house's flaws. "We've been working on the house, making it nice for—well, for whoever."

Molly bustled in, holding a feather duster.

"Well, hi." She sounded like she was glad to see them, and she probably was. Molly could see something good even in the worst people. "What can we do for you folks?"

"Like I said on the phone, we saw the land the other day, but we'd like to look at the house," the Dude said. "I was thinking on the way over here I'd like to see the furnace."

Like I said? He must have called Molly while Jess was outside hunting Hermy.

"The furnace? Sure."

To Jess's surprise, Molly nodded, then trotted off, straight down the hall and out the front door. Did she think the furnace was in the garage or what?

Jess thought about following her and fleeing, but she made small talk instead, hoping to stall the Dude long enough to make him forget about the heater. She hadn't been down to the basement for a while, but she had no doubt the rafters were festooned with cobwebs while the floor was gritty with mouse droppings. Then there was the furnace itself, crouching on a concrete block, spreading its ductwork arms like an ancient, grumbly king of the spiders.

"Is Val coming?" she asked.

"Didn't see any reason to bother her," the Dude said. "Your mom said it was okay."

Molly hadn't returned, so Jess led the couple through the kitchen toward the cellar door. The Dudette let out a little "*eep!*" when they passed the harvest-gold stove and the avocado fridge, but Jess hustled them through the cellar door.

The ancient heater predated Heck and possibly his grandfather. Constructed of rusting steel plates bolted together at awkward angles, it seemed to seethe when it was on, as if it might explode at any second. Fortunately, it was summer, so the beast was calm.

"The heater has almost as much character as the house itself," Jess said with a phony smile. "There aren't many of these babies around anymore. It's very, um, historic." Patting the side of the slumbering beast, she winced as a metallic clang echoed through the basement. "Um, I don't know much about it, but we kids used to love it. We played down here a lot, and…well…"

It probably wasn't a good idea to tell the buyers that they'd called the furnace the Beast. Depending on their game, it had been an undersea monster, an alien bent on destruction, or a giant spider. With its tubular steel arms, it had an octopus-like look that still haunted her dreams.

She heard a rustling sound and prayed silently that a pack rat or field mouse wouldn't choose this moment to show its furry head. She was relieved when Molly popped out from behind the furnace, wiping her hands on a rag.

Jess should have known Molly wouldn't desert her. She must have snuck down the outside hatch so she could tidy up, which explained the suspicious absence of mouse droppings on the floor. Jess noticed a few tools leaning against the wall—a broom, a mop, and hey, was that the manure shovel? Molly must have been using it for a dustpan.

"This heater sure works," Molly said brightly. "Keeps us snug as bugs in rugs. My husband cares for it like it's his own baby, so it's not only a rare antique; it's also in perfect working order."

The Dude looked a bit puzzled as he strolled around the Beast. Jess knew the constant care her father supposedly lavished on the thing actually consisted of a good swift kick now and then and hoped the Dude wouldn't notice the dents.

"I know it's warm today, but could you fire the thing up for us? We'd like to make sure it works."

Jess frowned. Turning on the heater for the first time in the fall usually sent clouds of stale-scented dust flying from the floor registers. Val might have known how to say no to a buyer, but Jess felt trapped.

"I have to warn you, we usually clean the ductwork at the end of summer." She flicked a switch. "It gets kind of stale."

Closing her eyes briefly, she said a little prayer and was rewarded when the Beast obediently rumbled to life.

But oh, the smell! Jess didn't remember it ever being this bad. Maybe something had died in the ductwork. Maybe *several* somethings. Maybe an entire pack of especially filthy rats.

That was actually the best-case scenario. Once, a whole gaggle of bats had flown into a vent and been unable to escape. One of the worst memories of her childhood was watching her father, her brother, and Cade fishing their small, winged bodies out of the Beast with a coat hanger. They'd had foxy faces and creepy little hands, and they'd smelled a lot like *this*.

The Dudette gagged as she stumbled up the stairs and out of the hatch. "What *eees* that?"

Molly stumbled up the stairs after her, and Jess heard them coughing outside. Beside her, the Dude scrunched up his face.

"I'm not sure I'd describe that as stale," he said. "It's more like—you sure something didn't die in there?"

Jess hit the *off* button, hoping the smell would go away, but it lingered in the air. Worse yet, the Beast had probably pumped its foul breath into every room upstairs. They'd have to air the place out as soon as the buyers left.

Actually, this might be a good thing. She'd been tempted to give these people a good dose of ranch reality, and here it was. Maybe it would drive them off.

The Dude, however, was made of surprisingly stern

stuff. He circled the Beast, sniffing now and then as he poked his fingers into various openings. Like a blood-hound, he seemed to be following his nose, snuffling around the intake filter, sniffing every riveted joint. Bending at the waist, he circled the machine, his nose seeming to lead him closer and closer to the floor until he knelt on the concrete, thrust his nose into the space beneath the monster, and gave a mighty *sniff*!

Jess had to bite her lips to keep from laughing as he scrambled back, his substantial derriere bobbing in the air.

"There's something there!" He paused to rub his nose. "Under-*cough*-neath. I *saw* it." He grimaced. "It had a *face*."

"Okay." Jess hoped he wouldn't ask her to look. "We'll, um, have to check that out."

"You ladies shouldn't do it," said the Dude. "Maybe call that young man next door."

Yeah, maybe not.

Jess almost asked him to take care of it. He was a man, after all, and he *had* said the ladies shouldn't deal with it.

But he was already halfway up the stairs, rubbing his nose. "Golly, I wish I hadn't smelled that. Not sure I'll ever forget it. Trapped in my—my mucous memory."

Jess had kept a straight face through this whole ordeal, but that put her over the top, and she burst out laughing. The Dude looked hurt for a moment, then joined in with a good-natured chuckle.

Dang, she was starting to like this guy.

The Dudette came around the side of the house with Molly.

"The smell, what *was* it?" she asked.

"Dunno, but when I looked at it, it looked *back*." The Dude shook his head. "Something crawled underneath, I believe. Died. Been there a while."

The Dudette was getting paler by the minute.

"I suggested they bring that young man over to take care of whatever it is," the Dude explained. "Not a job for ladies."

"That is a good idea," the Dudette said.

Jess had had enough. These people had intruded on her day uninvited, and now they wanted her to invite her ex-boyfriend, ex-lover, ex-*everything* over to *her* house, just so they could see some hideous thing that was lurking beneath the furnace.

No way.

She opened her mouth to object, but Molly beat her to the punch.

"Oh, you mean Cade?" Molly asked.

Jess folded her arms over her chest, ready to enjoy the pleasure of hearing her stepmother tell these folks they could forget about dragging Cade into their uninvited visit.

"I already called him," Molly said. "He's on his way."

Chapter 34

HEADING FOR THE DIAMOND JACK, CADE WONDERED WHAT Molly needed. He had to come, she'd said. Something had died.

She'd sounded breathless but not agonized, so he assumed it wasn't Heck. Maybe it was Jess's baby calf. If so, Jess might need comforting.

Yeah, sure. And he'd be the person she'd turn to, right?

Wrong.

But in spite of all his resolutions, something stupid inside him longed to see her. Every cool gaze, every polite word, was a stab in the heart, but he wanted her anyway.

There was a rental car in front of the barn. Cade hoped to God it wasn't the Dude and his wife, but Molly had said something had died. Maybe the Dudette had been stomped to death by a horse. The woman didn't mean to maltreat them, but horses didn't mean to fight back, either. It would be divine retribution.

"Down here," Molly called when he rapped on the screen door. "We're in the basement."

Cade poked his head downstairs to see Jess, the Dude, and the Dudette standing around the furnace. They'd called it the Beast when they were kids, and right now, it smelled like one. The whole house did.

Oh no. Not bats again. Dead bats make Jess cry.

He remembered the tiny bodies, the gaping mouths,

the once-bright eyes dull in death, and shuddered. Why did guys always have to deal with this sort of stuff? It wasn't like testosterone made you immune to sorrow, and it sure as hell wasn't making him immune to the awful smell.

Trying not to breathe, he headed downstairs.

The room was warm. They must have had the heater on, and whatever was inside it had cooked a bit. The scent was so dense in the air, he could taste it. He wished he could spit.

"It's under the furnace." The Dude was pinching his nose closed and sounded like Bob Dylan. "I could see it, but I couldn't reach it."

"What is it?"

"Not sure. It's got fur, though. And it's *smiling*."

Glancing around for a tool, Cade found a manure shovel leaning against the wall near the hatch. Shoving the blade beneath the heater, he realized he was just pushing the thing deeper beneath the Beast, but by turning the shovel over and scraping, he managed to haul out a grinning creature, flat as a doormat and dead as a stomped bug.

"Raccoon." He shook his head. "What's a raccoon doing in here?"

"Oh no." The Dudette had edged down the stairs after Cade. Now, she approached the flattened corpse, clutching Cade's shoulder so she could peer at it. "The poor theeng."

Cade shoved the blade of the shovel under the flattened corpse and lifted it. The paws stuck out in all directions, as if the critter was playing airplane. It had been dead for a long, long time.

"He must haff crawled under there to *die*," the Dudette said.

"Yeah." Cade kept his face somber. "Maybe he committed suicide because all the other raccoons teased him about the tire tracks on his back." He glanced around the room with a hard, accusing gaze. "Something's going on here. Somebody's playing games." He let his gaze linger on Jess, who was leaning against the wall, studying her fingernails. "And I bet I know who it is."

Jess knew exactly what Cade was thinking. She'd made that dumb joke about giving the buyers a dose of ranch reality, and then she'd accidentally shown them poor Hermy's behind. Cade probably thought she'd done that on purpose, which meant he thought she'd put the road-killed raccoon under the heater, too.

She narrowed her eyes. Cade himself could have done it, just to keep her around so he could make more stupid excuses for having slept with his ex-wife. But how would he know to put it under the heater? And when would he have been in the basement?

Sighing, she watched him carry the crispy critter up the steps and head for the dumpster behind the shed.

"Put that manure shovel in the barn, okay?" she called after him. "I've been looking for it."

"Yeah, right."

She didn't deserve his sarcasm. She was working her tail off, fixing the house so her dad could sell it. It wasn't what she wanted, but she knew it was the best solution to her family's problems. She was staying here to help, endangering a promotion she desperately wanted, so it ticked her off that he could accuse her of playing juvenile pranks that went against her dad's best interests.

Molly cleared her throat and gave the buyers her most winsome smile. "Would you folks like some iced tea?"

Say no, say no, say no. Jess wanted them gone, but the Dude gave Molly a grin.

"That would be just fine," he said.

The Dudette rubbed her nose. "Can we sit outside?"

"We could sit in the gazebo," Molly said.

The gazebo, built by some imaginative Bailey around the turn of the century, had been another of Dot Bailey's favorite places, probably because it was loaded with Victorian curlicues and performed no ranch-related function at all. Like Dot herself, it was merely decorative.

"That would be perfect."

Jess had crossed the gazebo off her list just the other day, slapping a coat of white paint over the wood so it was ready for its close-up.

"Oh, yes, so pretty. We might put a hot tub in eet."

The Dudette tripped girlishly down the porch steps and headed for the gazebo. Apparently, she expected Molly to get the tea on her own, like a servant. Jess loaded glasses with ice while the Dude poked around the kitchen, running the water and watching it drain, testing the disposal, flicking the stove on and off.

His examination was interrupted by a shrill scream from outside. Jess felt like she was having an Amber Lynn flashback, but this was real, it was now, and it was coming from the gazebo.

"Hermy!" the Dudette shrieked. "Oh, *Hermy, no!*"

Great. The missing calf had probably wandered off to

die, and the Dudette had found her second corpse of the day. Jess was all for ranch reality, but even she thought that might be a little harsh.

She raced outside, fighting tears and cursing herself for loving the doomed little calf. Cade was right behind her, along with the Dude, who was huffing and puffing like a steam train.

"I'm coming, princess-darling-sweetheart! I'm coming!" he shouted.

Jess braced herself for the sight of a deceased Hermy. The little guy had a trusting way of looking up at her while he took his bottle, batting the longest eyelashes of any animal she'd ever seen.

She reached the gazebo and found that Hermy wasn't dead at all; he was very much alive, standing spraddle-legged in the center of the gazebo. He eyed Jess shyly, blinking those long-lashed eyes like a shy but proud student presenting an art project.

He'd certainly been, um, productive. The gazebo was polka-dotted with proof the calf had been there quite some time.

Jess couldn't help it; her eyes teared up to see her little friend still alive. Kneeling in one of the few poop-free spots, she opened her arms. The spindly calf stumbled toward her, bawling pitifully and butting her with his head.

"Oh, Hermy, you're okay!" She looked up at the Dudette, whose mouth hung slack, maybe in horror, maybe in preparation for another operatic scream. "He must have wandered out to look for his mother and gotten stuck in here. Cows normally won't go up stairs, because they sure don't like to go down. It looks like he's been here all day."

The Dudette wrinkled her nose at the poop-spattered floor. "He ees still sick."

"Actually, he's getting better." Jess pointed at a mini cow patty near her foot. "You see? His stool is actually formed. It was runny before."

The Dudette blanched, and Jess remembered most people weren't used to analyzing animal poop. But it was an important way to gauge their health. Ranch reality struck again.

"There is so *much*," the Dudette said. "And it *steenks*."

Jess had to admit she was right. Normally, the vine-covered gazebo smelled like honeysuckle, but today it smelled strongly of slightly sick cow. That wasn't quite as bad as eau de deceased raccoon, but it came pretty close.

"Mrs. Swammett?" Molly was doing her best to keep smiling. "How about we have our tea on the porch? There's a lovely swing up there, with a honeysuckle vine. It's the nicest place to sit on a summer day."

"Long as there is no steenk." The woman tottered back to the house in her high-heeled cowboy boots, her face twisted in a grimace.

Cade stuck his head into the gazebo and frowned. "What a mess."

"I know," Jess said. "I just painted it, too."

Cade shot her a level stare. "Surprised you'd put him in here, then."

She felt heat flush her cheeks. "I didn't put him here. I was looking for him when they showed up."

"Right," he said. "And that raccoon crawled into your basement to die."

Jess scowled. "You know what? You've got a lot of nerve, accusing me of lying. You had your ex-wife at your house for what, a week? And you didn't tell me. And now…"

He was halfway to his truck before she finished speaking. She wanted to chase after him, make him understand, but why bother? If he thought *she* was lying—when she'd never lied to him, ever—what did that say about *him*?

She'd be a fool to believe nothing had happened between him and Amber Lynn. He'd said it himself— *men are weak.*

Well, she was strong. And she wasn't going to go chasing after Cade Walker.

Not anymore.

Chapter 35

JESS FOUND THE DUDE ON THE FRONT PORCH STARING UP at a colony of wasps that was constructing a multifamily condo in the eaves.

"I swear that wasn't there yesterday," she groaned.

He grinned. "Guess the wildlife's not always cooperative. The swing's purty, though."

She flashed the Dude a quick smile. Despite the phony western lingo, he was a pretty nice guy.

And he was right. The swing, also newly painted, looked fresh and clean against the green of the garden. Dangling honeysuckle issued a fragrant invitation to sit down and swing a spell.

"Try it out, honey," he said to the Dudette.

"No, thank you." The Dudette still hadn't unwrinkled her nose. "I could get a spleenter. They can get infected, you know. If they are *dirty*."

The look she shot Jess was hurt and accusing, as if Jess were somehow responsible for all the cow manure in the world.

Well, good. The woman didn't like dirt, and that meant she wouldn't like ranching. That meant she wouldn't buy the Diamond Jack, which meant Jess would never have to see her again. Settling onto the swing herself, Jess pushed off with one toe to make it sway in its restful, easy rhythm. The chains creaked, and the sound, the scents, and the motion brought her back to the magical evenings she'd spent there with Cade. The thought forced her to gulp down a sudden sob, and she struggled to steer her train of thought onto another track.

As if answering her prayer, Molly burst from the doorway and nearly dropped a tray of glasses.

"Don't sit there, Jess. Let Mrs. Swammett."

"She doesn't want to get a spleenter."

Smiling, Jess pushed off with her toe again, then lurched and gripped the seat as a loud *crack!* tore the silence. The world tipped sideways, and the far side of the swing seemed to rise in slow motion as her own seat sank. Her brain ground slowly toward understanding as the sound of splintering wood filled the air.

Glancing up, she saw the bolt that had been holding the chain above her head had torn from the wood. The other bolt held fast, but it was taking the entire weight of the swing—and of Jess. Time seemed to slow as the beam that held it tore from the ceiling and the whole porch began to collapse.

Acting on instinct, Jess grabbed the Dudette's arm and flung her down the steps, where she landed in a heap of angles and elbows. Jess dove after her but was too late to avoid the hail of wreckage. Covering her head with her arms, she felt the sharp broken end of a board slash her forearm. When she pulled her arm down to assess the damage, a beam crashed down on her unprotected head.

Crawling on her hands and knees, she tumbled down the steps and crab-walked backward across the lawn. The Dudette was already on her feet, her perfect face stretched into a panicked grimace.

"Zis place is falling *down*! How can you *dare* to sell zis house? Eet smells and eet is *dangerous*!"

"Now, honey," said the Dude. "The young lady saved you, and now she's hurt."

"Oh. She *deed*?" Margo's face immediately smoothed into its customary perfection, and she gave Jess a quick, flashing smile. "Zenk you."

Jess, freezing cold despite the summer day, hugged herself and shivered. That made her brain rattle inside her skull, and it hurt. She looked around. There was a strange quality to the light. Had some sort of storm struck? Everything was flickering.

"Oh no." The voice was wobbly and weird, like a slowed-down tape, but the soft hands that stroked her hair were familiar. "She's bleeding."

Molly. It's Molly. Everything will be okay now.

Gingerly, Jess touched the back of her head. Something felt wet and slick, and when she looked at her hand, it was coated with a bright-red glove of blood.

Her head grew hot, too hot, and the world rushed away as if she were falling down a well. Bits and pieces of the ranch streamed past while her vision narrowed to a tiny hole. Her ears filled with static, and the voices around her gabbled like geese.

"Run upstairs, hon." Only Molly's voice rang strong and clear. "There's a first-aid kit hanging over the toilet."

Jess pictured the plastic box with a red cross on it that had hung in that spot, unused, as long as she'd been alive. The Band-Aids would probably shatter at a touch, and the gauze would turn to dust in their hands.

Molly's face floated before her, smiling. "I restocked it."

She heard her father pounding down the stairs.

"Thanks." Molly barely looked at him. "Now bring

me a warm washcloth. There're some in the powder room, in the cabinet under the sink."

Wonderingly, Jess met her stepmother's eyes. Normally, there was nothing but sweetness there, but what she saw now was steely determination.

"Good job bossing Dad around."

"I'd boss the queen of England when you're lying there hurt."

The last word stretched out, low and long, as Molly's face rushed backward down a tunnel and became very, very small.

Jess gave the face a comforting smile while she tried to figure out who this nice woman was. She'd known just a minute ago. She looked so familiar…

"Jess?" The woman shook her shoulder. "Honey?"

"That's right." Jess tried to nod, but it hurt too much. "Jess. That's my name. You got it right, Mom." She stifled a sob as the face blurred and faded. "I'm surprised you still remember."

She felt like she might throw up, so she let the darkness wrap her in a soft cloak of unknowing and slept.

Chapter 36

CADE CRANKED UP THE HOTTEST SHOWER HE COULD STAND and let the stink of the dead raccoon and the sick bull calf run down the drain. Too bad the uncomfortable knowledge that the woman he loved was a liar and a schemer wouldn't wash off.

Jess knew her dad was sick and needed to sell the ranch so he and Molly could live someplace safe, with no horses to race or hay to buck. So why was she trying to chase these buyers away? He didn't like them either, but it could take years to sell a property the size of the Diamond Jack. Jess had to know that.

Letting the water beat hard on the back of his neck, he ran his fingers through his hair as if that could erase his doubts and worries. He was toweling off when his pager leapt to life, jigging around on the vanity before throwing itself to the floor like an exhausted toddler.

Shoot. He didn't feel like going on a call. He strained to interpret the staticky voice as it droned code numbers, commands, and assorted gibberish.

"185 County Road 17," it squawked. "Woman down, possible head injury."

Holy crap. That was the Diamond Jack.

"Female, age twenty-six, sustained a blow to the head from a collapsing structure. Scene may be dangerous. Proceed with caution."

Age twenty-six? That was *Jess*.

Collapsing structure? Blow to the head?

Suddenly, he forgot she was a scheming liar. She was just Jess, *his* Jess, and she was hurt. Pocketing the pager, he shoved his feet into his boots and slung the canvas bag that held his bunker gear over his shoulder. He stumbled toward the door like a hunchbacked monster, zipping his boots as he ran.

His buddies always appreciated his calm response to emergencies, but he wasn't calm this time. He ground the key in the ignition, cursing as the engine caught, then fishtailed down the gravel road.

When the house came into view, his heart leapt to his throat and died. The place looked like it had been hit by a tornado.

Once he stepped out of the truck, he realized it wasn't as bad as it looked. Only the porch had collapsed. The house stood firm, the front door opening to a three-foot drop. Six feet away, the porch steps stood, a short flight to nowhere, and between them and the house lay a mess of beams and boards beneath the drooping halves of the fallen roof.

On the lawn, Molly and Heck crouched over a prone figure. Almost falling out of the truck in his haste, Cade raced across the yard and skidded to a stop beside her like a runner sliding into home.

Jess lay with her head in Molly's lap, her eyes half-closed, her expression serene. She looked like she was sleeping, but there was blood on Molly's skirt. A lot of blood.

Heck wrung his hands. "Glad you're here, Son. A beam came down, hit the back of her head. I wasn't there. I couldn't protect her."

"It's all right." Cade did his best to sound calm. "You couldn't have stopped it."

He put a finger on Jess's neck to feel her pulse. It was faint but steady. "How long has she been unconscious?"

"Not long," Molly said. "She came to pretty fast, but then she touched her head. When she saw the blood on her fingers, she fainted."

"Okay."

Cade did his best to follow procedures as he would with any other patient. He checked her pupils; reactions were normal. Blood pressure was good, and the gash in her head wasn't deep. Scalp wounds bled a lot, but she'd be okay.

In a terrible way, this was a gift. He'd resolved to stay away, to take the lesson Redline had taught him to heart, but he hated to leave Jess believing he'd cheated on her. Somehow, he had to convince her of the truth. She knew he wouldn't lie—she had to—but he needed to clear the air between them before he left.

Deep down, though, he was hoping for something more. For absolution, followed by adoration, followed by the life he'd always dreamed of. With Jess.

Stupid. Goddamn stupid. How many times does she have to say no?

Pushing his dad's voice out of his head, he touched an alcohol-soaked pad to Jess's wound.

"*Ow!*" Her eyes flipped open like a doll's, then narrowed. "What are *you* doing here?"

Well, her reflexes were all right. Her face was flushed with pain, though—or was that anger? He'd always been an idiot when it came to reading her emotions. That was part of the problem.

The other part was that she'd caught his ex-wife in his bed and was determined to believe the worst of him. All these problems needed to be solved, but right now, he needed to do his job.

He raised his index finger in the air. "How many fingers?"

"Too many. Because they're *yours*."

"Now, sugar, you be nice," Heck said. "Cade's trying to help."

"I'm just not up for this right now." Shrugging off Cade's hands, she rose to her feet and swayed, pale as a daylight moon. She had to grab something to steady herself, and the closest something happened to be Cade.

"Careful," he said. "You've been hit in the head, and..."

"Yeah, no kidding. I figured that out on my own. What I want to know is what happened?" She turned to face the house and staggered. "Who knocked down our house?"

"Eeet just fell *down*." The Dudette was sitting on the ground by the porch steps, her husband hovering over her like an anxious bumblebee. "This house, it is falling apart."

Cade hadn't even noticed she was there. "Oh, sorry. Are *you* okay?"

"I am fine." She looked sulky and put out, probably because he'd rushed to Jess and ignored her. He had a feeling Margo was used to being first in line when it came to male attention. "I want to go home."

"We will, sweetheart princess," said the Dude. "Just rest a minute."

"I'm okay, too," Jess said. "So, Cade, you can go now."

A thin trickle of blood chose that moment to stream out from under her hairline. It trailed down her cheek, joined by a tear that slipped from the corner of her eye.

"You have a cut on your forehead, too." Ignoring her anger, he stroked her curls back from her face and examined a small but raw-edged wound. "This needs to be cleaned up. Once the ambulance gets here, I'm betting they take you to the emergency room. A head injury's nothing to mess with."

"*I'm* nothing to mess with. Just *go*, okay? I'm *fine*."

The Dude was poking through the broken beams.

"Got to be dry rot." He held up the chain from the swing, with the bolt that had once been screwed into a beam. "This pulled right out of the wood."

"I worked on this porch last summer, and it was fine," Cade said. "There's no dry rot." Distant sirens grew louder, and a rusting, rattletrap milk truck swung up the driveway. A picture of a cheeky smiling cow was barely concealed under a red cross painted on the side. As the makeshift ambulance skidded to a stop, two men jumped out of the back, bearing a stretcher.

"Oh no." Jess stood, swaying dangerously. "You're not loading me into that deathtrap." Cade was glad to see her grin at the ambulance attendants. "I know you, Fletcher Kincaid. I've seen you drive."

Fletcher, whose father owned a ranch beyond the highway, was just a couple of years out of high school, but he'd already earned his EMT certification. Though he was still a skinny kid, his training gave him an air of confidence as he took Jess's arm and lowered her to the ground. Cade felt pride warm his heart. He'd mentored Fletcher since the kid was sixteen.

"You're pale," Fletcher said. "How do you feel?"

"Bad." Jess shot a killing glare at Cade. "But I'll be fine if you can just get Cade to leave."

"You want Cade gone?" Fletcher looked stunned. "I thought you two were…"

"You thought wrong."

Even with blood trickling down her cheek and fury in her eyes, dressed in old clothes with Hermy's hair decorating her shirt and blood on her face, Cade couldn't help admiring Jess's fiery beauty. The Dudette had flawless makeup and perfect nails, but Jess had an indefinable quality that made her eclipse every woman around her without even trying. Her beauty wasn't the perfect-princess type—not at all. But she struck Cade speechless with her glorious imperfection.

She was unique. She was special. She was his—or ought to be.

Give it up, boy. You said you'd stop.

Cade shook his head, trying to dislodge his father. *I never made you any promises.*

Shoving his hands in his pockets, he let the scent of crushed honeysuckle fill his senses, calling up a long-ago summer night on that porch swing with Jess. He'd held her, swaying in the flower-scented night, and been sure they'd be together forever. Now, just looking at her made his heart hurt, as if it were trying to grow fingers so it could reach for her.

But he'd probably never hold her again, because the real forever he faced was going to be just like the last couple of years. Judging from the way she was behaving, she'd condemned him to a life sentence of missing her.

He needed to accept that fate and go.

Chapter 37

JESS SWATTED AWAY ONE FIREMAN, THEN ANOTHER. THEY were neighbors, well-meaning and kind, but she didn't need their help. She could stand up just fine. Somebody'd sped up the rotation of the earth, but she could handle it. Sure, she was staggering a little, but that was because the lawn was uneven. When had it gotten so lumpy?

Maybe around the time her life grew speed bumps. Her dad was sick, they were selling the ranch, Cade had cheated on her, and her house was falling down. She felt like covering her eyes and peeking through her fingers to see what was coming next, but for her dad's sake and for Molly's, she needed to face her obstacles head on.

Turning, she scanned the wrecked house. The porch was gone, just *gone*. The smell of crushed honeysuckle tangled in the wreckage was suddenly overwhelming; the world spun faster, then slipped out from under her feet. A hand gripped her elbow, and she stumbled against a male body—a young one, angular and thin. Barely man enough to hold her.

So not Cade.

Why did her heart sink at that realization? How could she still want him after what he'd done? Why did she want to tuck her head beneath his chin, rest her palms against the hard plane of his chest, and melt into his warmth?

Her head injury must be worse than she'd thought.

"Ma'am?" It was Fletcher again. "You probably shouldn't be walking just yet."

"Maybe not." She let him help her to a seat on the back of the milk-truck ambulance and shrank into the shadowed interior.

Cade had joined Molly and Heck up on the porch. He'd taken off his hat, and the way sunlight glossed his blond hair made it look like he had an actual halo, but she knew he was no angel. She didn't want to look at the man or talk to him, ever again. She didn't want him to hold her or comfort her.

But it sure was cold for a summer day.

She let Fletcher fuss with the gash on her head while she stared straight ahead, pretending she wasn't listening to Cade and her parents.

"I saw it happen," Molly said. "This side pulled out, and the other side held, but it was like the weight of the swing was too much for the beam and pulled the whole roof down."

Cade knelt to examine the beam. "Look. You can still see the marks of the screw most of the way. The wood's only torn up in the last half inch or so." He examined the bolt. "I think somebody set this up. Unscrewed it partway so it would fall."

"Why would anybody do that?" Heck looked puzzled.

Cade glanced around for the Dude and Dudette, but there was no sign of them. Turning back to Heck, he lowered his voice. "Somebody's trying to discourage buyers."

Molly and Heck didn't respond. Molly just stood there, twisting her hands in her apron, while Heck stared down at the ground and scuffed the dirt with one foot.

"You know who I'm talking about, right?" Cade asked.

Jess slid deeper into the ambulance and pulled her legs to her chest. Wrapping her arms around them, she leaned against the cool metal and closed her eyes. The man said he loved her, but he so readily believed the worst of her. Then he expected her to trust him with Amber Lynn playing pajama party in his bedroom.

It wasn't right. As far as she could see, she'd been the target, not the perpetrator. Nobody'd expected the Dudette to sit in that swing. The trap had been set for Jess, and whoever had done it was sneaky, underhanded, and mean. Jess wasn't like that—but she knew somebody who *was*.

The world wavered before her like an underwater dream. As she closed her eyes, she felt strangely confused, but somewhere in the stew of her slipping, sliding thoughts floated an image of Amber Lynn Lyle. She wasn't screaming, like the last time Jess had seen her. She was leering with triumph.

Winning Cade back wasn't enough for his ex-wife. She was trying to kill off the competition.

It was late afternoon when Jess woke to the roll of thunder. In intermittent flickers of lightning, she tried to figure out where she was. Dark wood, cream upholstery, the scent of furniture polish—she felt like she'd landed in a Victorian ghost story, but it was just her mother's parlor.

Great. She was languishing on the antique fainting couch like an old-timey virgin with the vapors. How appropriate.

A second thunderclap made her sit up. She watched

a streak of lightning tear across the sky, lighting up the rain-drenched pasture and the windblown trees beyond. Swollen thunderheads loomed over the mountains, and fat raindrops splatted on the windowpane.

Another flash lit up what was left of the porch.

"Shit." She didn't cuss much, and when she did, she tried to be creative, like her dad. It was a family tradition, but tonight nothing came to mind but *shit*.

"I feel the same way," said a voice from the shadows.

Cade. He was sitting in one of her mother's fussy slipper chairs, watching her.

Shit again. And double *shit*.

Jess started to stand so she could head upstairs to bed with her nose in the air, but the walls wobbled and the floor began to spin. Grabbing for something, anything, she grabbed *him*.

A wave of heat and nausea washed over her, and she slumped gracelessly onto the fainting couch. Nothing like demonstrating the function of an antique with some vintage feminine behavior.

"Jess? Talk to me. Please."

Maybe those Victorian women were onto something. Nobody could bother you if you weren't conscious. She threw her head back and let her forearm fall over her forehead to shield her eyes. Cade might think he had something to say, but she wasn't listening. She was done. Done, done, done with Cade Walker.

"At least let me know you're all right."

"I'm not," she mumbled.

She felt his hand brush her shoulder. "What hurts?"

"Nothing. I'm not all right with you being here."

"I know. And I'm sorry about that."

She felt him take one of her curls between his fingers. He gently pulled it straight, then let it bounce back into place. It was a tender signal between them, one of the many declarations of love they'd worked out over the years. Her tears, already threatening, brimmed over as another clap of thunder shook the house. The raindrops grew fat, then fatter, and then hailstones hammered the window like a thousand tiny fists.

"Look, I almost lost you," Cade said over the racket. "I mean, I know I lost you, but you could have been killed. It made me realize—I just need you to be okay. Don't know if I ever will be again." He sighed. "I guess that's up to you."

She didn't answer, hoping he'd go away if she ignored him.

"I wasn't sleeping with Amber Lynn. I wouldn't do that, and I think you know it."

She shifted and cracked one eye open. The so-called slipper chair, dwarfed by his long legs and broad shoulders, looked like something from a dollhouse. He had his elbows on his knees, his hands clasped before him, and was looking at her so intently, she felt naked. She closed her eyes and prayed he hadn't caught her peeking. She didn't want to face him. Didn't want him to look her in the eye.

Because deep down, she was dumb enough to believe him.

Outside, the hail ceased, and the sudden silence amplified his words.

"I'm not leaving til you talk to me," he said. "I'll sit here all day if I have to. You know I'll do it, same as you know I wouldn't cheat on you. Can't say it's much of a hardship anyway. There's no place I'd rather be than with you. You know that, too."

"Not really. Because you weren't with me. Not really. You were going home to her."

"I didn't want to."

"Then why did you keep it a secret?"

"I don't know. That was stupid. I just—I didn't think you'd understand." He paused. "Looks like I was right."

She peeked again. His hair was disheveled, with a boyish cowlick sticking up in the back. It reminded her of the boy he'd been, and that made her turn toward him, just the slightest bit, and meet his eyes.

There was so much sorrow there, her insides softened and twisted. A shiver skittered up her spine, born of dread for the conversation to come and fear of her own weakness, but there was something else—something that warmed her soul. It felt a lot like love, but that couldn't be.

How could you love a man who'd broken your heart?

She wished she really was a Victorian virgin. Then she wouldn't know what it was like to lie in his arms. She wouldn't remember the last time he'd looked at her that way, up in the hayloft, where they'd reignited the love they'd shared almost all their lives. Love that had faded like a banked fire but never died.

Closing her eyes, she channeled the unconscious damsel again and prayed for oblivion.

Chapter 38

CADE COULDN'T HELP SMILING AT JESS'S DRAMATIC EFFORT to convince him she was sleeping. She was draped over her mother's fancy couch, limp as a silk scarf. The contrast between the stiff old furniture and graceful Jess, with her tumbling curls and rumpled blanket, made him love her all the more.

He'd never been much for talking, especially when it came to emotions, and he'd sworn he was done trying with Jess anyway. But the thought of losing her had woken something deep inside him—something that didn't care about logic or common sense or what anybody thought. Something that simply loved Jess Bailey and always would.

Working with horses had taught him to take a chance and try when an unexpected opportunity arose. But what could he say?

He remembered something Heck had said years earlier.

A pony ride's always the way to that little girl's heart. A pony ride or a good horse story.

Setting his hat on the floor, he began. "Once the real estate agent turned up, I knew I'd lost you. And all I could think to do was work, get with the horses, so I'd feel better. So when I was done with those calves, I took that sorrel mare your dad bought into the round pen."

Her lashes quivered, just the slightest bit, and he knew she was listening.

"She could tell I was upset," he continued. "Skittered 'round the ring like a mosquito on a windowpane, trying to get away from me, and I don't blame her."

"Me neither," Jess said. "I know just how she felt. Wondering how to get loose, wishing you'd just leave her alone."

Ouch. That hurt, but at least it was a sign the old Jess was in there. It was a pretty good insult, after all.

"I finally calmed her down. Thought about leaving here myself, giving up, and that seemed to calm us both. But you know I'm not the type to give up."

No response.

"Later on, I tried to do some chores," he continued. "Simple stuff you wouldn't think I could screw up, but I kept dropping things, breaking things. Tripping over my own big feet." He sighed. "I can block this out for a little while. Focus real hard on work. But it doesn't last. I'm not going to be good for anything until I make things right between you and me, so here I am."

Uncovering her eyes, she turned and faced him.

"Just stop, Cade. It's done. I can't forget what I saw."

"So you're not interested in why Amber Lynn was there or what I have to say about it." He struggled to swallow a bolt of anger that had snuck up and surprised him. He couldn't be mad at Jess—could he?

He loved her. He wanted her back. But she wouldn't let him explain, and it was making him crazy. She knew what kind of person he was. He'd been true to her all his life. Why couldn't she trust him enough to at least listen?

"Well, it doesn't look like you're going anywhere," he said when she didn't answer. "Guess I'll just keep talking to the walls, telling them what I have to say. You can listen or not. But if you won't even listen, you're not the person I thought you were."

Her face flushed. "You're not the person I thought you were, either. You had your ex-wife in your house, sleeping in your bed, while you were carrying on with me. What kind of person does that?"

"A stupid one." He picked up his hat and spun it one way, then another, telling it everything without once looking at Jess. "Amber Lynn showed up the day you got home. I was surprised. She took darn near everything I had and went off with some other guy. I never expected to see her again, and that was fine with me. But I didn't realize what the guy was like. He *hit* her, Jess." He swallowed. The thought of a man hitting Amber Lynn—hitting any woman—made him feel sick. "Once she was sitting in my kitchen with a black eye that took up half her face, I couldn't send her away."

"A black eye? Really?" Jess raised a skeptical brow.

"Really." He looked down at the hat again. "I told her to go to her dad, but she said the guy would find her there, so I let her stay. I didn't want to. I told her to leave every goddamn day, but I had to go to work at the Vee Bar every morning, and when I'd get home, there she'd be, spouting some lame excuse for staying."

Jess sighed deeply.

"I know," he said. "I should have changed the locks. But I didn't want to carry her out, and since she'd already been hit by a man—well, I didn't want to damage her."

Jess turned, her gaze hard. The hat stopped spinning, and he slapped it on his head.

"You know, Jess, I care about people." He leaned in,

resting his elbows on his thighs. "Am I supposed to stop when it comes to Amber Lynn? I mean, she's just about my least favorite person in the world, but she was still a woman who'd been hurt and was in danger. So I let her stay, but I slept on the sofa. Never touched her."

"Right. Sure."

"You don't believe me?"

"No, I don't. I *saw* you, Cade." Her eyes filled with tears, and her face crumpled. "On the steps of Molly's trailer. She was climbing you like a tree. Is that your little love nest?"

"Aw, geez." Removing the hat, he ran a hand through his hair. "Molly rented Amber Lynn the trailer to get her the hell out of my place. She called and asked me to bring Amber Lynn's suitcase over. You can ask her. I was just dropping it off, and Amber Lynn grabbed me." He sighed. "I've never been inside that trailer, swear to God."

Replacing the hat, he rose and paced the length of the room. "If you'd stopped, seen what was going on, you would have known that. But you took off, thinking the worst of me instead." Reaching the far side of the room, he paced back. "Some guy *hit* her, Jess. What did you want me to do? And frankly, I didn't treat her that great myself. I don't love her. I don't think I ever did, and that means I wronged her, in a way." Returning to the chair, he slumped into it, letting the brim of his hat slant over his eyes. "I never should have married her. Should have gone to Denver instead and chased you down. Should have fought for you."

Jess let out a faint little mew, like a cat trapped in a closet, then looked away as if she'd like to take it back.

But he'd heard her, and he knew now at least part of

what was wrong. The problem went back further than he'd thought and had been festering all this time. He looked down at his hands a moment, gathering strength.

"Guess I should explain why I didn't." He gave her a wry smile. "Kind of smacks of self-pity, so I never talked about it."

She blinked, and he caught a faint shift in her expression. Maybe she wanted to hear this. Hard as it was to say, it might be the missing piece that was keeping them from understanding each other. Shoving his hands in his pockets, he spoke to the window, wishing his words could float off and carry all his baggage to the mountains and beyond.

"You knew my dad, but you never saw the worst of him. The beatings? Those I could take. Bruises fade. But he was a mean drunk, and it was his goal in life to convince me I was useless and stupid and should never have been born." Removing the hat, he sat down and spoke into the crown. "He drilled it into me, day after day, night after night, so I could never believe I was worth a damn thing. I always thought I was just damn lucky you thought so much of me, so when you left— well, I thought you'd figured it out, that's all. So I did you a favor and let you go on to better things."

Jess looked puzzled. "But he was gone by then."

Cade looked up, meeting her eyes. "I still hear his voice *now*, Jess. It's in my head every day. I don't listen, for the most part, but he's still there, in every board and shingle of that house."

She sat up, facing him, her knees touching his. "I thought you didn't care when I left. You never tried to change my mind, and you moved on to her so fast…"

"It wasn't Amber Lynn I moved on to. It was whiskey. She was just a by-product, which wasn't exactly fair to her." He sighed. "Everything my dad told me came true, so I figured I might as well follow in his footsteps and be a drunk. It's nothing I'm proud of, believe me."

He ran a hand down his face, wishing he could just erase himself. There were too many memories, and there was too much at stake. It was exhausting. He stood and stretched.

"I need to go home. I don't need you feeling sorry for me, okay? I just thought you deserved to know why I gave up so fast."

She stood, staggering a little, and paled. Clutching his arm, she let him ease her back onto the couch. A faint flutter of hope made him sit beside her.

Neither of them spoke for a long time. Occasionally, her eyes would scan his, as if she was reading his thoughts.

What she ought to be reading is my heart. Because her name's branded on it so big, there's no room for anybody else.

He stilled his emotions just as he had for Redline and a hundred other horses, and like the horses, she finally gave in. He felt the air around them calm, the tension dissipating.

So now what? Should he touch her? Kiss her? She seemed uneasy for some reason.

She cleared her throat.

Oh boy, here it comes.

"Um, there's just one problem with all that. You said Amber Lynn had a black eye?"

"Yeah." He sighed. "Guess I should've taken a picture."

"No, I believe you, and I know you couldn't turn her

away when she'd been hurt." Jess looked away. "She knew that, too."

He nodded. "She knows me pretty well."

"But when she came to the window—Cade, she was fine. There was no black eye. She was pretty as ever."

He stilled, but his mind was churning, churning, working at his memories, untangling the truth from the mess Amber Lynn had created. He remembered her clad in her sheer nightie, pointing to the window and screaming. How had her face looked?

He wasn't sure. His mind worked at the knot a little more, and he remembered telling her to go. He'd been firm, almost cruel, and she'd looked at him with wide, hurt eyes...

Wide, hurt, and perfectly normal. No bruising, no cuts.

"Holy smokes." He felt like he'd been punched in the chest. "There *was* no black eye."

"That Amber Lynn always was a whiz with makeup."

Cade stood and paced the length of the room. He felt a fool, but he also felt *free*, liberated from the stone that had been weighing him down ever since he'd seen Amber Lynn at his kitchen table.

"I'm an idiot, Jess." He joined her on the couch. "But I don't lie, and I don't cheat. Never have, never will."

She nodded, but after all they'd just shared, he'd hoped to see trust in her eyes. Instead, he saw fear.

It didn't surprise him. Jess wasn't scared of much, but she was scared of love. The way her mom left had broken her heart, and she'd carried that pain like a shield all her life. Behind it, she was wary and liable to bolt, like an animal that had lost a limb in a trap.

She looked down at their joined hands, then up at him.

The lines in her face, forged by worry, had smoothed out. But that fear—there was no getting past it.

He thought of Redline, standing at his shoulder, trusting him at last. That moment, that decision, was the end for a horse. They gave their whole hearts.

Women? They were a little more complicated.

Chapter 39

JESS WANTED TO BE WITH CADE AGAIN, TO LIVE IN THE perfect circle that had held the two of them, bound by a lifetime of love. She longed to put this whole Amber Lynn mess behind them. But things weren't quite that simple.

For one thing, seeing Amber Lynn at his window had reminded her of how wrong love could go and how much it could hurt. For another, she'd believed the worst of him way too easily. On top of all that, he'd believed the worst of her, too, and still did. He actually believed she'd put Hermy in the gazebo, unscrewed the swing to make it fall down, and flashed the Dude and Dudette with Hermy's messy backside on purpose, all so she could have her way, like some spoiled princess. She'd told him over and over she hadn't done any of those things, but he wouldn't believe her. And then he had the nerve to be insulted that she thought he'd cheat with Amber Lynn. Why did trust only work in one direction?

His eyes were probing hers, trying to read her mind, but her thoughts were swirling and tangling like threads in the wind, unknowable even to her. Maybe she was wrong. Maybe she was crazy.

Maybe she was tired.

"I'm sorry. I need time to figure things out." A tangled mass of curls flopped over her forehead and into her eyes. She swept it aside with one hand. "I've been wrong about everything, ever since I got home. You know, I even thought I could run the ranch by myself at one point."

"You could."

"Not without help. I was arrogant and stupid."

He smiled. "I thought you were independent and brave."

"Well, I thought Molly was a gold digger. And when I overheard her talking to the school principal on the phone, I thought she was cheating on my dad."

He gave her a wide-eyed look of disbelief.

"I know." She let her shoulders slump. "I think the worst of everyone, and I'm wrong every time. I was mad at Molly, at you, at life in general, but most of all, I'm mad at myself. I'm watching everything good in my life stream away behind me, like a long road in a rearview mirror, and I'll never be able to go back."

"You're right," he said. "We can't go back. But we can move forward, and when we do, we'll make everything better, I promise."

She swiped at a renegade tear. "You can't know that."

"Yes, I can," he said. "I'll make sure. I'll make *damn* sure. And I'll start with your porch." Standing, he hiked up his belt, as if preparing for a job. "It's too big a job for me, with work backed up and waiting, so I'll call Riley."

"Okay." She thought a moment. "Cade, there's one more thing we need to fix."

He grinned. "Just one?"

She smiled, but it was a sad smile. "You know who really did all that stuff—the raccoon, the porch, that business with Hermy?"

"Yeah, I know." He sat and took her hand, his eyes

warm with understanding. "But why didn't you just tell me? Don't you feel better now?"

With a rush of anger, she realized he thought she was confessing.

"Geez, Cade, I told you, it wasn't me. *Think*, okay? Who could it have been?"

He looked around the room, giving the deer head over the fireplace a suspicious squint, as if it might be guilty, then locked eyes with her. That was his answer.

He still believed it was her.

"It was Amber Lynn," she said. "It *had* to be."

"Yeah, right." He smiled, as if they were sharing a joke.

How could he not see it had to be his ex? The woman might as well have signed her name in red paint. After the fake shiner and all her obvious efforts to manipulate him, he still couldn't see her guilt.

Didn't that mean she still had a hold on him? He claimed he'd never loved his ex, yet he still believed the best of her—and the worst of Jess.

He'd explained why Amber Lynn had been in his bed. He'd explained the embrace at the trailer. But things still didn't feel right. And while she believed his explanations, he wasn't offering her the same level of trust.

And that wasn't right.

Molly couldn't help smiling. Judging from his enthusiastic off-key singing in the shower, Heck was excited about the trip they were taking. The Loose-Ends Gang had been invited to summer riding camp at Decker

Ranch, so she and her husband were headed to one of the retirement communities she'd found.

Life was moving forward, change coming at them fast. The Rhinestone Cowboy had surprised them by making an offer on the ranch despite the epic porch disaster, and Val had recommended they accept it. Molly had seen Heck's face pale at the thought, but he seemed happy enough now. He was concentrating on shaving when she stepped up behind him and wrapped her arms around his wide middle. He made a gasping noise, and she quickly glanced at him in the mirror. He thrust out his tongue and made a face.

"Don't scare me like that."

"You worry too much." He patted her hands. "Maybe you'll relax once we see what Old Fogey Bottoms has to offer."

"I guess." She sighed. "I'm not sure I want to leave this place, though. Especially not with those people taking over. I was sure we'd lost them when the porch fell down, and that was fine with me."

"It's a lot of money, sweetheart. We'll have a good life and be able to help the kids, too."

She gave him an appreciative squeeze and tried to feel happy, but who cared about money when you had a home like this? The Diamond Jack was a legacy, passed down through generations. How could they put a dollar value on that?

Resting her head against his back, she breathed deeply. The antiseptic smell of the hospital was gone, and he smelled like her cowboy again.

"Maybe we should tell them no. Cade and Jess talked

some, and he didn't look so hopeless when he left. They might save the place yet."

Heck turned and took her hands in his, and for once, his expression was grave. "Molls, it's getting mighty late for that. That big-bellied fella and his wife want the place, and you and I—we'll be fine."

"Cade said they don't know a thing about ranching."

"Once we leave here, it won't be any of our business what they do. We'll have a whole 'nother life. This one'll be behind us, and that's okay." Dropping her hands, he embraced her, rocking from side to side. "We'll build a new life, and I'm lookin' forward to it, long as it's with you."

She twisted out of his arms to stare up into his face. "You are?"

"Sure." He chucked her under the chin and grinned. "So come on, woman. We'll check out this place, and if we don't like it, we'll move on 'til we find one that's just right."

"Okay." She gave him a quivering smile. "So you're not mad?"

"'Bout what?"

"I talked you into dragging Jess back here, pretending we wanted to sell the ranch, and now we're selling it for real." She bit her lower lip. "I never meant for that to happen."

"Well, it's sure not your fault. I'm the one with the bad ticker." Grinning, he smacked her lightly on the butt. "Now, let's get going. I'm hoping this place has a horseshoe court. Or shuffleboard."

"You are?"

He shrugged. "Not really, but I'm trying to think

positive." He gently elbowed her in the ribs. "And you should do the same. Nobody likes grumpy sad sacks."

"All right." Breathing deep, Molly sucked in her stomach, stuck out her chest, and gave him a flirty grin. "How's this?"

"Fine as a fox and sexy as a badger," he said.

"Badgers are sexy?"

"Well, the lady badgers are. If you're a boy badger."

Laughing, she headed down the stairs. "Just let me tell Jess we're going."

She found her stepdaughter in the middle of the parlor, legs set wide apart, fists on hips. Jess's brows were drawn low over her eyes, and she looked so fierce, Molly took a step back.

"What are you up to, hon?" Molly knew Jess didn't want to sell the place and was upset the Swammetts had made an offer.

Jess's smile was almost scarier than the scowl.

"I'm fighting ghosts."

"Um." Molly glanced around the room, but no filmy wraiths lounged on the furniture or floated in the air. "What ghosts?"

"Just one, really." Jess gestured toward the fainting couch. "I'm getting that out of here—guess I'll put it on Craigslist. That too." She pointed at a fussy tea table. "And those stupid slipper chairs."

"But those are your mother's things. Don't you want to keep them?"

"This isn't my mother's house anymore." Jess bundled her curls into one hand and tugged them away from her face. "It's not ours either, not for long, but I want her gone before I leave."

"It's actually a beautiful room," Molly said.

"Do you ever sit in here?"

"Well, no. I like the back porch, and in the winter, the family room."

"With that ugly plaid sofa? That thing smells like every dog we ever had."

"It's *cozy*."

"Exactly. And nobody who belongs here feels comfortable on this prissy furniture."

Molly felt her heart go light. "Not you or your dad."

"Or you." Jess reached over and gave Molly a side hug, kissing the top of her head. "You belong here, too."

"Oh, sweetheart."

Jess grinned. "Oh, Molls."

Molly had been hoping for *mom*, praying for it nightly. But to have her stepdaughter use the pet name her husband had invented squeezed a flood of motherly warmth from her heart.

"I just hope we're doing the right thing," she said. "I feel like we're taking your home away from you."

"Don't worry about it, Molls." Jess relaxed onto the hated fainting couch. "The way things are with Cade, I don't really want to stay." She noticed Molly's stricken expression. "It's for the best, really. I'm up for a promotion—to Hawaii!"

"Oh my." Molly tried to look excited, but she knew that if Jess went to Hawaii, they'd never see her. It would be too far for them to visit, and she'd never have time to come home.

"Amazing, right? And I'll be free to enjoy myself. Maybe I'll meet a hot surfer."

As Molly headed back to the kitchen to pack some

snacks for the trip, she thought of her old life. Before her marriage, she'd been free, but it hadn't brought her happiness. It was loving other people that made life matter. Despite Heck's illness, despite the way she worried about him, loving him made her whole.

Freedom wasn't the answer. Not for her, and not for Jess.

Chapter 40

FOR JESS, A TRIP TO WYNOTT WAS ALWAYS A WALK DOWN memory lane. The dusty, papery smell of the library, the slow signals of the single stoplight, and the scent of the diner's delicious and wildly unhealthy food carried her back to a simpler time.

But the cloud of nostalgia that enveloped her at Boone's Hardware was overwhelming. The place smelled like childhood, like shaking old Ed Boone's dry and papery hand, like choosing a hard candy stick from the glass jar he kept on the counter.

When Riley James had moved into the apartment behind the store to help Ed and his sick wife, she'd added a few modern touches. There was a wider assortment of paint now and a larger selection of tools, but the most noticeable changes were the creative window displays. Right now, passersby were treated to a collection of pitchforks, scythes, machetes, and hatchets below a banner that read *Your Zombie Apocalypse Headquarters* in dripping, blood-red letters.

That was a customer's first hint Riley wasn't your average small-town hardware entrepreneur. A city girl from Denver with a history as wild as the tattoos that snaked up one arm and curled around her neck, she had silvery-blond hair and pale-gray eyes that made her look like a fairy from some fantasy film. Despite her ethereal appearance, she spoke as bluntly as a man, and her gaze was equally direct.

"Hey, I'm glad you're here," she said. "Cade called about your porch. You want it restored or replaced?" Her voice, low and husky, broke on the upturned question.

"What's the difference?" Jess asked.

"If I restore it, it'll look like it did before, only sturdier and fresh-painted. If I replace it, I could get a little creative. Design something interesting."

Jess wondered what "interesting" would mean to someone like Riley.

"I don't know. Our house is pretty interesting as it is." She chewed her lower lip, watching Riley wipe down the cash register. "Oh, what the heck? Every other generation managed to put their stamp on the place. Why not us?"

"Sweet!" Riley beamed, eyes aglow. "I love your house for just that reason. I'll build you something special, I promise."

"Don't get too crazy," Jess said. "Or too expensive. We're selling it, so the new buyers have to like it."

"I have an idea to tie all the elements together," Riley said. "Make the place look like something special, instead of just *interesting*."

"That would be great." Jess didn't see how the house could get any weirder, and it would be fun to see what Riley came up with. "Call me when you can get started. In the meantime, I need some painting supplies."

Riley led her to the paint department at the back of the store.

"I need to pick a nice off-white for our front room," Jess said. "My mom used to call it the parlor, and it's all fussy and pink."

"Can't have that," Riley said. "You hear from your mother much?"

Riley could be socially clumsy sometimes, maybe because she'd had even less mothering than Jess.

"No, she's busy."

"Oh." Riley leaned over and plucked a color card from the rack. "These are warm whites. Good for a parlor." She stood there, twisting one foot like an awkward child, while Jess scrutinized the colors. "What about your brother? You hear from him?"

"Not much." Jess frowned, comparing the colors against the white shelves. One looked too pink, another too yellow. "He's never been big on communication."

Riley grinned. "Still an asshole, I guess."

Jess couldn't help laughing. "You obviously know Griff well."

"Not real well. But I text him on What's App sometimes." Riley looked down at her toes, suddenly shy. "I'm not sure he wants to hear from me, but I don't care."

When Jess turned to answer, she realized, with a sort of stunned amazement, that Riley *did* care. About *Griff*. Spots of color rode high on her cheeks, and she avoided Jess's eyes.

"You *like* my brother?"

"No. I don't know." Riley shoved her hands deeper in her pockets and frowned at the floor. "I thought he was brave, going off like that. I always feel like I'm hiding in this town. It's so safe, you know? But Griff doesn't care about being safe."

"No. If he hadn't joined the Army, he'd probably be a bull rider or maybe a smoke jumper."

"Yeah." Riley busied herself straightening the color

samples. As far as Jess could see, they were in perfect order, but Riley took out one, then another, put them back, and pulled out more. "You know when he's coming home?"

"No. I just hope it's soon."

"Me, too."

They stuck to small talk until Jess had paid, but Riley took her time putting the paintbrush in a bag, glancing up at Jess while she fooled with stuff behind the counter.

"What?" Jess figured the girl had more questions about Griff.

"Nothing. It's just…you know who could use your help?"

"No, but I'm sure you'll tell me."

Riley laughed, a short, raspy sound as if she was unaccustomed to humor. "I do tend to say what I think." She paused. "Cade Walker."

Jess groaned. "I really don't want to go there."

"Okay," Riley said and plunged forward as if Jess hadn't objected at all. "But you're not worried about Amber Lynn Lyle, are you? Because she was at the bar the other night, swatting all the guys away, talking about how she doesn't have time for a relationship."

"She was?" Jess hadn't wanted to talk about Amber Lynn either, but what the heck. Gossip was always tempting.

"She got a job at her dad's bank, so now she's a career woman." Riley forked her fingers into scare quotes. "Glad I don't work there. She must be a holy terror for a boss, and you know her dad wouldn't make her a mere teller."

"No, I doubt that." Jess started for the door again.

"Just so you know, this probably isn't the last you'll hear about Cade," Riley said. "The old guys at the diner are laying bets on you two."

"Hey, my dad's one of those guys," Jess said.

"Yeah, I'm pretty sure it was his idea."

"And you think small towns are safe." Jess gave Riley a narrow-eyed stare. "Did *you* bet?"

"No, but if I did, I'd bet on you getting what you want. You're Griff's sister, after all." Popping open the cash register, she busied herself counting bills again. "From what I've seen, you're brave, too. It's just a Bailey thing."

Jess felt tears spring to her eyes and had to turn away. She wasn't sure why the comment touched her so deeply.

Maybe it was because she wasn't brave at all. Every time she thought of Cade, her heart leapt and spun like a figure skating champ—until she thought of Amber Lynn at his bedroom window. Then her heart would fall on its ass, skid across the ice, and slam into the wall.

She was scared. She knew that was what it was. She didn't think Cade had slept with his ex, but he believed Jess had messed with the Swammetts and was unwilling to even suspect his ex-wife. That made Jess wonder just how he felt about his ex and whether they could build a relationship where there was no trust.

"You know Cade loves you, right?" Riley grinned. "Everybody says you could do just about anything, and he'd never quit." She sobered a bit. "I'd give a lot to have a guy like that. Not looking, but hey, if it happens…"

Jess sighed. "It's complicated."

"Sorry. I guess it was rude to bring it up."

"It's okay." Jess noted Riley didn't look sorry at all. "But you know what?"

Riley cocked her head, letting her silver ponytail flow over her left shoulder. "What?"

"You should probably change your bet. I'm not even sure I *know* what I want."

Chapter 41

A FEW DAYS PASSED WITH NO COMMUNICATION FROM JESS. Cade spent his nights staring at the ceiling, trying to figure out where he'd gone wrong. Why wouldn't she just admit she'd tried to drive the Dude and Dudette away with her "ranch reality" pranks? He'd thought things through a hundred times, and it *had* to be her.

Maybe blaming Amber Lynn was some sort of test for him. But she'd never been like that before—making him jump through hoops to prove his love. That was more Amber Lynn's style.

There had to be something else. Some other reason she couldn't let him into her life.

The phone rang, and he answered to find Molly on the line.

"Hey, Cade," she said. "Heck and I'll be gone for a few days, checking out one of those retirement homes."

"Okay," he said. "You need me to take care of anything while you're gone?"

"You could take care of Jess."

He almost groaned aloud. "She doesn't think she needs taking care of."

"Well, she does. And she shouldn't be alone here, after that head injury. I was thinking maybe you could invite her over to your place, give her a break."

Now it was his turn to smile. "You never give up, do you?"

"Not when something matters. And you shouldn't, either."

She had a point. Things hadn't ended well with Jess the other day, and he needed to mend some fences. He doubted he could get her to his house, but maybe if he stopped by, tried again, she'd listen to him.

"I'll try, Molly."

"I knew you would."

She knew him well. Once he thought about seeing Jess, the rest of his plans for the day took second place. He dressed hastily and rushed his breakfast.

"No boiled bacon today," he told Boogy. "You get a ride, though."

When they reached the Diamond Jack, Jess's car was parked beside the barn and Buster was grazing in the pasture, but there was no answer to his knock.

He tried the knob and stepped inside, followed by Boogy.

"Jess?"

She was home. He could hear her yodeling some sort of gibberish in the parlor. Boogy laid his ears against his head, yipped once, and dodged back outside. Maybe Molly was right about Jess's head injury. It sounded like something was terribly wrong.

He strode down the hall and burst into the parlor like John Wayne slamming through the doors of a Wild West saloon.

Jess was on a stepladder, paintbrush in hand, cutting in a pretty cream color next to the ceiling. Dot Bailey's "civilized" furniture was stacked in the middle of the room, draped with sheets.

"Jess?"

She didn't answer. Didn't even turn around. He realized why when he noticed wires dangling from her ears. Tinny tunes crackled from her earbuds as she shifted her hips from side to side and yelped out the lyrics to a Keith Urban song.

"*Bloo, oo-oo-oo, oo-oo-oo, looks good on the sky-yi-yi...*"

Jess had many skills, but singing wasn't one of them. She sure was enjoying herself, though. Leaning against the wall, he settled in and waited for her to notice him.

She carried on, hollering about how blue didn't match her eyes—which was wrong, because it did. On the second verse, she jerked her arms outward, splashing paint on the wall, on the sheet-draped furniture, and on Cade.

Dancing wasn't one of her skills, either. The ladder rocked, and the paint can tipped dangerously. Grabbing it, she half fell, half jumped to the floor, right in front of Cade.

"*Aaaaieee!* Holy crap!"

Jerking the buds out of her ears, she flushed pink all over. Maybe she was upset at seeing him. Either that or she was embarrassed to be caught murdering poor Keith.

Then again, it might be her outfit. Her plaid shirt must have been Heck's once; it hung to her knees, and the shoulder seam was halfway to her elbows. An equally ancient pair of jeans ended at her ankles, making her feet look huge in her old pink Chucks. She'd completed the look by corralling her curls with a bandanna that gave her a Rosie-the-Riveter, we-can-do-it look.

Cade plucked one of the buds from around her neck and held it to his ear.

"You're going to go deaf." He pulled a long face. "Wish I could go with you."

"Hey, I never claimed I was Mariah Carey, but at least I'm not sneaking up on people and embarrassing them."

"You're embarrassed?"

She cocked her head, considering the question. "No, I'm not embarrassed. You already know I can't sing."

"Or dance." He took her paintbrush. "Especially not on a ladder, balancing a full can of paint."

He set the paint can and brush on the drop cloth she'd spread over the floor. "This looks nice." He gestured toward the one finished wall. "Sure beats that ugly wallpaper."

"I spent all night tearing that stuff off. Lucky it was just some temporary stick-on crap Mom bought online. What do you think of the color?"

"I like it."

"It's called Unicorn. I'm painting over all my bad memories, most of which involve my mother." She waved toward the sheet-draped furniture. "Maybe you could help me carry all that crap out to the barn."

"What are you going to put in here?"

She shrugged. "I'll leave it empty. Let the Rhinestone Cowboy and his pretty, pretty princess decide."

"Oh no. They made an offer?"

Pressing her lips into a thin line, she nodded.

"Damn." That was bad news, but at least she hadn't said her bad memories involved him. They'd left things on a sour note the other day, but she seemed to be in a good mood now. Maybe he could turn things around.

You never give up, do you?

Shut up, Dad.

"Need help?" Picking up a Boone's Hardware bag, he found a second paint roller and tray. "I wouldn't mind erasing this room myself. Your mom used to call me in here while you were upstairs getting ready so she could tell me I didn't deserve you."

"I didn't know that."

"Now you do." He grabbed the paint can and poured a thick, smooth runnel of Unicorn into the pan, then slid a cover on the roller. "There's a lot of the past I don't want to erase, though. Like…well, a lot of things."

He'd been about to mention their recent roll in the hay but thought better of it.

"Heck and Molly got off okay?"

"Uh-huh. They're in a rush to find a place now. Apparently, the Swammetts are in a hurry."

"Shoot. I'm going to have to move."

She barked out a mirthless laugh. "Molly said the Dude wants you to run the place and teach his wife to ride."

"Not happening."

They finished two walls before Cade started to get restless. Covering up bad memories was fine—but he'd rather create some good ones.

———

Jess felt something poke her between her shoulder blades and whirled to see Cade with his roller held high.

"That shirt just needed something."

"You!" She fought back, slashing a wide, cream-colored streak across the front of his shirt.

A paint fight was the kind of thing they'd done when

they were kids—silly, fun, and competitive. Neither of them liked to lose, so what might have been harmless fun always turned into a high-stakes battle as they became desperate pirates on a gangplank, fighting above a shark-infested sea.

Jess was quick, but Cade was more aggressive, so she wasn't surprised when he accidentally poked her in the cheek with the end of the roller. She wasn't hurt, just breathless and flushed, but he reached for her, cupping the back of her head, and *oh*, he was so close, gazing at her with such grave concern. Her mind swam, her body yearned, and as usual, her brain shorted out.

Everybody says you could do just about anything, and he'd never quit.

Riley had been right about that. So how could Jess resist? *Why* would she resist?

She couldn't remember what they'd been fighting about. Probably something stupid. Because what could possibly matter more than this, them, together, now?

His eyes went soft, and just like that, love flowed over her like a wave, filling her heart, swamping her mind, and drowning all her anger. The barriers she'd erected buckled under a tsunami of emotion as he bent his head and paused, his lips inches from hers, a question in those eyes.

Closing the distance, she said yes.

Midkiss, he swept her up in his arms and carried her out of the parlor while she stripped off her oversized shirt and tossed it aside. In the front hall, he set her down, and she pulled his paint-splashed T-shirt over his head, tossing it out the open door. It caught a breeze and drifted down to the tumbled chaos of the wrecked porch and lay there like a white flag of surrender as he hoisted her to his chest, slammed the door with his foot, and carried her, like a Wild West Scarlett O'Hara, up the stairs.

Chapter 42

RHETT BUTLER HAD IT EASY. SCARLETT'S STAIRCASE HAD been a wide, sweeping affair, while the staircase at the Diamond Jack was so narrow, Jess's feet kept banging against the wall. To make matters worse, Boogy was following much too close. Cade managed to avoid tripping over the dog or bashing Jess's head on the railing, but just barely. He was panting harder than the dog when they reached the top.

He'd planned to gentle Jess the way he'd gentle a difficult horse, with sensible choices, careful deliberation, and a cautious eye on her mood. He'd told himself she had to make the decision to give in on her own. It didn't matter that his body ached for her every minute of the day or that his heart had barely recovered from their last breakup. What mattered was creating a bond, *the* bond, that would last.

Unfortunately, he felt like he'd just carried a horse upstairs. There wasn't much room on the landing, and somehow his body wound up pressing hers against the wall.

She sure didn't feel like a horse.

She scanned him with sparkling eyes, her body writhing against his in a struggle that could have been mistaken for refusal if her fingers hadn't been working on his belt while her breath came fast and hard.

"Bedroom," she muttered.

He thought of her lacy canopy bed and pale pink walls, and a jolt of heat surged from his mind to his heart and then to some far less appropriate organs. He and Jess had found all sorts of secret hookup spots in their teens—the hayloft, the treehouse, the line shack in the north pasture. Pretty much any shady sheltered spot had worked, as long as it was far from prying eyes.

But once or twice, they'd found themselves alone at the ranch, and Cade was almost ashamed of the way he'd taken advantage of those opportunities. It was in Jess's bedroom they'd made the shift from friends to lovers, and he wanted to relive that, over and over, for the rest of the day, the week, the month, the year. For the rest of their lives, if she'd let him.

Taking her hand, he pulled her through the door while the dog watched mournfully from the top of the steps. Jess only pretended to resist; when they reached the bedroom, she fell back onto the bed, bouncing among the frilly pillows. Why did women always have so dang many pillows?

Maybe because they knew they looked sexy draped over a heap of puffy lace. Jess wore nothing but a silky tank top now, and it fit her lithe body like a second skin. He could have stared at her forever, memorizing the casual toss of her limbs, the careless curl of her fingers, and the tumble of her crazy curls fanning over a pale-pink pillow. Indulging themselves in this bed was like making love on top of a strawberry Frappuccino with extra whipped cream.

"I was thinking we'd stay friends for a while," she said, eyes closed, lips barely moving.

"We've always been friends." Settling beside her, he traced a finger across her forehead, then let it trail down the side of her face. "Now we'll be really, really *close* friends again."

Letting his finger wander to her lips, he traced the seam of them and shivered when the pink tip of her tongue flicked out and licked them.

"No promises, okay?" She propped herself up on her elbows, looking much too serious. "Everything's too complicated, because…"

He set his finger on her lips. "No promises, no demands. You're in charge, okay?"

"Seriously?" Her eyes flashed with a devilish spark from under almost-shuttered lashes. "I'm driving this trip?"

"Yep." His finger drifted down to trace her collarbones, the delicate dip between the light-boned wings.

She reached up and cupped the back of his neck. "I like to drive fast."

As she pulled his head down to her and set her lips to his, he realized pink frilly canopy beds probably ought to come with seat belts.

Jess paused in the middle of a passionate kiss and looked at Cade, really looked at him. He was all rumpled, sexy hair, eyes filled with love so strong, it warmed her down to the bone, and a lean and muscled body ready for action. There was something bothering her, some reason she shouldn't give herself entirely to him right now, but darned if she could remember what it was. "Where are we going, Jess?" he whispered.

"I think you know." She smiled up at him. "We've been there before, but I'm thinking we need to find a shortcut."

Cade didn't seem to be looking for a shortcut, though the man could move from zero to sixty in half a heartbeat. She felt his body tighten with desire, muscles growing rock-hard under her fingers. The angles of his face seemed to alter in some subtle way, making his deep-set eyes look deeper and intensifying the heat of that broken-crystal gaze. It carried her way beyond wanting him; they were in needing territory now.

Skimming her hands over his bare chest, she felt the cool air from an open window stroke her own skin. He'd pulled down the straps of her camisole, and it hung dangerously low. If she hadn't been so aroused, the filmy shirt would have slipped right down her body, but the peaks of her nipples held it up and kept her decent—if you could call anything decent that made her desire so clear.

With a quick tug, he stripped it to her waist and lowered his head to her breast. She wasn't sure what exactly happened after that. There was a pull at her breasts, a tug deep inside her, a struggle with his belt and jeans, another struggle with her own, and then the two of them were rolling, gloriously naked, on her bed.

They'd had their first time in this room. They'd started in the truck but had to cut their make-out session short for her curfew. When they'd gotten home, they'd discovered Heck had gone to Cheyenne for a cattleman's meeting, so they'd had the house—and her pink poofy bed—to themselves.

"Do you remember?" she whispered. They'd been so in love that day, with feelings that were pure and uncomplicated. "It was so easy then."

"It's still easy. I'll show you."

And he did.

He touched her like he had all those years ago, when they'd been so unsure of what was right, of what would work. From there, he took her steadily forward through the years, reviewing every phase of their relationship and reminding her, with desperate, rushed touches and sweet, slow interludes, that the lifetime they'd spent together hadn't always been smooth. There'd been doubts and pain, but they'd always found solace in each other.

The boundaries between them always disappeared when they made love. He was hers, and she was his. Together, they were stronger than they'd ever been apart. And when he slid inside her, she felt his joy in her own heart, and they cried out in one voice.

It had always felt good, but this time, it felt momentous. In spite of saying she could drive, he'd gently taken the wheel and led her to a place so warm and right, she wondered why she'd ever left it.

They stayed there until the breeze from the window softened and stilled. Twilight dropped a dark curtain over the plains, and in the hush of the country night, she lost her sense of time and all her doubts. Cade had carried her up to the stars and back and set her, sated, on solid ground. It was always solid at his side. She could count on that.

Right then, right there, she knew, despite the doubts that prodded the back of her mind, she was right where she belonged.

Chapter 43

JESS'S HEAD FIT NEATLY IN THE HOLLOW OF CADE'S shoulder. Resting there, she savored the velvety peace of the night. A soft breeze wafted over her body, echoing the sound of Cade's slow breathing beside her.

The last hour had cleared her mind of all her fears. In the light of their lovemaking, everything else seemed small and insignificant. It was as if her life was a stew that had simmered for hours until only its essence remained, only what mattered—and what mattered was Cade.

Because he was *Cade*. He loved her. They just needed to have a talk about what mattered to her—not her own goals, but her goals for her father. He needed to understand the roles had shifted, and she was taking care of her dad now. He'd see the truth then and realize she wasn't the one playing those pranks.

He stirred, opened one eye, and smiled.

"We probably ought to get cleaned up," he said. "Your folks are coming home tonight, right?"

"Maybe. They weren't sure how long they'd stay. Depends how much they like it, I guess." Absently stroking his hair, she let the real world flow back into her mind, a little at a time. There were horses to feed, chores to be done, a meal to be made, but she didn't want to move.

Sitting up, she twisted her hair in one hand and

glanced at the mirror. There was a streak of Unicorn decorating her cheek. She laughed.

"Guess you're right. Cleanup time." She jumped to her feet. "Let's use Mom's crazy bathroom."

Cade threw on what clothes he could find and stepped into his boots, but Jess didn't bother to get dressed. Giggling wildly, they stepped over the sleeping Boogy, scampered down the stairs, and tiptoed, for some reason, through Heck and Molly's main-floor master bedroom to the fancy en suite bath Dot Bailey had simply had to have.

"Man." Cade gaped at the floors, the ceiling, the walls. "This is really, um, something."

Like Dot Bailey herself, the room was in questionable taste. Pink marble floors veined with white were polished to such a high shine, Cade and Jess had to shuffle like old folks to keep from slipping. The walls, tiled in the same blush marble, reflected the two of them in their rose-colored depths. It was like seeing themselves in some alternate dimension where they were always pink, always naked, and just a bit blurry. Jess wished life was really like that.

Sitting on the edge of the enormous jetted tub, she cranked the hot water on high.

"Are there life jackets?" Stepping out of his jeans, Cade gaped up at the beaded chandelier, reflected forever in multiple mirrors set in heavy gold frames. "I feel like I'm in Vegas." His eyes fell on Jess, and the wonder turned to smug satisfaction as he sank down beside her. "And I beat the house tonight."

He swept a dangling lock of hair back from her face, tucking it behind her ear, and they kissed while steam from the hot water plumed from the tub.

When Jess came up for air, she turned to check the water level, took a deep breath—and gagged. Gesturing wildly, she tried to wave away the sickening odor that rose from the steaming water. She staggered across the room, sliding dangerously on the slick floors.

"You all right?" Cade looked up, caught the smell, and coughed.

"It *stinks*."

"Sure does."

Steam rose in veils from the water, and with it the smell, powerful and impossible to ignore. It filled the room like a living thing but smelled like a dead one.

Gasping, Cade plucked a Kleenex from the vanity and put it over his nose. With his nostrils clamped shut, he dared to bend over the tub long enough to turn the water off.

"What the hell is it?" Jess's eyes were watering as she wrapped herself in a towel. She worried she might never take an untainted breath again. "Sulfur?"

"Worse. I'm not sure, but it's bad. It smells like dirt."

"It smells like death."

"It smells like death dirt. I guess we'll find out. Molly sent a sample of the water to the state, so they can test it for the Rhinestone Cowboy." He wrapped a towel around his waist. "Seems he read a Louis L'Amour story about alkaline water cows can't drink."

"Seriously? Louis L'Amour?"

"Taught that man everything he knows about ranching."

Jess snorted, her laughter blending with the dog's sudden barking. Cade put a finger to his lips at the sound of a vehicle crunching ominously up the gravel drive.

"Holy crap! They're *home*. And we're *naked*."

They raced to the stairs. Cade's first step sent his towel cascading to the floor. He tripped on the end of it, barely catching himself, but they kept right on going. They could explain a damp towel on the stairs, but it would be hard to explain a naked Cade—especially when Naked Cade was accompanied by Nearly Naked Jess.

Or not so nearly. As she dragged him up the stairs, the corner of her own towel, neatly tucked in above her breasts, worked its way free. In slow motion, the oversized bath sheet unwrapped until it, too, lay undone on the stairs.

"Just get to my room," she hissed as Cade dipped to grab it, then played a quick tug-of-war with Boogy, who'd grabbed the other end.

"Gotta get dressed," she fretted.

"You think?" He grinned as she shoved him into her room ahead of her.

"I *do* think. Sometimes. But it's hard right now."

"You're right, it is."

Giggling, she smacked him and stepped into a pair of panties from her top dresser drawer. She pulled a T-shirt from the middle one, but the bottom drawer stuck, so there was a quick wrestling match before she hauled it open and found a pair of jeans. She was hopping around on one leg, pulling them on and trying not to trip over the dog, when she noticed Cade was still naked, sitting on the side of the bed with a smile on his face as he watched her reverse striptease.

"Get dressed!" She swatted him with a pair of clean socks.

He regarded her with a sexy grin, and she wondered why she was putting clothes on instead of taking them off.

"I'm trying to remember where I left my clothes."

It all came back to her in a rush. The two of them making love in her bed. Running a bath in her parents' bathroom. Cade had felt shy about running around naked in Heck and Molly's house, so...

A car door slammed.

"Shit!" Jess hissed. "Your stuff's still in the bathroom!"

Cade glanced wildly around the room, then lunged for the bed. "Here. I found my hat."

She couldn't help laughing. "That's not going to help! Hold on."

She raced downstairs, disappearing into the bathroom as the front door swung open.

"Jess?"

"Just a minute!"

Jess snatched up Cade's jeans, boxers, and socks. She glanced wildly around for his T-shirt, then remembered tossing it onto the front steps.

Oh no.

"I saw Cade's truck outside. Is he in the barn?"

"I don't think so." Jess clutched the clothing to her chest and did her best to sound happy and welcoming as she raced back upstairs to the bedroom. "You guys are home early! Hold on. I'll be right down."

Shit, shit, shit.

She was halfway up the stairs when she remembered Cade's boots, standing in a corner by the tub. They'd be a dead giveaway if her folks used the bathroom—and they would, after their long car ride.

Racing back down into the bathroom, she slipped on the shiny tile and went down. Grimacing and clutching her knee, sure a bruise would blossom by morning, she grabbed the boots—and dropped the bundle of clothing.

Reaching on the run, she grabbed his clothes, except for one stubborn sock that escaped her grasp. Trying to catch it as it fell, she slipped again. This time, she caught herself, but the tap dance took its toll. Could a hip get dislocated? It sure didn't feel right.

She limped through the bedroom as fast as she could, but Molly was already in the downstairs hall-way. Startled, Jess raced past her and up the stairs, stumbling when Cade's boxers escaped from the bundle and draped themselves over the steps like an expiring damsel. Sweeping them back into her arms, she looked down at Molly, opening and closing her mouth like a starving goldfish, struggling to find something to say.

"Did everything go okay while we were gone?" Molly asked.

Jess couldn't help it. She had to smother a laugh. Cade, still in the bedroom, didn't, and she prayed her stepmother hadn't heard him. She longed to throw a boot at the door but smiled brightly down the stairs instead.

"Oh yeah." She tucked Cade's clothes behind her back as her father stepped up beside Molly. "Everything went fine."

Still smiling, she bent to pick up the boxers—and dropped a boot.

Thumpity thump, down the stairs it fell, end over end over end. Eternity seemed to stretch on and on before it landed at her father's feet.

Her dad picked up the boot.

"Well, hey. This is nice. It's a Tony Lama, right?"

Chapter 44

HECK TURNED CADE'S BOOT OVER AND OVER IN HIS HANDS, examining the stitchery while Jess, still frozen at the top of the stairs, cursed her dad's passion for fine leatherwork and tried to roll Cade's clothes into a bundle behind her back.

"I didn't know you had these, hon." Propping one foot on the bottom step, her dad set the boot beside it. "Dang, honey. I think this'd fit me." He chuckled fondly. "You always did have big feet, even when you were just a snippet."

Jess glanced down at her stepmother and realized Molly knew exactly what was going on. The woman was turning from red to purple as she struggled to hold in her laughter. Clawing through her mind for a distraction, Jess found one.

She executed her best spoiled-princess hair flip and scowled. "My feet aren't big, Daddy! And I'm not a *snippet*." Blessing her dad's inexhaustible capacity for tactlessness, she did her best to channel outrage. "Get with the program, Daddy. Women are not *objects*. It's the twenty-first century."

Heck held up Cade's boot. "Sorry, hon. You want your boot back?"

"I don't care about any old boot. I care about being treated like a human being."

Before she was half done answering, he tossed the boot up the stairs. Startled, she reached out to catch it and dropped Cade's clothes. The bundle unrolled to reveal each item in turn—first Cade's jeans, then a sock, and then the boxer shorts. Cade was a serious guy, but his boxers were another story. This particular pair was red, with little white hearts all over them.

The final sock was kind of an anticlimax.

"Oh, Jess!" Molly shook her head, looking grave. "Are you doing Cade's laundry again? That man ought to take care of that himself." She gave Jess a wink. "Get with the program, hon. It's the twenty-first century." She let out a long, theatrical sigh. "Men can do their own laundry. Right, Heck?"

Heck nodded. "Sure. I mean, I guess so." He gave her a sheepish grin. "Never tried."

"Yeah, because *I* always did it," Jess said.

She frantically gathered Cade's clothes, but her panic had given way to laughter. Her folks loved Cade, and she suspected they'd cheer if they found him naked in her bedroom. Still, it seemed disrespectful to parade your afternoon delight in front of your parents.

Slamming the bedroom door behind her, she closed her eyes and let Cade's clothes fall at her feet while she gained control of her laughter.

"I think I love my stepmother," she gasped. "I couldn't ask for a better friend."

Cade sat naked on her bed with his cowboy hat clamped strategically over his unmentionables. "Thought you'd never get here."

The dog, looking equally aggrieved, sat at his feet. Jess's laughter rose again, and she doubled over, giggling helplessly as he set aside the hat and grabbed for his clothes.

Sitting on the bed, she watched him dress, laughter bubbling like a creek after an all-day rain. But her heart was turning toward more serious thoughts, moved by the reverse striptease of a handsome cowboy who made love well up in her heart and overflow, warming her to her toes.

———

Cade managed to smother Jess's giggles with a couple of well-placed kisses before she headed downstairs. He waited a while so they wouldn't emerge from the bedroom together. Then he and Boogy took the back stairs, Boogy moping outside the back door while Cade entered from the hall.

Molly, still in a rollicking mood, pointed at him and burst into a fit of giggles. He looked down at his clothes, wondering if he'd left his fly open or buttoned his shirt crooked.

"You're fine," Molly said. "It's just so funny when you kids try to act all innocent." She lowered her voice. "For heaven's sake, Cade, we left you two alone on purpose! Just tell me it went well."

He gave her a quick thumbs-up.

"Best news ever." Standing on tiptoe, she pulled his face down and gave him a smack on the cheek. "Although I thought you were taking Jess to your house."

"Yeah, well." He felt his face go hot. "We never made it."

As the two of them walked into the kitchen, he did his best to act casual, clapping Heck on the back and shaking his hand in greeting.

"How was Shady Acres?"

"Great," Heck said.

Cade strained to hear any false note in his neighbor's hearty tone, but Heck sounded like himself. The man wasn't much of an actor, so apparently Shady Acres truly was "great."

"It was a little rough at first. Got myself into a poker game at the clubhouse and lost a bundle to those vagina men."

Cade shot Jess a questioning look.

She giggled. "It's Viagra, Dad."

"Whatever. They're sharp, even with those four-hour erections. Thought we might've lost our down payment 'til Molls joined the game. Tell 'em what happened, Molly."

"I won it all back, plus a little more." Molly sat down and reached for the bread basket, constructing a sandwich as if there was nothing remarkable about a schoolteacher trouncing a bunch of men at poker. "I had to punish those guys for having the nerve to take Heck's money."

"You're a card sharp?" The idea of Molly, with her fluffy hair and pink tracksuit, raking in the pot at an all men's poker game made Cade smile.

"I used to play with one of the boys I tutored—a third grader on the autism spectrum." She squirted mustard on her bread in looping curlicues. "It turned out he didn't need my help with math skills or probability." Spearing slices of ham from the plate of cold cuts, she laid them across the mustard like a Subway sandwich artist. "He ended up tutoring me."

"I think she counts cards," Heck said proudly.

"Are you allowed to go back?" Jess asked.

"Oh sure," Heck said. "They want a rematch. Couldn't believe a woman could soak 'em like that, so they're convinced it was a fluke."

Molly chuckled. "Those who question history are doomed to repeat it."

The phone rang, and Jess raced to the hallway. She was gone for a few minutes, and when she returned, her face was pale.

"Who was that?" Cade asked.

She gave him a startled look. "Oh, nothing. Nobody." Scanning the table, she lunged for the glasses of ice water Molly had set at her place and Heck's.

"Hey," Heck said. "That was mine."

"It was just *water*, though." Jess speed walked back to the table and grabbed her own glass, shooting Cade a wide-eyed glare. "That's not special enough. It's a big day, right? We need to drink something *fancy*!"

Her chirpy tone was as convincing as her phony smile.

"I'm not sure what you're celebrating, hon." Molly gave her an impish grin. "Would you like to tell us about it? You seem awfully happy."

Heck looked puzzled. "We don't do fancy. Gimme my water back."

Jess ignored him, bending over to rummage in the refrigerator. Cade stared a moment before he remembered his manners.

"Ah, you need some help?"

"I'm fine." She emerged, waving a green bottle in the air. "I found just the thing!" Bustling to the counter, she fiddled with the bottle for a bit, then put it between her legs and grimaced as she tugged desperately at a plastic cork.

"Jess, be..."

There was a loud pop, and the cork shot across the room, hitting the ceiling hard enough to send a small shower of plaster cascading to the floor.

"Champagne!" Ignoring the damage, Jess waved the bottle. "We're celebrating, right? Those folks made an offer on the ranch, and you two found a place you like!" Setting the bottle on the table, she raced to a cupboard and pulled out wine glasses. "Too bad we don't have champagne flutes. Then we'd be *really* fancy!"

Heck picked up the bottle. "This isn't champagne. It's sparkling grape juice Molly bought for New Year's last year." Turning the bottle in his hands, he squinted at the label. "Matter of fact, she mighta bought it the year before or the year before that. It's expired. Might actually *be* champagne now." He sniffed the neck of the bottle. "Or vinegar."

"Daddy." Jess started to wind up her princess act, then realized she shouldn't make her family drink expired grape juice. "How 'bout soda? Come on, who likes Mountain Dew?"

Molly and Heck glanced at Cade, who gave them a shrug, but he wasn't as puzzled as he tried to look. He suspected the phone call had been from the water authority, warning Jess about the death dirt lurking in the well. In all the excitement and nakedness, he'd forgotten all about it.

Cade followed Jess out to the garage, where a spare fridge held water, soda, and beer. "Was that the well inspector?"

"It sure was." Jess glanced at the door and dropped her voice to a whisper. "He said the water has *E. coli* in it and lots of other stuff."

"Did he say what it's from?"

"He said maybe an animal got in there and drowned, but I don't see how. Daddy's got bricks on the well box so nothing can get in." She gave him a wide-eyed, innocent look. "Maybe whoever did all that other stuff did something to the well."

Cade rolled his eyes. "Yeah, maybe."

She didn't seem to catch his sarcasm, so he grabbed two Cokes while she snagged a Mountain Dew for her father and one for herself.

"You have to tell your folks," Cade said.

"I know. I just wanted lunch to be nice, with no bad news, you know? Dad seems so happy." She sighed. "I can't believe something else went wrong. We'll never get this place sold."

They really needed to have a talk. She needed to see how important it was for her dad to get the ranch sold— even if it went to the Swammetts. Cade didn't much like them for neighbors, but maybe that would be the push he needed to get in touch with John Baker, see if that job was still a possibility. Maybe Jess could go with him. Maybe the hotel chain she worked for had a location nearby.

Maybe turtles had wings.

"I'll check the well after lunch, okay?" Cade turned at the door. "Whatever it is, we'll get it fixed."

"Thanks," she said. "I'll help."

Yeah, I'll bet. They'd have a chance to talk—really talk—and straighten everything out. Surely, she'd admit to whatever she'd done to the well and all the other pranks. Surely, she'd stop playing this game.

Because it *had* to be her, and it bothered him that she wouldn't admit it. Was this part of what she'd learned in the city—how to lie without blinking? Jess had always been smart, and she'd always been mischievous, but she'd been open and honest, too.

"Cade?" She looked puzzled.

He realized he'd been staring at her for what, five minutes? Without saying a word?

"Nothing." He smiled. "You're just pretty."

She smiled back, but his heart sank. Now *he* was being dishonest.

This couldn't go on. They were going to have to have that talk, and the sooner, the better.

Chapter 45

THE WELL WAS HOUSED IN A WOODEN BOX HECK HAD fashioned out of scrap lumber. As Jess began removing the concrete blocks stacked on the lid to keep out animals, she swatted an eager Boogy out of the way.

"He smells something," she said. "Guess dogs like death dirt."

Cade pitched in, removing one block, then another. "So some critter took these off, unlocked the top, climbed inside, and drowned itself?" He gave her a teasing grin. "Must have been a bear. A really smart one." He put on a goofy Yogi Bear voice. "Smmmarter than the average bear!"

Jess wasn't amused. "Obviously, somebody's messing with us. Somebody human." She glanced up at her parents' bedroom window, which overlooked the well. "Nobody could have snuck in and done this at night, though. Molly's a really light sleeper. I've caught her way after midnight, roaming around the house humming to herself. I think she likes late-night snacks."

Removing the last block, they lifted the heavy lid and peered down the long vertical tube of the wellhead. Boogy propped himself up on the side, sniffing for a good whiff of death dirt, then leaned inside and snatched a torn cardboard box.

"Oh no, you don't!"

The dog raced away with Cade in pursuit. By the time

he snatched Boogy's trophy from his drooling jaws, both were out of breath. Staring in disbelief for a moment, Cade burst into laughter. "Gorton's frozen fish sticks."

"*What?*"

He handed her the box while Boogy followed it with his eyes. "It's a fish sticks carton." Bending down, he sniffed at the well opening, then jumped backward, rubbing his nose. "Never liked those things, and I like 'em a lot less now."

Jess didn't particularly want to reacquaint herself with the death dirt smell, but she figured she ought to check. One hesitant sniff was enough. "I didn't notice it smelled fishy, but now that I know…"

Cade leaned over the box. "Ugh. Here's a stick that didn't make it in." Without thinking, he picked up the breaded morsel and tossed it over his shoulder. Boogy, eyes alight, snatched it out of the air and swallowed it in one smooth motion.

"Oh, Boogy." Jess felt a little green. "That's bound to come back up."

They worked together to replace the heavy lid without losing any fingers or crushing Boogy's nose, then collapsed together against the well house.

The two of them sat side by side among the wildflowers, staring at the sky. They'd always been comfortable sharing silence, but Jess didn't feel comfortable today. Cade kept glancing at her, taking a breath as if he was about to speak, then looking away.

"*What?*" she finally said.

He sighed. "I just need you to tell the truth, Jess. Nobody else could have done this."

He was acting like some stern schoolteacher, like

she was a naughty child telling a lie. Jess raked her hair back from her face, clenched it into a tight ponytail, and gave it a tug.

"I told you, it had to be Amber Lynn."

He laughed. "She's just a little slip of a thing. She could never move those blocks."

"Oh, I see." She stood and hoisted a brick onto the well house. "And I'm an elephant."

"You're a goddess." He grinned, as if everything was just fine between them. "And a pretty tough one."

There'd been a time when she'd have taken that as a compliment, but he was still accusing her of lying. Besides, the "little slip of a thing" comment stung.

"I doubt Amber Lynn knows what a well looks like," he said, rising to help her replace the blocks. "She probably thinks faucets are magic. Besides, how did she get Hermy in the gazebo? She's pretty helpless when it comes to *ranch reality*."

A tear trailed down Jess's cheek, because dammit, she always cried when she was mad. She reached up to bat it away, but he beat her to it, running the back of one finger down her cheek.

"Hey, it's nothing to cry about." The smile faded, the gray eyes turning grave. "Just *trust* me, Jess. Tell me."

"I *did* trust you." Crying probably made him think she was sad or sorry, but that made her madder, which made her cry harder. "I made up my mind to believe you about Amber Lynn, because that's how we are. We don't lie to each other. We don't cheat."

"Exactly." He smiled gently, as if encouraging a fractious child. "So don't you have something to say?"

She kicked viciously at a rock, which skittered across

the hard-packed dirt and hit the house with a satisfying *thunk*. "Why bother? You wouldn't believe me anyway. You're the one who decides what *reality* is, and I don't have a say."

Striding into the house, she slammed the door.

They were done.

———⌇⌇⌇———

Cade stared at the door that had just slammed behind Jess.

What the hell had just happened? He felt like he'd ridden a roller coaster to nirvana, one that chugged up, up, up to the heavens and then slammed him back down to earth. It happened over and over, and he was tired. Jess just wasn't ready for a relationship, and maybe she never would be. He knew she'd been behind the pranks, and it was ridiculous that she wouldn't admit it.

He needed to get off the roller coaster and stand on solid ground. Go back to his original plan, and concentrate on his business.

Patting his thigh, he gave Boogy a soft whistle and headed for his truck. As always, the dog rode shotgun, grinning and panting. Boogy loved truck riding. Maybe Cade should be more like that, taking pleasure in simple things.

Stopping at the rusty mailbox at the foot of his driveway, he pulled out several days' worth of junk mail. Flipping through the stack, he tossed advertising circulars and mail order catalogs on the floor.

"Junk, junk, junk, bill, junk, junk—whoa."

He stared down at the last envelope. It bore a graphic logo in the corner that represented a running horse with a few simple lines. The envelope was heavy stock, and when he opened it, it contained a letter on equally classy paper.

The letter was from John Baker.

No doubt the trainer was rescinding the offer, wondering why Cade hadn't even had the decency to write back. Scanning the note, he braced himself for disappointment—but wait.

Wait.

He started at the beginning again, and a mounting excitement dizzied him as he stared through the windshield.

It wasn't a kiss-off letter. It was another offer, higher than the last, along with a brochure showing the Baker Equine Center. It was a ranch straight out of Cade's dreams, with heated stalls, indoor arenas, and a tack room piled floor-to-ceiling with high-end saddles, bits, and bridles.

Letting the letter fall to his lap, Cade shifted gears in his brain, from loving Jess to dedicating himself to his work. Baker was famous for overworking his clinicians, and eighteen-hour days in the stables and the round pen would occupy his mind and heal his heart. He'd lose himself in one horse after another, and maybe the brand Jess had burned on his heart would start to heal.

It would never go away altogether, but it would hurt a whole lot less.

Chapter 46

HECK SQUINTED DOWN AT TWO ALMOST IDENTICAL PLUMBING fittings and wished he'd had the sense to bring the broken parts from his irrigator with him to the hardware store. A lifetime of penny-pinching had made it hard for him to spend an extra buck if he didn't have to, but he'd have to buy both and return one.

Dad blast it, he'd spend any amount to get Molly flowers, and while plumbing fittings were hardly romantic, keeping the ranch going was part of taking care of her. He needed to get the place sold, get his wife the home she wanted.

Too bad that wasn't the same as what *he* wanted. He'd told Molls what she needed to hear, but when that fat man had ogled the Diamond Jack like he already owned it, Heck had felt a pang of regret so sharp, he'd thought his heart was acting up again.

But Jess was up and down with poor Cade, and if she couldn't commit to a man, he doubted she'd stick with cattle. A ranch would break her heart a hundred times, with droughts that starved the livestock and hail that wrecked the crops, summer heat that seared the soil bone-dry and winter snows that made the cows pile up at the fence lines and freeze. He wasn't sure she could handle it, and nobody could handle it alone.

Lost in his thoughts, he almost didn't notice Riley James peering into his basket.

"You got a Zimmatic irrigator on your place?" she asked.

He shook his head. "Reinke."

"That's what I thought. You won't be needing this, then." Plucking one of the fittings from his basket, she returned it to the shelf and gave him a lopsided grin. "You're welcome."

"Thanks."

Riley Sue James was a peculiar little thing, but she was smart. Ethereal as a ballerina in holey jeans and a tank top, with tattoos all down one arm, she looked as out of place in the hardware store as the Sugar Plum Fairy at a Superfund site, but she could fix just about anything.

"How the bejesus do you know this stuff?" he asked. "There must be a thousand little pieces here, and I swear, you know where every one of 'em goes."

"It's my job." She shrugged. "Ed taught me a lot, plus he works here in the afternoons so I can take on outside projects around town. That's how I learn. I like home renovation jobs best, but I've fixed some irrigation rigs."

He stepped up to the counter. "What do I owe you?"

"Two dollars and eleven cents."

Rummaging in his pocket, he found three crumpled bills. Riley rang up the sale, then flipped back a lock of silver-blond hair and cocked a hip against the counter.

"Heard you're selling the place."

"Couple from California made an offer." He sighed. "You'll probably have to help them with their irrigators, too, and just about everything else. They're fancified folks, worked in the media business. Don't know a cow's ass from a combine."

"Doesn't that bother you?"

"Sure it does, but life goes on." He shoved his hands in his pockets to keep them from shaking. "My health isn't what it used to be, and Molly can't run the place."

"What about your son?"

"Griff never took to ranching. He's raiding terrorist training camps in Afghanistan, last I heard."

Keeping his hands in his pockets, Heck clenched both fists hard. His brain felt like a terrorist camp lately, with rebel memories ambushing him from every side. Time to change the subject.

"Hey, you hear about our porch falling down?"

"Yeah, Cade called me, and Jess stopped in earlier. I told her I'd take the job."

"Good."

He'd heard the rumors—that Riley had been involved with drugs, booze, even sex addiction—but what mattered was she'd gotten over it and had a fine reputation for home repairs. Heck believed everyone deserved a second chance.

Danged if he wouldn't like a few himself. Especially with Griff.

"I'll be out to take a look at it," Riley said. "How did it fall down?"

Heck kicked at the floor, scuffing the old pine boards. "We're pretty sure somebody pulled out a screw here, loosened a bolt there."

"Why would anybody do that?"

"Trying to stop the sale, I guess."

She wrinkled her forehead, thinking. "You think it was Cade, trying to keep Jess around?"

"More likely Jess herself. She's not ready to let go."

"Jess isn't like that." Riley sounded awfully sure. "If

she wants something, she comes right out and takes it."
Another cockeyed grin made her look surprisingly girlish. "I mean that in a good way."

He smiled back, warming to the girl. "Seems to me
you're the same kind."

"I guess I am. Wasn't always, though." She turned
away, fooling with the blank key forms that hung on
a turntable next to an ancient duplicating lathe, then
glanced up with a speculative light in her eyes. "You
must be real proud of Griff," she said.

"Sure."

Actually, it hadn't occurred to Heck to be much more
than mad at the boy. Griff was the reason Heck was in
this mess; if he hadn't run off, he'd be home taking care
of the ranch, and Heck wouldn't have to sell. "I'm proud
of him. But I miss him."

"Me, too."

"You?" Heck regretted his tone as soon as the words
left his mouth. "I mean, I didn't know you even knew
him. He never mentioned…aw, shoot. I'm messing
this up. I just didn't know you two were friends." He
flushed. "There's a lot I don't know about Griff."

"It's okay," Riley said. "I didn't know him that well.
Just met him at some parties out at the quarry."

Heck knew about those parties. Young folks gathered there to drink and probably do drugs. The sheriff
rounded them up once in a while, called their parents.
Griff had never come home in a patrol car, so Heck had
convinced himself his son was a straight arrow.

So much for that.

"He used to talk about how he wanted to go overseas,
see the world. Save it, I guess." A faint blush colored her

cheeks. "I thought he was brave, going after his dreams like that. This town's so small, and he never lived anywhere else." Shaking open a small bag, she dropped the parts inside. "Sounds corny, I guess, but most people don't have the guts."

"Guess I never gave much thought to what Griff wanted." He looked down at his boots, embarrassed. "Always thought ranching offered a big enough world for any man—the cows, the clouds, the canyons..." He turned away. "I'll let him know you asked about him when I write him."

"Oh, that's okay." Her voice, low and husky, broke like a teenage boy's. "I found an app where you can text soldiers overseas, so he knows."

She was blushing again, and Heck wondered if Griff had ever noticed how pretty she was. If you could get past those tattoos, there was a strange beauty underneath and an unexpected sweetness.

"I think he's a good guy, that's all," she said. "I figured a soldier might need a note now and then." She turned back to the key machine, touching the blanks absently. "It's stupid, I guess. I barely knew him. Lots of times, he doesn't message me back."

"It's not stupid," Heck said. "It's kind of you. But he doesn't write back to me, either, so don't take it personal. You keep writing him, or typing him, or whatever it is you kids do." He huffed out a little laugh. "Maybe you can talk him into coming home sometime."

"I doubt it. I think he's gone for good." She caught herself, too late, and waved her hands as if she could erase the words in the air before they reached his ears.

"Not necessarily, though! I'm sure he'll come back. Yeah, of course. You're his dad, and he loves you."

"Did he say that?"

Heck knew the question made him sound pitiful. But although he'd thought he was still mad at Griff, it turned out he was hungry for every word the boy might have said.

"He never said it right out, but that doesn't mean sh—anything." She let out an awkward laugh that was a little too loud. "He's not exactly the emotional type, you know? And hey, if you move, he might be more likely to come. He never liked the cow thing much."

This time, she looked like she wanted to swallow the words, but Heck felt like she'd thrown him a life-line, because she was right. Griff hadn't liked "the cow thing," and he was probably afraid his dad would start pressuring him to take over as soon as he came home. If there was no ranch—well, maybe things would go better. It felt like a consolation prize, but it was the only light in a dark sky. He'd take it and be grateful.

"You've got a point." He knew he should just shut up, but it had been a long time since he had a line to Griff, and he was reluctant to let it go. "The Diamond Jack's been home all my life, but now, that's wherever the kids are." He shook his head slowly as the truth rose in his mind, so obvious, yet somehow hidden for so long. "All my life, I've been focused on the land, but it's family that matters. Put me in a trailer on the backside of town, and I'll be fine, long as my family's there."

He realized, a little too late, he was talking to a woman who didn't have a family of her own. But she smiled, dismissing his embarrassment.

"I know just how you feel," she said. "Me and Ed, we're family now. He's like the dad I never had."

"Well, that's mighty nice for him," Heck said. "He and Ruthie always wanted that, and she'd be pleased. You take care, now."

"You, too. And hey, I could show you that app if you want. I bet Griff would be glad to hear from you."

Heck could only nod in answer. The bells on the door jangled as he closed it behind him, and he hustled down the sidewalk, praying the ache in his throat wouldn't explode with some sort of embarrassing outburst before he made it to his truck.

Chapter 47

JESS WALKED INTO THE BANK WITH A KNOT IN HER STOMACH, a catch in her throat, and a throbbing ache behind her right eye. She'd promised to move some money from the ranch account into her dad's personal savings, in case he and Molly decided to put a down payment on a place at Shady Acres.

She didn't see why Heck couldn't do it himself, since he'd insisted on driving her into town despite the fact that she was over her head injury, but Molly had wanted her to go to the bank while her dad shopped at the hardware store. It wasn't like Molly asked for a lot of favors, so Jess figured she'd put on her big-girl jeans and go.

She'd rather put on one of the big-girl business suits that hung in her closet in Denver before taking a chance on running into Amber Lynn Lyle. Jess's suits were her armor, a costume that let her pose as somebody other than her ordinary, countrified self. But she hadn't figured on needing them this trip, so they hung neatly in the closet back in her apartment, awaiting her return.

Looking down at her holey jeans and loose cotton shirt, she felt the knot in her stomach turn into a whole darn macramé project. Amber Lynn, no doubt, would be dressed like a cross between a high-priced lawyer and a streetwalker.

She glanced up at the bank's lighted sign as she walked inside.

Wynott Bank and Trust.

Hey, maybe she could buy herself some trust. A big dose of it, as a present for Cade. He didn't seem to have enough of it, for some reason.

Shifting from one foot to the other, she glanced around, hoping to avoid Amber Lynn. Her nemesis was nowhere in sight. When the single teller on duty finished with a grizzled rancher, she motioned for Jess to step up.

"I need to move some money around." Jess fished for her ID in her purse while she rattled off the ranch's account number.

"I'll take care of this," said a familiar voice.

Jess looked up from her purse and felt the blood drain from her face.

"Hi," said Amber Lynn. "Welcome to Wynott Bank and Trust."

She was dressed in a black pencil skirt that was a little too short for business wear, but Jess doubted the men who frequented the bank minded that one bit. A stylish matching jacket was pinched at the waist, emphasizing Amber Lynn's hourglass figure, and a pair of four-inch heels completed the outfit. She looked put together and poised, if a little too sexy for serious work. Jess felt like a Hereford cow standing next to a Thoroughbred.

"Sorry." She started to turn around. "Changed my mind."

"Oh no. Please, Jess, don't go. This is my *job*. My dad'll be mad if you leave just because it's me. Besides, I've changed. Just ask Molly."

"Molly?"

"Sure. She's helping me turn over a new leaf."

Jess felt the betrayal like a punch to her solar plexus.

Everyone was taking Amber Lynn's side—first Cade, now her stepmother.

"I confess, okay? I set this up because you and I need to talk," Amber Lynn said. "Molly helped, because she knows there are things I need to say."

Jess groaned. Amber Lynn hadn't just duped Molly into taking her side; she'd schemed to force Jess into a confrontation. Now she'd dole out some insincere apology, declare her intention to remarry Cade, and make Jess look ungracious for slapping her across the face—which Jess most sincerely wanted to do.

"Come into my office." Lifting a hinged section of countertop, Amber Lynn headed down a white-walled hall, gesturing for Jess to follow. Jess started to balk, then noticed the bank had filled up. It was lunchtime, and six people now stood in line. Six pairs of eyes were watching Jess's every move, while six sets of ears listened in on the conversation. Every word she said would be all over town in five minutes.

She followed Amber Lynn down a narrow hallway to a plain, undecorated office. Cade's ex fluttered around, brushing invisible crumbs from the seat of a plastic chair, gesturing for Jess to sit down.

Jess sat but slowly, her mind racing with escape plans.

Knock her down and make a run for it. Holler "Fire!" and skedaddle. Fake illness. Better yet, just slap her smug mug and run like hell.

Unfortunately, Amber Lynn's father wielded a lot of power in Wynott. Jess needed to keep this meeting on a professional footing.

"Your stepmom's nice." Standing behind a faux

wood desk, Amber Lynn twisted one toe into the deep pile carpet, looking sheepish. "She's letting me rent her trailer until I find a place of my own."

Jess nodded, pressing her lips into something like a smile.

"I know you don't want to talk to me, but we really need to."

"Right."

Jess loaded the word with sarcasm, but Amber Lynn didn't seem to notice. In fact, Cade's ex looked a little pale herself. Maybe she knew Jess was going to find a way to prove she'd done all that mischief at the Diamond Jack. Maybe she knew Jess was going to somehow force a confession out of her, right then and there. Jess would prove her innocence to Cade and everyone else—and her father would know, beyond a shadow of a doubt, that she cared about the ranch as much as he did.

With a subtle John Wayne–style tug at her belt, she lowered herself into the chair and faced Amber Lynn Lyle.

———

Leading Redline from the barn, Cade glanced around at the improvements he'd made to Walker Ranch. He hadn't had much time, but the place looked good. As he stroked the mare's pretty copper-penny coat, he tried to let the joy of a sun-drenched bluebird day sink into his soul.

He almost succeeded.

Redline, for sure, was getting a new life, a happy, civilized horse life with warm stalls, veterinary care, and a job to do. She had a lot to learn, but Cade had even more. He'd be working for a boss, something he hadn't done in years. He'd be moving to California, where the climate was completely different. But the biggest change would happen in his heart, because he was going to learn to live without Jess Bailey.

"We're getting there, girl," he muttered to the horse. "It'll be all right."

Redline shuddered as he adjusted the saddle and fastened the girth, but she'd learned to stand firm, her feet planted solidly on the hard-packed ground.

For Cade, that was more of a challenge. It seemed like the earth under his feet had been spinning and shifting for months, changing with Jess's every mood.

Fortunately, that all stopped when he was working. In the barn and the round ring, he knew who he was and what he needed to do. Consistency and calm were the keys to good training; it was a regimen that would do him good.

Baker had wanted him ASAP, but Cade had needed to tie up some loose ends. He'd had two roping horses to finish for neighboring ranchers, and he'd had to find homes for Heck's charity cases. Two of them, geldings, would go to a local woman who ran a horse rescue, turning older horses into dependable mounts for children. She'd finish their training and sell them to families who'd take good care of them.

As for Redline, she'd be going back to Heck, broken to saddle at no charge as a thank-you to a man who'd been more father than neighbor for the past few years. Saying goodbye to Heck would be his last task and the hardest—unless Jess decided to speak to him long enough to say goodbye.

He doubted she would. She hadn't called, hadn't answered any of his messages, hadn't even texted him. He wasn't surprised—not anymore.

Settling a hackamore over the horse's head, he glanced over at the house. It didn't look nearly as disreputable as it had when his dad died. Cade had cleaned it up, painted the siding, and repaired what was broken as best he could. It was a respectable ranch house now and a fine place to live—for somebody else. For him, no amount of paint and polish could exorcise the ghosts peering out every window and lurking behind every door. Some of them looked like his mother. Others looked like his dad. But these days, most of them looked like Jess, and he was tired of being haunted.

Setting a firm hand on the saddle, he slipped one foot into the stirrup and tested the horse's response to his weight. She stood quietly, one ear flicking back then forward again.

She was ready.

Swinging his leg up and over, he settled in, speaking softly all the while, then clicked his tongue and nudged the horse into a slow walk around the ring. One circuit, two, then three. A little more speed, a little more control each time.

She was ready to go forward, trotting into her new life.

Hopefully he was, too.

Chapter 48

JESS SAT ACROSS FROM AMBER LYNN, WATCHING HER shuffle papers almost as if she knew what she was doing.

"Okay." The woman gave Jess a perky grin. "First, I want you to know we're on the same side now. I mean, I work *here*, at Your Friendly Neighborhood Small-Town Bank!"

The way she repeated the slogan told Jess Jasper Lyle must have drummed it into her head every morning at breakfast.

"Here we go." Amber Lynn fooled with her computer, thrusting out her chin and squinting at the screen before popping back up with her perfect posture intact. "We can move that money for you if you just give me your ID."

Jess fished out her driver's license, stifling the urge to whip it back when Amber Lynn pinched it between her shiny, Barbie-pink nails.

"I met that Mr. Swammett that's going to buy your ranch." Amber Lynn propped Jess's license on her computer. Squinting, she punched the keys with two fingers. "He's a big deal in Hollywood, did you know? He produces 'Redneck Wives.'"

It figured. Jess hated that show. The so-called rednecks were supposed to be cowboys but were actually a bunch of horse-challenged gym rats looking for their big break into show business.

"I was pretty excited to meet him," Amber Lynn continued. "I'd have asked about trying out for the show,
but my dad needs me here at the bank."

"Not to mention that you're not a wife anymore, and
Cade's not a redneck."

Jess hadn't meant to get combative. Amber Lynn
would be more likely to confess if she believed they
were friends.

Amber Lynn hesitantly tapped a few more keys.
"Sorry," she said. "This is a new position for me. I'm
really just a trainee."

Of course it was new. Amber Lynn had never held
a job in her life, so her previous "positions" had come
straight from the *Kama Sutra*. Jess smiled at the thought,
then scolded herself. Being catty was Amber Lynn's
job. Jess was supposed to be the nice one.

"There." Cade's ex flicked a couple more keys and
sat back. "Done. Now here's what I wanted to tell you.
Take a look at this office." She swept her arm around the
room as if it was a corner suite in Trump Tower rather
than a dumpy, drywalled cube in a small-town bank. "I
owe this all to Cade."

"Really."

"Uh-huh." Amber nodded hard, like a child. "I never
thought I was good for much more than looking pretty,
you know? But Cade said I was smart and good at getting people to do what I want."

Jess knew. "Yeah, you manipulate folks really well."

"Thank you." The woman preened. If Cade thought
this woman was smart, he must think women kept their
brains in their boobs.

Argh. Be nice. Think nice thoughts.

"So my dad had a job he wanted to offer Cade," Amber Lynn continued. "But can you see him behind a desk, under these lights all day?" She tinkled out a lovely little laugh. "He'd lose his mind."

"If he hasn't already." Jess frowned. "I don't want to talk about Cade, okay?"

"Okay. I just wanted to tell you how he believed in me, you know?"

Jess huffed out a bitter laugh. "I'm glad he believed in someone."

"Oh. Molly said you were having trust issues." Amber Lynn gave Jess a sympathetic moue. "I'm sorry about all the stuff that's happened at the ranch, and *double*-dog sorry he thinks it was you."

Jess blinked hard, forcing back tears. How could Cade have shared their intimate secrets with Little Miss Slip-of-a-Thing when she was responsible for the whole mess? It was obvious whose side he was on.

To heck with getting Amber Lynn to confess. Jess just wanted out.

She rose. "Sorry, I have things to do."

Leaping from her chair, Amber Lynn slammed the door closed and stood with her back against it, bosom heaving. She lifted a finger and pointed it at Jess's face.

"I'm not letting you out of here until you listen to me, Jess Bailey."

"Oh, stop. You can have him, okay?" *Damn this woman, anyway. And double damn Cade Walker.* The tears were on the verge now, and the last thing Jess wanted to do was cry in front of Amber Lynn. "Just treat him better this time, okay? He deserves a good life."

"I can't give him that. That's what I'm trying to tell

you. Jess, you *have* to forgive him." Amber spread her arms across the door, barring the way like the heroine in a bad melodrama. "That man has loved you all his life. *All* his life. And that includes his wedding day, our honeymoon, and every day of our marriage."

Jess started to speak, but then Amber Lynn's words sunk in, and all that came out was a stunned croak.

She finally managed to push words past her aching throat. "Did he call out my name or what?"

"Not during sex. But he muttered it in his sleep all the time." Amber Lynn's eyes filled with tears. "Do you know what it's like, knowing your husband misses another woman like that? Knowing he dreams of someone else every night, while you're right there beside him?"

"No." Jess was having trouble keeping up with the conversation. "I mean, I don't know. I—I'm sorry?"

"Are you? Because you *should* be. Not for me, but for *him*. The man is messed up, Jess. You've gone and wrecked him for any other woman, and now you're making it worse, just because he thinks you did some mischief. What was it, something with a calf? A porch swing?" She huffed out a sarcastic little laugh. "Who *cares*? You did a lot worse to that man than poison his water. You ruined his life when you left him the first time, and now you're doing it again."

"He was hardly ruined," Jess said. "He married you within the year."

"He was *drunk*. And besides, he didn't have much choice."

Jess cringed, remembering the mythical baby.

"That man didn't know which way was up." She

met Jess's eyes with a challenge in her own. "Think about the Cade you knew. Would he have allowed any woman to do the things I did? Spend all his money, cheat on him?"

Jess bit her lip and stared at the floor.

"No," Amber Lynn said. "He wouldn't have. Not before you left. But when you went away, you *broke* him. He just didn't care anymore."

"Amber Lynn, just *stop*. My life is none of your business, and I'm sure your dad wouldn't approve of this conversation on bank time."

"My dad won't care." Amber Lynn raised her chin. "He *values* me now, as an employee. I'm the first person here and the last to leave, and when I'm home, I'm studying. I've learned so fast, Mary Lou's training me to do mortgages already. But you know what? I'd give it all up if that would make things right between you and Cade." Her lower lip wobbled, and it took her a moment to master it. "I care about him. You might find that hard to believe, and I guess he would, too, but it's *true*. He deserves happiness, and I'm not letting you out of here until you understand Cade loves you, and you belong together. I'm not doing this for me. I'm doing it for *him*."

Jess decided Amber Lynn deserved a job with Mr. Swammett. She sure had the chops for it—because this was all an act. It had to be. The woman had never cared about anyone but herself.

Still, she was awfully riled up, so maybe Jess could get her confession now.

"It's not what he did," she said. "It's what *you* did."

"Me?" Amber Lynn mimed shock. "I'm sure he

explained I was just staying with him to escape my abusive boyfriend."

"Right." Jess had had enough. "The one who gave you that magical disappearing black eye."

"Oh my gosh, you figured that out?" Amber Lynn collapsed against the door, her eyes wide with admiration. "I always knew you were smart."

"I figured out more than that," Jess said. "I figured out you were behind the fish sticks."

"Fish sticks?" Amber Lynn cocked her head and bit her lip as if deep in thought.

Geez, what an actress.

"Oh. I remember now. Cade doesn't like them. But I didn't have anything else in the house."

Jess felt a surge of triumph. "So you admit it."

"Yes." Amber Lynn's jaw jutted rebelliously. "But I never told him I was any good at cooking. And Daddy used to make them for me all the time. I didn't know they were kid food."

"What are you talking about?" Jess's head felt like a top was spinning inside, reeling around and crashing into her skull before careening off in another direction and slamming into the other side.

"Fish sticks," Amber Lynn said. "It's like the Spanish Inquisition or something. I mean, that meal was over a *year* ago. And he ate it all right. Even without any tartar sauce."

"I'm not talking about a meal, and you know it," Jess said. "I'm talking about the ones you put in the well."

"The well?"

"Yes, the *well*. Someone could have gotten sick." She rubbed her nose, still dealing with the remnants of the death dirt smell. "But of course Cade refuses to believe *you* could *possibly* do such a thing, because you're so *little* and *helpless*. So it would go a long way if you'd admit to him that you did it and get me off the hook."

"If I told him what? That I put fish sticks in the well?" Amber Lynn leaned toward Jess. "Is that what you want? For me to tell him I did that?"

"Yes. And about the porch swing, too."

Amber Lynn looked as if the light was dawning at last. "That I made it fall down?"

Jess nodded.

"And then you'll forgive him? You promise?"

"I don't know." Jess flopped down into her chair. "Even if you tell him the truth, that doesn't change the past. He still *thought* I did it. He still thinks I'm the kind of person who hurts people to get what I want. And that's not me. That's *you*."

Amber Lynn flinched. "Okay. I deserved that. But why *wouldn't* he think that?" Her eyes grew hard. "That man lived with me for over two years, and I put him through hell." Returning to her chair, she smoothed her skirt. "I was a nightmare, Jess, and he probably still hasn't gotten over it. Why would he trust anyone? He doesn't think you're a bad person. He just thinks that's how women are."

Jess stared at Amber Lynn, stunned, gears turning in her mind.

"He doesn't trust *anyone*," Cade's ex continued. "His dad treated him like crap, and his mom let him do it. I took advantage of him, too, and so did my dad. So he's been cheated all his life. Give the man a break, okay? Teach him he's wrong."

Jess sat back, feeling like she'd just been tumbled in a dryer and tossed into the chair, all wrinkled and hot, her innards still spinning.

"Wow, Amber Lynn. I think you might be right."

"I *know* I am. And so do you."

Amber Lynn nodded. Slowly, Jess nodded back.

"Okay. Now. Business." The bank's newest employee shimmied in her chair, as if settling into a new persona. "I moved $5,000 from the Diamond Jack account to your father's savings account." She pressed a button on her keyboard, and a spiral of paper came out of a printer on her desk. "Here's your receipt. Now go home and tell Cade Walker you love him. You *know* you do." Folding her arms over her chest, she leaned back in her chair, slipping easily into a pose eerily reminiscent of her father. "You definitely don't have to worry about me. I'm busy with my career. I plan to be a vice president of this bank within two years."

Jess rose, which wasn't easy, because her knees felt strangely weak. She'd known all her life that Cade had been misused and abused, but she'd thought it was what made him strong. She'd certainly never thought of herself as one of the abusers. But now that Amber Lynn had painted the picture, it was clear as a country day.

"Thank you." She squeezed the words past a lump in her throat. "I—I appreciate what you said."

"You're welcome. It's about time I did something for Cade." The woman looked up with such a stark, pained look that Jess actually ached for her. "Save him, okay? He deserves to be happy. Even if it's not with me." She sighed. "He's yours and always will be."

I'm yours and always will be. Jess remembered Cade

saying that as he'd handed her that ruined flower outside the barn. She remembered the look in his eyes at that moment—so earnest that love had swelled in her heart like an orchestra soaring into song.

Now, her heart felt more like a string section tuning up, screeching and sawing at all the wrong notes. But musicians had to do that before a symphony, right? Sooner or later, they set their bows and played in perfect harmony.

"Okay. I'll call him or something." She had to blink so fast to hold back tears that she could barely see as she fumbled for the doorknob and stumbled out the door.

Pausing in the hall, she turned to face the woman who'd always been her nemesis. "And Amber Lynn? I hope you do real well here at the bank." She offered a tremulous smile. "I hope you really succeed. And I think you will."

———

Stepping out of the bank, Jess blinked in the afternoon sun. She felt as if she'd been in some alternate universe—one where the most insensitive, selfish person she'd ever known had turned the tables and revealed that Jess wasn't much better.

Amber Lynn was evolving, apparently, while Jess was stuck in place. She'd become the greedy one, the one who wanted more than Cade could offer, the one who demanded perfection in every aspect of their relationship. The one who wanted everything at once—the ranch, her job in the city, Cade, her independence—everything.

It was time to choose. And as she climbed into her father's truck and breathed in the stuffy, horse-scented air of the cab, with its subtle notes of dog, saddle leather, and sweat, she realized there was no contest. Sitting in the sunbaked pickup, watching the wind blow a scattering of leaves down the empty sidewalks of Wynott, she thought about Cade and the love she'd almost tossed away and wondered what on earth had made her leave.

Maybe it had been that show on TV where four city girls made sleeping around seem sophisticated. She'd fantasized about men with culture, men with money, men with high-powered careers. She'd pictured herself married to one of them, balancing a sophisticated social life with an important job of her own.

She'd wanted a life filled with loft apartments, sleek minimalist décor, cultured friends, and gallery openings where she'd sip wine and make intelligent observations about the latest avant-garde works by the hottest new painters. She'd gotten most of that—although she never had learned to enjoy avant-garde art—but it hadn't made her happy.

So she'd moved on to wanting Hawaii, a life on a beach. But she had a feeling that wouldn't make her happy either. She could spend the rest of her life seeking happiness in work, in travel, in success, and never find it. And now she knew why.

Cowboy was her culture, and that meant money was for paying the bills, not impressing the neighbors. It meant your morning routine was in a barn, not a coffee shop, and your nightly soundtrack was played by night birds and crickets, not cars and trucks. It meant you worked under the open sky, not a drop ceiling, and the sun ruled your day instead of flickering fluorescent lights.

Most of all, it meant that love mattered more than any

riches in the world. The love of family, of neighbors, of a hometown so small, everyone knew your business, and the love of a good man, one who was a true partner rather than a piece of arm candy or a hot date dressed to impress. Cade's thoughts might be focused on bovine bloodlines and equine equanimity, but he was as smart as any of the stockbrokers and bankers she had met, and his heart was capable of a love so great, it had dominated her life from the time she was a girl.

She'd never be as pure of heart as Cade. She could be petty and argumentative, demanding and impetuous. But she loved him back. She always had.

It was time to apologize for all she'd put him through. More important, it was time to tell him *yes* and pray he'd still want her in spite of it all.

Then it would be time to tell her boss, who'd been so patient with her long absence, that she was staying here, at home, in the world where she'd always truly belonged. At least Treena would be happy.

And so would Jess—at last.

Chapter 49

Cade was leading Redline to the round ring for one more ride when the hum of an engine cut through the still air. Soothing the mare as she shifted and balked, he shaded his eyes with one hand to see who was coming.

Little red car.

Jess.

Third chance?

He felt his internal optimist perk up and slapped it down. How many times was he willing to torture himself? The slightest thought of Jess could still make his heart burn high and bright—and that was why he needed to let her go.

He'd known this moment might come, and he'd figured out how to handle it in a way that was right for him and best for her as well. He'd show her he was moving on without casting blame. He'd hide his pain and swallow any last-ditch pleas his foolish heart coughed up.

It was the last gift he could offer and the hardest to give. But he was ready.

She slipped from the low car and stood tall, all long legs and loveliness, with her wild curls tumbling in the breeze. His heart turned over, groaned once, and died. How could he think he'd ever get over her? Saying goodbye felt like losing a limb. But he'd be damned if he'd show it.

She looked around the ranch, and he wondered what

she was seeing. All his hard work, the improvements
he'd made? Or the gaping difference between his simple
old house and the elaborate Diamond Jack? Pretending
he didn't care, he plucked a blade from the tall grass
growing by the fence and let it dangle from his lips like
James Dean's cigarette. Beside him, the mare bumped
his shoulder.

"What's up?" he asked.

"Not much. What's up with you?" She smiled, and
his heart battered his chest like an animal that wanted
out of its cage. "Dad said you found a home for those
two geldings of his. He wanted me to thank you for him.
So, um, thanks."

She seemed strangely shy, and no wonder. She was
probably afraid he'd try to start things up again.

God knew he wanted to. He wanted to haul her close
and kiss her senseless, but that wasn't what she wanted,
and he'd never been the kind of man to press himself on
a woman.

Setting his face in firm, neutral lines, he nodded.
"No problem. They were the last ones. Well, besides
Redline." He tilted his head toward the mare. "I'm putting the last ride on her right now. Then she'll go back
to your dad, and I'm off to California."

"Redline?" She laughed. Last time Jess had seen the
horse, it had been hopping around like a kid on a trampo-
line. "Good name. Try not to get yourself killed, okay?"

The sun was setting behind him, lighting her face with
late afternoon light, turning her curls to burnished gold.
Cade's heart ached, swelling his throat nearly closed.

"Wait." She squinted, confused. "Did you say
California?"

"Yep." He looked away, faking absorption in the sunset. "Got a job with John Baker."

"A job?" She stilled, staring at him wide-eyed. "*The* John Baker?"

This was the one part of saying goodbye he'd been looking forward to. The offer from Baker was hard, cold proof of his success, and it felt good to leave her with that big, fine feather waving in his cap—even if he was dying inside.

"He's looking for new clinicians," Cade said. "I'll be working with him over the winter, getting up to speed on his techniques. Then I'll hit the road, travel to different ranches and fairs all around the country, running clinics."

"Wow." She rocked back on her heels, clearly stunned by his news.

"You're probably heading out soon, too, right?" The ache in his throat threatened to strangle him, but he swallowed it down, busying himself with the horse, patting her neck and fussing with her mane. "Good luck with that promotion."

"What? No. Wait." She shook her head. "You're leaving? Just like that? What about your horses?"

"I've got most off 'em finished. Rehomed those strays, and Pride'll go with me. Boogy, too."

"John Baker's letting you bring Boogy?" The faintest hint of a smile quirked her lips. "Did you warn him?"

He grinned. "I told him about the cow chasing, but the killer farts'll be a surprise."

Jess huffed out a little laugh, but it didn't sound happy. "How long are you going to be gone?"

"Six months, a year." He gathered Redline's reins in

his hands and headed for the round ring. "Maybe for good, if things work out."

Jess followed. "Won't you miss this place? Won't you be, I don't know, sad?"

Sad. Was she clueless or what? Of course he was sad. "Cade?"

Her voice sounded hoarse, and he wanted to turn, to see if she was sorry, to see if he had one more chance left. But he'd vowed to let her go, and he would.

"I won't miss it." He opened the door to the pen and turned, looking hard into her eyes as if on a dare. Looking but not seeing, his heart locked tight in an iron cage. "The place is full of ghosts. You had the right idea when you left this town."

"I'm not so sure of that. I was thinking…" She glanced at his face, but he kept a mask in place, impassive. Her gaze flicked back and forth, and he knew she was searching for the old Cade, the one she knew. The one who loved her and couldn't leave her.

That Cade was still inside him, but he wouldn't let him out. Not ever again. He didn't smile, didn't soften, just clutched the reins tighter and prayed the horse wouldn't give him away. It was a mark of her training that she held firm, shifting quietly beside him, ignoring the emotions coursing through the air.

"Won't you miss *anything*?" Jess asked.

You. I'll miss you.

He looked down, gnawing on the inside of his cheek, searching for something safe to say. He and Jess had danced a little too long, stepping in, stepping out, coming together, and spinning apart. Lately, they'd been stumbling around, stomping on each other's feet, and falling around the dance floor. He didn't want to be cruel, but he needed to end this, firm and hard.

"There's nothing I'll miss." Meeting her eyes squarely, he pulled the grass stem from his mouth and tossed it to the ground. "I'm through with this place."

"Okay." She stood motionless in the drive, looking stunned.

He wanted to run to her, swear he wouldn't go, beg her to go with him, something. Anything. Instead, he looked away, fooling with the gate.

"Wow." She folded her arms over her chest and beamed. "Congratulations. That's awesome. I know you'll do well."

"Hope so."

"Baker doesn't know how lucky he is," she said. "You're one of the best. Wasted here, really."

"Thanks." All this time, he'd waited to hear her surprise, her praise. And now, it was the last thing he wanted. That bright smile cut like the blade of a knife. "I'd better get to work."

"Okay. Well." She paused. "See you."

"Yep."

Leading the horse into the round pen, he closed the gate and let her go.

He heard Jess's boots crunching over the gravel. The sound faded toward the Miata, and the little car's engine roared to life.

A cloud of dust rose from the spinning tires, floating over the round pen like the ghost of summers past. Cade leaned against the rough wooden panels and watched it drift away. It was carrying his old life, his old self, letting it vanish with the wind. That's what he had to believe.

When the cloud cleared and the sound of her engine faded away, he took a deep breath and bent at the waist, holding his head in his hands. He struggled to calm himself for the horse's sake and for Jess's, too. Collapsing against the pen's rough wooden walls, he slid to the ground and drew in one ragged breath, then another.

The horse walked over and stretched her neck to huff at her new friend, wondering why he was acting so strange. He felt her muzzle, velvety soft, stroke the side of his face before she backed away, puzzled.

For the horse's sake, he didn't move, and he wouldn't until he could master his emotions. For Jess's sake, he'd stay in the pen, let her go without laying on guilt. He'd never show her how much this hurt, how it always would. He'd never done anything harder in his life, but it was the best gift he could give to the woman he'd loved all his life and the only way he could see to save himself.

Chapter 50

JESS DROVE AWAY AS FAST AS SHE DARED. ONCE SHE'D rounded a curve that hid her from Cade's view, she parked in a pullout by Willow Creek and shut off the engine. Folding her arms over the steering wheel, she rested her head on her hands and stared unseeing at the road ahead.

When she'd left Amber Lynn at the bank, she'd had a plan. Go to Cade's, apologize prettily, tell him she loved him, and watch his eyes light up. They'd celebrate, probably, by making love in his bed, with the window open. They'd hear this very creek flowing past. She'd always loved that.

Then—and she'd found herself looking forward to this part, too—she'd call her boss and give him her notice. Maybe they'd manage to save the Diamond Jack, or maybe she and Cade would live at Walker Ranch. One way or another, she'd go back to the life she'd been born to live. Her roping would get better. Her riding, too. And someday, she'd be one of those old ranch women, wise in the ways of the wind.

The relief she'd felt at the thought of quitting her job surprised her. She'd worked so hard at Birchwood, she'd lost sight of the fact that she didn't actually enjoy it. Sitting in that stark, brightly lit office, she'd missed the wide sky over Wyoming every day. She'd missed the friendly people of Wynott. She'd missed her family, her horse, and Cade. Quitting would be like getting out of jail and going home.

But she'd realized the truth too late.

Now, she'd have to make a different kind of call. Go back. Keep gunning for promotions that would lead her ever farther from home. Go back to her second-choice life.

She knew she was getting exactly what she deserved. She'd asked too much of life and far too much of Cade. His love was deep and real, but she'd taken it for granted and pushed for more. No matter what he did, it was never enough.

He was the kindest man she'd ever known, but he was still a man. There was a limit to what his pride would bear, and she'd poked and prodded until she'd pushed him over the edge. She'd demanded perfection. Total trust. All the while, she'd never given his past a thought—how everyone who should have loved him had failed him somehow or even hurt him. And she'd been one of the worst.

Exiting the car, she stumbled down an embankment and plunged into a grove of cottonwood trees that bent dark, crooked boughs beside the creek. After staggering through the underbrush, she stood at the water's edge and watched the water make its mindless way to Colorado.

She could hear a pinging sound coming from the road, where she'd left the car door open, the keys in the ignition, but she didn't care. Climbing onto an old cottonwood that leaned across the stream, she edged along a thick branch that arched until she found a rough-barked seat where she could dangle her legs over the water.

It was the same water that had flowed past Cade's

bedroom window, singing to them when they'd made love. It had borne the little boats they'd fashioned out of leaves when they were kids. They'd sat in this very spot through long summer days, shoulder to shoulder—Jess reading her Trixie Belden mysteries, Cade his battered horse magazines, the same ones over and over. He'd kissed her for the first time here and countless times thereafter. Now, she had to face a world without him.

Would she ever get over this? Would she ever be able to stand her own face in the mirror again? The more she thought about it, the more she realized she'd been as bad as Amber Lynn, taking and taking, never giving an inch. She'd been wrong. And it had cost her the world.

Well, at least she'd be busy. She could drown herself in managerial tasks and think of nothing but success. She'd die a little inside, but she'd become the person she'd wanted to be all those years ago, when she'd chosen her mother over her father, city life over Cade, success and self-importance over love and a giving heart.

Idiot.

Shifting her hips, she let the toe of one boot dangle in the water, creating an eddy that hypnotized her as it spun to a smooth backwater and disappeared. She wished she could calm the tumult in her heart that easily.

Maybe she should go back, talk Cade into staying. Amber Lynn said he'd always be hers. Riley, too. Maybe she could still save the life she wanted.

But all she could see was his face as she'd seen it just now—the set of his jaw, the jut of his chin, the shield drawn over his eyes. He hadn't looked like a man who'd wanted his mind changed. He'd looked like a man with a mission—a strong, successful man who'd gotten the opportunity of a lifetime, who was about to reach his professional goals.

Those horse magazines.

She smiled at the memory. Cade had bought those magazines whenever he had a few dollars. *Western Horseman*, *American Quarter Horse Journal*, the rodeo papers—he'd worn them out, cover to cover, and told her he'd be in those pages someday, a famous horse trainer.

He'd never really expected to succeed. He'd assumed he was doomed to slave at his dad's dwindling cattle ranch until Tom Walker frittered away the rest of it. But every boy has a dream, and Cade had dreamed of horses. He'd wanted to help them and their people, like his idols Buck Brannaman, Tom Dorrance, and John Baker, and now that dream was coming true. Jess had no doubt a job at John Baker's California ranch would carry him to the kind of stardom he'd imagined all those years ago. Manipulating him into staying, denying him that chance, might be a win for her—but it would be a huge loss for Cade.

If she really loved him, she'd let him go. She had a chance to be unselfish for a change. To do what was right for Cade.

Sliding off her tree-branch seat, she dropped into the water and stood ankle deep in the stream. She was ruining her boots, but she didn't care. She didn't care about anything but Cade and the painful knowledge that she had to let him go, had to let him have this chance.

Covering her face with her hands, she stood in the water, leaned against the tree, and cried for a long, long time.

Molly heard Jess returning before she saw her. The screech of brakes, the crush and spit of gravel—the girl drove as if pursued by demons. Plucking a towel from the stove handle, Molly watched her stepdaughter climb up out of her car.

Something was wrong. Jess staggered like she could hardly find her feet and walked like she'd been blinded. As she neared, Molly realized the girl really couldn't see. She was crying too hard. And her boots were soaking wet.

Without thinking, Molly raced out the side door and caught her stepdaughter in her arms. Jess fell against her, crying harder, and Molly nearly fell over with shock. She and Jess had been getting along lately. She'd flattered herself that there was even some love developing between the two of them. But until now, Jess had never come to her with her troubles.

"He's leaving," Jess moaned. "I chased him off. My stupid, stupid pride. He's had enough, and I don't blame him."

She made a small whimper deep in her throat, a sound as helpless and hurt as an animal caught in a trap. Easing Jess down onto the stoop, Molly sat beside her.

Jess hunched over her stomach as if it hurt. "Who cares if he trusts me one hundred percent? Who cares if he thinks I did all that stuff? He's *Cade*. Nothing else matters." She clutched her stomach and rocked. "What have I done? What have I *done*?"

"Hush, sweetheart," Molly said, stroking Jess's bright curls. "Cade loves you. You'll work it out. You always do."

The girl shook her head, curls flying. "Not this time. He's done. He's got such a good chance, Molly. He's going to California, to work for John Baker."

Molly tried to look like she knew who that was, but Jess apparently caught her blank look.

"He's the most famous quarter horse trainer in the country. Cade's going to work with him, learn all his techniques. He'll be famous, Molly." She sat up and brushed her tears away as best she could. "You wait. We'll see him on TV, in magazines."

"That's good, honey, but he can do that later. You need to get things worked out between the two of you first."

Jess shook her head, hard. "No. This is his chance. I love him, Molls, but I've been so selfish. I have to let him go." She sniffed. "I'm no good for him. I always asked for too much. Like he should be perfect, agree with everything I do. When really, how could I expect him to trust me? He doesn't trust anyone. He's been hurt so many times. His dad. His mom. Amber Lynn. And me."

Molly thought that was probably true, but it didn't seem wise to say so. Jess collapsed for a moment, sobs shaking her shoulders, but quickly took a deep breath and wiped her eyes.

"I learned a lot about myself today, I'll tell you that."

"Like what?"

"Like that Amber Lynn's a better person than I am. She understands him. I just think of myself."

"That's not true." Molly looked up at the blue sky that arched over them and thanked God and all the universe for bringing her this child. Jess might be a grown woman and a difficult one at that, but for now, she was

Molly's little girl. Stroking the pretty blond curls, Molly felt her heart swell until it felt too big to hold.

She'd solve this problem for Jess. She would.

She had to.

"Jess, you know all that now. Tell him you're sorry. Tell him you'll change."

"But I can't." Jess sniffed and slumped her shoulders. "I'm such a bitch, I *still* can't get over it. Why does he think I did that stuff?" Jess's face was so earnest, it hurt to look at her. "How could he think I'd mess with the porch? Someone could have been hurt. Or the well. You and Dad could have gotten poisoned. I'd never do that."

"I know, honey. I *know* it wasn't you."

"Amber Lynn even admitted she did it. But it doesn't matter now."

"Amber Lynn admitted it?"

Jess nodded.

Molly stared off across the field as the world spun off-kilter. She'd only wanted to save her husband's life and to help Jess find her way back to Cade, back to the life she loved. She'd had the best intentions, but she'd made one hell of a mess. And it was time to come clean.

"Honey, we need to talk," she said. "Let me go get your father."

"Don't tell Dad. He'll just worry."

"There are things he needs to know. You, too." Molly took both the girl's hands in her own. "I think I can help, okay? You have to trust me. Just this once."

Because you'll probably never trust me again, once I tell you what I did.

"I trust you." Jess sniffed. "I just don't want Dad to see me cry."

"Then I guess you'd better get hold of yourself."
Molly reached up and patted her cheek. "Go clean up,
okay? Meet us on the back porch when you're done. We
can straighten this out, trust me."

Trust me. Trust me. The words rang in Molly's mind
like a bad joke while Jess slouched off to the powder
room, meek as a newborn lamb.

Heck, ensconced in his usual chair on the back porch,
looked up from his paper and grinned as Molly entered.

"What's up, darlin'?" The surgery had done him
good, and she paused to admire the glow in his cheeks,
the light that had returned to his eyes.

"We need to have a talk," she said.

The healthy color faded fast. "You're not leaving me,
are you?"

She smacked his arm. "Of course not, silly. You
know better than that."

"Thought I did," he said. "But when a woman says
she needs to talk…"

"It's not about us. Well, not really. It's about Jess and
Cade and the plan." She took a deep breath. "It's time to
tell Jess what we've done."

His forehead creased. "You kiddin'? I never want her
to know how we fooled her. And there's no reason for
her to know."

"Oh yes, there is." Molly sat beside him and took his
hands in hers. "Because there was more to the plan than
you knew. And I need to tell you both all about it." She
looked down at their joined hands. "By the time I'm
done, *you* might leave *me*."

"Good lord, woman." He snorted. "You kill somebody?"

"No. I just took things way too far."

"So you've been sneaking around and manipulatin' folks again? What am I gonna do with you?"

His smile was fond, his manner kind, but Molly wondered how he'd feel once he heard the whole truth. Looking around at the homey porch, with her craft table in one corner and Heck's easy chair in another, she wanted to cry herself. But she had some truths she needed to own, so this was no time for tears.

Those would come later, after Heck and Jess chased her off the place. Because although she knew the deep-down goodness of her adopted family, she doubted they'd tolerate the things she'd done, the lies she'd told. The way she'd hurt them both—and Cade most of all.

Heck watched his baby girl step onto the porch, looking more like her childhood self than she had in years. Her face was pink and fresh, as if she'd washed off all her sophistication with clean, cold water. He wished she knew how beautiful she was, even when she didn't try.

"How's my girl?" He stood and gave her a loud smacking kiss on the cheek.

"Okay, Daddy." She gave him a smile so shaky, it nearly broke his heart, and he noticed her eyes were puffy. "Well, sort of. Not so good, really."

"Well, me and your mom are here to help."

For once, Jess didn't correct him when he called Molly her mom. He'd been ready to make that argument, because Molly was more of a mother to her than Dot Bailey had ever been, and it was time Jess learned that blood only went so far. Look at that Arabian horse of

Cade's if you wanted proof. The animal was pure hoity-toity breeding, but put him in the corral with a bunch of cow ponies, and you had yourself a cutting horse.

Jess was the same. Put the girl in the country, and the country filled up the girl.

But when Dot Bailey left, she'd taken Jess's heart with her—the clear, golden heart of a cowgirl. In its place, she'd left a hollow shell dead set on striving for the finer things in life—the things that cost money. Stuff. Money. Prestige—whatever *that* was. His ex-wife had damn near destroyed the girl, but Molly had helped coax his cowgirl back to life, and whatever happened, that was a good thing.

"Molly says she's got something to say," he told Jess. "Guess you and me are going to listen."

He could tell Jess about the plan, of course. It might have been Molly's idea, but he'd signed on with more enthusiasm than he liked to admit. Getting Jess home, by fair means or foul, had seemed like a fine idea. And getting her together with Cade had seemed even better. It was what he wanted, and just like with Griff, he hadn't thought about Jess's plans.

"Me first," Jess said. "I have something to say."

"But…" Molly was leaning forward with her hands clasped as if in prayer. She was biting her lower lip so hard, its berry-pink hue had turned to white, and her face was drained of color.

"But nothing." Jess set her hand gently on Molly's arm, softening her words. "Me first."

"All right."

"Okay." Jess swiped at her thighs as if brushing off crumbs. "I just want to apologize to both of you."

"Oh no." Molly sounded genuinely dismayed. "You don't need to do that. In fact, once you hear what I have to say…"

"Nothing you say could change my mind," Jess interrupted. "Dad, you were right when you told me I wasn't giving Molly a fair chance. I fell for that 'evil stepmother' crap hook, line, and sinker, and I couldn't possibly have been more wrong." Smiling, she reached across the table and took Molly's hand. "You're a better mother than my mom ever was, and I love you, okay? I think you're the best person I know, and I hope you'll accept my apology for being such a brat."

Heck's heart soared, but then he saw Molly's smile tremble and break.

"Oh, Jess, I think you're saying that way too soon." She swallowed something—a lump in her throat, maybe even a sob. "You need to hear what I have to say. What I did. You'll probably change your mind."

Chapter 51

Heck watched Molly blink back tears.

"I lied," she said.

"Oh, come on." Heck turned to Jess. "What Molls is trying to say is that *I* lied. Me." He grinned like he was proud of himself. "She might have suggested the plan, but I executed it. See, when I told you I wanted to sell the ranch, we weren't planning any such thing—not for real. I just wanted to get you home, and we figured losing the ranch would put a burr under your butt."

He glanced over at Molly, hoping she'd pick up the conversation, but she was staring down at the tabletop as if she could read her fortune in the wood grain, so he continued.

"See, your stepmother and I, we thought you and Cade belonged together." He held up a hand to stop her protests before they could start. "Now, I know that's not how it's necessarily worked out, but we thought the boy ought to have a chance."

Jess glanced from him to Molly. "So you weren't planning to sell? But..."

"Not at the start, we weren't," he said. "But then I had that blasted heart attack, and you and Cade weren't getting along, so it seemed like it was the best thing for everyone after all."

"Oh no." Jess looked stunned. "So if Cade and I had worked it out..."

"We never wanted you to do anything but what feels right to you." He sighed. "Just goes to show, you shouldn't mess in other folks' business. The world turns as it turns, and a man can't change the course it takes."

He knew old ranchers were supposed to be full of homespun philosophy, and he was proud of that bit. Maybe he ought to write it down.

"I'm just sorry it didn't work," Jess said. "I made a lot of mistakes. I don't know, maybe leaving in the first place was a mistake. I got everything I wanted in my professional life, but there was always something missing. I didn't know how precious this life was until I lost it. Same with Cade."

This conversation was about to turn into one of those sob fests women were so fond of, where everybody wept and said how much they loved each other. He hated that stuff, so he shoved his chair back and stood.

"Well, I'm glad we had this little talk. Now, if you'll excuse me…"

"Stay right there." Molly hauled him back into his chair with a grip like an iron claw. "There's more."

"Dang." He sat.

"It was mostly my idea," she told Jess. "Your dad had his first heart attack and didn't see how we could keep the ranch. But I thought if you and Cade could get together, you two could run it, and Heck and I could stay here. I planned out your life to fix my own, without even asking, and then, instead of suggesting it to you, I manipulated you." She sighed. "It sounds like I was being selfish, but I swear to you, I was only trying to make your father happy, and I thought it would make you happier, too."

"But the good news is, it all worked out," Heck said.

"End of story. We're moving to Happy Snappy Acres, and you and Cade—well, what are you and Cade doing, hon?"

"Nothing," Jess said grimly. "Not together, anyway. He's leaving, Dad. He doesn't trust me. He thinks I did all that stuff, to the gazebo and the porch and the well."

"So, didn't you?"

"What?"

He shrugged. "I don't see how anybody else could've done it."

"Dad, I did *not*." Jess leaned across the table, her face flushed. "It was Amber Lynn Lyle. She *confessed*."

Holy moly, if the girl wasn't careful, her hair would light on fire.

Molly stood. "I have more to say."

Heck, sensing something momentous about to come, took her hand. He and Molly had faced a lot of trouble in the past few months, and he'd learned that they could deal with anything if they confronted it together.

But as he started to stand with her, Molly slipped her hand from his and pressed him back into his chair.

"No, Heck. This is all me." She took a deep breath. "I know I shouldn't have messed with your love life, honey. I know I was being manipulative and sneaky. But I wanted what I wanted, for you and for your dad. I wanted it bad, and I was blinded by it."

Heck squinted up at her. With the overhead light beaming over her head like a halo, she looked beautiful and sorrowful and hurt. He reached over and squeezed her hand, and she seemed to draw strength from it, closing her eyes and drawing in a deep breath before she spoke again.

"I know you didn't do those things. It wasn't Amber Lynn, either. It was me."

Heck's mouth dropped open. He knew he should shut it—it was that time of late summer when the flies were drowsy from the cool nights and tended to bumble into you when you least expected it—but he didn't seem to be capable of movement.

"You?" Jess looked dang near as stunned as Heck felt. He was probably a little safer from the flies now that her mouth hung open, too. Gave 'em another option.

"Yes, me." Molly's eyes were shining with tears, but she stood tall. "I was sure if you and Cade just had more time, you'd come to your senses, so I tried to hold off the sale." She sighed, seeming to deflate as she slumped back into her chair. "I know it was none of my business. But I love that boy so much, and honey, I love you even more—more than you can imagine. I never meant to hurt you."

"I know that," Jess murmured.

"So you did all that stuff?" Heck gaped. "The porch swing? The calf in the gazebo?"

Heck pictured her sneaking around, causing mayhem, and couldn't help chuckling. His wife was spunky, that was for sure. As the chuckle rose into a full-on laugh, Molly glared.

"This is *serious*," she said. "When those awful people came to buy the place, I knew I should be glad, but they were terrible." She swiped away a tear and turned to Jess. "I never meant to hurt you. I just untwisted that bolt on the porch swing a tiny little bit. I had no idea it would take the whole porch down." She looked into her lap, flushed with shame. "And I tried to get that woman to sit in it. I thought she deserved it, after how she made Cade's horse rear, but it was wrong. I can't believe how mean I was, and then it was *you* who got hurt, Jess. I never felt so bad in my life."

"Aw, she's fine, aren't you, hon?" Heck smacked his chest. "Bailey blood. We're tough."

"Yeah." Jess slumped in her chair. "Cade thinks I'm tough, too."

Heck didn't see what was wrong with that, but he knew better than to say so. Words and women together brought him nothing but trouble.

"So it was you who stole my manure shovel, right?" Jess asked. "To scoop up that road-killed raccoon?"

"Yes, that poor thing. I saw him on my way home from the hospital and knew he might come in handy. Then, when the Swammetts wanted to see the furnace, I went around the back way and slid him underneath."

"But how'd you get Hermy in the gazebo?" Jess asked. "That calf hollers if you touch him."

Heck wondered about that, too. He couldn't see his wife carrying the bull calf across the yard. Plus, like Jess said, the calf was always bawling for more milk.

"I just got him a bottle and dragged him over there with it. He was too busy drinking to be loud."

"Damn." Jess looked up from the table, a faint light in her eyes. "You'll be a rancher yet."

"I don't know about that." Molly flushed. "What kind of rancher would put fish sticks in the well?"

Heck burst out with a loud guffaw. "Fish sticks?"

Molly turned to Jess. "I told Cade he should get you over to his place. That way, no one would drink the fish-stick water until the test came back. I thought they'd thaw slowly, you know, and take a while to, well, ferment." She sighed. "I didn't expect an offer on the place so soon. I was so desperate to slow things down, and when they asked for the well test, I thought—now there's an idea."

Jess sat back in her chair and crossed her arms over her chest. A series of opposing expressions crossed her face in quick succession, ranging from anger to amusement. To Heck's great relief, amusement won the fight. She tossed her head back and laughed, clapping her hands.

"I can't believe it," she said. "It never even occurred to us it could be you. We ruled you out, every time, without even *thinking* about it." She gave Molly a sharp glance. "You're not the sweet innocent you seem to be."

Molly hung her head.

"Hey, don't worry," Jess said. "I might not approve of your methods, but I like that you tried so hard to keep the ranch for my dad."

"It wasn't all for him," Molly confessed. "Once you came, I started to love the place, too, looking at it through your eyes. So I was trying to save it for my own sake, too. And yours." Sitting cautiously on the edge of her chair, she took Heck's hand. "But I almost ruined everything, and now you're on the outs with Cade, all because of me."

"It's not because of you," Jess said. "It's because of me. It wasn't enough for me that he loves me or that he doesn't care if I do stuff like that. I wanted him to trust me, believe everything I say. One hundred percent. And I wouldn't bend." She sighed. "To be honest, it still bothers me. I told him over and over it wasn't me."

"Hell, *I* even thought it was you," Heck said. "Didn't seem like it could be anybody else. 'Course, I didn't know I'd married a criminal mastermind." Molly winced, but he squeezed her hand. "Just joking, hon."

Molly fiddled with the hem of her apron, glancing from Heck to Jess and back again. "Jess, I just have to ask one thing."

Jess nodded.

"When Cade thought you'd done those terrible things—the ones that I did—was he mad at you?"

"Not really. He seemed to think it was funny. But—"

Molly stopped her with a "halt" gesture. "Now you take a look at your dad." Heck felt the room heat up as both women stared at him. "He knows now what I did. And does he look mad to you?"

Jess grinned. "No. I think you could shoot the Dude and Dudette and bury them in the manure pile and he'd forgive you."

"Hell, I'd help you dig the hole," Heck said. "You did everything for the right reasons, hon. I love you anyway."

"There." Molly flashed Jess a triumphant smile. "That's what it's all about. I'm happier in this marriage than I've ever been in my life, because I found a man who loves me for who I am." Her eyes softened. "Cade might not have trusted you, honey, but trust is *hard*. What matters is that he wasn't mad, because he loves you anyway, like your dad loves me." She reached up and ruffled Heck's hair, giving him a tousled baby-bird hairdo. "We can't expect our loved ones to be flawless." She admired her handiwork and grinned. "Lord knows I don't."

"Hey," he said.

"But I know I messed up. I spoiled your chance with Cade." She leaned forward, touching Jess's leg. "Tell me how I can fix it, honey."

"I know how." Heck pointed a finger at Jess. "You need to run to that boy and beg him to stay. You do whatever it takes." Looking at Molly, he thought of her kind smile, the touch of her hand, and knew love was more precious than pride, than trust, than anything in the world.

But right now, the woman he loved was frowning and, thinking over what he'd said, he understood why.

"Sorry. I guess if I learned one thing from all this mess, it's that I can't force Jess to feel what I want her to feel, do what I want her to do." He took Jess's hand and squeezed. "So I'm sorry, hon. I can just hope and pray and be here when you want me. The rest is up to you."

Chapter 52

As Heck looked into his daughter's eyes, a lone cricket started up a rhythmic chant in a corner of the room. It seemed it was the only creature on earth that wasn't holding its breath, waiting for her to figure out her next step. But a ringing phone startled the cricket into silence, and she leapt to her feet to answer it.

"Yes?" Heck heard her saying. "Uh-huh? Well, okay."

There was a long silence before she spoke again.

"That's all right. I hope they're very happy there. And hey, I'm sorry. I know that's not good news for you."

She paused.

"Sure. There'll be somebody else."

When she returned to the room, she stood motionless at the door, the phone still cradled in her hand. "That was Val."

Molly's hand flew to her lips on a quick intake of breath. "The real estate agent?"

"That's right." Jess's somber expression transformed as her lips twitched into a smile and her eyes began to sparkle. When the smile became a full-on grin, she lifted her fists into the air in celebration. "Sale's off, folks. The Dude and the Dudette found a different ranch to wreck, so the Diamond Jack is safe." She turned to Molly and saluted, grinning. "Good job, Mom."

Molly, who'd gone white as a ghost, collapsed against Heck. "Oh God," she said. "I'm so relieved. It's wrong, I guess. I don't know what we'll do now. But I'm so glad."

"I know what we'll do." Jess pulled out a chair and joined them at the table. "We'll start again and fix what's wrong. I've learned a few things."

Heck wasn't much for lessons and morals, but here came another one. Maybe he could add it to his new collection of ranch-raised philosophy.

"I made all these assumptions." Jess ticked items off on her fingers. "I assumed Molly was an evil step-mother. I assumed Cade was sleeping with Amber Lynn. And I assumed Molly was—well, that she was up to something, one time."

He didn't know what that was all about, but he didn't care. All that mattered was the conspiratorial gaze that passed between his wife and his daughter—a look that seemed close enough to the kind of love he'd wished for them a hundred times.

"You made some other assumptions about Cade," Molly said.

"I know." Jess's smile faded. "I assumed he'd believe me, no matter what, and that was asking too much of him. Because you're right. He might not believe me, but he loved me, and that's what mattered." She looked down at her lap. "I also assumed he'd always be here, and I was wrong about that, too."

"What?" Heck asked. "Of course he'll be here."

"He's moving to California, Dad, to work for John Baker." She put her hands over her face, pressing her fingers against her eyes. "He gave up on me, and I don't blame him."

"John Baker? Wow." Heck blew out his cheeks.

"That's somethin'. But—wait. You want me to talk to him? Get him straightened out?" He slapped a hand on the table. "I'll tell him what's what. He needs to stay here with you."

Molly chuckled. "Well, I guess there's one person here who didn't learn much tonight."

Despite being near tears, Jess laughed, too, and Heck felt a bit put-upon. But the two women he loved most in the world were laughing together, so he swallowed his pride.

"You know, speaking of assumptions," Molly said to Jess, "you should look at the assumptions you've made about love." She glanced at Heck, then back at Jess. "It's not perfect, hon."

That was news to Heck, but he sure didn't want to get into an in-depth discussion about it.

"You can love each other half to death and still be mystified by the other person half the time," Molly said. "I mean, why does your dad want to hang out with that crowd down at the diner? Why does he spend so much money on boots?" She gave him a critical up-and-down scan. "And why does he wear such ugly shirts? It's a mystery to me."

"Hey." He looked down at the yellow-and-red number he was wearing. "This is one of my favorites."

"And that's fine. I'm just saying, I don't know everything you're thinking, and you don't always understand me, either." She took his hand and squeezed it. "You didn't understand how much my job mattered to me. That's pretty important, Jess. He should have understood it, don't you think?"

Jess nodded. "I guess."

"So do you think I should leave your dad because he didn't understand how much my work mattered to me?"

"Wait, what?" Heck widened his eyes, panicked. "Don't do that. I get it now, I promise."

Jess laughed. "No, of course you shouldn't."

"So if Cade doesn't understand that you wouldn't play those tricks on the Dude and Dudette, it's just one of many things he doesn't know about you yet. Just like you didn't understand he wouldn't sleep with Amber Lynn again."

"Ouch." Jess felt a jolt of shame.

"You have so much to learn about each other." Molly squeezed her husband's hand. "The learning never ends, and it's the best part. Life would be dull if I knew everything about this guy." She grinned at her husband. "No surprises. Think how boring that would be."

Jess's brows arrowed down, and she put a hand to her forehead.

Molly frowned. "Does your head still hurt from that business with the porch? I feel so bad about that."

"Oh, it's not that. It's just—I can't absorb all this information." She gave her dad a smile. "I kind of want to do it Dad-style, go over there right now and tell Cade how to feel, but I think I'd better sleep on it."

Molly took Jess's hand. "You do that, sweetheart. And try to see Cade's side. He's just confused, like most men. They're all confused, you know, and it's our job to set them straight."

Heck started to protest, then realized there was no point. His wife would just run her verbal steamroller over him again.

But he loved her anyway.

———ᴡᴡ———

Morning crept stealthily through a gap in Jess's bedroom curtains. Outside, the grass glowed with a silvery light that made her think of fairies dancing on the lawn. Rising, she slipped on a pair of jeans and stepped into her boots.

She'd slept little the night before, and she'd thought a lot. Now she had a mission to accomplish. She might succeed, she might fail—but she had to try.

Buster nickered softly as she swung his stall door open.

"Ready for a ride, old man?" She looped a bridle over his head, tugging his ears through the tooled leather headstall. As they left the barn, she stopped him at the fence and climbed on board.

Holding the reins loosely, she relaxed while Buster set off at an ambling walk. Somehow, he knew where she needed to go. Maybe that meant she was doing the right thing. Horses had their own wisdom, after all, and it worked in mysterious ways.

Their slow pace gave her time to enjoy the magic of morning. The sun was hovering just behind the mountains, staining the peaks with a peachy glow. Dew clung to the seed heads that topped the long grass, droplets glinting like diamonds.

Buster's hooves swept a dark path through the dew. It curved like the wake of a slow boat meandering across the pasture, and that was fine. She was in no hurry, because what she was about to do probably wouldn't be easy. And it mattered more than anything she'd ever done.

Buster paused at the gate, letting her lift the latch. He stopped again when they'd passed through, but she urged him onward.

"We'll leave the gate open. We might need to make a fast getaway if this doesn't go well."

She knew she was offering Cade too little, too late. Concentrating on the job with Baker had to look like a better bet than counting on her. Working with a famous trainer and traveling to ranches all over the country would propel Cade into the top professional ranks, where he could help more horses and their people.

She needed to support his choice any way she could. Just as the ranch sale was about what was best for her dad, this was about what was best for Cade. As for herself—well, she could find a way to adapt. She'd have to.

Hopefully, when this day ended, she'd be able to look at herself in the mirror without gagging. Instead of Heck Bailey's spoiled little princess, she'd see a woman who thought of others before herself. She didn't feel noble and selfless. She felt like she was finally on the right path, caring for the people she loved.

Buster's hooves thumped the dirt of Cade's driveway, flinging small stones that clattered across the ground. A few horses nickered from the stable as Jess slid to the ground, lifted the bridle from his head, and turned him into the paddock by the barn.

Showtime.

Moving quietly, she tiptoed through the wet grass. When she reached Cade's window, she tapped gently on the glass.

No answer.

Her stomach clenched. Maybe he'd left already, and she was too late.

Silly, there are horses in the barn.

She knocked again. A blind over the window hid whatever was going on inside.

There was a thump and a rustle. Something fell, and a muffled curse made her smile despite the nerves that shook her hand as she tapped the glass again.

This was it: her last chance at happiness. She didn't know how he'd react. Her mistakes might have destroyed the love he'd had for her. He might tell her to get lost.

Deep down, she knew that was exactly what she deserved.

Chapter 53

CADE WAS DREAMING ABOUT THE STABLES AT JOHN BAKER'S ranch. He dreamed he wasn't allowed to work with horses after all. He had to build new stalls, and he was tapping nails into the wood.

Tap, tap, tap.

Blinking awake, he realized the sound was real. Somehow, the dream had followed him into the waking world.

There was a movement at the window and more tapping.

No. It couldn't be.

He lifted the shade, squinting against the light of dawn.

Jess.

His heart rose like a hawk cresting a ridge. "Jess?"

She had one foot behind her, ready to run. "Can I—can I come in?"

"Of course." He stumbled out of bed, tripping on last night's discarded clothes and almost falling on his face.

What could she want? He hoped she wanted him, but that was crazy. When he'd told her he was leaving, she'd seemed unfazed by the idea. She'd congratulated him, once she recovered from the surprise of his success. He remembered that smile, bright and cutting as a knife, and vowed once again that whatever she wanted, he'd make it quick and clean. There was no point in prolonging the agony.

"Give me a hand." She was halfway in the window, with one long leg draped over the sill, but a splinter had caught her hair. She tilted her head, grimacing.

"Hold on." He pulled the blond strands from the rough wood and helped her climb inside.

"There." She stood beside him, her hair a golden tumble, her eyes sleepy but glowing. He felt a stirring of excitement and knew whatever wisdom his mind had to offer was about to be swamped by the needs of his body.

When she sat down on the side of the bed, he settled beside her, and then instinct took over. Instinct, need, and a love that had lasted all his life.

As their lips met, he lowered her gently until she lay beneath him, her eyes shining up into his. That bright smile was gentle now and brought the past flooding back. It closed over them as if memories were water and could shut out the world.

Holding his breath, he took the dive one more time, deep down into the heart of their shared history, and felt the past close around him, uncomplicated and pure.

—∽∽—

Cade had said his house was full of ghosts, but Jess couldn't sense a single one. Now that Amber Lynn's mess was cleaned up, she saw he'd stripped the place of his parents' things and made it his own. The walls in the bedroom were paneled with white-painted wood. The furniture was rough and utilitarian but warm, hand-built of local pine. Nothing seemed familiar—not even the window dressing.

"There were curtains here."

"After what happened, I wanted them gone."

She nodded, wondering how much it had hurt him when she'd seen Amber Lynn and assumed the worst. Without even thinking, she'd held him to a higher standard than she could reach herself.

Thinking. That's what she needed to do. Think of Cade and not herself. Make him happy, even if it was for the last time.

Leaning toward him, she lowered her lashes, inviting him in.

When he kissed her, she felt the same thrill she always had, a heady rush that prickled her skin and sent a rush of sensation from her body to her mind. Whatever complications had come later, it hadn't affected the chemistry that throbbed between them now.

Every part of her body thrilled as he touched and stroked and soothed her skin. They were face to face, chest to chest, and hip to hip, and she couldn't resist the urge to shimmy just a little, warming to the friction as their bodies met, heating with the thought of what might come next and what would come after that.

Breezes drifted through the open window, raising goose bumps, but Cade's hands warmed all the right places, triggering feelings she'd done her best to bury when she'd realized he might be gone for good. Feeling overwhelmed, she put up her hands to push him away but found herself smoothing the planes of his chest instead. The feel of him was familiar yet new; he was rangy as ever, but stronger, with new and very interesting muscles to explore.

He stroked a hand down her side, following the

curve of her hip and sending shivers—the good kind—
all through her body. This man knew her, with all her
quirks and weaknesses, her peculiarities and strengths.
He knew what she liked and why and did his best to
touch her as she liked to be touched.

Other men didn't give a damn about what she wanted.
It always seemed like they'd learned their moves out of
a book, or worse, from watching dirty movies. They'd
done things to her, not with her, and she hadn't trusted
them enough to give herself away.

But this…this was what she needed. *Who* she needed.

The urgency of another kiss sparked an answering
warmth in her own, and the sweet, slick stroking of his
tongue made some very interesting demands on other,
more intimate parts of her body. While his clever hands
moved down the front of her shirt, slipping open one
button then another, she explored his bare chest with
greedy fingers, savoring the brush of the soft hairs that
flecked his chest against the palm of her hand.

Everything about him was familiar but somehow
new, because this time, she was committed. She gave
herself to him completely, trusting love, really *trusting*
it, for the first time in her life. She had no questions, no
doubts. The rightness of it felt pure and complete.

Gently, he opened her shirt and kissed her jaw, her
throat, her collarbone, the tops of her breasts. Moaning,
she arched her back and strained against the confines of
her lacy bra. Cade, who'd never been known to hurry
these things, traced the outline of the lace with one
finger, making her gasp with need as she slipped into a
fast-flowing river of memory, sensation, and love.

He was smiling into her eyes in a way that told her

he knew exactly what he was doing, so she slowed her own wandering hands and concentrated on his flat, smooth nipples, brushing them with her fingertips until he moaned and closed his eyes. The river met the sea, and she lost herself in surging waves of sensation. Then the front clasp of her bra came open somehow, and then her jeans were unsnapped, the zipper down, the rough cloth skimming her thighs.

Next thing she knew, they were lying there naked in the shadow of the climbing rosebush that draped the window. She could smell the fading flowers as they nodded on the breeze. They smelled of memory and sorrow, overlaid with a melancholy sweetness. Somehow, the thorny bush pulled all that from the dry Wyoming soil, season after season.

"I've always wondered how you kept those roses alive," Jess murmured. "Didn't your mother plant them?"

Too late, she realized she'd invited a ghost into the room, but Cade didn't seem to mind.

"My dad took care of it. Pruned it every spring, watered it through every summer."

"That doesn't sound like him."

"I know. It almost made me think he loved her."

"He must have. It's just sad that he couldn't show it. Sad they didn't have what we have."

His expression softened. "What do we have?"

"Love." She smiled and brushed his hair back from his face. "I love you, Cade."

He looked into her eyes, and he didn't have to say a word. She knew. She'd always known. He was steady and solid, and she never should have doubted him.

She reached for the nightstand drawer and drew out a

foil packet. Once he was sheathed, they dove down and down again, rolling together in the waves. There was no uncertainty now, no questions or doubts. Every touch flowed into the next, telling them how to move, where to touch, how to buoy each other up.

They'd danced to this wild, sweet tune a hundred times before, yet every step was new again. They were older now and wiser. The years apart had made them strangers in some ways, but that only skimmed a sweet layer of excitement over the comforting familiarity they'd always shared, like jam spread on a homemade biscuit.

She opened to him, and he filled her. Clutching the sheets while he rocked above her, her body was bowed by the stress of holding in her joy. Did she dare to let go? Cade might leave, walk away, leave her holding a broken heart. It would be fair and right, after how she'd treated him.

But whatever happened, she was his, and he needed to know. Looking in his eyes, she felt her heart fly true as an arrow, straight to the soul of the man she loved.

Cade made a sound, animal and uncontrolled, as the two of them met and merged. Jess cried, literally cried in his arms. All around them, the walls turned gold in the morning light, and the breezes gentled and died.

Spent, he tucked his chin into the soft curve of her neck. The sound of the creek outside filled her ears, along with the birds' morning chatter. She felt the water flowing in her veins as if she was part of the earth and the earth was a part of her.

She'd never felt so whole, so complete, and knew she'd never forget this day, no matter how it ended. It would always be a precious gem, glowing in her memory as the day she became her true self: the woman who loved Cade Walker.

The one who'd never leave him.

The love they'd shared all their lives, starved for so long, came back to life and set her heart aflame, refining it with a healing fire. The world felt young again, full of possibilities, glowing with the light of a new day as all her doubts and uncertainties drowned in the rippling waters of Willow Creek.

Chapter 54

CADE DIDN'T THINK HE'D EVER FELT SO RELAXED. FAMILIAR sounds drifted through the window—the last harrumphs of the night-singing bullfrogs, the shushing sound of a breeze stroking his mother's roses, the trilling of bluebirds singing up the sun. Beneath it all, keeping time, there was his breath and Jess's, slowing together, slipping into the rhythms of their shared world. Being with her felt new every time, as if his old, dull self rose from a stupor, gilded by love.

This wasn't goodbye. He'd made up his mind, and she'd have to do the same. Whatever plans she had would have to be changed, and if she was mad at him for some trumped-up reason, she'd just have to get over it. The two of them belonged together, wherever in the world they decided to go. California, Denver, Hawaii— they'd carry home with them.

He knew it was a gamble. Despite the magic of their coupling, she might never forgive him for the past. Marrying Amber Lynn had driven a wedge between them, and nothing would ever be the same. But that didn't mean it had to be worse. Having lost each other, they should learn to value what they had more highly, hold each other tighter. He hoped so.

Oh God, he hoped so hard.

Taking a deep breath and letting it out, he let his worries stream away like water flowing down his back. He knew what love was. He knew its challenges, knew how heartbreak could hurt, but he also knew this woman was worth every jerk and pinch of his poor battered heart.

Nothing mattered but the soft swell of her breasts under his calloused hands, her tender need against his wild, pent-up desperation. They'd made love in the past few weeks, but that second chance love had been torn apart so fast, he'd almost lost the feel of it. This time, he'd held tight to every taste, every glance, every touch. The way she took the tip of her tongue between her teeth when she closed her eyes and smiled. The way the sun set her curls alight with gold. The way her body warmed and opened to let him in.

He vowed to think less of tomorrow or the next day and just work on today. They'd talk, they'd touch, and maybe they'd somehow sort things out.

"Wait." She broke the silence and stilled his thoughts. "Hold on."

He opened his eyes, his heart pounding. Forever could slip from his grip like a snake, intent on its own journey and impossible to grasp. They'd found lasting love once before, hadn't they? And it had slid away, dying on the rocks of Jess's ambition and his own stupidity.

He must have looked as scared as he felt, because Jess laughed. "Don't worry." She twisted so her right hip lifted, dumping him unceremoniously on the mattress. With one palm on his chest, she pushed him back down on the bed, then tossed a leg over him with the ease of a lifelong horsewoman. As she knelt above him and placed herself just so, his doubts died, and his body came to life. Again.

Rising above him, she rocked, flexing her hips. The

bedsprings, squealing in rhythmic protest, were lost in the harsh duet of their ragged breathing.

She sure wasn't in a hurry. She played with him, a wicked grin on her face, and just when he thought he'd explode if she didn't go faster, harder, she gave a little hint of what he wanted. Then she gave him more, and then more, until they were lost in a new rhythm, hard and fast and needy. This wasn't giving, this was taking, taking what they needed, but as long as they were both greedy for it, it was incredibly, wildly *right*.

She arched above him, gold skin glowing, a goddess flushed with victory as she tightened around him. Her cry pierced his heart, and he felt himself climb, climb, fly, and then let go, tumbling from the sky.

She collapsed over him, and he rolled them over, partly to let her rest but mostly so he could bury his face in her shoulder while a crazy urge to weep passed by. He was a man. He never cried, but he was happy, so damn crazy happy.

Brushing her curls back from her forehead, he kissed her temples, one side and the other. He thanked her, not in words but with a look.

She took his gratitude and smiled, and he felt golden in her gaze and right with the world for the first time in years.

"So," Cade said. "Is this a goodbye? Like last time?"

Jess smiled up at him, arms stretched high above her head, curls spread across his pillow. "No, it's nothing like last time. For one thing, I found the right person in the bed."

He shook his head. "I didn't mean *that* time. Let's forget that ever happened. I'm talking about that Christmas Eve."

"It sure felt like Christmas." She ran one finger down the side of his neck, across his shoulder, and down his arm. Who knew biceps were an erogenous zone? "It felt like Santa came and gave me everything I wanted."

She was giving him that smile again, with her tongue between her teeth. He kissed her nose and gave her a cockeyed scowl. "Seriously, though."

"It's not goodbye unless you want it to be." She tilted her chin up, and her eyes seemed to glow with love and light. "It could be *bon voyage*, see you later, or it could be hello."

He didn't dare take anything for granted. "What kind of hello?"

"That's up to you." She lowered her lashes. "I was hoping for the kind of hello where we never have to say goodbye again. At least not for long."

Love scrambled his brain. Could she really mean what he thought she did?

He'd promised himself he'd take it slow, follow her lead, protect his heart. But if there was the slightest chance they could build a life together, he'd dive in headfirst. If he hit bottom, it wouldn't matter, because if he lost her again, there'd be nothing left of him.

She cocked her head, still smiling. "Of course, you're going to California, so..."

He answered quickly, without thinking. "Not if this is hello I'm not."

"No, Cade, you need to go." She ran her hand down

the side of his face, a tender gesture that warmed him to his toes. "You'll learn so much. It's the chance of a lifetime."

"But what'll you do?"

She sat up, and he could see the excitement in her eyes. "Well, I've been in the running for a promotion to Hawaii."

He swallowed hard. Hawaii was a long way away—even if he moved to California.

"Well, there's one other candidate for the job, and he runs the Birchwood Suites in Malibu."

He sat up, too, catching her mood. "That's not far from Baker's place."

"I think it's about a half hour drive. So if Ted—that's the guy who's up against me for the Hawaii job—if he gets it, I could take over his hotel. My boss would probably be pretty happy with that solution."

"But what about the Diamond Jack?"

"I think I figured that out, too." Excited, she was gesturing with her hands. "Dad needs to thin the stock. Whoever ends up running the ranch probably won't want Highlanders, and it's the right time of year to sell them. Then he and Molly could take a cruise. I was thinking about booking one for them, as a present. Help my dad get used to relaxing a little."

"That's a good idea, but what about the horses?"

"Riley could stay at the house while she's working on the porch. She'd still work for Ed, of course, but she'd have a home of her own for a little while." She smiled. "Riley's always full of advice for me, but I think she needs to make some changes. She can't live with Ed forever. It's like she's married to that store."

Cade nodded. "Does she know anything about livestock?"

"You know Riley. What she doesn't know, she can learn. So what do you think?"

"I think it's good, short-term. But when do the Swammetts take over?"

"Oh yeah. So much has happened. You don't know, do you?"

"Know what?"

She grinned. "Sale's off."

"Off?" He felt like a new sun had risen, shining for them alone. "That's great news."

"I'll work for Birchwood as long as you're in California, and once you're done, I'll give my notice." She looked down at her hands, twisting in her lap. "Then maybe you'd want to come back here and run it. With me. As partners or whatever."

"Not partners," he said. "*Whatever*."

Slipping out from under the sheets, he slid to the floor and knelt beside the bed. Her eyes widened, and he wondered if he was making a fool of himself.

But hey, of course he was. He'd prepared for this moment in his mind a hundred times, and he still couldn't do it right, because dammit, he'd forgotten something. Rising, he crossed the room to his dresser, forgetting he was naked until he felt her eyes following him, tracing his every move.

It didn't matter. Naked was good, because he had nothing to hide. Besides, she was naked, too, and he wanted her to stay that way.

Rummaging in the top drawer, he found what he was looking for, palmed it, and returned to kneel again.

"Jessica Jane Bailey."

Her eyes widened. "This sounds serious."

"It *is* serious." He took her hand, looked into her eyes, and felt his brain go blank. "Shoot. I had a speech."

"You did?"

Swallowing hard, he nodded, wondering what had happened to his brain. It had been a really good speech, one he'd worked on for years, and it was gone — just *gone*.

He looked in her eyes and did his best to dig down under his emotions and find the words he'd cobbled together so carefully over the years, but there were no words, just love, so that would have to do. It was plain, honest, cowboy love, and it wouldn't dress up in a fine vocabulary or turn itself into poetry. He'd have to hand it over as it was, with no rules or reservations.

"Well, what did this speech say?" Jess asked. "Roughly, I mean."

"It said I love you. It said it a lot of different ways. When we were six, it said you were my best friend. When we were twelve, it said I finally noticed you were a girl, and I was a boy, and maybe we could go to a movie sometime."

"I remember that day. It was a Star Wars movie."

"That's right."

He was surprised she remembered. Usually, he was the romantic one, the one who remembered anniversaries and special events. Jess tended to forget that kind of thing. Big emotions overwhelmed her, maybe even scared her. That had something to do with her mother leaving, but he was no psychologist, and it didn't matter where it came from — it just mattered that he understood, that he knew he needed to take care of her heart so well, she'd come to trust someday.

"When we were sixteen, I knew I wanted to spend the rest of my life with you." He ignored the pain of the hardwood floor against his bare knee. "But I never said it. I just assumed we'd be together."

"I messed that up. I shouldn't have left."

"You had to. You needed more people around, more excitement. Hospitality work suits you, and you might miss it if you give it up. So coming back isn't something written in stone, okay? When I leave Baker, we'll decide what works. If you want to keep going with your career, I'll sell the ranch and go with you. Hawaii, whatever."

Her eyes widened with shock. "You'd do that for me?"

"Sure. I can train horses anywhere," he said. "There's only one thing I won't do for you, and that's let you go. Our life can be whatever you want, but it'll be us, always, together."

She smiled. "Is that a promise or a threat?"

"It's both." He uncurled his fist to reveal a ring with a small diamond nested in a filigree setting. Fumbling with his big, work-hardened fingers, he lifted it from his palm. "But mostly, it's a promise." He took a deep breath. "Jess Bailey, I'm asking you to marry me. No matter what happens, I want my life to be with you. No matter what you want out of life, I'll do my best to see you get it."

He took her hand. She let him. He figured that was a good sign and found a better one when he slipped the ring onto her finger and caught her smile.

—◦◦◦—

Jess bit her lower lip, looking down at the ring. It was lovely, small but ornate, and she knew it meant a lot to him. It had belonged to his grandmother, who had died when he was young. He'd loved the fierce old woman, who'd been his one defender while she lived. Though Jess had been half afraid of her, it meant a lot to have her ring.

She looked up to find him still kneeling there, still naked.

"This is a very nontraditional proposal," she said.

"Not really," he said. "I knelt. And I had a ring."

"But you're naked."

"I guess that might be nontraditional. But then, our marriage will be nontraditional, too."

"So we're going to be naked all the time?"

He grinned. "I hope so. But seriously, what I mean is that you're not some rancher's wife. You're my wife, a rancher, a hotelier, an executive—whatever you want to be, okay? Whatever pie-in-the-sky notion you come up with, I'll make it happen. And I'll be there, right beside you." He turned her hand in his, admiring the ring. "So that's settled. All that's left is my apology."

"What apology?"

"Amber Lynn called me last night. Told me she was the one who put the fish sticks in the well and did all that other stuff." He sighed. "You were right all along."

"No, I wasn't." Jess grinned. "And Amber Lynn didn't do it, either. I kind of made her say that."

"What did you do, threaten to ruin her life?"

Jess smiled. "I think she was worried I'd ruin yours."

Cade looked confused. "So who was it?"

"Molly."

"*Molly?*"

She laughed. "Turns out she didn't want to let go. She says she was desperate, knowing how much Dad loves the place, plus she's started to love it herself." Jess flushed. "I guess she really wants you to marry me and help Dad run the place."

"Maybe that's what we'll do, but it has to be what you want, okay?" He paused, making sure she met his eyes. "You don't have to decide now, but you need to know this isn't about the Diamond Jack. It's about you and me. All I need is you, and anyway, I've got this." His broad gesture included his house and the stables, the acreage he still owned, the round ring and the horses. "It's not much, but all this will be yours."

"Ours." She patted the bed, and he stretched out beside her. Turning, she tucked herself against him, drawing his arms around her waist and holding them tight. He pulled her close, breathing in the sleepy, sexy scent of her.

"You know I was thinking?" She sounded as if she'd slip off into sleep any moment. "Maybe it's crazy, but I thought maybe the Diamond Jack could be a dude ranch someday. There's plenty of room." Her drowsiness seemed to fade as she talked. "We could fix up the bunkhouse and host families. Teach kids to ride. Hold clinics, too, for folks with problem horses. Heck would be the host. All the men would love him. And Molly could teach the kids, maybe. Or run the poker games." She sighed. "I guess that's crazy, huh? Pie-in-the-sky." She laughed. "You'd probably rather have one of Molly's pies."

"Nope. I like yours." He held her close and kissed the

back of her neck. "Sky pie's the best kind. You left me once to get it, but crazy as it sounds, the reason I lost you is the reason I love you. You're meant for something big."

"Yeah," she murmured. "A big *family*."

He pictured little Cades and Jesses running around the place and felt as if his heart might burst. "Whatever your dreams are, we'll make them happen."

"They already did—the ones that matter." She snuggled against him. "A little time away, so you can work with Baker and I can tie up loose ends. Then all I want is you, me, some horses, and this old house, Molly and Dad next door, and the land spread all around. That's more than enough for me."

Epilogue

JESS STOOD BEFORE THE FULL-LENGTH MIRROR IN HER mother's ridiculous bathroom. Behind her, the glowing pink travertine reflected bride upon bride upon bride, receding into the distance, in a haze of blush pink.

"You look so pretty." Molly brought her fist to her mouth, blinking back tears. "I thought I might never see this day."

Jess turned, grinning. "You made this day, Molls. It was your plan that got us here."

"I still feel bad about that, but it came out okay, didn't it? But I still think Dot…"

"Hush." Pushing her veil to one side, Jess bent and kissed her stepmother's cheek. "You're all the mother I need. Mom's always too busy. This is a new life, *my* life. She wouldn't understand."

A tap on the door interrupted them, and Jess opened it to find Riley James standing stiffly in a blue bridesmaid's dress. With her silver hair and pale, hooded eyes, she looked startlingly lovely.

"Cade wants to see you," she said.

Jess stared. "Holy cow, my brother wants to see *you*. I'm sending pictures, and he's gonna wish he'd made it home so he could see you in that dress."

"Don't laugh," Riley said. "This is the first time I've worn a dress in public since—well, since I can't even remember. I feel like a little girl playing dress-up, and then I look in the mirror, and I'm like, *who's that?*" She swayed, hands clasped behind her back, and stared down at her toes. "But I wish Griff *could* come home for this. His own sister, married to his best friend. Darn Army."

"I'd have liked that, too," Molly said. "And I'm sure Griff would have come if he could. But Riley, go tell Cade he can't see Jess. It would be bad luck and against convention."

"Cade's always good luck for me, and this isn't a conventional marriage." Molly had been a handy human etiquette book through the wedding preparations, but she'd forgotten Jess wasn't a rule follower. "Besides, he probably has some sort of crisis going on. I'm betting it's his tie. Where is he?"

"In the barn," Riley said.

Molly made sweeping motions with both hands. "Go, then," she said. "Go be unconventional, you wild bride, you."

Picking up her billowing white skirt, Jess kicked off her shoes and raced out the front door, Riley following with her own high heels in her hand. Summer had ended, and the yellowed grass was coarse and spiky, but they barely felt it as they sprinted across the yard, slowing as they neared the barn.

"I always thought Cade was pretty conventional," Riley said.

"He seems that way, and then he surprises you."

"Like how?"

Reaching the barn, they paused for breath.

"Like when he proposed. It was definitely not conventional."

Riley raised her brows in an unspoken question.

"He was naked."

"Go, Cade." Riley burst into giggles—another girlish miracle from the least girlish woman Jess knew. Riley was delicate and beautiful to look at, but she was tough as nails and had the hammer to prove it. Still, there was something fragile there, something sweet. She and Jess had become good friends when the porch design blended into the wedding preparations.

They found Cade waiting in the barn, shifting his weight from one foot to the other, clearly impatient.

"I brought her." Riley punched Cade in the arm. "Don't say I never did anything for you, buddy."

Giving Jess an up-and-down look that reminded her of Boogy sighting bacon, Cade staggered backward, almost falling on his tightly tuxedoed butt as Riley slipped away.

"Wow. You're wearing a wedding dress."

"News flash." She grinned. "I'm getting married. You seen a groom around here anywhere?"

"There's one right here, and he's all yours. But he's got a crisis." He gestured toward a stack of hay bales that rose halfway to the ceiling. "We're not either of us dressed for it, but we need to move this hay."

"What?" Jess stared at the mountain of hay. "When did it come?"

"Last night. Help me out?"

She looked down at the dress, then back at Cade. He wasn't the sort of man who'd mind if she had dust on her wedding gown or hay in her hair. And a rancher had to be ready for anything, anytime. So did a hotel manager or a horse trainer's wife. This was her chance to prove herself.

"Sure."

Reaching high, she grabbed a bale from the top of the stack. The two of them worked in silence, stacking the bales against the wall across from the horse stalls. She had no idea why it had to be done right then, but she and Cade were partners now, or would be in…she checked her watch. Two hours.

"Hey, look." Cade pulled a bale aside to reveal a slab of wood, painted white. "There's something back there."

Aha. Catching the glint in Cade's eye, Jess grabbed another bale and tossed it aside, then another, not bothering to stack them. He'd hidden something back there, and judging from his expression, it was some sort of surprise.

Gradually, they revealed a sign—a big, square sign bearing a bold, professional jack of diamonds, with the words DIAMOND JACK below it.

"Oh, I love it," Jess breathed. "Cade, it's beautiful. The one by the drive is so worn out."

She wouldn't mention how her brother had painted it—her brother who was off at war. She'd long had a superstition about the sign, believing keeping it safe would keep her brother from harm. But Cade didn't know that, and anyway, it was silly. They could have *two* signs.

"Keep going." He grinned. "We have to get this hay moved. All of it. I want you to see the whole thing. I wouldn't replace Griff's sign for nothing, you know."

Like a terrier digging for mice, she tugged the remaining bales aside. At the bottom of the sign, two more words gave the gift a new meaning.

"Diamond Jack *Dude Ranch*," she breathed. "Oh, Cade."

He grinned. "I got you some pie."

Jess stared a moment and then spoke in a rush. "I'll work up a website while we're in California and some brochures. I've already talked to Molly about it, and she wants to learn chuck wagon cooking. You can do clinics—week-long ones, and you won't have to travel. Folks will bring their horses to you."

"To us," he said.

She took his hand, squeezing it so hard, it hurt. "We'll fix up that old bunkhouse, okay? And the back wing of the house—nobody uses those rooms. I'll fix that old fireplace...but what about Molly and Heck?"

He loved her for worrying. He loved her for everything.

"Your dad's all in. He figures the extra revenue stream will pay for an RV. They'll take off on vacation whenever they want."

"He thinks dude ranching will make that much money?"

Cade laughed. "No, he figures your stepmother will fleece the guests at poker every night."

Jess laughed. "She will. But Molly should be in charge of the kids, and Riley..." She turned left, then right, looking for Riley. "Where'd she go? I was thinking she could do some renovations. We need..."

"We need nothin'."

Cade stepped up and stopped her with a kiss. She hushed, remembering this wasn't a time for planning. She needed to stop thinking and let herself fall—into love, into Cade, into the happiest life she could imagine.

And she did, just two hours hour later, when Jessica Jane Bailey and Cade Thomas Walker stood before God and the entire town of Wynott and repeated the vows they'd written, which said nothing of obedience but plenty about love.

And when they finally kissed as husband and wife, Jess felt the golden light of all her Wyoming summers glowing around them, summers filled with Cade smiling, Cade working, Cade helping and laughing and, most of all, loving. Cade never giving up on her, no matter how foolish or selfish or crazy she got.

Through the twin miracles of love and forgiveness, he'd promised to hold her heart in his own, sharing all the wins, losses, and unexpected disasters of a country life that would fit them like a perfect pair of boots for the rest of their lives. There'd be some time away, right at first—time for learning and planning. And then, for the rest of their lives, it would be Jess and Cade, living the life they were born to live, always and forever at the Diamond Jack.

Acknowledgments

It's been a while since Wynott turned up on your GPS, I know. Things have been a little complicated in my life lately, but Cade and Jess have been with me all along. I'm happy to be bringing them to your bookshelves at last.

As many of you know, I'm a breast cancer survivor. While my treatment was successful and I'm blessedly cancer-free, the side effects from treatment were severe and long-lasting. That doesn't happen to everyone, but "chemo brain" is real, and I was one of the few who just couldn't seem to shake it. I finally had to take a break from writing and concentrate on my recovery.

When it seemed like I'd never be able to get this story done, I called my editor at Sourcebooks and offered to send back my advance. But Deb Werksman wouldn't take it. She told me she believed in me, and she knew I'd get better. Her generosity and confidence helped me through some very dark days. Everyone else at Sourcebooks has been incredibly supportive as well, especially Susie Benton, my hummingbird friend.

I also want to thank Wyoming writers Amanda Cabot and Mary Gillgannon. Not only did they encourage me through the darkest of days, but they took time from their own busy writing schedules to check my manuscript for memory blips. They are my dearest friends, supportive, generous, and understanding, and they never ask for anything in return.

Last but not least, my husband, Ken McCauley, stood beside me through the whole journey. It wasn't always easy, but he never let me down or stopped believing in me.

Cancer and its aftermath make you grateful, and I know how lucky I am to have a happy life, good friends, and great love. I hope some of my good fortune touches you through this story about second chances and the kind of love that never gives up.

And for all you cancer survivors out there—if you're struggling with side effects from treatment or you just need some support, drop me a line through my website. We need to stick together and support each other.

—Joanne Kennedy
May 2018

P.S. Cade's dog Boogy is a real dog. His owner, a local veteran, became too ill to care for him, but Boogy found an angel in my friend Janet Marschner. Janet's nonprofit, WY Pets Matter, serves the animals of southeastern Wyoming and the people who love them.

Janet won Boogy's star turn as a romantic hero at Cheyenne Animal Shelter's annual Fur Ball Auction with a generous donation to Cheyenne's homeless animals. She's truly a remarkable person who lives the Wyoming lifestyle to the fullest, all while saving homeless animals.

You can learn more about Janet's organization on the WY Pets Matter Facebook page.

About the Author

Joanne Kennedy is the RITA-nominated author of ten contemporary western romance novels, including *Cowboy Trouble*, *Tall, Dark and Cowboy*, and *Cowboy Tough*. The first book in her Decker Ranch trilogy, *How to Handle a Cowboy*, was named one of *Booklist*'s "Best Romances of the Decade." She lives in a secret mountain hideout on the Wyoming border with too many pets and a retired fighter pilot. The pets are relatively well-behaved.

Joanne loves to hear from readers and can be reached through her website, joannekennedybooks.com.

Can't get enough of Joanne Kennedy's charming cowboys? Keep reading for an excerpt of RITA finalist

Chapter 1

THE COWBOY BOOT WAS THE MOST PATHETIC PIECE OF FOOT-wear Charlie had ever seen. Upended on a fence post, it was dried out and sunbaked into dog-bone quality rawhide. She glanced down at the directions in the dude ranch brochure.

After pavement ends, go 1.6 miles and turn right. Boot on fence post points toward ranch.

The boot's drooping toe pointed straight down toward the ground. Evidently, Latigo Ranch was located somewhere in the vicinity of hell.

No surprise there.

Still, the boot was a welcome sight, signaling the last leg of the weird Western treasure hunt laid out in the brochure, and putting Charlie one step closer to getting done with this cowboy nonsense so she could go home to New Jersey where she belonged. Back to New Brunswick, with its crowded streets and endless pavement, its nonstop soundtrack of whining sirens, its Grease Trucks and commuter buses. Back to the smog-smudged brick of New Jersey and the slightly metallic, smoky scent of home.

Wyoming, on the other hand, smelled disturbingly organic, like sagebrush and cowflops, and offered nothing but endless expanses of featureless prairie with a few twisted pines wringing a scant living out of the rocky ground. If this was home on the range, the deer and the antelope were evidently taking the summer off. She hadn't seen so much as a prairie dog at play since she'd crossed the Nebraska border.

Cranking the steering wheel to the right, Charlie let her back end spin up a plume of dust, then winced as the Celica jerked to a halt. Yanking on the emergency brake and flinging open the door, she stomped around the front of the car to watch the right front tire hiss out its life in a deep, jagged pothole.

She pulled in a long breath and let it out slow. She could handle this.

Reaching under the seat, she hauled out the jack and climbed out of the car. After a fair amount of fumbling around, she managed to set the jack handle and start cranking, ignoring the itch that prickled between her shoulder blades as the sun leached sweat from her skin. The car rose, then rose some more. Then it shifted sideways, groaned like a tipping cow, and slammed back onto the ground, its wounded tire splayed at a hideously unnatural angle.

This was no ordinary flat tire.

Charlie knelt in the dust, staring at the crippled car. What now? She was in the middle of nowhere with a screwdriver, a roll of duct tape, and a 1978 Celica hatchback that looked as if euthanasia would be the only humane solution.

She pressed the heels of her hands into her eye sockets to push back the tears. She wasn't scared. She really wasn't. That couldn't be her heart pounding. Couldn't be. It was…it was…

Hoofbeats.

Hoofbeats, drumming the road behind her. She turned to see a Stetson-topped silhouette approaching, dark against the setting sun. Lurching to her feet, she fell back against the car as a horse and rider skidded to a stop six feet away, gravel pinging off the car's rear bumper.

The sun kept the horseman's features in shadow, but Charlie could see he was long-boned and rangy, with pale eyes glimmering under a battered gray hat. She could almost hear the eerie whistle of a spaghetti Western soundtrack emanating from the rocky landscape behind him. She'd have been scared except one corner of his thin lips kept twitching, threatening to break into a smile as he looked her up and down.

It had to be her outfit. Saddle Up Western Wear called it "Dude Couture," but she was starting to think "Dude Torture" would be more appropriate. The boots were so high-heeled and pointy-toed she could barely drive in them, let alone walk, and she was tempted to follow local tradition and upend them on a fence post for buzzard bait. Then there was the elaborately fringed jacket and the look-at-me-I'm-a-cowgirl shirt with its oversized silver buttons. She cursed the perky Saddle Up salesgirl for the fourteenth time that day and straightened up, squaring her shoulders.

"Whoa," the rider said, shifting his weight as the horse danced in place. "Easy there, Honey."

"I'm not your honey." She tossed her head and her dark hair flared up like a firecracker, then settled back into its customary spiky shag. The horse pranced backward a few steps, then stilled, twitching with restless energy.

"I know. Easy, Honey," the rider repeated, patting the horse's neck. "Tupelo Honey. That's her name," he explained.

"Oh." Charlie looked up at the animal's rolling eyes and flaring nostrils and blushed for the first time in fifteen years. "I thought you meant me."

"Nope. The horse. So you might want to calm down. You're making her nervous, and she's liable to toss me again." Honey pitched her head up, prancing nervously in place as he eased back on the reins. "It's her first time."

"Her first time," Charlie repeated blankly.

"First time in the open under saddle," he said. "Doing just fine, too." He bent down to fondle the horse's mane. "Doing just dandy," he crooned softly.

Charlie watched him rotate his fingers in tiny circles, rubbing the horse's copper-colored pelt. Honey's long-lashed eyes drifted shut as she heaved a hard sigh and loosened her muscles, cocking one hind leg.

"Niiiice," the rider purred. Charlie felt like she'd interrupted an intimate encounter.

"Sorry." Dammit, she was blushing again. "I'm

trying to get to Latigo Ranch. My car broke down." She gestured toward the crippled Celica.

"Latigo? You're already there," he said. He swung one arm in a slow half-circle to encompass the surrounding landscape. "This is it. You a friend of Sandi's?"

"A client," she said. Sandi Givens was listed as "your hostess" in the glossy dude ranch brochure that lay on the Celica's front seat.

He straightened in the saddle and widened his eyes. "You came all this way for Mary Kay?"

"Mary Kay?" Charlie shook her head. "No way. I'm not into that stuff. Makeup, yeah, but more like Urban Decay. I came out here to do some research on so-called horse whispering." She attempted a smile. "I'm a grad student. Psychology."

The rider bunched the reins in his fist and backed the horse a step or two. The horse moved cautiously, one foot at a time, nodding her head and laying back her ears. "Well, Sandi could sure use a shrink, but she's not home. And don't let her tell you she knows anything about horses. Whispering or otherwise."

Charlie shrugged. "Well, duh. She's just the hostess."

"Hostess of what?"

"The dude ranch. I'm going to a Nate Shawcross clinic."

The cowboy narrowed his eyes. With his battered hat and the two-day growth of stubble on his chin, he bore an uncanny resemblance to the young Clint Eastwood. That eerie, fluttering whistle pierced her subconscious again.

"Nate Shawcross doesn't do clinics," he said.

"Yes, he does. I have a reservation." She set her fists

on her hips and squared her shoulders. "Is there some kind of problem?"

"Kind of." He leaned forward and pointed a thumb at his own chest. "Because I'm Nate Shawcross, and I don't know a damned thing about any clinic."

Charlie stood stunned, her mouth hanging open. "But...but I'm Charlie Banks. From Rutgers. I came all the way from New Jersey. My boss sent a deposit."

"To Sandi, I guess," he said. He looked down and fiddled with the reins. When he lifted his head, a muscle in his jaw was pulsing and his gray eyes glistened. He swallowed and looked back down at his hands. "Sandi's my girlfriend," he finally said. "She up and left, though. Went to Denver. I guess that makes her my ex-girlfriend." He shook his head, still looking down at the reins. "Sorry. She didn't tell me anything about this."

"I'm supposed to stay here for three weeks," Charlie sputtered. "And my boss expects me to come back with enough notes for a paper. There's a conference..." She shook her head and blinked fast, pushing back tears. "I got lost, and now the car's broken down and..." A single tear welled up in one eye and she flicked it away, praying he hadn't seen it. She was angry, not scared, but she always cried when she was mad. And the madder she got, the harder she cried. It made her look weak, and she didn't want to look weak in front of this stupid cowboy.

Because that's what he was—a cowboy. No matter what the brochure said about "horse whisperers," the man in front of her was a cowboy.

And she didn't like cowboys.

She'd tried to explain that to Sadie Tate, but Sadie really didn't care what Charlie liked.

Three days earlier, Charlie had parked her butt in an orange vinyl chair and devoted a solid half-hour to convincing Sadie Tate that the trip to Latigo Ranch was a bad idea.

The orange chair was part of the psychology department's sixties vibe—a decorating concept as attractive and up-to-date as Sadie herself. The woman looked like an advertisement for *What Not to Wear* in her shapeless gray sweater and high-water pants.

"So you want me to spend the summer on a dude ranch, harassing innocent animals with a bunch of cowboys." Charlie grimaced. "Please. I'm begging you. Don't make me do this."

"But it's perfect." Sadie's nasal voice meshed perfectly with her appearance. "You love animals. And this is valuable field research." She pushed her heavy glasses up the long slope of her nose and glanced down at the research proposal on her desk. "You'll be assessing the parallels between the training techniques of Western livestock managers and the nonverbal cues with which humans communicate their wants and needs."

Charlie snorted. "You can't fool me with your academic double-talk, Tate. I know what a Western livestock manager is. It's a *cowboy*." She shoved the glossy brochure under Sadie's nose, tapping one crimson fingernail on a color photo of a man in Wrangler jeans and a Stetson. "I'm a PETA member in good standing, Sadie. That's 'People for the Ethical Treatment of Animals.' I won't 'bust a bronc,' and I don't want to deal with anyone who does." She sighed. "Can't we just experiment on a few more freshmen instead?"

"Times have changed, Charlie." Sadie dismissed her last question with an imperious wave of her hand. "They're not called 'cowboys' anymore. They're called 'horse whisperers.' They use nonverbal cues to communicate with another species. They soothe them and gain their confidence by mimicking the body language the animals use to communicate with their own kind. It's exactly the sort of thing we need to understand."

Charlie sighed. Her summer was ruined, but she'd stand on her head and whistle Dixie for Sadie Tate if she had to. Sadie was the only professor who'd been interested when Charlie shopped around for grad schools. The others figured out that her choice of psychology as a field of study was an afterthought. She'd majored in biology with an eye toward veterinary school, but she'd never make it with her mediocre grades. She'd spent too much time at PETA protests and not enough at her desk.

At least a degree in psychology would lead to some kind of meaningful work. No way was Charlie going to end up like her mother, sacrificing her life to making a living in a succession of dead-end jobs. Waitress. Receptionist. Hostess.

Mom.

Charlie knew her mother loved her, but being saddled with single motherhood at seventeen had been the equivalent of a life sentence to New Jersey's minimum wage gulag. Mona Banks could have escaped, but she'd saved every penny she earned for her daughter's education. That's why she was still waitressing herself half to death on the night shift at the All-American Diner, still pushing

Charlie to succeed at something, anything. *There'll be time enough for fun later, after you get your education,* she'd said. *Make some sacrifices.*

But cowboys?

That was going too far.

"Do you realize what you're asking me to do?" Charlie demanded. "You're asking me to spend half my summer with men who make their living subjugating helpless animals. Men who think getting ground into the dirt by angry bulls is the ultimate proof of manhood. Who swagger around in chaps and cowboy hats, chewing tobacco and looking for 'buckle bunnies.'"

"Exactly," Sadie said. "I'm glad you have such an accurate grasp of the concept. Your flight leaves in three days."

"Flight?" Charlie blanched. "Oh God, Sadie. Don't make me fly. I hate flying. Can I drive? Please let me drive. I'll take my own car."

Sadie smiled and slit her eyes like a satisfied cat. "Why certainly, Charlie. I'm so glad you've agreed to go."

Charlie cursed herself silently. She'd fallen right into Sadie's trap.

"But you'll need to leave tomorrow since you're driving," Sadie said. "It's at least a two-day trip, and I arranged for you to arrive early in order to receive some individual instruction."

Individual instruction? That meant Charlie would be on her own—all alone with a cowboy who would no doubt try to tell her what to do. She pointed a finger at Sadie and took a deep breath, preparing to plunge into verbal battle.

Sadie stared back, calm as a Buddha, and Charlie felt her anger fade into hopelessness.

"I need to pack," she mumbled and slouched out of the office.

Reaching the doorway, she turned. "But if they abuse their horses, I'll—"

"You'll observe and report," Sadie said, raising her eyebrows and stabbing the air with a ballpoint pen. "As a student of psychology, you will maintain an objective perspective and will eschew any personal involvement with your subjects."

"Yeah, that's just what I was about to say," Charlie muttered.

"Good." Sadie shoved the pen behind her ear and nodded sharply. "I'm glad we understand each other."

Charlie's mother tossed a plastic-wrapped package into Charlie's suitcase.

"Here," she said. "I got you these."

Charlie scanned the model on the cover. "Mom, these are granny panties," she said. "Yuck." She flipped through her underwear drawer and pulled out a pair of polka-dotted hi-cuts and a matching bra. "I wear pretty stuff."

Her mom flipped her waist-length gray hair over her shoulder and peered into the drawer, picking through the satin and lace pretties. Pulling out a flimsy scrap of lace, she held it at arm's length and eyed it as if she'd found the decaying corpse of a dead trout.

"What is *this*?"

"A thong," Charlie said, snatching it out of her hand. "It's so you don't get panty lines." She tossed it into the suitcase, but her mom immediately snatched it out and flipped it back into the drawer.

"Don't you have any *regular* underwear?"

"This *is* regular," Charlie said, holding up a scanty bikini panty with lace panels in the side. "I like pretty things, Mom. It's not a big deal."

"How do you expect to be taken seriously in your career when you dress like that?"

"I'm not going around in my underwear, Mom." Charlie rolled her eyes. "It just makes me feel good to be pretty underneath, you know? I'll be wearing jeans and stuff the whole time. I need a little pick-me-up."

"Just don't let anyone *else* pick you up."

"They're cowboys, Mom," Charlie said. "I told you. I'm not going to fall for some dumb bronco buster."

"I didn't think I'd fall for a football jock either." Her mom sat down on the side of the bed. "But it happened. And you know where it got me."

Where the football jock "got" Charlie's mother was the state of single-motherhood. A year after Charlie was born, he moved away, never to be heard from again. Charlie barely even knew what the man looked like. If she passed him on the street, she'd probably walk on by—and he'd probably run away. He'd never paid a dime in child support.

"Just don't get involved with anybody until you finish your education."

"I know."

"Because men are different. They can just walk away, even from their own child." She slipped the panty package back into the suitcase. "Men don't love like we do. Just remember that."

"Maybe they're not all like that," Charlie said. "Maybe there are a few good ones out there."

"Maybe," her mom said. "But it's not worth the risk. Not for you. Not now."

She set her hands on Charlie's shoulders and looked her daughter in the eye. Charlie looked up and offered a quick prayer for patience, then met her mother's gaze.

"What's The Plan?" her mother asked.

It was their own private catechism, and Charlie had the answers down pat.

"Get my degree."

"And after that?"

Charlie sighed. "Get meaningful work. Work that fulfills me. Work that helps people."

"Right." Charlie's mother patted her shoulders twice and beamed at her. "Just keep your eyes on the prize, and you'll be fine."

"Okay," Charlie said.

"And keep everyone else's eyes off your underwear."

"No problem." Charlie grinned. "They're cowboys. I'm not interested, and anyway, I've heard they only have eyes for sheep."

Chapter 2

NATE EYED THE CRIPPLED CELICA AND SHOOK HIS HEAD. THE right front tire was completely flat, angling the front end into a painful twist, and the left rear wheel was perched up on a rock, accentuating the car's absurd position.

"How were you planning on getting up to the house?" he asked.

"I'm going to walk," the woman said decisively. "It can't be far."

She was unconsciously mimicking the pose of the car, with one hand fisted on a cocked hip and her torso twisted to survey the wide expanse of prairie. She was a tiny little thing, with short black hair hacked into a ragged, choppy shag. She'd rimmed her green eyes in thick black eyeliner, and her lips were painted a deep shade of crimson. Any self-respecting Mary Kay lady would faint dead away at the sight of her, but Nate thought she looked exotic, like a strangely attractive alien from Planet Jersey.

"Ranch house is ten miles that way," he said, pointing down the road. He looked down at her boots and stifled a smile, picturing her teetering across the rugged landscape in her fashion footwear. "It's getting dark. Don't you think you'd better ride?"

"I don't ride," she said. "I'll call the ranch." She tugged a cell phone out of the back pocket of her painted-on jeans. "They'll send somebody."

He watched, amused, as she flipped the phone open and stared in dismay at the "No Service" notice that lit up the screen.

"Shit," she said.

"Those don't work here," Nate said. "And besides, who's 'they'? Don't tell me Sandi made out like we had a staff or something." He swung a leg over the horse's back and eased himself to the ground.

"Okay. I won't tell you." She glanced over at the car, then flicked her eyes back to him. He followed her gaze and spotted a glossy brochure in the passenger seat. "Live the Western Dream at Latigo Ranch," it said. Dang. It had Sandi written all over it. He wondered how many more of them were out there.

Sighing, he jerked his stirrups short and looped them over the saddle horn.

"What are you doing?" she asked.

"Taking Honey's saddle off. Can I put it in your car?"

"Why? The car's stuck."

"Right. And that's why." He turned and met her eyes. "Honey'll carry us bareback, no problem."

"I told you, I don't ride," she said.

"It's up to you," he said. "Either you ride, or I leave you here and the coyotes pick your bones." He shrugged. "Your choice."

"But I can't," she said. "It's morally wrong, forcing animals to serve us. Nobody has the right to..."

"Look." He wedged one finger in front of the bit and lifted Honey's upper lip into a horsey snarl. "See those teeth? And look at those feet." As if to emphasize his point, Honey stamped one heavy hoof. "She weighs almost a thousand pounds. If she didn't want to carry me, she wouldn't." He stroked her muzzle and she nosed his ribs, snuffling at his shirt. "Honey and I have a deal. I keep her warm and fed and spend a fortune on vet bills, and once in a while she takes me somewhere."

The woman studied the horse, then turned to survey the featureless expanse of land surrounding them. "Okay," she said uncertainly.

He heaved the heavy Western saddle into the Celica's hatchback, then tossed a thick saddle blanket into the front passenger seat. The blanket released a puff of white dust onto the black leather upholstery, and the brochure rose into the air and flipped out the car window. As Nate and Charlie watched, it fluttered across the landscape on a gust of wind, resting briefly against a clump of sagebrush, then continued on its random, breeze-blown journey across the plains.

"Oh, well." Nate hadn't really wanted to read what Sandi had written anyway. Swinging up onto the mare in one easy motion, he tightened the reins and backed up until Honey stood right next to the car. "Step up on the hood and I'll help you up."

Charlie looked down at her boots, then up at Nate. "I can't. The boots will scratch my car." He wondered why she cared. The car looked to be ninety percent Bondo and ten percent rust.

"Take 'em off," he said. For some reason, the phrase summoned up a picture of Charlie Banks taking off a lot more than just her boots. He gave himself a mental slap. Women were nothing but trouble—this one more than most, he was willing to bet. She struck him as a bad attitude, all wrapped up in a pretty package.

He'd better keep his wayward imagination under control.

The bad attitude rested her shapely ass on the car's fender while she jimmied off the boots and tossed them into the hatch with the saddle. Rummaging around on the floor behind the driver's seat, she found a pair of sparkly flip-flops and slid into them.

"Now, up on the hood," he said. "Give me your hand."

"I don't know," she said, hoisting herself onto the car. "I don't even know you."

His lips twitched again, and this time he let them curl into a smile. "You want an introduction?" He held out his right hand. "Hi, I'm Nate Shawcross."

"Charlie Banks," she said. "Nice to meet you." She reached up for a handshake and yelped as he grabbed her right hand, tucked his other palm under her left armpit, and swept her up onto the horse's hindquarters in one smooth, practiced motion.

Honey snorted and danced sideways as Charlie flailed her legs and struggled for balance. Nate reached back to steady her and felt some soft, yielding body part give way beneath his hand. Good thing she was behind him. He could feel his face heating in a blush.

"Okay?" he asked.

"Sure." She sounded breathless, and he wondered if she was scared of horses.

Maybe she was scared of him.

He hoped so. Because he wasn't scared of grizzly bears, rattlesnakes, or charging bulls, but he was definitely scared of women.

"Hang on around my waist," he said.

She set one hesitant hand on each of his hips. Honey pawed a front hoof and snorted again.

"No, I mean really hang on." Nate grabbed her wrists

and pulled her arms around his waist. She clasped her hands tight, her knuckles whitening. Good thing he was wearing his granddad's old rodeo buckle. If it weren't for that two- by three-inch plate of chased silver, she'd have hit the danger zone.

Honey bunched her hindquarters and gave a little hop to the right, bouncing his passenger up into the air and back down hard on her tailbone.

"Ow!" she said.

"Shhhh." Nate stayed firmly in place and patted the horse's shoulder. "It's all right," he said.

"Oh, I know," Charlie said. "I mean, I've ridden before. When I was a kid." She sighed. "Before I realized how wrong it was."

Nate glanced back at her, then returned his attention to the horse. "I figured that."

"You did?" She sounded pleased.

"Yeah. It's Honey I'm worried about."

He felt her stiffen against him. That probably wasn't what he was supposed to say, but heck, if the woman had ridden before, it must have been a birthday party pony ride. She sat the horse like it was an electric chair on death row.

"Honey's just new to all this, so try not to be nervous. She can feel it."

"Okay."

Nate murmured a few sweet nothings in Honey's ear and felt her blow out her tension in a long, slow breath. At a click of his tongue, she stepped out briskly, nodding her head in time with each step.

The woman squeezed him tighter despite Honey's easy gait.

"Just relax," Nate said. "Relax your thighs."

He fondled the crest of Honey's mane and tried not to think about Charlie's thighs. She was squeezing the mare's flanks so hard she was liable to urge the horse into a jog, and that would probably land both of them in the dirt. With any luck, he'd land on top of her. He shut his eyes tight, banishing the image of the two of them wrestling in the dust.

"Don't worry, Honey," he murmured. "We'll take this real slow. There's nothing to be afraid of."

"I know," Charlie said. She hung on a little tighter, and he felt an involuntary flood of warmth wash over more than just his face this time.

He didn't like this woman. He wished she'd go away. But some part of him was glad she didn't mind being called Honey anymore.

Unfortunately, it was the wrong part of him, and it was harder to control than a hungry horse hell-bent for the barn.

Also by Joanne Kennedy